THE DEMON CABAL

The Demon Cabal

VOLUME 2 OF THE HY BRASAIL CHRONICLES

Kass Williams

ABLE Communications

ISBN 978-0-9947848-3-4 (pbk.)
ISBN 978-0-9947848-4-1 (epub)
ISBN 978-0-9947848-5-8 (mobi)

www.kasswilliams.ca

Cover art, design, typesetting:
Magdalene Carson, New Leaf Publication Design
http://newleafpublicationdesign.ca

Printed in Canada

Dedication

This book is dedicated to Lola,
whose time in the world was much too short.
My girl, may you forever chase balls
in the great dog park in the sky.

Contents

Once Upon A Time...

. . . a book called *The Elf Conspiracy* told the story of how, every Christmas Eve for a thousand years, Kris Kringle has crossed the dimensional rift between his universe and ours to bring gifts to children.

To conceal and protect his world, Kringle placed secret elf operatives in key human organizations such as the Central Intelligence Agency. When four young hackers, Harald, Bart, Princess, and Shugger, discovered the rift and threatened to reveal it, Kringle sent his special elf operative at the CIA, Candace Batonne, to stop them. After her cover was broken, she was hunted down and captured. When doctors examined the badly injured elf, the American government realized she was an alien.

Meanwhile, a discontented elf named Twinkle stole Santa's sleigh and reindeer and crossed the rift. Convinced that humans wanted to return to the pre-electronics world of yesteryear, he infected all electronic systems on Earth with a virus that shut down almost everything: power plants, military and civilian satellites; even the Internet.

As if that wasn't bad enough, demons in a neighbouring dimension planned to launch a genocidal attack on Kringle's world on Christmas Eve. With their conquest secure, they would turn their murderous attention on Earth.

In the nick of time, Twinkle saved Candace's life. The world's electronic systems were restored and the demons' inter-dimensional portal destroyed just in time to prevent the invasion.

At a New Year's Day party, Kringle revealed to all his friends that the rift between his world and ours was about to shut forever. But the four youths and elf scientists came up with a way to open a wormhole between the universes so that, every Christmas, Kringle and his sleigh can continue to visit our world.

The Demon Cabal picks up six months after these events.

Cast

Kris Kringle: Also known as Santa Claus, the Master, Father Christmas, and Bishop Nicholas. The real deal.

Candace Batonne: Real name, Candy Cane. An elf woman prone to near-death experiences. Lover of Paul Gironde.

Paul Gironde: An unstoppable force. Former CIA agent, lover of Candace Batonne.

The Lady Yseult: Immortal Guardian of the Rings of Hy Brasail.

Hubert Rothsay: Wizard, and significant other of the Lady Yseult.

Rigel: Part human, part alien representative of the Silchar people. An enigma.

Harald, Princess, Shugger, Bart, and **Tiddleums**: Five youths struggling to balance brains and hormones.

The King: Demonic life form and royal pain in the butt. Scared of Candace.

The Queen: Demonic life form. Vicious and lethal. Scares Candace.

The President of the United States. Not number 45.

Assorted elves, demons, college students, religious fanatics, secret agents, heroines from the book that follows *The Demon Cabal*, and **people presumed dead**.

THE DEMON CABAL

"The secret to success," Candace told her lover, "is not to fall off."

"I think I've figured that out for myself," Paul Gironde called across the space between them. The very empty space with several hundred feet under it and rocks lurking at the bottom. Thick white drifts of snow didn't soften the view.

Candace clapped her heels against the sides of the reindeer she bestrode and sped ahead, laughing. Gironde gritted his teeth, checked surreptitiously that the safety belt around his waist was securely fastened to the saddle, and followed, reflecting that the thrill of chasing a lovely elf woman across the skies of a fantastical planet was worth any risk.

He just wished it wasn't quite so far to the ground.

"There's John!" Candace turned in her saddle with the confidence of someone who had learned to ride before Gironde's great-great-great-grandfather was born. She pointed down toward the margin of a lake, where a small human figure stood in front of an artist's easel.

"I see him." Gironde pressed his knees against the reindeer's sides and the animal responded to the signal by descending in a series of hops and skids. The deer had only recently been trained to fly and gave his rider a clear impression of being not a little terrified, too.

"Good boy," Gironde said, leaning forward to deliver an encouraging pat, which the deer interpreted as a command to drop faster.

They fetched up together, mainly due to the safety belt, on a flat rock some five feet from the edge of the lake. Violet sparks flew from the deer's metal shoes, which weren't made of steel but of some gravity-neutralizing substance alien to Gironde's distant home planet.

"God, you're brave," said the man at the easel. His eyes were wide with admiration. "You'd never get me on one of those things."

Gironde grinned and tried to hide his shaking hands. During his previous career as a CIA officer, he'd faced armed and deadly enemies determined to kill him and had never once lost his nerve. He'd parachuted from aircraft at night into hostile territory and, with steely focus, thought only of completing his mission. Riding a mythological beast across an otherworldly sky was different. He knew he'd become accustomed to it eventually, but wished 'eventually' would hurry the hell up.

"You came here by reindeer," he said, releasing the safety belt and sliding gratefully from the deer's back.

"That was different." John wiped his paint-spotted fingers on a rag as he came over to shake hands. "I was inside a sleigh all the time."

As the men greeted each other, Candace and her mount demurely floated the last few feet and came to a neat halt. Her eyes were sparkling and her smile was definitely smug.

"Show off," Gironde said, walking over to give her a hug and a warm kiss. Here in her own world, no longer needing to constantly disguise who and what she really was, Candace could let her playful side shine.

"How are the plans going for the wedding?" John asked, coming over for a hug and a rather more platonic kiss.

"Oh, not bad, all things considered," she said. "The Mothers' Council has finally agreed that the Master will perform the ceremony."

"I thought that was a given," John said in surprise. "Santa Claus was a bishop, after all."

"And still is." Candace strolled over to scrutinize the painting. "But this isn't merely our first elf-human marriage;

it's our very first wedding ever. All the members of the Council want to take part, and they all have opinions on how it should go."

John grinned at Gironde. "See what happens when you marry into a matriarchy?"

Gironde pulled off his riding gloves and tucked them into his belt as he walked over to study the painting. "I lie awake nights thinking of how many mothers-in-law I'm going to have."

"You do not lie awake nights." Candace's sidelong glance was roguish. "You sleep the sleep of total exhaustion."

"Ah, yes." Gironde managed to look both embarrassed and delighted. Elf lovemaking was exhilarating. He turned to the artist. "Is Princess still thrilled about being the bridesmaid?"

John began to pack up his palette, brushes, and paints. "Thrilled is an understatement. At seventeen she's already a pro at intriguing and scheming. I understand that she's getting along famously with the Council."

"Good thing it's summer vacation time back on Earth." Gironde squinted at the canvas. "This is interesting. What're you going to call it when it's finished?"

"'Lake of the Rainbow'. Or, possibly, 'Lake That Looks Like A Rainbow'."

"This is what I so admire about humans," Candace said dryly. "Your powers of wild imagination."

The artist put on an affronted expression. "What do elves call it?"

"Rainbow Lake," she answered with a grin.

"Seriously, what causes this effect?" Gironde looked across the expanse of still water. Distinct stripes of glistening green, blue, orange, and purple created an image that was prismatic in pattern, if not in colour.

"It's due to an organism that on Earth would be algae-like, but not algae," Candace said. "Colonies of different not-algae stay together and don't mix with other types. You see this most often close to the equator, but this lake is fed by a hot spring. It's quite warm by human standards."

Gironde dipped a toe into the water. Tiny ripples made the nearest colour stream tremble. "What would happen if I jumped in?"

"You'd get wet. Also, you'd die."

He jerked his foot away.

"Just kidding!" A leap, a multi-hued splash and she was in the water, fully dressed and laughing.

"Elf humour," John said, thoughtfully moving his easel back a couple of feet. "Going in?"

Gironde already had his leather jacket off and was tugging at his boots.

"Right," the artist said. "I should tell you two to go find your own lake, but I see my taxi coming." A distant dot in the sky resolved into a small sleigh drawn by two reindeer. An elf about the height of John's knee perched on the driver's seat. He brought the vehicle to a tidy stop, jumped down and saluted.

"Here as promised, sir!"

Gironde, stripped to his jeans, looked back. "I think we've met. You're Gumdrop, aren't you?"

"No sir!" The elf, small as most males were compared to the tall and willowy females of their species, saluted again. "My name's The Elf Who Used To Be Known As Gumdrop."

"Oh, right. I'd forgotten." For centuries, the elves had been given names relating to Christmas. Recent changes to the tradition had led to an an explosion of new names, but not to a firm grasp of how naming worked.

"You can call me The for short," the elf chirped. "Does sir need help with sir's belongings?"

"Just hang onto the painting for a moment, please." John handed the canvas to the elf, who held it as a pilgrim might the Holy Grail. Like others of his race, The was caught between awe of humans, to whose creative powers elves owed their sentience, and a proud, newly gained independence from centuries of human influence.

Gironde came over to help the artist squeeze himself into the vehicle between the easel and supplies bag, with the canvas braced on his knees.

"See you at dinner tonight," he said, as John tried to wriggle into a more comfortable position. "Have a safe trip back." Gironde turned eagerly toward the lake but paused in surprise. "Candy?" There was no sign of the elf woman. The water was smooth and not even a small ripple marked where she had jumped in. The shattered colour bands had reassembled themselves and hid any view into the depths. Cold prickles slid down his spine.

"She must be holding her breath," John said, catching the other man's unease. Turning to the driver, the artist asked, "Elves can hold their breath under water for a long time, can't they?"

"Only for a minute, sir," The said.

Spray fountained as Gironde arrowed into the lake. Below the layer of coloured bands, the water was limpid. He surfaced, gasping for air. "She's not here!" He dove again and again, seeing nothing but schools of small fish darting through the grass-like weed at the bottom.

John squirmed out of the sleigh and hurried to the water's edge. "A prank?" he said hopefully as Gironde splashed ashore after his fourth long dive. "More elf humour?"

"She's not there. Not a sign. You, The Elf Formerly Known: can you sense her?"

The driver extruded his antennae, until then sheathed discreetly under his scalp. The thin, silvery filaments waved purposefully toward the water. "I can't detect her, sir. I should be able to feel her presence. Requesting permission to panic, sir."

Gironde stood dripping on the bank. A light, chill breeze

from across the lake raised the hair on his skin. It carried the faintest whiff of sulphur.

"Granted," he whispered.

The meeting chamber of the Mothers' Council ought, Princess decided, to have been solemn and stately, with pure white marble thrones circling a noble rotunda, high windows letting in floods of light, and an inspiring ceiling that went up forever.

Big, comfy, slightly shabby chairs, lots of thick rugs, no windows at all in the underground room, drinks dispensers scattered randomly about and a general sense of an informal, well-used clubhouse didn't meet her expectations for the meeting hall of the royalty of a race.

On the other hand, the chairs were really comfortable.

"More cocoa?" asked Crystal, the elf who was acting as the young human's guide. Her hand hovered near one of the dispensers. Elves lived mainly on liquid foods and had metabolisms rather like those of the hummingbirds of Princess's own world. Sugars of various kinds formed a key food group, along with vegetable and fruit juices and the occasional meat or fish bouillon.

"I'm good," she said. "Stuffed, in fact. Lunch was wonderful."

Crystal smiled in satisfaction. Cooking was a skill that only a few elves had acquired, mainly those serving the planet's de facto leader, Kris Kringle, known to elves as the Master and in the human world as Santa Claus. Arranging for lunch to be brought in had required complicated negotiations with the elf woman in charge of the kitchen.

The question of who would have the honour of escorting the visiting heroes who had helped save their planet from a genocidal demonic invasion had sparked a competitive squabble among Council members. Candy Cane, as a personal friend of the guests, was of course the official host after the Master himself but couldn't be with all of the visitors all of the time.

Normally stationed on Earth at a concealed Arctic installation that monitored developments in the human world, Crystal had exploited her own small role in the victory to claim one of the coveted positions. She was enjoying the opportunity to tour her planet, plus a respite from days spent analyzing the tsunami of information that poured into the Arctic installation's electronic eyes and ears. The only downside was that in drawing lots, she'd pulled the girl's name and not that of the young man who had given off such interesting signals a few months earlier.

Still, she was now better placed than other Council members to learn about Earthly marriage customs, a new and consuming interest for every female on the planet. They were few in number compared to the males and filled a niche that Kringle had once described as similar to queen bees in a hive, though elves were not insectile.

"Please tell me about blue," she said, pouring a cup of cocoa for herself and sinking into one of the big chairs. "We've gone over why the bride needs something old, something new, and something borrowed, but why something blue?"

"It's lucky," said Princess. In fact, as the colour of the Virgin Mary's robe, blue was associated with purity, but Princess was the kind of girl who felt free to invent her own interpretations.

Crystal asked, "Any particular shade?" and they plunged for several minutes into a happy discussion.

"But it's really Harald you should ask about colours," Princess said. "He's going to be a famous fashion designer some day. He says so. Often."

"Is it true that he's designing the wedding dress?" Crystal's private corps of spies had already ferreted out that information, but had been stymied in its efforts to get a glimpse of the concepts. Elves were telepathic and Crystal could've picked the information from the young woman's mind, but refrained out of genuine consideration for human sensibilities.

"I think so," the girl replied. She'd seen the designs, but even at her tender years knew that knowledge is power.

Crystal, at a hundred and fifty years of age, seventy-five of them spent as a member of the Council, knew that Princess knew and only smiled politely. One thing that elves did very well was to bide their time.

"How are your friends Shugger and Bart enjoying their visit here?" she asked, pleased with herself at the casual way she said Bart's name. The youth had just turned 18 and, as Crystal knew from her long study of human culture, was now legally of age. Those signals six months earlier...

"Oh, they're both having a wonderful time," Princess said placidly. Her quick ears had picked up on the lack of inflection. "By the way, Shug's calling himself Martin now."

"But which name is his name?" Crystal's interest shifted momentarily from the impending wedding to the equally fascinating subject of nomenclature. She'd decided to keep her own name as it suited both the elven and human worlds. Many of the other females were trying to follow the example of Candy Cane, who used both her given name and Candace Batonne, the name she'd adopted among humans and seemed to prefer.

Princess launched into an explanation of nicknames that quickly devolved into why she didn't like her own name. "I mean, Sandra's just, you know, so blah," she said to the attentive elf. "Daddy calls me Princess and so do all my friends, except Alison at school; she calls me Sandy to annoy me, as if I'd ever let her know! and she thinks math is stupid but when she went shopping with me she borrowed her mom's credit card, except she didn't tell her mom, and bought something she thought was only ten dollars and didn't know enough math to understand about decimal points and boy, was her mom mad about that and she had to return the stuff, and she said it was my fault because I was a geek and should've told her—"

"Flowers," Crystal said, gently interrupting what threatened to be a long foray into the intricate social dynamics of senior high school. "How many should the bride carry, and what kind, and should they be edible?"

A universe away, Candace fought suffocation, for a few terrifying seconds re-living hours of torment six months before as the prisoner of a psychopathic CIA officer.

The water surrounding her rushed away. She fell, hit a hard surface and lay for a long moment drawing air into her lungs in shuddering gasps. The air spoke to her: odours of incense and beeswax candles. Male human pheromones. Decaying pizza. Dirty socks.

Candace opened her eyes.

"I command thee, succubus," intoned a young man's voice. "Thou shalt do my bidding."

She pushed wet hair out of her eyes and, keeping her antennae tucked under her scalp, reached out with her mind. There were three humans nearby; no others within range. "Where am I?" she said. "What the hell is going on?"

"Speak not until thy master doth command," the voice intoned. It came from the middle of three cloaked and hooded shapes about five feet away. "Did I say that right?" the owner of the voice whispered to one of the other figures.

"You're doing fine," the figure whispered back. "Get on with it."

"Right, right," the first speaker said. "Um, thou shalt do my bidding, succubus, and, uh, do my bidding."

The second figure shook its hooded head in disgust.

Candace stood up. "I'm in a dorm room," she said. "You're college students."

"Hey, how'd you know that?" The middle figure edged backwards.

"It was the socks. You have some explaining to do."

The three shapes turned from one to the other in consternation.

"This isn't how it's supposed to go," the middle one complained. "I thought she'd be all submissive and, like, naked."

"She's wearing a T-shirt and jeans," said the hulking figure on the far left. "I mean, the wet T-shirt's great, no complaints about the shirt, but why the jeans?"

"It's the latest fashion among succubi," Candace said and immediately regretted the levity. All three minds lit up like fireworks.

She took a step forward and bumped into something soft and resilient. Reaching out, her hand pressed against an invisible surface that grew harder the more she pushed. A force field. Looking down, she saw that she was standing in the centre of a pentacle, a five-pointed star surrounded by a circle. *I've been invoked*, she thought in amazement. *Also kidnapped and subjected to illegal imprisonment and possibly sexual assault.*

"You boys are in a lot of trouble," she said, putting her hands authoritatively on her hips. "Tell me where I am."

"No, we're your masters," insisted the middle speaker. "That's how it's supposed to go."

"Unclothe thyself," droned the right-hand figure. "I bid thee do it now."

Candace folded her arms and glared at him.

"This isn't right," said the one that she was starting to think of as Middle Idiot. "We must've made a mistake in the ritual."

"Impossible." That was the right-hand speaker again. Candace tagged him as Mr. Nasty. Without extending her antennae she couldn't be positive, but he gave off the sour mental whiffs of psychopathy. "I did the research myself. I don't make mistakes."

Yep: psychopath, she told herself, and fought back the sharp bite of fear.

Perhaps an appeal to normal behaviour would jog the three into a more cooperative frame of mind.

"Look, boys," she said, "I was having a lovely day with my fiancé until you dragged me here. We were going to have a picnic and talk about our wedding plans. Send me back. Now."

"Thou belongest to me—to us," snapped Mr. Nasty. "Bare thy breasts. I command thee!"

Candace expressed her opinion of him in words that left all three open-mouthed and goggling.

"I thought you said she'd be submissive," whined the big youth, whom Candace tagged as Dork. "This isn't going right."

"Let me out of here and I won't press charges," she said in a firm voice.

"No, we can't do that," Mr. Nasty replied quickly. "Succubi are demons. She'll devour our souls."

Candace rubbed a temple. Her head was starting to throb. Elves couldn't dominate alert and hostile minds; the three had to be relaxed and unafraid of her before she could use her telepathic abilities to influence them. But first, she had to get out of the pentacle. "I'm not a succubus!"

"You said that jeans and T-shirts were the fashion among succubi."

"I was joking." She nodded at the speaker, Middle Idiot. "What's your name?"

"Don't tell her!" That was Mr. Nasty. "She'll use your name to control you."

No, I'll only use part of your hindbrain, Candace told herself, with a flash of distaste.

"Uh, I've gotta get to football practice," muttered Dork. "Maybe I'll catch you guys later."

"You don't have practice today," retorted Mr. Nasty.

"Yeah, well..." Dork shuffled his feet. "Look, this isn't going the way you said it would."

"It worked, didn't it? We summoned a succubus!"

"She doesn't sound like one. I mean, what she just called you: would a succubus say that to her master? That was like what your girlfriend said when she dumped you."

"I dumped *her!*" Mr. Nasty threw back the hood of his cloak with a melodramatic flourish, revealing a thin face, pale blue eyes, and straggling, mouse-brown hair. "I, Lord Dragonfire, command thee to yield to me thy name."

"What, you don't know it?" Candace raised an eyebrow. "Don't you need to know a demon's name to summon it?"

"She's got a point," mumbled Dork. "Maybe that's why the ritual went wrong. You just said 'succubus'. You didn't use a name."

Candace wondered if the spell had swept her up, instead of the intended succubus, because she'd been looking forward, rather intently, to being alone with Paul in the iridescent lake.

"Well, it worked." Mr. Nasty's jaw muscles clenched. She noticed that he seldom blinked, another trait of psychopaths. "If anyone made a mistake, it was one of you guys."

"Hey, we did it exactly like you said," Middle Idiot sputtered.

"Boys, boys." Candace held up both hands in a gesture that arrested the burgeoning spat. "You're all whiz kids, I'm sure. You're going to be rich, famous, and popular. Inventing a teleportation system: wow, that's so cool." *And thank you, Harald, Bart, Martin, and Sandra,* she said to herself, *for the geek vocabulary.* "Look, you probably should run out and patent your teleporter before someone else does. I'll be glad to provide a testimonial that it works, okay?"

Middle Idiot tentatively poked a sneaker-clad foot toward the rim of the circle. *Break it,* Candace willed him. *Break the circle and let me out and I guarantee you'll wake up with no memories of today. I hope one of you has a car, because I'm going to steal it.*

"No!" Mr. Nasty shoved his friend away from the pentacle. "She's playing us. Demons are deceivers. They can't be trusted. Watch: I'll prove she's a demon." He dug into a pocket of his robe and produced a wooden crucifix. He thrust it toward Candace's face with a cry of "Avaunt!"

"Nice carving," she said. "Looks old. Central European, perhaps? I'd say Czech, at a guess. Probably valuable."

"Yeah: how'd you know that? I mean, how didst thou ken such knowing?" Disappointed at her reaction, Mr. Nasty lowered the crucifix. The body language of his friends suggested relief.

"I took a course in Art History," Candace said. She didn't add, at the Sorbonne in Paris. In 1903. "By the way, 'ken' means the same as 'knowing'. You need to work on your imitation medieval syntax."

Mr. Nasty shot her a dirty look as he shoved the crucifix back in his pocket. "There must be something wrong with this thing. I'll have to try another one."

"The priest at Holy Trinity would be glad to have it back," Candace said encouragingly. She'd caught his vivid memory of stealing the holy symbol from a church.

His head jerked up. The unblinking eyes flashed fever-bright. "How'd you know *that*?"

Oh damn, she thought.

On top of the tallest skyscraper in the elves' home, called simply the City, Bart and Shugger leaned against the parapet and talked in low voices about the one thing that is always on the minds of youths aged respectively 18 and 17.

"The food's great, isn't it?" Bart hacked, spat, and watched as the Arctic wind froze the glob into an irregular snowflake.

"Yeah, it's great. You know, you might hit someone."

"I aimed for the roof of that building." Bart looked around for another target.

"Does your mom let you do this at home?"

"Where at home is there a skyscraper at the North Pole?"

"Good point. That aurora's something, isn't it?"

"Makes it almost as bright as day. You'd hardly know it was night."

Shugger stood on tiptoe and tried to lean as far as his friend but lacked the necessary inches. *It sucks to be short*, he thought. "What do you suppose sex is like with an elf lady?"

"Ha! You want to know what sex is like, period."

"As if you'd know! *Do* you know?"

"Hey, you're the one who shoplifts skin mags."

"I promised Gram I'd stop, and I have. Anyhow, I only stole them to keep my dad from beating on me. Do you think it'd be better than with a human girl?"

"Ask Mr. Gironde."

"I did. He just grinned."

"We kinda had sex with Candace," Bart mused, thinking back to a night six months earlier. "Group sex. Seven humans and one elf." He puckered, spat, and watched the result drift downwards.

"I'd say it was more like giving first aid. She'd have died if we hadn't transferred all that energy to heal her. Nobody knew it would also make her pregnant."

"True." Both youths were silent, remembering. "It was still weird," Bart said after a moment. "Imagine giving someone CPR and afterwards getting hit with a paternity suit."

"Candace wouldn't do that. I think Crystal likes you."

"Hey, man, she must be all of thirty years old. Maybe even forty."

Shugger sniffed. "I thought you liked older women."

"With elves, how do you tell?"

"I heard Mr. Kringle say to your mom that elves grow up really slowly," Shugger said. "An elf two hundred years old, like Candace, would be about thirty in human years." He shot a sidelong grin at his friend. "I guess that would make her kid sister, Crystal, about eighteen."

"Uh, yeah. Yeah." Bart gave up his hobby and turned to go indoors. The intense polar cold penetrated even his heavy fur parka.

Shugger followed his friend into the room they shared with Harald, shedding garments as he went. Heaters kept the room at a temperature that was pleasant for the humans, if steamy hot for elves. "I wonder if there are any teenage girl elves."

"Crystal told me that females only happen every couple of hundred matings," Bart said. "Mostly it's male elves. Currently, there are no girls."

"Think Candace will have one?"

"You willing to wait that long for your first date?"

A round of mock fighting followed.

Bart broke it up by throwing himself onto a lavishly carved and upholstered sofa and trying to look like he was just bored and not getting the worst of it. Since moving in with his grandmother, Shugger had filled out. Good food, enough food, and the regular exercise she insisted on were rapidly turning a skinny, malnourished geek into a well-muscled and energetic geek. "She still has six months to go," Bart said. "My mom says that if she'd had to be pregnant a whole year, she'd have grown me in a bottle."

"What, she didn't?"

More mock combat.

"Hi, guys. What's up?" Harald came in, his eyes peering above an armload of cloth. A toy helicopter hovered a couple of feet above his head. He dumped his load on a table and looked up at the toy. "Thanks a lot, Officer Ensures Traffic Goes In The Proper Directions Without Collisions."

A tiny arm waved from the pilot's side of the toy and the helicopter sped through the door and disappeared down the hall.

"Got lost," Harald said. "Had to ask a traffic cop for directions. Half this city is underground. Look what I found. Man, some of this stuff is hundreds of years old and yet it's in perfect condition. Must be the cold."

"How do you remember those names?" Shugger released a red-faced Bart from a half nelson. "It's killing me to keep them straight."

"I just do. It's no big deal."

"Is this for Candace's wedding dress?" Shugger picked up a length of brocaded scarlet fabric and wrapped it around his shoulders.

"Oh, that's you, it's really you," Bart said, flopping again onto the sofa.

"I can't picture her in something that heavy," Harald said, sorting through the pile. "I see her in a finer fabric; cloth of gold or silk."

Shugger tried on another length of brocade. "Yeah, something sort of, you know, elven."

"Oh, very funny. No; this is for Mr. Gironde's suit. Hey, careful with that. It's made of real silver foil."

"Would he even notice what he's wearing?" Shugger tossed the fabric onto Bart. "He doesn't see anything but her."

Bart rolled up the strip of cloth and pitched it to Harald. "I guess that tells you what it's like to do it with an elf."

"Nah." Shugger dropped onto the carpeted floor and sat with his back against an ottoman. "I think it's that thing called 'love'." He blinked. "Did I just say something deep?"

"Are we talking about sex?" Harald refolded the bundle carefully. "Elf ladies do it with their antennae, you know.

Direct stimulation of the pleasure centres of the male's brain. The female in turn takes some energy. Plus they do all the other stuff with the, you know, other parts."

Bart stared at his friend, wide-eyed. "How'd you know that?"

"I asked the cleaning elf, No Dirty Spots Allowed. He's five hundred years old and knows everything. A great guy."

"How would he know how a human and an elf do it?" Bart sat up, impelled by a mighty curiosity.

"Well, it stands to reason, doesn't it? I mean, for hundreds of years the elves' evolution was influenced by human thinking. No Dirty Spots says that 'cause we thought of female elves as sexy ladies, that's what they eventually became."

"And male elves are little green men." Shugger started to pick his nose, thought of his Gram, and stopped. "But do lady elves have babies like human women?"

"Crystal says no," Bart said. "There's a limit to how much we could change them. Basic biology stayed the same. They have buds. Crystal says she had twelve after her last mating, which is a real good number. If she'd had a girl, she'd have been elevated to the top rank of the Mothers' Council. There's only a handful of ladies at that level. Her mom's the head of the Council. She's had two girls."

"You and Crystal sure hang around a lot together."

Bart went red in the face. "Hey, we're just friends."

"Baaaarrrt has a girrrrlfriend," Shugger chanted and this time got the worst of it when the taller youth landed on him.

Harald skipped aside as the pair rolled in amiable combat across the carpet. "Don't knock over the furniture. When I'm a famous fashion designer, I'm going to have a sideline just for furniture and maybe I'll have it made here."

"I fink 'ers fumone at fdoor," Bart said from under his friend's arm. He wriggled with eel-like flexibility out of Shugger's wrestling hold and bolted, laughing, for the apartment's entrance.

A small, slightly translucent elf stood in the hallway outside, tiny fist raised to knock again. Imps, elf children, were often used as messengers and could be seen scampering about the City, full of earnest self-importance.

"C'mon in," Bart said.

"Really?" The imp's eyes, already large, bugged. To be allowed to carry a message to the honoured human guests was glory in itself. To be welcomed into their company was bliss undreamed-of and a coup that would make him the envy of every other imp in his crèche.

"Sure." The human stood aside to let the little creature enter. "What's your name?"

The imp gulped. "Please, sir, it's Ted."

"Ted? Nothing else?"

The imp bobbed anxiously from one foot to the other. "Is it too long? I could shorten it."

"No, no, it's fine. Do you have a message for us?"

The elf's face crumpled. "I've forgotten it!"

Harald wandered over. "Is it about dinner time?"

Ted rocked from side to side. "I don't know."

"Who gave you the message?"

"My mother."

"Candace?"

"No, sir." The imp quivered.

"Crystal?"

"No, sir." As Harald rattled off the names of elf women he'd met, the imp progressed from moderate distress to awareness of impending social disaster and eternal condemnation in the eyes of his peers.

"Was it about something animal, vegetable, mineral, or digital?" Bart crouched on hands and knees to be on the same level. The imp was vibrating so fast that he blurred.

"Vvvvvvvvvvvvgetaaaaaaaaaaablllllll," he managed to say.

"Must be dinner time," Harald said. His stomach rumbled in agreement. He carefully picked the imp up in both hands and awkwardly laid it on his shoulder like a baby needing to be burped. He patted the heaving little body, trying to remember how his aunt, a new mother, cared for her infant when it cried. All he was sure about was that human babies were soggy at both ends. "It'll be all right. Gosh, you don't weigh anything at all."

Shugger asked anxiously, "He's not shrinking, is he?" Distressed male elves were wont to do so. "Do imps shrink?"

"How would I know?" Harald bounced up and down on his toes and tried to recall the words his aunt used to sooth her baby. "There's a sweet little tiddleums."

"Really?" Ted's head popped up. "You're giving me a new name? A human-chosen name?" The traumatized expression vanished in the face of beatific joy. "I am Tiddleums!"

Bart took a sudden interest in the pattern of the carpet. Shugger found fascinating things to study on the ceiling.

"I didn't mean—" Harald began, but the imp was now regarding him worshipfully.

"Our mothers name us," he said. "No elf has ever had the honour of being named by a human. That means you are my mother, too. My human mother." The imp's antennae flattened against his head. "I make obeisance to you, oh my mother. I will love and obey and honour you for as long as I live."

Harald opened his mouth. Nothing emerged but a faint squeak.

"Good; that's settled." The newly named Tiddleums hopped down. "I just remembered what I was supposed to tell you: for dinner tonight you have a choice of vegetarian platter or curried fish." He led the way proudly to the door.

"After you, Mom," Bart said.

"...never live this down," Harald muttered, trailing after the imp.

"Try living it up instead," Shugger said. "Princess is going to spit nails, she'll be so jealous. I bet she'll have half the city re-named by dessert."

"Yeah." Harald brightened. "She'll be *imp*-patient to start because she's so *imp*-petuous. But I'm sure it's *imp*-possible to rename them all." Grinning, he hurried after his friends, who fled the series of increasingly bad puns in the direction of the dining hall.

It is worse than I feared." Kris Kringle stroked his silver beard with a gesture that Gironde had learned meant he was very concerned. The two men stood side by side, studying a glowing holographic chart floating above a rock crystal table in the city's Hall of Advanced Learning. To Gironde, who had tracked the old man to this location, it was a university and the Senior Natural Philosopher demonstrating the chart was a research scientist.

Still damp and chilled from his headlong homeward gallop, he pulled a blanket more tightly around his shoulders. "Why is that?" Fear for Candace made his heart clench.

"Lad, I'm sure you feel, right now, that it can't possibly be worse. Professor Einstein's Left Eyebrow, would you please explain."

At another time, Gironde would've been curious about the story behind the elf's new name. Now, he strained not to erupt with impatience as the scientist stepped forward, fiddling with a miniature loudspeaker. The fact that he was three inches tall meant only that he'd been selected months before for the honour of mating and was growing back from microscopic size. Unlike the women of their race, male elves could change size. Where the mass went was one of the mysteries that Gironde had yet to solve about his new home.

On Kringle's other side stood Glitter, his operations manager. At almost five feet, he was the tallest male elf Gironde had seen and had held onto his original name. There were likely hundreds of other elves in the room. Objects sometimes moved apparently by themselves, shifted by handlers too small to see.

A faint creak came from the megaphone. The scientist shook it and tried again. "Sorry, sorry, batteries getting low. Yes. The situation." He waved at the hologram. "As you know, sirs, the demon universe swings about ours in an orbit that is erratic, but more or less elliptical. Now and then the universes brush in passing and when that happens, it's possible for the demons to open a gate. If the contact is strong enough, they can send through an army."

"They've done so in the past," Kringle interjected for Gironde's benefit. "If the touch is glancing or the portal too small to admit a large force, they try to use it like a trap to catch whomever they can."

"Do you think that's how they took Candace? Were they hunting her?"

"I doubt it. John was probably their target: all alone at the lake with no witnesses around. They must've been about to spring the trap when you two arrived."

"And Candy did them the favour of jumping into the lake. Why do you say it's worse than you suspected?"

The elf scientist cleared his throat. "Sir, I can answer that question. If my calculations are correct, the orbit of the demon universe will shortly bring it into prolonged juxtaposition with ours."

"How prolonged?" Kringle bent forward. To the elf, it must've been like standing under an impending avalanche of snowy white beard.

"A year, perhaps. It is difficult to give a firm estimate, because the mathematics are very complex and there's no way to actually get out there and measure. Their attempted attack on both our world and Earth half a year ago may have been only a prelude."

Kringle clasped his hands behind his back. Turning to Glitter, he said, "Where is Peter?"

"In the south, sir. He's mapping the fire snake country."

Gironde knew that the geography of the elves' world matched that of Earth closely. Where the two worlds differed radically was in the course that evolution had taken. Elves, adapted to cold, didn't like to venture into warmer climes and as a result their knowledge of the planet below the temperate zone was not very good. Peter, Kringle's former servant and now friend and colleague, was in the process of mending the lack with a centuries-long program of mapping and exploration. The fire snake country lay in what would've been Mexico on Earth.

"Send for him posthaste," Kringle said. "Inform the head of the Mothers' Council that I would like to meet with her at her earliest convenience." He turned to Gironde. "What the Professor is telling us is most grave. Although we've beaten back invasions in the past, they've always cost us dearly. Very dearly." His ruddy face paled with remembered grief. "Have you ever led an armed force?"

"I was an air force major before I joined the Agency. Served overseas."

"You're now Air Marshal."

"I appreciate your confidence in me," Gironde said, "but isn't there an elf with more experience? Glitter, for instance?"

Kringle shook his head. "Get an elf into a hand-to-hand battle and you couldn't ask for a more bonny fighter, but they're not strategists. Their natural impulse is to attack, fight, and stop when no enemy is left. That's a good way to protect the burrow against invading predators, but not adequate against an organized army. My elves have come a very long way since acquiring sentience a thousand years ago, but under some circumstances they're still strongly governed by instinct. That's why I would like you to take command of the Air Force."

"We have one?"

"We will shortly."

Gironde nodded. He'd witnessed the incredible manufacturing capabilities of the elves. "I'll need to know the history of the previous wars. The enemy's tactics, weapons, forces."

"Glitter will see to it that you have what you need."

"What can we do for Candace?"

"I've been considering that. Won't do to leave her in the hands of the demons."

"They are real demons, are they?"

"Well, it's what we call them," Kringle said. "Or what I call them. Legacy of being a bishop in medieval Europe. If it's spooky, scary, doesn't go to church and tends to burst into flames, it's a demon."

"They're a life form, then."

"Can't say what they're like when at home. In this universe, they're more energy than matter. Hard to kill with blades, which was all we had in the past. On Earth, they're able to hold material form for a short period before they convert entirely to energy. As young Sandra discovered, a fire extinguisher will do them in handily."

Gironde had a quick mental picture of fighter jets strafing an enemy with foam, pushed it aside, angry at himself for having a frivolous thought at such a serious moment, then retrieved it for closer inspection.

"What about our friends?" he asked. "Should we send them home?"

Kringle tugged at his beard. "They'd be safer on Earth, yes."

"Excuse me, sirs." Professor Einstein's Left Eyebrow waved for attention. "While I cannot disagree with you about the danger, I could do with the help of the honourable young lady guest. Her talent for mathematics is most impressive."

Kringle nodded. "True. She did the calculations for the wormhole."

"The other guests may want to assist," the miniature elf said. "Such is the nature of heroes, after all. The artificers

Bart and Martin are peerless at their craft. They collaborated with our best people to design the wormhole terminals and establish the inter-dimensional linkage, and I recall that young Harald seamlessly coordinated everyone's efforts."

"True, true." Kringle rocked back and forth on his heels. "I will ask them, and their parents, of course. If an invasion does happen, they can be whisked back to Earth and the gateway closed." He turned to Gironde. "My friend, when I invited you to emigrate to this world and become a citizen, I did not anticipate throwing you into a war."

Gironde clapped the other man on his broad shoulder. "You couldn't have kept me away. My home is where Candy is."

"Speaking of whom." Kringle tugged at his moustache. "There's an option we must consider. A way to save her. It will take our joint efforts, yours and mine."

"How?"

"It will also require us to leave this world, at a most crucial time."

Glitter stepped forward. "Sir, I believe I know what you're thinking. If you and the Air Marshal give me your instructions, I can see to all the necessary preparations. General Peter will be here soon, too, and of course you won't be gone very long by our reckoning."

"Gone where?" Gironde looked from elf to man.

"There is a path," Kringle said slowly, "a route out of this world. I don't know if it's a true wormhole or something else. I was privileged to be granted its use centuries ago, by one whom I hold in the highest esteem. I have used it a few times. The thing is, Paul; it leads to yet another universe, one that can take us in turn to the demons' world. With courage and luck, we may find Candy Cane and rescue her."

Gironde pulled the blanket from his shoulders. "You know what I want to do."

"The advantage of this route," Kringle said, eyeing the man from Earth, "is that time does not run the same in every dimension. If we live and all goes well, we could be back in a couple of days. The problem is that the route is one way. To return here with Candy Cane, we'll have to use the demons' own wormhole. They may not want to cooperate."

Gironde offered no vain boasts, no oaths that nothing would keep him from saving his love. He'd seen death often enough to know that no boast is proof against fate. "I will go," he said. "You must stay. You're the real leader here."

Kringle shook his head. "The portal will open to none but me. Even if you could cross by yourself, I doubt you'd get very far. The guardian of that realm looks upon trespassers with a cold eye. Besides," he said, "Candy Cane may be your betrothed, but all elves are my responsibility. I'll lose no more of my people to those demonic savages. Never again. Never." He turned abruptly on his heel and walked to a window that overlooked the City.

"Oh, sir," Glitter called after him, pointed ears fluttering with emotion, "I know you'll succeed. You always do. You rescued my mother when she was a prisoner under that mountain on Earth. You'll save her again, I'm positive!"

"Candy's your mother?" Gironde regarded the elf with surprise and a flash of contrition; he forgot, sometimes, that he was not the only one who cared about her.

"Yes, sir," the elf said proudly. "From her first mating." He leaned closer and in a confiding voice added, "Five hundred years ago, there was a great raid from the demon world. We fought it off and my own great-grandmother, Star, personally rescued scores of our people who were prisoners of the demons. But at the very last instant, as the dimensional portal closed, she was dragged through. I've heard it said that she and the Master were close. People thought they might even—" The elf coughed, looking embarrassed and a touch guilty. "I shouldn't gossip. Suffice it to say that he was devastated. When he sensed her death, it hit him very hard. He almost abandoned Christmas that year. His sense of duty pulled him through, but it was a near thing; very near. He hasn't so much as looked at another woman since. Except that horrid witch he married, and she ensorcelled him. It's a relief to all of us that she's dead." Glitter pulled a large handkerchief from a pocket and blew his nose. "I don't think anyone could hold him back now. You'll take good care of him, won't you, Air Marshal?"

"My word of honour," Gironde said, wondering privately who, in a dangerous venture across strange universes with unknown natural laws and creatures, was going to take care of whom.

How did you do that?" Dork stared at Candace open-mouthed, a pizza box in his hand, the door open behind him. "I mean, get upside-down."

"Oh, we demons are very flexible," she said, a little out of breath. Squirming into a handstand inside the cramped space of the pentacle had indeed been a challenge.

Dork let the door swing closed and walked nearer, cocking his head to the side. "Why are you doing that?"

"Gravity is different in hell," she said solemnly. "For me, this is standing upright." What she was really trying to do was to distract, confuse, and entice him closer.

"I like what it does to your breasts." The pizza box started to slide, unnoticed, from his fingers. "You're really sexy. I think Sco—Lord Dragonfire, I mean, is right and you're a succubus. You were only pretending to be a person."

"Well, I had to try to take your souls," Candace said. "It's a demon thing."

She'd picked their real names from their minds: 'Lord Dragonfire' was Scott; Middle Idiot was Morris, and Dork was Doug, when he wasn't trying to live up to his online cognomen of Thumper the Humper. She could imagine what her four young friends would've had to say about their choice of aliases.

"Make them jiggle." The young man sat on a dirty cushion on the floor, pizza box covering his lap and the tumescence starting to make itself visible. "You have to do what we command. Scott said so."

Candace obligingly twisted a little. A tidal wave of hormones was taking control of his brain. *Lean closer,* she suggested, pouring into the projected thought all the subtle appeal she could. *So close, almost within reach. You don't need to be afraid. Reach out. Break the pentacle. Touch her.*

"Doug!" The crash of the door slamming against the wall shattered the trance. The young man leaped up, spilling pizza at Scott's feet. Concentration ruined, Candace lost her balance and collapsed into a heap. "What the hell do you think you're doing?" Scott's face was white with fury.

"I was just trying to cop a feel," Doug replied in a surly tone. "I wasn't letting her out or anything."

"You'll have to eventually," Candace yelled, patience torn to shreds. She used the slightly elastic walls of the pentacle to help push herself upright. "How are you going to explain to people that you're holding a woman prisoner in your dorm?"

"We won't," Scott said. "It's summer term. There's no one on this floor but us."

"I hope there's a washroom on this floor," she replied. "Don't look so surprised. Doesn't it stand to reason that if I have human form, I'm built like one internally? We drink. We pee, and I'll need to pretty soon." Candace pointed at the waterlogged carpet. "Air and light pass through the barrier. So does water. I had lots to drink. Lots and lots."

"That will not work." Scott's eyes glinted. "No demon will make a fool of Lord Dragonfire. You are a creature of air and darkness, not of the flesh. I know this to be true."

He did, too. He knew it like he knew his heart was beating and that gravity was 'down'. Her appearance inside the pentacle had confirmed, irrefutably, a life-long belief that he could work magic.

"You'll be sorry." Candace gave up for the moment and sank cross-legged onto the floor. She knew a good deal about psychopaths, partly from two centuries of reading human minds and also from the psychiatrists' briefings she'd attended during her former job as a CIA analyst. Six months earlier, she'd been in the power of one for several of the worst hours of her life.

The briefings had taught her that psychopaths' brains were physically not like those of normal humans, which explained why Scott's thoughts seemed to squirm away when she tried to influence him. They typically acquired a pair of helpers; either lower-level psychopaths or normal people who could be dominated. She'd pegged Doug in the second category but wasn't yet sure about Morris.

Setting that aside, she focused instead on the urgent question of why she was there. She'd never heard of anyone on Earth successfully invoking an elf, though demons were known to try. She'd heard all her life about the ancestor who had fallen victim to a raid from the demon world.

But none of that explained why she was on Earth.

"What are you studying?" she asked Scott after a while. The young man was now sitting at a desk, thumbing through a battered old book that to her sensitive nose reeked of mildew.

"This is the grimoire of Demetrios the Thaumaturge. It is herein that I found the lore on how to raise a succubus. He was the greatest of the demon masters and you will, of course, know of him. I expect that I will find your name in his Demon List and once I have that, you will be compelled to obey me in all things."

"Can't say that I've ever heard of the man."

Scott sniffed. "Of course, a demon would deny the power of a demon master."

"I keep telling you: I'm not a demon."

He smirked. "Then what are you?"

"I'm one of Santa's little helpers."

"Demon, I find your attempts at humour feeble."

And I find your pompous arrogance contemptible, she thought. Longing for Paul, for the safety of his arms, briefly overwhelmed her. *No;* she told herself, *Paul would tell me to learn everything I can about them, and the Master trusted me as one of his own secret agents, even if I did screw up. I can handle these jerks.*

"Oh most exalted sorcerer," she said aloud, "may this lowly succubus know what you intend to do with her?"

The other two young men, eating pizza while they viewed pornography on a computer, turned to listen.

"Well, I...that is..."

Hah! Candace said to herself. *Didn't think you'd get this far, did you?*

"I plan to start with some whipping. Then—"

She listened, eyes growing wider, while he rambled on inventively. After a minute, Doug crossed his legs and dropped a hand onto his lap. The perspiring Morris plucked incessantly at the thin fuzz on his upper lip.

"—and finish with the triple twist, of course."

"Of course," Candace echoed in a stunned whisper. Sometimes, it's possible to learn too much. She drew up her knees and hugged them tightly. *You're never getting me out of this pentacle,* she silently promised him. *Never ever.*

General Peter has arrived." Glitter cocked an antenna in salute and stood up straighter. The man whom he announced strode into the room. He was of compact build and average height but heavily muscled, and in his snugly fitting flying leathers radiated strength.

"I came as fast as I could," Peter said, shaking hands firmly with Gironde before turning to throw both arms around Kringle's shoulders in a hug that drove the breath from the older man's body. "Are we under attack?"

"Not yet." Kringle led him to the viewing table where the holographic representation of the universes floated. The room had now become an operations centre. "An attack may be imminent, however." He quickly briefed the other man about the situation, then said, "General, I want you to take command of the land forces and set up our first line of defence at Rainbow Lake. I have a crew draining it. If the rift is still active, we will attempt to use it for our return from the other side, and I anticipate that we could have company. Perhaps a whole hostile army of company."

"I understand. We'll be ready. I was told of your plan to rescue Candy Cane." After centuries of familiarity with his friend's personality and thinking, Peter didn't question the decision, even if he might privately disapprove of it.

The day and night that followed were among the most intense of Gironde's life. Snatching catnaps when he could, he spent the time in consultation with elf engineers, designers, and fabricators, as well as with newly minted flying officers and crews. In between he attended strategy sessions with Peter, Kringle, and Holly, the formidable head of the Mothers' Council. Like pending mothers-in-law everywhere, the statuesque elf was not convinced that any man could know or do what was best for her daughter.

"I lost my mother to the demons," she said at one point, fixing Gironde with an icy blue, intimidating stare. Her finely pointed ears twitched warningly. "I know of the horrors that my child faces. Bring her back safely, man, or by the Magi, I promise you, I will never—" The stern, frosty features collapsed and Holly covered her face with her hands. "Please bring her back," she whispered. Nearby elves flinched from her unintentionally broadcast anguish.

I have loved Candy for a few years, Gironde thought, sobered. *These people have loved her for centuries. But if we succeed,* he told himself with fierce determination, *I may yet have the joy of loving her longer than anyone.*

Zraxion."

"No."

"Zpados."

"No."

"Zuzurus."

"Nope."

"Zygurn."

"Not even close."

Candace lay on her back, legs propped vertically against the force field. It sent a not unpleasant tingle through her skin as long as she didn't lean on it too hard. Finding a comfortable position in the confines of the pentacle was difficult.

Scott, red-eyed with weariness, slammed his grimoire shut. His mouth compressed into a narrow, angry band. "I have read every name in the Demon List. Yours must be one of them. It has to be."

"Do you enjoy wasting your time?"

"Mock thou me not, demon!"

"Good grammar learn you, mortal man."

A rasping snore interrupted them. Scott shared his room with Doug, while Morris had a room of his own down the hall. Candace had learned that the three were graduate students, taking extra courses during the summer. She'd also discovered that this suited their families just fine.

"You should go to sleep," she said, yawning to give him a hint. Fatigue threatened to send her to dreamland first; stamina wasn't an elven virtue. Worse, her earlier threat to cause a flood was not just a gambit. She really did need the washroom. The sooner Scott passed out, the sooner she could make him or his friend open the pentacle and release her.

She began to sing in her pleasant contralto, "Lullaby, and good night..."

"Stop that." Scott came and stood by the edge of the circle that penned her in. "You want me to go to sleep. Why?"

"I think sorcerers are adorable when they're all tucked in."

He stared at her for a moment, then spun on his heel and

left the room. When he returned half an hour later, he was carrying an unmarked spray can.

"I've decided you're right," he said. "I need to sleep. Also, you were correct in what you said earlier, about air passing the barrier."

Candace stood, trying not to show apprehension. "What's that?"

Scott's mouth twitched up in a triangular smile. "Something from the chem lab." He raised the can, pointed it at her and pressed the plunger. "Chloroform."

Ready to leave, lad?" Kringle hitched at the waistband of his sturdy new red trousers, made in a matter of hours by a team of elf tailors. He wore a matching jacket abundant with pockets, a jaunty cap, and new boots. The gear contained no metal at all. Gironde's own clothing was a considerably trimmer copy in grey.

"I'm ready."

Kringle took one last look at his reflection in a large mirror in his suite. "Dapper, if I say so myself. Well, let's be on our way. Not that way, lad."

Gironde halted en route to the entrance. "To the roof?" Most buildings in the City had reindeer landing pads.

The old man grinned. "Closer yet. Over here." Kringle walked through his bedroom to a short corridor linking it to the bathroom. He pointed at a narrow door. "Looks like a linen closet, doesn't it?" Eyes twinkling, he turned the knob and pulled the door open. Neat stacks of sheets and towels filled the closet. "Now, watch." Shutting the door, he gripped the knob again and closed his eyes, focusing. "I have to think of a series of images in the right order. It's been a while—" He twisted the knob, pulled, and the door opened onto a garden. A pebble-covered path led from the threshold into a green and fragrant summer vista. Warm golden sunlight suffused a cloudless blue sky.

Gironde whistled, impressed.

"After you," Kringle said with a courteous gesture. "I need to hold the door open."

Gironde stepped across, yelped in pain and clapped a hand to his cheek.

"Metal filling?" Kringle followed him, closing the door. It remained there, an unimposing door in a pathway.

"Metal post." Gironde poked the unhappy tooth with his tongue. Raised in the Age of Fluoride, his teeth were cavity-free. The now missing titanium screw had anchored a tooth cracked during a parachute drop into a hostile country one dark night during his career as a CIA officer. He'd miscalculated how close the ground was and landed hard, the shock driving his jaws sharply together. The tooth now felt slightly loose.

"Well, it's probably on the floor back home. Quite safe there. Pure metal can't pass the portal, which is why I'm sure it's not a wormhole." Kringle gestured broadly. "Welcome, my friend, to Hy Brasail."

"I've heard of it. Isn't it supposed to be a mystic island in the western ocean?"

"Mystic, certainly. The sea in which it floats is infinity." Kringle led the way down the path. Fifteen minutes' walk through the garden brought them to the top of a low rise, where a park bench waited. The old man sat down with a *whoosh* of breath.

"Too fat for all this exercise," he said as he made himself comfortable. "Have a seat, lad. We may have a wait ahead of us."

Gironde didn't join him. He was studying the view hidden until then by the trees. In the distance a wide river dotted with boats large and small flowed parallel to the hill. On the far side a city spread out. It reminded him of pictures he'd seen of medieval London: low buildings, architecture of a distinctly hand-built cast; streets that meandered in patterns set by ancient footpaths. Surprisingly, two other hallmarks of medieval cities were missing: smoke and stench.

"What's that city called?" he asked, turning to Kringle.

"Hant, the same as the name of the river. But most people call it the City of the Lady."

"The lady who...?" Until recently the citizen of a democracy, Gironde automatically assumed a generic meaning for the title.

"Her proper title is The Lady Yseult, Guardian of the Rings of Hy Brasail," Kringle replied. He waved vaguely at the surrounding gardens and the palace crowning a nearby hilltop. "This is her home."

"Why are we here?" Gironde tried to control his impatience.

"To ask permission to go further." Kringle heaved himself to his feet. "We are in luck: she is in residence."

A woman was approaching from the direction of the palace. She wore a long gown made of some emerald green fabric that flowed gracefully with her movements. Her auburn hair was woven with pearl strands into a thick braid. Gironde estimated her to be in her mid twenties, until she came closer. A power of age and wisdom shone from her dark brown eyes.

An immortal, he thought. *Like Kris and Peter.* And, with the shock of recent memory, *Like me.*

The woman smiled and held out a hand. "Master Kringle," she said in a warm voice. "Welcome. It has been too long."

Kringle took her extended hand in his own and bent to kiss the back of her fingers. Gironde bowed also.

"Lady Yseult," the old man said as he straightened his back. "You grow more beautiful with each passing year. I mourn that my duties have kept me from your company for so long."

"Flatterer! You said the same thing a century ago."

"But not with as much sincerity as today."

The exchange gave Gironde the impression that he was being shown, in a subtle way, a very old friendship.

The woman turned to him. "Do introduce me to your companion."

"He is my friend Paul Gironde, a great warrior formerly of Earth and now a citizen of my world. I trust him and vouch for him."

"Your word is sufficient for me."

The ritualistic phrases somehow reverberated like echoes in a very large room. Kringle inclined his head. "You honour us both, Guardian."

"But I expect this is not a social call," the woman said. "Are you on a journey?"

"Yes. We wish to go through the Sixth Ring to the World Tree and thence via the Moon Track to the Way of No Return."

"Ah. That world." Yseult's sober gaze turned to Gironde. "Do you know of what he speaks?"

"I can't say that I do, ma'am."

"My realm is a bridge to many others. He requests permission to travel through it. There is no retreat from that path and the world onto which it opens is deadly."

"Yes, ma'am. Enemies have my lady. I mean to find her and bring her safely home."

"She is also one of my people," Kringle said. "I will not abandon her or let my friend walk that path alone."

"Then you have my permission to journey through the Rings as you wish, and may your quest end with your heart's desire." Yseult turned to Kringle and in a less formal voice said, "Kris, do you need a guide? It has been a long time since you walked the Rings."

"A guide would be appreciated."

She raised a hand and a scarlet bird dropped from the sky and landed on her outstretched arm.

Gironde managed to keep his jaw from sagging. The creature was the size of a large hawk, but covered with scales, not feathers. The wings were like bats' wings, the eyes shone like opals, and a thin trickle of vapour flowed from the flared nostrils.

Kringle grinned. "Never seen a dragon before, eh, lad?"

"They weren't common back in the States."

Yseult smiled, a youthful expression oddly harmonious with her ancient eyes. "My friend will show you the way." She tossed up her arm and the little dragon fluttered to a nearby tree branch. Coming closer, she put a hand on Kringle's shoulder. "Kris, you must attend my next WinterFeast, of course when your quest is completed. I have missed you." She stood on tiptoe to kiss the old man on each cheek.

He responded in kind. "I shall look forward to it."

"Bring your friends," Yseult said, with a smile for Gironde. "My dining hall is capacious and you know how I love stories." Just for an instant, she looked almost shy. "Fare well."

Gironde bowed again as she turned to walk back the way she had come.

Kringle sighed as she vanished from sight. "One of the sweetest and most charming beings you will ever meet," he said. "Also, one of the most powerful. My contemporary, as a matter of fact."

The dragon spread its wings and glided a score of paces down the path. Both men set out in pursuit.

"She's a thousand years old?" Gironde asked as they walked.

"Very nearly, I think. From Earth, like us. Scotland. Keep your eyes on the dragon. This garden is her creation and its many ways lead to many worlds. We don't want to get lost."

"How did she come to be here?"

"Well, now, that's another tale. If we—no, *when* we return home, I'll tell you."

"What are these Rings she mentioned?"

Kringle tugged at his moustache. "You already know that there are many universes. Hy Brasail is a stack of universes, like a cake—or perhaps, more like an onion. Yes, an onion: layer wrapped around layer. The deeper in you go, the higher the energy levels. We are on the outermost Ring, number nine. It corresponds closely to the environment you'd find on our world. The energy we call magic works here, but to use it requires special talent and training. The deeper you go into the Rings, the more magic becomes part of the fabric of reality and of the creatures dwelling there. Ring Eight is the home of centaurs and such-like beings. In Seven you find what humans call fairies. I've never been to Six, Five or Four. Three is the home of dragons and I doubt we'd live very long if we ventured there without our guide. I've been told that Ring Two is the home of elementals and other beings of pure energy. Very, very dangerous level. No one other than the Lady knows what's in Ring One."

"She's the ruler here?"

Kringle snorted. "Can you imagine what a nightmare it would be to try to rule nine worlds like these? No; the peoples govern themselves according to their own laws and natures. The Guardian's role is to keep the Rings from merging. She intervenes only when magic is grossly misused and the balance threatened."

"I look forward to meeting her again."

"As do I. Odd, though..."

"What's odd?"

"I was rather expecting an invitation to stay a while. She does love visitors. Must be something happening. I hope it's not serious."

They followed their guide for several more minutes, the landscape subtly changing around them, when the sound of pounding hoofs made them pause. The little dragon perched on a tree branch and preened itself as the pursuer rode up.

Galloped up? Gironde's jaw did sag.

"Gentlemen," the newcomer said, a bit breathlessly. "The Lady bade me bring you these supplies for your journey and begs your pardon for her lack of courtesy, but she is much preoccupied."

"I understand completely." Kringle walked over and, with the confidence of long experience, shook the centaur's hand. "Let me help you with those." He caught Gironde's very wide-open eye and nodded at the bundles slung over the dapple-grey back. "You'll see stranger than this, I promise you."

"The Lady told me you're from Earth," the young centaur said, twisting around to pull at the leather strap securing his load. "Which one?"

Gironde shook off the paralysis and offered his own hand. The centaur's grip was firm, warm, callused and not at all mythological. "There's more than one?"

"At least three, or so I'm told. Is it true that on Earth you can fly without magic? I'm sorry; where are my manners: my name this year is Hint of Spring. Do you like gardening? I'm an under-gardener here. What kind of flowers do you have at home?"

"They're a chatty people," Kringle said some time later, after the centaur had made his elaborate farewells and galloped back the way he had come, black mane flying in the wind.

"No kidding." Gironde squatted to examine what the Lady had sent them. "Are we going to need all these weapons?" He slid a slender knife into his boot, picked up a belt from which hung a matched pair of long daggers, and buckled it around his waist.

"It seems the Lady thinks so." Kringle frowned. "On my previous visits, all the protection that I needed was her welcome." He selected a sword and baldric that fit over his ample frame, plus a short dagger. "Take that spear; it'll be useful as a walking stick as well as a weapon."

Gironde hefted the spear. The killing tip was elegantly leaf-shaped. A spike on the butt offered both support and a means of poking out an opponent's eye. Kringle took a shorter staff with a handgrip that could serve as walking stick or club, and Gironde added a baldric and slim sword to his own armament.

The bundles contained cloaks and knapsacks stuffed with dried fruits, meat, and hardtack, as well as flasks of wine. A small, heavy bag held a selection of tokens; some of metal, some of crystal, and a few of substances that Gironde couldn't identify.

"That's money," Kringle informed him. "We may have to stop at inns."

"Is it far?"

"Subjectively, a few days. I know you're impatient, lad, and so am I, but in terms of the passage of time in our world, unless something seriously bad happens to us on the way, we'll be home in a couple of days."

Gironde tried not to sigh. *Every step takes me closer to Candy,* he told himself as he shouldered the heavier of the knapsacks and took a firm grip on the haft of his spear.

"After you," he said to Kringle and followed him into the lands of Faërie.

It was fortunate, Candace considered, that her elf metabolism didn't react to chloroform like a human's would.

On the other hand, she wanted to throw up everything she'd eaten in the last hundred years. Her eyes burned, too. Elves had no tear ducts; a transparent membrane like an extra eyelid moistened their eyes. She blinked rapidly to slide the membranes across her dark blue irises and the stinging effects of the gas gradually eased.

The room was quiet; even Doug's raucous snoring had

tapered off. Scott stretched on his bed, shoes kicked off but otherwise fully dressed, and she sensed that he was at last deeply asleep, confident that she was out cold.

Faking unconsciousness had been easy, and air blowing from the open door to a window had cleared the gas from the pentacle and helped quiet her stomach. It was now or never. Candace extruded her antennae and reached out gently to touch Doug's dreaming mind.

She entered a fantasy of football, food, beer and her. She tweaked the images, adding a cheering crowd and goal posts made of cheese strings. After a second's thought, she dressed her dream self. Normally, the sex fantasies of human males didn't bother her but this had become personal. In the dream she waved at Doug and held up a football that was a foaming beer globule.

His attention assured, she reached deeper, finding the neural pathways that controlled his muscles. Doug stirred, sat up, swung himself out of bed and shuffled slowly toward the pentacle.

Candace changed the dream images. He was now on the goal line, knuckles down, the football tucked under his arm and seconds left to cross the line and win the game. On the edge of the pentacle, Doug dropped into a crouch.

Here, her lack of knowledge about football almost woke him; a linebacker didn't carry the ball. As consciousness stirred she quickly sent a row of cheerleaders cavorting across the end zone and put herself at the front. Reluctantly, she deleted some clothing. Doug grunted and slid back into deeper sleep.

She built the goal line into a white bar; a frustrating barrier between himself and his desire that had to be beaten down. Doug's arm clumsily batted at the chalked circle, smearing the powder. Candace made her dream self dance closer, beckoning. His hand lurched forward and she almost cried out in relief as it scraped through the chalk, breaking the circle.

The force field disappeared. She jumped out of the pentacle and over Doug's now slumped form, and ran for the door.

But half-way there, she paused. To complete her escape she'd need money, perhaps a car, and there was still an urgent need to attend to. Across the hall was a washroom. She detoured into it and soon emerged, much relieved.

The two young men continued to be deeply asleep. Candace studied them for a moment. Invoking her would've taken power, energies that she was certain were not natural to Earth.

The instincts she'd developed as a secret agent, living for years among humans and constantly playing a role, were still very much alive in her. Moving as quietly as she could, her stiffened antennae constantly monitoring the men's states of mind, she began to search the room.

She found money quickly enough: a wad of bills in Doug's wallet. A large plastic box in a closet was filled with the appurtenances of sorcery: vials of what looked like blood, an ornate dagger, black candles, amulets, all of them off-the-shelf magic shop rubbish, plus a dried chicken's foot good only for soup, a shrivelled human finger that she dropped back with a shudder and a desire not to know how Scott had come by it, and a few well-thumbed books on demonology.

Candace sat back on her heels beside the open box and wondered where an aspiring sorcerer would keep his greatest magical treasure.

Rising to her feet, she went to the side of Scott's bed. A quick visual inspection revealed no enchanted rings or mystic bracelets on his hands, but there was a chain around his neck, the end tucked under his shirt. An odd shape under the cloth rose and fell with each movement of his bony chest. When she bent nearer, her antennae tingled with the energies seething about the hidden object.

Candace pinched a fold of cloth at the collar between two fingers, lifted the shirt and, with utmost delicacy, began to draw up the chain.

She had no warning before Morris's wiry body crashed into hers and carried her across the room, to land on Doug's sprawled form.

Winded, she fought back, writhing to get out from under him, jabbing with elbows and knees as he struggled to pin her down. She felt the other two men's minds rousing and lashed at Morris's, trying to stun him.

Nothing happened. She used her teeth instead, biting down as hard as she could into the flesh of his arm. He didn't seem to notice.

An instant later she was hauled to her feet, Doug's muscular arms wrapped around her waist. She struck again with her mind and the football player screamed, clamped his hands to his head and dropped to his knees.

Her freedom lasted only a second. She caught a glimpse of Scott's shocked expression before Morris's bloody forearm whipped across her face. The lights went out.

This is so, like, totally cool," Princess said in a whisper to her friends, forgetting that the pointy ears of the many elves in the operations centre could pick up every word, not to mention their ability to read minds. "It's like having a front-row seat when history is made."

"Yeah; or like being in a movie," Harald agreed. "A sci-fi movie where all the special effects are real."

"Mother is so clever," said Tiddleums proudly, sitting at ease on the youth's shoulder.

Out of the elf's sight, Princess mimed gagging.

Shugger had his nose pressed against the floor-to-ceiling window. "Would you look at that; they've already built a helicopter squadron." He turned to Harald. "Isn't your pal, Officer Ensures Traffic Et Cetera, in command?"

"He's changed his name to Group Captain Fiercely Smite the Foe From The Skies."

"Easier to remember. Not."

Bart wandered over. "I think they've adapted the helicopters from existing models. Weren't those on TV last Christmas? Not that I watch the kids' channels, I mean. I just heard about them from someone whose, um, little brother likes remote-controlled toys."

"Couldn't have sold well. There's a lot here." Shugger waved as the flight soared past the window.

"Don't be idiots," Princess said. "If they shot at you, you'd die. Daddy said they've ripped out the innards and replaced them with real stuff. He's at the factory, helping with schematics. Maybe they couldn't hold off the invaders for long, but they could slow them down until the bigger guns arrived." She swallowed through a suddenly tight throat. "I think you'd have to be really brave to go to war in a helicopter the size of a grapefruit."

Bart nodded. "Do you think they'll have full-size jets built in time for the invasion? If one happens, that is."

"Mr. Gironde and Santa seemed pretty sure of it," Shugger said. "That there'll be an invasion, I mean."

Princess lowered her voice. "Do you think Candace is all right? Everybody looks so, you know, grim and scared when they talk about her." She bent down, picked up the loose end of a bolt of delicate cloth that Harald had brought with him, and wiped her eyes.

It said much for Harald's own state of mind that he didn't grab the cloth away. "She was a secret agent for years and years," he reminded his friend, casually nudging the bolt out of reach with his foot. "I'm sure she'll come home safe and I'm going to keep working on the wedding clothes. When I'm not helping with the war effort."

"Mother is wonderful," Tiddleums said. With his real mother's blessing, the imp had attached himself to the human youth as general assistant and personal messenger. Bart and Shugger now and then eyed him speculatively and in the back pocket of Princess's jeans was an already thick list of new names. Tactfully, she'd decided to hold off for a while on an imp naming spree.

"I wish there was something we could do," Shugger said, ramming his fists into the depths of his pockets.

"There is," Princess said. "I've been listening to people. They know there's an inter-dimensional portal at the lake but they don't know where, exactly, it is. What if we could come up with some way to detect it?"

"I've already got some ideas," Bart said. "Shug, what do you think?"

"It's Martin now," the youth said. "Yeah. We'll need access to a tech shop, though."

Princess turned eagerly to Harald. "You know everyone. I bet you can find us a place to work. One that's not microscopic, I mean."

"Plus some helpers," Bart said.

"I can arrange that," Tiddleums offered. "My other mother will help."

"Good." Harald rubbed his hands together. Excitement brought a rosy pink flush to his cheeks and mental flow charts began to coalesce in his head. "Let's get busy. We have a world to save," he said, understating the true situation by cosmic degrees of magnitude.

In the university dorm, Candace returned with profound reluctance to the waking world.

"C'mon, c'mon," goaded a testy voice. Her face stung; someone was slapping her. She could taste blood in her mouth: human and her own. She opened her eyes.

Scott was the assailant. He backed away as soon as he saw that she was awake. Behind him stood Morris, blood from the bite in his arm drying to the colour of brick. His face was empty of emotion. Doug sat on a chair, holding a bag of ice to his head. His look was both murderous and fearful.

Candace realized that she was lying on Scott's bed. When she tried to sit up, she could barely raise her shoulders off the rumpled sheets. She was wrapped, mummy-like, in duct tape from neck to feet.

"Try getting out of that," Scott said with satisfaction. He eyed her warily. "I'm not sure you're a demon after all. Even with these." He tugged one of her ears. The tip, once kept trimmed by cosmetic surgery when she needed to pass as human, was growing back. She twitched it out of his grip and spat some blood. Morris's blow had split her lip. For the second time in half a year, the colour of her blood had betrayed her non-human nature. A green drop landed on Scott's hand and he wiped it fastidiously against his jeans.

Doug lowered his bag of ice and growled, "I saw a website about aliens living among us. The guy who runs the site claims to be a former CIA agent. He says the government's covering it up. I thought he was nuts but maybe he knows what he's talking about. He says that aliens have green blood and antennae sticking out of their heads and that they can read minds and want to take over the world."

Kevin Finnegan, Candace thought. The man who had held her prisoner and tortured her, and whose mangled form she had last seen being loaded into an ambulance, after a thorough trampling by some of Santa Claus's reindeer.

"I didn't invade your world," she said. "You brought me here."

Scott's knobby fingers gripped the object under the thin cotton of his T-shirt. "Heed my warning, demon or alien or whatever you are: You cannot harm me. I am protected. Strike again at my follower—at my friends, and I'll make you regret it."

"A sweetheart like you?" She flinched as his fist flew toward her face, but he didn't land the blow.

"That was a warning. Tell me: What are you?"

"Bored."

Scott's lips compressed and his eyes narrowed. Morris stepped closer, whispered something into his ear. The young man's mouth stretched in a predatory smile. "Yeah; good idea. Hey, bitch: I bet I can get you interested." Reaching out with his free hand, he stroked her hair.

No; not her hair: her antennae. A strip of duct tape pinned both delicate organs against her head, exposed and vulnerable. She shivered involuntarily at the touch and then again at the thought of what it would feel like when the tape was ripped off.

"Like that, don't you?" Smiling, Scott ran a finger the exposed length of a filament.

To Candace, the intimate touch was both deeply repulsive and, at the same time, intensely erotic. In her entire life, she'd allowed only two men to touch her antennae: Paul and one other. The psychopath's fondling was a kind of rape.

"I've never killed anyone," she said in a choking voice, "but I'm starting to think there's a first time for everything."

"You can't harm me."

She glanced toward Doug. "Ask him if he agrees." The big youth jumped to his feet, face white.

Morris muttered again in Scott's ear. The psychopath grinned, reached into the drawer of a nearby desk and took out something silvery.

"No." Candace's mouth went dry. "Don't."

Scott sneered and worked the handles of the nail scissors he held, making the blades click suggestively. "Where are you from?"

I hate psychopaths, she thought in terror, grasping his intention. Adrenaline rushed into her bloodstream and panic broke her self control. Half driven by instinct, she gathered her mental strength and hurled her fear and anger at Scott's brain.

He shrieked, dropped to the floor and thrashed violently. Doug stood petrified, staring down at him.

Morris sidestepped the convulsing man, plucked the nail scissors from his hand and strolled toward Candace, clicking the blades and smiling. He leaned over, slid his bitten arm around the back of her neck and under her chin and dragged her head hard against his stomach, holding it immobile. She struck again; hit what felt like a thick glass wall. A wall through which something dark looked back.

She'd made a mistake: Scott wasn't the leader of the group, as he himself thought. It was Morris; bumbling, biddable, easy-to-overlook Morris.

Possessed Morris.

The chime of a cell phone stopped Morris as he began to snip at the shaft of one of Candace's antennae.

"Now who could that be?" He released her head and stepped back, reaching into a pocket of his pants for the phone. "Hello?"

A small drop of blood rolled down her forehead from the cut. Candace wondered in despair if screaming would do any good. Doug stood rigid with indecision beside Scott, who lay moaning on the floor, blood trickling from his nose. She couldn't detect anyone else close enough to respond to a shout.

"Yes, I have the elf," Morris said. "I was about to neutralize her." He listened for a moment and so did Candace, her attention wholly captured. "Is that wise?" Morris turned to look at her. "She's dangerous. She just laid out a human." He listened again, nodding reluctantly. "All right, bring the limo around to the back entrance. We'll be down in a minute." He put the phone away and said with a grin, "You're in luck. Someone wants to keep you intact."

"What are you?" Candace whispered the words through a throat tight with fear.

"The leading edge of a new order." Morris, or the

Morris-being, opened a cabinet, removed a roll of duct tape, tore off a piece and pressed it firmly over her mouth. "We're going on a trip," he said. "Can't have you squeaking. But before we go—" Producing the nail scissors again, he separated the sharp blades with a quick twist. As Candace and the still frozen Doug watched, he knelt beside Scott and with efficient, brutal speed ripped open the young man's throat. Bright red blood spurted across the room.

Candace screamed behind the gag, her brain lashed by the horror in the dying man's mind. Through a haze of intense pain, she saw the smiling Morris stand up and strike at Doug's neck. All that saved the young athlete's life were his automatic reflexes. His head jerked back and the blade only grazed the skin over his jugular. The paralysis holding him broke; he bellowed in rage and lunged at Morris.

Candace tried to help, reaching out to stimulate his brain and pour energy into his muscles. Doug pounded big fists into the smaller man's body; wild, smashing blows.

Abruptly, Morris stopped fighting and hung like a puppet under the flailing fists. Candace's eyes widened. The man wasn't dead or even unconscious. Morris was simply gone. She could sense echoes of him; scraps of memory and personality, but nothing more. The presence that had lurked in the background had disappeared, too.

"Mmmph!" She thrashed, trying to draw Doug's attention. "Mftop!!"

To her relief, the youth did stop. He dropped the limp form, stood up and stepped back, foot splashing in a puddle of blood. The blind rage in his mind drained away and a numb blankness took its place.

"Ug!" Candace lightly stroked his mind, trying to calm him. "Issen oo ee."

He turned slowly. The blankness was like a sheet of paper on which anything could be written. She was acutely aware of her helplessness.

"Ug?" she tried again, raising an eyebrow. The tiny gesture, so normal, so feminine, seemed to jar him from the trance.

Doug moved stiffly to her side and with clumsy fingers tugged at the gag. It came free, re-opening the split lip.

"There's a knife in the plastic box," she said, licking away blood. Doug's eyes followed the movement of her tongue and his mind trembled, overwhelmed by strangeness. "We can't stay here, Doug. We have to get away."

"No." He sat down on the side of the bed. "No, if I run away they'll think it was me who killed him. My best friend." Tears ran down his face. "I'd never hurt him. They won't believe me."

"You didn't kill him," Candace said, reading all too clearly the fears surging up from the depths of the young man's mind. "I'm a witness. They won't blame you."

"My dad—"

"—always criticizes you. I know. You're innocent. Morris was crazy. He killed your friend. You acted in self defence. But we still have to get away."

"I should call 911." Doug looked at Morris, breathing harshly through a broken nose. "Yeah; I have to call 911. When they get here, you'll tell them what happened."

"How will you explain me?"

"Oh." Doug was starting to think, although slowly, as if using his head was as difficult as walking in a river of molasses. "Yeah. The duct tape." He scrabbled in the box of magic trinkets and retrieved the dagger. The sharp blade slid easily through the sticky wrappings. Candace tried not to wince at the occasional nick.

Peeling the strip off her antennae was every bit as painful as she'd feared, but soon it was added it to the wadded, silvery ball in Doug's hands. With relief she retracted the filaments into their protective sheaths.

"I'm going to call 911 now," Doug said.

"Listen to me." Candace put a restraining hand on his

arm. "We can't. Didn't you hear what Morris said on the phone? Someone is coming. They may be here now."

"Yeah, but—"

"Someone who wants me alive, but who expects you to be dead. Like Scott. Someone who might finish what Morris failed to do."

There was a childlike, hurt quality in his mind. "But why? Why would someone want to kill me?"

"Do you want to stay and find out?"

Doug looked around at the carnage on the floor, the chalked pentacle, the huffing, unconscious form of Morris. "I don't know what to do. Scott always tells me."

"Listen, Doug," Candace said again. "I work for a man who can help you. A very kind man. We'll straighten things out, I promise you."

Stepping carefully around the pool of blood, she crossed to Morris and eased the chain off his neck. The object he'd tried to conceal was a large crystal that looked like an ordinary chunk of milky quartz, one end of it wrapped in silver wire with a loop for the chain. Junk jewelry like it could be purchased at any psychic fair or shop in the country. She had a strong suspicion that it wasn't the product of an amateur jewelry maker, and very probably not even a product of Morris's world.

She held it up. "Doug, do you know where this came from?"

The young man rubbed in a dazed way at his forehead. "Scott got it from his aunt. He said she was a sorceress. She died and left her magic stuff to him."

"Do you know her name?"

"I think it was Gloria or Gladys or something like that."

"Gladys—" Candace caught her breath. Kringle's late, unlamented wife had borne that name. She'd also known how to raise demons and had sent one to murder Candace and her four young friends. *This cannot be coincidence,* she thought. The little pendant seemed somehow much heavier and full of nightmarish portent. "You wouldn't happen to have any lead foil, I suppose?"

"Uh, yeah, I do." Doug opened a cupboard and pulled out a grey packet. "It's from the physics lab," he said, handing it to her. "Scott asked me to steal it for him. I don't know why."

Candace didn't point out the futility of trying to lie to a telepath. But Doug really didn't understand what his friend had been planning, though he knew it involved radioactivity. She had a hunch that Scott's death might have been a very lucky break for some innocent people.

Careful not to touch the crystal, she wrapped it in several layers of foil, stopping only when she couldn't sense its energy. Slipping the heavy little bundle into a pocket of her jeans, she nodded toward the door. "Let's go." The sound of an elevator grumbling slowly up its shaft caught her attention and she reached out toward it. The brief mental contact with the sole passenger hit her as hard as a kick in the stomach. There was no mind in the elevator. What she felt was like a hole, a terrifying, icy void.

But Doug still demurred.

In growing fear, Candace put her hands on the big youth's back and tried to push him out the door. It was like shoving an elephant. "Company's coming! We have to go down the stairwell."

"I shouldn't go," he mumbled. "Running away is for cowards. My father—"

"Go, damn it! I'll stay with you, Doug; I'll help you."

"But if we call 911—"

"Go, Doug, or I'll fry your brain! I will, and you know I can." Doug paled and stumbled toward the door.

To the right was the elevator and a chill like the depths of outer space.

To the left, a stairwell. Candace half pushed her companion

along the hallway. She looked back as the elevator ground to a halt. Clear to see on the floor behind them were red prints from Doug's blood-soaked sneaker.

They reached the fire door, almost fell against the release bar and tumbled through into the stairwell. Candace sprinted down four floors to ground level and Doug, catching her panic, this time didn't linger.

At the exit door she stopped and listened with all her senses. Reassured that there was no reception party on the other side, she pushed the door open.

Mild air. Bright sunlight. Palm trees. Ocean winds.

"Doug," she said, "where are we?"

"School," he replied dully. Reaction was setting in, his mind withdrawing from the recent horrors.

"No; I meant, where in the country?"

"California."

"Calif—!" Candace caught her breath. Her escape plan, formulated during her stay in the pentacle, had been to steal a car, drive to John's house, and use the wormhole in the garage to go home. The problem with the plan was that she'd assumed she was on the East Coast. "I don't suppose you have a car?"

"Yeah, I do."

"Where?"

"Student parking lot."

"Got your keys? Please, please don't say they're still in your room."

"No." A bit sullenly, Doug produced a keychain.

"Good." Footsteps echoed in the stairwell behind them. "Let's go!"

She guided herself by picking the route out of her companion's mind. Candace was a fast runner but Doug kept up easily, loping along with a grace not usual in linebackers.

As they neared the student parking lot, she slowed in dismay. "Where is your car?" The lot was huge. She'd heard that no one walked in California and now believed it. A scattering of vehicles dotted the vast space, mostly vacant during the summer term.

"Over there." Doug pointed toward a small cluster of cars in the distance, close to a massive building.

"That's half a mile away!"

"It's by the sports complex," he said in a reasonable tone. "I'm there most of the time so that's where I park."

"That doesn't make sense—oh, let's just run."

Doug trotted stolidly ahead. Candace, following, looked back frequently, feeling dangerously exposed in the open space. Morris had said 'bring the limo', but to her relief no sleek black shape showed itself, which said something about her inexperience with Californian culture. She didn't at once connect the long, pink shape gliding across the lot with danger.

Not, that is, until it suddenly accelerated toward them. Fifty feet away it slowed and doors sprang open on each side. Men leaped out.

"Seize the elf," barked a voice from inside. "Kill the man."

"This way!" Doug grabbed Candace's hand and almost dragged her toward the cluster of vehicles parked by the sports complex. Reaching the cars, they dashed through ranks and across open lanes, gaining a little distance on the silent pursuers.

"Where's your car?" she gasped, badly out of breath.

"Here!" Doug vaulted over the side of a bright crimson convertible and slid with the accuracy of long practice into the driver's seat. Candace scrambled in beside him and reached for the seat belt.

Power roared under the hood and the car leaped backwards in a sharp hook, crunching into the front left corner of the pink limo as it attempted to block them in. Doug changed gears, spun the wheel and the sports car tore down the lane.

Candace screamed as hands snatched at her, closing on an arm. One of the men from the limo was sprinting beside the car, legs pumping inhumanly fast and face contorted by effort. Only the seat belt saved her from being dragged out. The man lost his grip, fell and rolled away. She caught from his mind a veneer of humanity over something terrible.

Doug cursed, took the next corner on screeching wheels and thundered toward the exit. Looking back, Candace saw the runners abandoning their chase. From the limo rose a grey cloud that she guessed meant something important had suffered during the collision.

"I hope you've got insurance!" the young man shouted. "Somebody's got to pay for the damage." Now secure behind the wheel of his car, his confidence was soaring, images of the carnage back in the dorm shunted aside by the excitement of speed and escape.

"It'll be taken care of," she shouted back. "Can you drive me to the East Coast?"

"What!"

"It's where I was when you invoked me." Explanations about other universes could wait. "I've no other way to get there." With the separation of the human universe from her own, half a year earlier, the only point of contact that she knew still existed was the wormhole in John's garage. No longer needing to protect his world from human curiosity, Kringle had pulled most of his secret operatives from their assignments on Earth. The only installation still active was Otherside Station, located at the North Pole near where the two universes had formerly touched. The station still collected children's letters to Santa and monitored human attitudes toward Christmas. Candace knew that the staff had gone home for their annual holiday. A few elf women remained in the human world, but all were in Europe and out of reach.

Doug drove for a few moments in silence before saying, "I could give you some money for a plane ticket."

"No good. Can't tell you why." Flying would require going through a security check, and facial recognition technology could immediately flag her as a wanted fugitive or, more accurately, as a wanted fugitive extraterrestrial alien and spy in whom the American government was extremely interested. According to Crystal, who eavesdropped regularly on the country's top-secret communication channels, Candace's escape from custody six months earlier had created waves that were still reverberating. With all her human friends visiting her world, there was no one she could phone for help.

"I'll take you to the train station, then."

"Doug, you owe me!"

He thrust out his chin. "It was Scott's idea to try magic."

"Do you want another headache? A really bad headache?"

"I bet you won't do that while I'm driving. Look, I'm sorry, but it's you they're after, not me. I'll take you to the bus terminal, OK?"

"You'd be dead now if I hadn't made you leave the dorm! Besides, just now, I clearly heard someone in the limo say, 'Kill the man'."

"No, no; it was 'Seize the wealth. Kill the engine'. They were carjackers. Just carjackers."

"I think you know better than that."

"Don't be silly." A mulish expression slipped with the ease of long practice onto Doug's face. "There are no elves."

"Sure, and every girl you know has antennae sprouting from her head."

"You're an alien, of course. Everybody knows about Roswell and Area 51."

Candace could feel the walls going up as Doug struggled to protect his sanity by cobbling together a story he could believe, and abandoned that tack. "How will you explain what happened in your dorm?"

"Dad's a lawyer. Mom's a judge. They'll figure something out. They've gotten me out of trouble before. I mean, it's obvious, Morris went mad and killed Scott and yes, I ran, because I thought I'd be next, but my fingerprints aren't on the nail scissors."

Candace slid down in her seat, defeated. *It took three billion years of evolution to produce someone like Doug,* she told herself. Then again, it had also produced Paul. She sat up straighter.

"Do you want to put me on a bus with forty people who could be killed if those 'carjackers' track me down?"

"Well..."

"I've a better idea." She stroked a hand across the leather dashboard. "I like your car. I really do." Doug's face squinched up like that of a child about to cry. "Oh, relax; I'll leave it somewhere safe and you'll get it back. I'll also need your credit card."

"I think the bus—"

"And I won't tell your grandparents that you were mixed up with sorcery. Leaders of the Right is Mighty Christian fundamentalist sect, aren't they?"

"How the hell did you know that? Are you a mind reader?"

"Yes," Candace said serenely, catching the guilty memories rushing through the young man's brain.

She got the car and the credit card.

Las Vegas at night, two days later. Candace guided Doug's sports car down the famous strip, enjoying the coolness of the desert night air and the brilliant lights. They made her homesick for the spectacular aurora of her own world. She passed the great casinos with regret; a few hours at the poker tables would've given her all the cash she'd need to get home. As a young elf in Europe during the Belle Époque, the golden age that preceded the First World War, she'd supplemented her earnings as a fashion model with the unwitting help of the elegant gambling salons of Paris and Monte Carlo. Avoiding games of chance such as roulette, she'd used card games and telepathy to build a fortune that, with over a century of accumulated interest, made her a millionaire several times over.

Not that she could currently access any of that money. Nor did she dare to enter any of the casinos. Her image would be immediately picked up by the omnipresent security cameras and it was very possible that a connection would be made to the FBI's register of known felons and fugitives. Even driving down the street was risky. She was already attracting notice: a lovely young woman all alone in a fiery-hot sports car.

Candace detoured into the less glamorous back streets and found a brightly lit, guarded parking lot. "I'll be back in a few hours," she told the attendant, handing him the keys and the required advance payment. Probably, most of the lot's clientele returned much poorer than they'd arrived. She knew that the car stood a good chance of finding its way back to its owner and in the glove compartment she'd tucked Doug's credit card, which had paid for gas on the journey. She kept the money she'd already stolen from his wallet back in the dorm room. Any purchases she made from now on had to be in untraceable cash.

Some of her funds she spent in a second-hand clothing shop, emerging with an old leather jacket that on her looked better than new, plus a shoulder bag, a cap that hid her growing ear tips, and dark glasses.

An inquiry at a convenience store directed her toward the highway she wanted. With the hunters now far behind, she could take the time to find cars or trucks going east. A touch of elf influence on the drivers' minds and they'd never know they carried a passenger.

At an intersection with the main strip she paused, overwhelmed for a few seconds by loneliness. All about her, people were enjoying themselves; flocks of tourists with cameras in hand and starry-eyed or anxious gamblers hurrying from casino to casino. The intense hubbub of human life rolled in an unending swirl. Longing for Paul cut like a knife.

"Move it, bitch," said a woman's voice. "This is my turf."

"What?" Caught in her thoughts, Candace hadn't noticed that she had company.

"I said this is my turf. Get your ass off my corner."

"I'm not—"

"She giving you trouble, baby?" A large man dressed mainly in gold necklaces and fake leopard skins loomed up suddenly.

"I saw her cruisin' earlier. Hot red car. She's nothing but low-down trash. Make her move her fucking ass." The prostitute put a long-nailed hand on Candace's shoulder and shoved.

"Keep cool, I'm going." The elf backed away. Getting into a brawl was not an option.

"Hey, wait, babe." The pimp turned toward her. "This is a friendly town. We always welcome a fresh face. What's your name?"

"Sorry to bother you. I'm leaving." Candace tried to step around him but the man blocked her path.

"Hey, pretty lady, I just want to know your name. You lookin' for work? I can get plenty of high rollers for a fine lady like you."

"Baby, what about me?" whined the prostitute.

The man turned on her with a flare of rage. "You want me to bash you?"

The hooker's reaction was so vicious and fast that Candace almost lost both eyes to the pointed nails. She ducked just in time but the lacquered claws raked across the tender base of her injured antenna, sending a jolt of agony through her already abused brain.

An instant later she was rolling on the pavement, struggling with the drug-addled hooker while the pimp tried to keep out of the way. Camera flashes blinded her as tourists recorded the free street theatre.

Hand-to-hand combat hadn't been part of her training and with so many onlookers, she didn't dare stun the woman. Or bleed. The best that she could do was to grasp the other woman's arms and try to hold off the raking fingers.

"Break it up!" Flashing red and blue lights and the voice of authority brought the fight to a quick conclusion. Someone dragged the frenzied hooker away and pushed her, cuffed and screaming obscenities, into the back of a police car. The pimp had vanished.

"You hurt, ma'am?" A policeman helped Candace to her feet.

She touched her split lip. Thankfully, the wound hadn't opened.

"I'm OK," she said. "Thank you, officer."

"She started it!" an excited tourist shouted. "They were fighting over territory! I was a witness. I saw everything."

"That's right," said another, nodding vigorously. "She was moving in on the other girl's pitch."

The policeman's hand reached around to his handcuff pouch.

Caspar's balls, Candace thought. *I hope Paul and the Master never learn of this.*

Very far away, Paul Gironde stood in front of a large painting in a town square and wondered what the hell he was supposed to do next. The painting's almost photographic detail showed a view of a city street. Nearby hung similar artworks, each depicting a different street.

He turned to Kringle, who was waiting at his side. "If this is a transfer point, how does it work?"

"You just walk toward the painting," Kringle said. "Takes a bit of getting used to, lad. I remember, the first time I tried it, I bruised my nose quite severely until I got the hang of it."

"We didn't have to do that in the garden," Gironde protested. "Just followed the path and came out here. In Ring Eight."

"The garden's a special place," Kringle said. "All we had to do to cross a level there was follow the dragon." He glanced at the creature in question, preening itself on top of the painting's frame. "Any fool who tries to use a garden path without the Lady's permission will end up, well, somewhere. Given her love of a good joke, I'm sure it'd be a place the trespasser would never forget. No; this is a communal transfer point, open to the public. Watch; I think that fellow is about to leave."

He nodded at a man who was intently studying another painting. The traveller finished his scrutiny and stepped back several paces. Keeping his eyes fixed on the painting, he walked toward it.

Gironde caught his breath as the man dissolved into the air.

"Where the hell did he go?"

Kringle pointed at a row of symbols running along the side of the painting. "That goes back to Ring Nine. He'll arrive at the place shown in the painting." The old man waved a hand at the gallery. "Transfer points can't be used to travel within a Ring," he said. "You have to walk or take whatever local transportation is available. But to travel vertically, from one Ring to another, all you need is a clear reference point for the destination."

"Is that why the paintings are so realistic?" Gironde asked.

Kringle nodded. "You keep the picture in your mind and move toward it. Easy, really."

"Can you cross from any place at all?"

"If you know *exactly* what to visualize," Kringle said. "Most people use already well-established transfer points. Not just for convenience; there are beings in some Rings who prey on travellers. Established transfer points are protected. Also, there are places where it's simply easier to cross over. Finding them is one of the jobs of the local magic workers."

Curiosity kept the questions popping from Gironde's mouth. "So the garden is the Lady's personal transfer station, then?"

"The Guardian can move as she wills through the levels of the Rings, though she's as restricted as anyone else in moving laterally. No; most of the garden paths lead to universes outside of Hy Brasail. You can see why she doesn't allow trespassers. Imagine what an evil wizard could do at large on a world like Earth."

"He'd make a fortune in Hollywood. Real magic would trump special effects any day."

Kringle's merry face turned somber. "*Evil* wizard, my friend. People would laugh off any suggestion that he wasn't an ordinary person. He'd be invincible."

Evil wizards...if I wrote that up and sent it to the editors of the CIA Factbook, *it would make an interesting chapter*, Gironde thought. *Except they'd think me insane; the guy who believes in elves and Santa Claus.* "Are there a lot of other universes?"

"Well, there's two or three very similar Earths, including yours; a strange universe where, I'm told, the stars are actually alive; plus the demons' world and perhaps a few more."

Gironde sighed, thinking of the linen closet portal. "It would've been handy to have a doorway directly to the demons' world."

"But dangerous," Kringle said. "Even for the Guardian. Rogue doorways between universes do form naturally from time to time or evil wizards create them. They're nothing to scoff at. Imagine if an army of demons came through right inside the Palace. Yseult can't be killed but she can be hurt.

For centuries the goal of many an evil doer has been to capture her and force her to use her powers for their wicked ends."

"Can the doorways be closed?"

"Yes. Or moved to the garden if she sees a reason to keep them active. Finding them is a big part of her job. But the Way of No Return is an exception. An enormous explosion centuries ago tore open a hole between the demons' world and Ring Five. Destroying it would've caused massive instability, so the Guardian left it open but made it one way only."

"And parked it in the middle of nowhere."

"Well, Ring Five." Kringle took a tighter grip on his walking stick. "It's just occurred to me; that explosion was the very one that opened the rift between our world and your Earth a thousand years ago."* His white brows dipped. "This smacks of what young Bart would call 'creepy synchronicity'."

From the top of the painting came a small yawn and an impatient rustle of wings.

"I'm going to try this!" Gironde went closer to the street landscape. Part of his training as a CIA field officer had sharpened his memory and powers of observation. He studied the picture for a minute, then, as the other man had done, walked toward it, keeping the image in his mind. It seemed to fade away; at the point where he should've bumped into the frame, his foot came down on a cobblestoned street.

He turned, triumphant, to welcome Kringle. But a minute passed and then another. Gironde's anxiety was swelling when the old man finally appeared. He was holding a handkerchief to his nose.

"A bit out of practice," he mumbled. The dragon hadn't crossed with him but nonetheless still perched on top of the picture frame, that now showed a painting of the street from

---

* As told in *The Elf Conspiracy*.

which the two men had come. A flaming snort greeted Kringle's statement.

"What now?" Gironde asked, fighting back a grin.

"We find somewhere to have lunch," Kringle said, cramming the now dappled handkerchief into a pocket. He pointed to a sign in the local symbols. "We're now in Ring Seven. The nearest safe access point to Six is quite a ride from here, at the World Tree. We—or I, at least—need to freshen up."

"And then down the Moon Path," Gironde said. *If I could follow the image of Candy in my mind I'd be at her side right now,* he thought, with knife-sharp yearning.

In her former career as a high-fashion model, photo shoots were an enjoyable part of her life, Candace reflected gloomily half an hour after the scuffle on the Las Vegas street. Mug shots were not.

"Turn to your left," the photographer ordered. "Perfect. You're a natural. You should take up modelling. OK, that'll do."

A female officer took her by the arm and guided her to the station's holding cell, pushing her inside with a light pressure on her back. "No fighting, you two," she warned, and slammed the door.

It was a slow night in Las Vegas. Candace and her recent opponent were the only guests of the city. The hooker huddled in a corner, shivering as whatever cocktail of drugs she'd consumed earlier wore off. "Leave me alone," she growled, and sank back into her misery.

The elf picked a spot on a bench across the cell. The smell of the place reminded her of hitching a ride in the back of an unsuspecting policeman's cruiser six months before. That adventure hadn't ended well.

How long will it take, she wondered, crossing her ankles

and trying to relax against the wall, *for my photograph to work its way through the system and into the hands of someone who will recognize it?* Who would arrive first to claim her; the government or the hunters? Candace listened with ears and mind to the human chatter down the hall. Her best chance to escape would be to coax one of the officers to open the cell door and let her out. She needed someone tired, who could be subtly persuaded that the prisoner's release was all in order.

But instead, strain caught up with her and she dozed off. She awoke an uncertain time later to the sound of her name.

"Ms. Batonne."

Candace blinked up at a man in a black suit who stared at her expressionlessly through dark glasses. She stood up stiffly, one hand braced on the wall. The hooker was gone and she was alone in the cell. "Gentlemen," she said, trying to keep her voice steady, "I've been expecting you."

Two other men, identically dressed and equally stony of face, moved slightly closer.

"We are aware that you can read minds," the first man said. Reaching into a pocket, he withdrew a small taser. The other men echoed his movement. "We are prepared to use these if you offer resistance or attempt to meddle with our minds."

"Why would I resist such handsome fellows as you?"

"Please stand closer to the bars. Put your left leg between them."

Reluctantly, she obeyed. Her last encounter with a taser had left her half paralyzed. She would've died if not for the heroic efforts of her human friends and her own rebellious son.

The man took a short, tubular object handed to him by a companion, knelt down and, with a quick movement, clipped it around her ankle. A small blue light began to wink on its side.

"Ms. Batonne," he said again. "You are wearing an anklet designed expressly for you. It contains a locator that can track your position anywhere in the world. It also contains a taser that will activate if you attempt to force it open. The taser is remotely controlled from a location well beyond what we believe to be the effective range of your telepathy." He touched a finger to the lapel of his jacket, to which was clipped the gleaming black button of a tiny video camera. "If it appears that you are trying to control our minds, the taser will be remotely activated. Do you understand?"

Candace sighed wearily. "Yes."

"Come with us." He unlocked the cell door and stood aside to allow her to exit.

Harald would love this, she thought, both of her hearts pounding. *The Men in Black are real.* Despite the warning, she did peer at their minds. Whatever conditioning the three had undergone was remarkably good; looking into their heads was like listening to static on the radio.

Humans. Ever adaptable. Candace tried not to succumb to despair as she was led out of the police station and put into the back seat of a black sedan, an escort sitting stoically and silently on either side. She closed her eyes and didn't look at the dawn-lit city.

The car stopped much sooner than she'd expected. She was surprised to see that they had rolled into an underground parking lot.

"Come with us." One of the men held the door for her and Candace climbed out. "This way." He led her into an elevator and used a key to activate the button panel. They rose twenty storeys and came to a stop at a level marked 'Suites'. "Follow me," the same man said—she was starting to think of them as Eenie, Meenie, and Minie—and opened a door onto luxury.

She wasn't given a chance to admire her new surroundings. "Sit here, please," said Eenie, who seemed to be the leader. 'Here' was an armchair set a few feet in front of a large flatscreen TV.

Candace found her voice. "This is a surprise. I was expecting rigorous interrogation, not entertainment. What's the movie?"

No one answered. Eenie spoke briefly into a cell phone, then touched the control panel. Light bloomed. The three escorts stepped to the side as a man's face filled the screen.

"Good morning, Ms. Batonne," he said.

Relief made her dizzy. She caught her breath and said, "Good morning, Mr. President."

It is good to see you again," the President said. "I regret that our last meeting was not a success."

"Well, I was dying at the time," Candace said, still giddy.

"I am very pleased to see that you have recovered. Ms. Batonne, the past six months have been supremely interesting for my administration. The presence in my country of an extraterrestrial alien and proof of the existence of other universes—let me just say that my science advisors have never worked so hard. I am, myself, very excited about the potential for learning and sharing between our peoples."

"Yet I'm wearing an ankle bracelet that could kill me."

"Yes, Ms. Batonne: That is because I also have security advisors. Allow me to recap." The President leaned forward a little. "For several years, you held a position of considerable responsibility within the CIA; a position that, with your telepathic abilities, gave you access to very sensitive information. You also controlled a communications device that could reach across dimensions."

"My snow globe."

"Very pretty it looked, too, before you knocked it off the table and smashed it."

"Accidents happen."

"I was told that the effort it took to do that almost killed you. Ms. Batonne, I do not wish to be your enemy. The impression I have of you is of a dedicated and very brave individual who will do whatever it takes to carry out her mission. But what is that mission? You understand; I must know."

Candace felt tension draining from her back muscles. "The mission is over."

"What was its nature?"

"Self defence."

"Against us?"

Years ago she'd been warned, when she started her assignment as a secret agent, that the longing to tell what she knew could become overwhelming. Isolation and loneliness could erode even the strongest will, and she'd been in the doubly difficult position of passing herself off not merely as an American, but also as a human.

Nonetheless she'd held out and even her growing love for Paul hadn't weakened her resolve.

Now, it no longer mattered. With the separation of her universe from the human realm, there was no more risk that the immense power of human thoughts, beliefs, and desires could control her people's destiny, as it had for centuries. With a sense of relief Candace talked, until the slant of light coming in the suite's tall windows said that over an hour had passed.

When she at last paused to sip a glass of chilled, sweetened water silently offered her by one of the escorts, the President sat back in his chair.

"So your role at the CIA was to intercept any information coming in about the existence of your universe and alter or erase it."

"Yes."

"Hm. Other than that, you have an exemplary service record and believe me, Ms. Batonne, the CIA has gone over it with a microscope. An electron microscope. Your analyses were always trusted, and with good reason. Not at all the activity of an enemy."

"I've never considered myself to be the enemy of your country. My job was simply to protect my people."

"From our dreaded power of imagination."

"Not dreaded, sir. Just powerful."

"I should like to visit your world some day."

"I hope that will be possible."

The President chuckled. "A neat answer. You haven't told me if there *is* a way to travel between the worlds. Is there?"

"I don't know how I was brought here. The students used a pentacle but, as far as I'm aware, it shouldn't have worked." Another rule of secret agents: Don't tell everything you know, even if you are cooperating. The wormhole in John's garage would remain hidden.

"Could it have something to do with this?" The President held up a familiar lead-wrapped package, taken from her at the police station. "Young Douglas Whallen said you were very interested in the stone inside."

Candace wondered how he knew about the youth. "Yes, sir. There's some kind of energy emanating from it. I suggest that you handle it with care."

"How do you know of this energy?"

What the hell, Candace told herself. *I've come this far.* "This is how." She extruded her antennae and was amused to see his eyes widen. "I can sense some frequencies."

"As well as thoughts."

"When necessary. May I ask a question?" At his nod, she said, "Is Doug all right? And Morris?"

"As to the latter, he is in hospital and appears to be catatonic. Very low brain function, so I'm told. His survival is questionable. Douglas is home with his family."

"I'm glad he's OK."

"You're more charitable toward him than he is toward you. His story is that you're a demon and that you caused his friend to go mad, commit murder, and then lose his mind. He's also accused you of kidnapping him and stealing his car and credit card. He implies that it was your plan from the start."

"*What?* Those boys abducted me, held me prisoner, and assaulted me! They even wrapped me in duct tape!"

"I know; the Secret Service has examined the room. Mr. Whallen claims it was merely kinky sex play and that you were a willing participant."

Her hearts skipped a beat. "Did he mention the men chasing us? The pink limousine?"

"He did. According to him, they had nothing to do with what happened in the dorm. It was an unrelated carjacking attempt. We've found no trace of the limousine."

The creative human imagination at work. How could she prove, even to a willing listener, what she'd sensed in the back of Morris's mind? Candace laughed bitterly. "What happens now? Am I to stand trial as a suspected killer? Or, perhaps, to be exorcised?"

The President looked uncomfortable. "My legal advisors have raised the question of whether or not you *can* be put on trial. Does the law apply to non-human persons? Can a non-human even be a person?"

She felt as if the world was dropping out from under her feet. "What is your opinion?"

"My opinion is that I am speaking with an intelligent person who is not human." He looked down at the long hands resting on his desk. "There's more that I think you should hear. Mr. Whallen confessed everything to his family. Or, at any rate, everything as he sees it. His grandfather is very highly placed in an organization with a strongly fundamentalist mandate. He is also a Senator. I do not know how he knew that you were in custody, or why he chose to call me, but we had a most interesting and, I have to say, disagreeable conversation. He, for one, does not believe that you are a demon."

"Well, that's a relief!"

"He thinks that you're a witch. In his view, not shared by

myself, a witch must not be suffered to live. Senator Whallen had a long career as a lawyer. He picked up at once on the possibility that our laws may not apply to you." The President's jaw muscles tightened. "He has demanded your immediate execution, and pointed out that both California and Nevada have the death penalty."

Candace couldn't speak for a moment and when she did, her voice shook. "That brightens my day no end."

"It will not come to that, I assure you."

"What will it come to?"

"For the time being, comfortable circumstances. The suite you are in is for your use. You are free to come and go, providing that you do not try to leave the city. An allowance has been made available for clothing and entertainment. You will, of course, be escorted, but discreetly and for your protection; I understand that there was an awkward encounter last night. It would please me very much if you would, from time to time, make yourself available to answer questions."

"I—I appreciate the kindness, sir. I wasn't looking forward to lying on an autopsy table. Again."

The President looked embarrassed. "That won't happen and should not have happened. We will be in touch." His hand moved and the screen darkened.

Candace sat for a moment. When she looked up, all three of her escorts—her bodyguards, her keepers—were silently watching.

"Gentlemen," she said. "Let's go shopping."

At a table in a Ring Seven eating house, Paul Gironde poked a spoon into the thick brown stew filling the steaming bowl in front of him and dipped out a shiny, round white ball. He looked across the table at his companion and whispered, "Do you know what we're eating?"

Kringle patted his mouth with a napkin and smiled. "It appears to be organic. Rather tasty, too. Try it."

"Looks like an eyeball."

"Might be, at that. The waiter said it was a local dish, very popular with the regulars." The old man scooped up a pale globe from his own bowl, popped it into his mouth and chewed with gusto.

Gironde sipped some of the gravy. The flavour was definitely brown. He couldn't match it up with any familiar taste. The other people in the hostelry's dining room didn't match any familiar shapes, sizes, or phenotypes, either. Some had wings. Many were furry. One looked like a small horse, except for its glowing, pupil-less red eyes and the prehensile tongue that conveyed fruit to its mouth.

Most of the other guests, accustomed to encountering highly diverse species in hostelries catering, like this one, to travellers crossing the Rings, ignored the two humans. They were far more interested in the dragon, exotic even here. The creature had its own little table and ate food served on dainty china plates.

Gironde set down his spoon and said, "I guess, over a thousand years, you've eaten some pretty unusual items." Making conversation held off the moment of putting one of the globes in his mouth. "There must've been bad years. Hungry years. Back in the Middle Ages."

Kringle smiled. "If you're wondering, did I ever starve, the answer is 'no'. As a priest and later a bishop I lived well, even in famine times. Before I took holy orders, I never missed a meal either. My family was quite well to do, for fisherfolk." He paused for a sip of the greenish beer that had come with the stew before going on.

"Noble boys who entered the Church could count on rising in the hierarchy, but it was unusual for a commoner lad like me to advance past the level of village priest. I had talent and a couple of noble patrons who took an interest in me, but what really boosted me up the ladder were the generous donations my family gave the Church. Add to that my lack of scruples, burning ambition, and considerable cynicism, and my future was assured."

Gironde paused in the act of reaching for his own mug of beer. "I'm hearing this from the original, real, authentic, one-and-only Santa Claus?"

Kringle's eyes gleamed with amusement. "I've mellowed considerably. By the time the elves contacted me, I was already a man sickened by his own vanity and greed. They made me reach into myself and find who I truly was."

"Children everywhere are grateful you did."

"You can't imagine how grateful I am to the elves."

Gironde put a sauce-coated ball into his mouth and tentatively bit down. The texture was firm and chewy. *I was a CIA officer*, he reminded himself. *On one of my missions, I ate raw snake in the desert. On another, I chowed down on bugs in the jungle. Why the hell am I squeamish now?*

Kringle might have read his thoughts. "I believe the term is 'culture shock'," he said. "Think what you've been through these past few months. Discovering that the lady you loved passionately was not only an exceptionally talented spy and double agent, but an alien to boot. Fighting demons. Learning that there are other universes. Emigrating to one. Becoming immortal."

"About that." A memory flashed through Gironde's mind: elves, thousands of them, surrounding him where he sat in the centre of an amphitheater, antennae focused on him with silent intensity. "Can't say that I feel any different."

"Oh, it'll hit you one day. I remember waking up one morning in the City and thinking that it was a hundred years since I'd eaten a perogie. My mother's were especially good. Glitter can tell you what that day was like; I'm sure he'll never forget it. Try some of this condiment. I believe it's pickled vegetable. Or possibly," Kringle went on with a twinkle in his eye, "rancid innards."

Really, the globes weren't half bad and the crusty bread that had come with the stew was both familiar and delicious.

Gironde finished his bowl and beckoned to the waiter, who scurried across the ceiling to take his order for a second helping.

"What's our next stop?" he asked.

"The World Tree. That will take us in turn to Ring Six and the Moon Track. Pity I couldn't bring my sleigh and reindeer, but they can't fly in all of the Rings. We'll hire mounts at a livery stable here and save ourselves a lot of walking. We still have a long way to go."

"Mounts like that?" Gironde nodded toward the horse-like being.

"Not a good idea to stare at a kelpie, lad. They don't like it and have a tendency to become aggressive if provoked."

"I have a lot to learn." Gironde couldn't resist another sidelong peek at the creature and was alarmed to see it staring at him. The scarlet glare sent prickles down his spine. *Probably curious too,* he thought as the kelpie's head quickly jerked away. *Not its fault that it looks like it belongs in a horror movie.* Out of the corner of his eye he saw the horselike being head at an urgent trot toward the restaurant's door. The kelpie roughly pushed aside a customer trying to enter and disappeared into the street. A few seconds later a waiter hurried after, waving an unpaid bill.

Gironde turned his attention back to what Kringle was saying.

"You're doing admirably," the old man assured him. "I can see why Candy Cane chose you."

"I think the choosing was mutual. Candy said she never tried to influence my thoughts to make me care about her. Other than in the conventional way, with the words 'I love you'." Gironde toyed with a piece of warm bread. "That matters a lot."

"Enough that you risked career and life to save her when she was captured by your people."

"Speaking of which, what nationality am I now? An

American Elfite? Elfadian? Elfman?" Gironde chuckled. "Perhaps I should change my name to Danny and learn how to compose great music."

Explaining the reference occupied the rest of the meal. Later, lying alone in a bed clearly designed for a much larger being, Gironde watched through a skylight the intricate dance of three moons and considered the journey ahead. *Every day brings me closer to her,* he thought, and fell into a deep sleep.

Fate is mysterious in his ways, Candace decided, floating on her back in the hotel's enclosed rooftop pool. She was deliciously tired after the day's shopping expedition. *Last year, I was a miserable prisoner in the country's most secure installation, under Cheyenne Mountain in Colorado. This year, I'm a pampered guest of the government.* Assuming, of course, that she obeyed the rules, because despite the generous expense allowance and luxury accommodation, she was really a prisoner. The anklet and the silently watchful presences of Max, Bill, and Joe—not, she was certain, their real names—were proofs.

On the other hand, she loved clothes and shopping and was in a town that catered to well-moneyed spenders.

The entire top floor of the hotel, containing two suites and the pool, had been reserved for her and the guards. They took turns sleeping in their suite, so that at least one was always on duty. A discreet look around had confirmed that electronic eyes and ears were also observing her, every minute of the day and night. Her ambivalent status couldn't be more clear: former spy and possible threat; potential ambassador of an alien civilization. Handle with care.

She swam leisurely to the pool's sunken marble steps and walked out of the water, aware that Max, formerly known as Eenie, was watching her from behind his dark glasses. He looked like an ordinary, if very well muscled, vacationer in his plaid swim trunks, lounging comfortably on a deck chair with a tablet computer on his lap and a communications device discreetly clipped to an ear. She was sure that he wasn't reading a novel and that the innocuous pouch on a nearby table held a weapon. She'd already worked out that the suggestive shape in the pocket of his trunks was a taser.

Human males usually reacted positively to female elf pheromones and with the added stimulation of her new and very expensive swimsuit, the men's libidos should've been twanging. The lack of any response suggested that the guards had taken drugs to neutralize or reduce sexual response, in addition to whatever conditioning and training they'd used to block her mind reading. Or perhaps they were gay. In the half year since she'd escaped her previous captivity, someone had done a lot of homework and preparation. The speed with which the suite had been acquired and wired was another sign of that readiness.

"Care to join me for lunch?" she asked as she reached for a towel.

"No thank you, ma'am." That summed up all the conversation she could squeeze out of the men: Yes, ma'am; no, ma'am; can't say, ma'am.

Lunch waited on a nearby table. She'd seldom seen such a varied collection of fruit and vegetable juices, sent up by a room service that was accustomed to satisfying the whims of very rich people capable of losing very large sums of money in the hotel's casino. There were even thin peeled sticks of sugar cane and she chose one to nibble on.

What if, she asked herself as she stretched out with her snack on a deck chair, *what if I can never go home? What if the wormhole closes forever and I'm trapped on Earth?*

She knew that life might even be pleasant, especially if she was willing to cooperate fully. After her years with the CIA, she could well imagine the uses to which the government might put a telepath.

Candace wriggled a little on the chair, feeling a slight pressure along both sides of her spine from the bud sacs developing deep within her body. In six months, her children would be born. What future could Earth offer them? Could they even survive, without the devoted round-the-clock care and feeding provided by male elves? Buds were very fragile in their early days. Could they survive well-intentioned human curiosity?

"Do you have any kids?" she called to Max.

"No, ma'am."

"I do." She watched as his fingers tapped on the tablet. No doubt, that tidbit was now entered into a data base marked Alien, Information About, Ultra Top Secret. "All boys," she added. "I miss them."

Tap, tap, tap.

"I have twenty. Most are from my second and third matings."

Tap tap tappity-tap.

"Actually, twenty-two."

Tap. Tap.

"Did I mention that they're all boys?"

"Yes, ma'am."

"I suppose someone will now try to figure out if I'm pulling your leg."

"Yes, ma'am." Tap tap tap.

"I'm not."

Tap.

She sighed. Teasing a living robot wasn't much fun. Lengthy reports would probably now be written and serious, well-thought-out analyses prepared on how to determine if an alien is telling the truth, or even if an alien perceived truthfulness as humans did. Cross references would be made to the medical information collected when she lay helpless and half-paralyzed months before, and serious discussions on the topic of alien psychology would fly back and forth on secure channels. Someone, somewhere, was certain to be calling him- or herself a xeno-psychologist and building an exciting new career based on her behaviour and the pearls that fell from her lips.

"Pearls before swine," she muttered. "I am not a lab rat." At the root of her defiance, as she knew very well, was the knowledge that everything could suddenly change. A new administration, a shift in policy, a bout of xenophobia, could turn her current comfortable situation into something wretchedly different. So could a failed escape attempt.

But staying on Earth wasn't an option, and not just because of her unborn children. There was also the terrifying presence she'd sensed in Morris's mind. Something new and awful was making itself known and only at home could she count on people to believe her.

Mostly, though, she missed Paul; missed him like she would one of her hearts.

"I'd like to go to the casino tonight," she said.

"Yes, ma'am."

"Blackjack, I think." An escape attempt would need money and the cash she'd stolen from Doug had been confiscated, perhaps with that concern in mind. Her shopping spree had been paid for by Bill, using a credit card that she wasn't allowed to handle. In the bustle of the casino, she might be able to hide a few chips or dollars. It was worth a try. "Or poker."

No answer. Tap, tap, tap.

"You do understand, don't you, that I'll be reading the minds of the other players?"

"Yes, ma'am." TAP tap tap.

"We aliens don't see it as cheating, as it's a natural ability we have." That was true. The tapping fingers paused. "Are you going to tase me if I read their minds?"

"Can't say, ma'am." Tap. Tap. Tap.

Max's earpiece must have signalled him. He cupped a hand around it and listened briefly. "Roulette, ma'am. Or slots. No blackjack. No poker."

She wondered who had made that decision. "Drat. I was looking forward to breaking the bank."

"Yes, ma'am."

Long pause.

"I'm pregnant."

Tap.

"Of course, I could be lying."

Short pause. Taptaptap.

"But I'm not."

Max again cocked a hand to his ear. "When are you due, ma'am?"

"Six months from now, and if you say 'ma'am' one more time, I will scream."

"Yes, miss. A doctor will be in to examine you tomorrow morning."

"Oh, good. Some brand-new expert in xenobiology."

"Yes, miss."

She gave up for the moment and flopped back on the deck chair, watching the intense blue sky through the skylight over the pool. Condensation gathered at the bottom of the windows. For her comfort, the air conditioning had been turned down as low as possible and she hadn't even needed to ask: another fruit of the knowledge gained during her previous incarceration. If she did manage to get the anklet off and slip away across the desert, she'd be all right at night but during the day, when temperatures soared, the heat might kill her. In her own world, elves lived only in the Arctic and temperate zones.

Mostly to see what Max would do, she extruded her antennae and waved them gently.

He stood up, drew his taser in one smooth movement

and pointed it at her. "Please put those away, ma'am."

A gust of air made her look around. Joe, taser in hand, had entered the pool room. She retracted the filaments, shaken by the men's reaction.

Max pocketed his weapon. "We will stay in tonight."

"All right, gentlemen, I get it: privileges revoked for scary behaviour."

"Yes, ma'am."

Joe left as silently as he'd entered.

Candace sat up and, in as calm a tone as she could manage, said, "You can't keep me here indefinitely. Aside from the fact that people you don't want to notice me will have the chance to do so, it must be costing the government a fortune."

"Which people?"

"I've already told—better answer your ear; it's about to ring." The fact that it did was a small triumph.

Max hadn't returned to his chair. "I am instructed to tell you that you will be moved to new accommodation soon."

"Where?"

Perhaps the men thought she could only read minds when her antennae were extended, because this time she glimpsed an image: a ranch house in a valley surrounded by mountains; an impression of remoteness and isolation. Cool temperatures, ample creature comforts, and an electric fence completely surrounding the property.

"I can't say, ma'am." Max sat down again, picked up his tablet and resumed whatever he'd been doing.

Candace threw her towel and the remains of her sugar cane onto the floor and jumped to her feet, not caring at that moment if her seething frustration showed. "I'm going to take a nap."

"Yes, ma'am," said the maddening Max.

"The trick to riding a wheeler is to approach your mount confidently," Kringle said to Gironde in the yard of the Ring Seven livery stable they'd found. "But not arrogantly. Just with confidence. Let me demonstrate."

"That went well," the younger man said a moment later, trying not to grin too broadly.

Kringle muttered something that did not sound like "Ho, ho, ho," and fingered the rip that a bony beak had made in his trousers.

"I'm sure we can find a tailor," Gironde said. "Perhaps also something that runs on gasoline."

"It *does* run on gas," Kringle said, summoning his dignity. "Methane." He eyed his mount. It stared smugly back with a scarlet-rimmed eye.

"My turn," Gironde said without enthusiasm. His own steed waited a few feet away. He'd ridden at Scout camp as a youth but suspected that the only thing this creature had in common with horses was the expression of bored docility concealing intent to buck. *At least it can't kick,* he reassured himself, but the deeply ridged circle of bone and cartilage that formed the creature's rear wheel looked like it could effortlessly shred human flesh. The front wheel's hub bore horn-like projections that, according to the stable hand who had saddled the beast, were used by males to fight off rivals. They'd been cut short but perhaps not short enough, Gironde mused, noting the scabs and scars on the groom's legs.

"Confidently," he said, and stepped forward just as Kringle's digestive system parted with an explosive amount of gas. As the mount's armoured head jerked toward the tantalizing odour, Gironde seized the opportunity to leap onto its back and grab the handlebar-like antlers.

The animal started but soon relaxed, growling in pleasure as Gironde squeezed the levers attached to the antlers, releasing into its nostrils a puff of gas from the tank strapped between his knees. As suggested by the groom, he guided it in slow practice circles around the livery stable's yard. The wheeler soon settled under him, perhaps grateful that it wasn't carrying Kringle, who was getting a boost into the saddle of the other animal with the help of two perspiring stable hands.

"I'm going down the street," Gironde called to him. "Back in a minute."

He turned the antlers toward the road and pressed his knees against the wheeler's sides to urge it on. Like a horse it responded to leg aids; the key to a smooth ride, he'd been told, was to coordinate the movements of his hands and legs with a methane reward.

He left the yard and merged into traffic. Most of the vehicles on the cobbled streets were carts pulled by larger wheelers, though now and then centaurs trotted past, drawing wagons or cabs. A giant thumped down the road, carrying on its matted head a house-sized bundle. Like the other travellers, Gironde prudently pulled to the curb to give it room. The peoples of the Rings might get along, he decided, but sometimes peace requires a willingness to yield right of way.

The road opened up and he nudged the wheeler to a faster speed, enjoying the smooth ride that the thick cartilage tires gave on the bumpy cobbles. *Candy would love this,* he thought, imagining her sitting behind him, arms around his waist, laughing into the wind. Or, more likely, he'd be trying to keep up with her as she raced ahead of him on her own mount.

A second later his wistful grin was wiped away as an arrow glided over his shoulder.

"What—" Gironde twisted around. The persistent staccato tapping behind him that he'd assumed was made by a centaur's hooves came from the kelpie, and it had brought friends.

Ring Seven's ruffians, thugs, brutes, hooligans, and muggers might have shared very little in physical form, but they all projected the same aura of intent to do a great deal of harm with the knives, swords, spears, and clubs they carried.

Another arrow, shot by a centaur whose right eye had been obliterated by a long-ago knife slash, wobbled past. The archer cursed and snatched a fresh bolt from the quiver strapped to his flank.

Ahead, an open road and a chance to outrun the pursuers. Behind, Kringle, alone and perhaps also under attack.

Gironde wrenched his wheeler's antlers, forcing the animal to spin around. He clapped his legs hard against its sides, released an encouraging gust of methane into its nose, and tore back along the road, straight toward the pursuers.

An arrow grazed his cheek. The centaur, cursing, lunged aside to avoid a collision but thumped into the kelpie. Both went down in a tangle of legs.

Flattening himself as low as he could, Gironde plunged through the pack. A spear nicked his jacket. Knives clutched in hands, paws, or tentacles jabbed at him but the attackers were off guard and most of the thrusts struck empty air. One lucky blow scraped the wheeler's flank and with an enraged squeal the animal swerved to gore a giant's shaggy leg with its blunted but hard horn. Gironde grabbed at the saddle and the antlers and held on for his life's sake.

Wheelers shared a conviction with horses that while in the stable the only place to be is outside, and while outside the only place to be is in the stable. It headed home at top speed.

Kringle was riding practice circles as Gironde skidded into the livery stable yard, heaving on the wheeler's antlers to bring it to a stop. The old man raised a bushy white eyebrow.

"Trouble, lad?"

"You could say that." Gironde glanced over his shoulder. The progress of his pursuers could be tracked by the oncoming uproar.

"Time to flee for our lives, I take it?"

"Informed persons would agree."

"Very well." Kringle nodded a polite dismissal to the grooms shadowing him, gripped the antlers of his beast and with commendable skill guided it into the street.

Gironde followed close behind. "Are we going in the right direction for the transfer point?" he called, praying that it did not lie on the other side of the hoodlum scrum.

"I believe so," Kringle replied, dodging around a wagon full of apples. "Beg pardon, ma'am," he added, almost running over a woman's long, black train. The woman shrieked, unfolded the train into huge wings, and leaped into the air.

"Never wise to annoy a banshee," Kringle shouted to Gironde, kicking his wheeler into a faster pace. The flustered banshee locked onto the strongest nearby sources of emotion and dove wailing and clawing into the pack of thugs.

"But sometimes useful," Gironde called back. The scrum had stopped in its collective tracks and within a few minutes was far behind.

Kringle dropped back to ride at his side. "That young centaur fellow, Hint of Spring, said that the Lady was 'much preoccupied'," he said. "I'm beginning to understand why. Someone doesn't want us here. Someone powerful enough to counter her protection."

Gironde said nothing. He concentrated on his driving and tried not to think of all the fairy-tale monsters he'd read about as a child.

Sleepless in Las Vegas. Candace lay in the centre of a large, seductively comfortable bed, and wondered what the hidden observers watching her through the not-very-well-concealed spy cameras would make of her restlessness. *Another scientific paper,* she decided morosely.

The silk of a new nightgown flowed across her skin as she turned on her side. She'd bought the garment partly to keep up her spirits, by imagining how Paul would enjoy seeing it on her, and partly to provoke her guards. A subtle power struggle was in progress and she was sure the men knew it.

So far, they were leading. In a city dedicated to luck, odds of three to one weren't really all that good when the other side had tasers, spy cams, and unseen minions.

Candace slid out of bed, went to the window and drew back the curtains. Las Vegas also didn't sleep. She'd already discovered that when the thick curtains were closed, the glaring, dancing lights couldn't penetrate. The only illumination in the room then was the blue flicker from the ankle bracelet.

Crossing her arms, she leaned against the glass and wondered what was happening at home. Paul would've gone straight to Kringle after her disappearance, she was sure, but what then? The Master always knew when an elf died or was very ill, but not where that elf might be. If she could somehow get a message home she'd quickly be rescued, but the kernel of the problem lay in 'somehow'.

Wide open spaces, big, sprawling ranch house; electrified barbed wire. How soon would she be moved?

The one place where she was reasonably sure there was no spy cam was inside the suite's luxurious shower stall. Max had told her that she was allowed five minutes of privacy in the bathroom for 'personal needs', though she'd have given good odds that if some researcher wanted to write a paper about alien bodily functions, her privacy wouldn't matter.

Going into the living room, she announced, "I can't sleep," to Bill, who had the night shift. He sat on a couch, the inevitable tablet in hand. "I'm taking a shower."

"Yes, ma'am."

"A long shower."

"Yes, ma'am."

"During which time I will formulate an evil plan to take over the world."

"Enjoy yourself, ma'am."

Swearing under her breath, Candace headed for the bathroom. The cold water soon streaming over her skin did feel good and under the cover of the lavish artificial rain she extruded her antennae. The cut made by Morris was healing, though still sensitive. She lathered her hair, using the scrubbing motion to help conceal the rising antennae as she investigated the surrounding area.

Bill's thoughts were like an alert, loud buzz. The slumbering minds of Max and Joe in the suite across the pool felt smothered.

Candace stretched her range downward. There were no minds on the floor below; presumably, the government had rented the space for security reasons. Below that there were people in plenty; most asleep, some fuzzy or over-stimulated with alcohol, some worried, a few happy; one like a hole in the fabric of space itself.

That mind was on the move. She tracked it heading toward the building's east stairwell, where it paused briefly. If the door was locked, it didn't delay the creature for very long because soon it was in the stairwell and rising.

Candace grabbed a towel and wrapped it around herself as she ran to the living room.

"Get your gun out," she snapped at Bill. "Something bad is coming up the stairs."

A pistol almost leaped into his hand. "Which side?"

"East."

"Wait here, ma'am."

"There's another. It's coming up the elevator; getting off two floors below." Her antennae stiffened. "Now it's moving toward the west stairwell. We're being bracketed. Wake up your friends."

Bill touched his earpiece, spoke briefly, but didn't leave her. She could feel his doubt, the suspicion of a trick. "Confirmed," he said. A security cam must've spotted the intruders. "Are there any more?"

Candace closed her eyes and concentrated. "Only two nearby. But I think there's more at street level. Tell your people to look for a pink limousine."

Bill relayed the message, showing no surprise at how far she could stretch her senses.

"Get dressed," he barked, as the suite's door opened and the other two guards entered, fully clothed and with weapons in hand. Max carried a sub-machine pistol.

Candace dashed back to her bedroom and scrambled into the clothes she'd been wearing when invoked by the three students, plus a pair of sturdy sandals she'd bought with an eye to a possible desert crossing. There was still soap in her hair and she towelled it out hastily as she rejoined the men.

Max eyed her antennae. "What can you tell us?"

"They have human form but aren't human. I don't know if they're armed, but I'd bet on it. I can't read their minds; I can only sense that they exist." She swallowed. "They scare the shit out of me."

For the first time, she saw the glimmer of a smile on his face. "Go into the bedroom," he said. "Lock the door. Get under the bed, if you can."

"One's on our floor now," she said as she backed toward her room. "It's going into your suite."

"Wait." Max held up a hand. "I need you to tell me where they are."

"The second one's reached this floor. Another is coming up in a passenger elevator. There may be one in the service elevator."

"Backup's on the way," Joe said.

"ETA?"

"Two minutes."

"It'll be over by then," Max said calmly. "Where are they now, ma'am?"

"The one in your suite is coming this way through the

pool room." A side door led from the suite to the pool. Bill moved to cover that entrance. "Three have converged on the landing in the west stairwell. They seem to be waiting."

"There's a disturbance downstairs," Joe said, hand cupped over his earpiece. "Street level."

"They're moving!" Candace's head turned toward the west stairwell. "Running down the hall—they're here."

"Get down!"

She dropped to the carpet and started to crawl backwards toward the doubtful safety of the bedroom. An instant later, bullets ripped through the drywall and layer of soundproofing, narrowly missing Joe, who was crouched behind a chair. Max's machine pistol stuttered in reply.

One of the empty minds flicked out like a candle flame in the wind. Bullets spurted through the poolside wall and Bill's gun replied.

"You got one in the hallway," Candace said. "The one in the pool room is moving to my left."

"The other two?" Max asked.

"They're retreating down the hall."

An instant later, an explosion deafened her and filled the room with dust and fragments of metal, plaster, and insulation. The attackers hadn't tried to force the locked door; they'd blasted through the wall.

The explosion flung Joe back five feet. Candace cried out and clutched her head, rocked by the man's pain. Her vision blurred for a few seconds.

When her sight cleared, Max's forehead was streaming blood from a deep gash. Gun in hand, he staggered to his feet and fired at a figure climbing through the hole in the wall. Candace saw a man in a cook's uniform, followed by another dressed in the suit of a senior hotel employee. The first shot shattered the cook's knee. He fell and began to crawl on his elbows, eyes fixed on her.

"Behind me!" Max pulled her to her feet and shoved her

into the bedroom, blocking the door with his body. Over his shoulder, she saw his next shot explode the cook's eye. Brains erupted in a red cloud from the back of the skull. The body flopped to the floor and Candace caught her breath as the weird not-mind winked out.

That left the man in the suit. Shots from Bill's pistol smacked three times into his chest, straight through the heart. He kept moving forward.

"Get the head!" Max followed his own advice and the man fell.

"Fucking zombies!" Bill turned with a fierce grin and died as a shot came through the poolside wall and slammed into his head.

Candace screamed as the death rocked her mind, wide open and receptive. She dimly heard more shots as a dark grey mist rolled over her, then nothing.

So that's the World Tree." Gironde tilted back his head and stared, not caring that his mouth hung open. The top leaves of the tree brushed the stratosphere. Its roots rippled as high as mountain ranges and the trunk filled so much of his field of vision that sky made only a narrow slice on either side. "What sort of tree is it? Other than incredibly, outrageously, huge."

"An oak, I believe," Kringle said, standing in his stirrups to ease his aching glutes. He cast a glance over his shoulder but their pursuers were not in sight.

"I'd hate to be here during the autumn."

"Why?"

"Acorns. They must be the size of cities. Not fun to be under one when it drops."

"Back when I was a lad, long before I took holy orders, I used to drive my family's hogs to the forest to fatten on the acorns," Kringle said with a reminiscent smile. "I wouldn't like to be here when the pigs come."

"There are giant pigs?"

"You don't see any little oak trees, do you? Something's eating up the acorns."

"Right." Gironde kicked his wheeler's sides. "Let's get a move on before we're stepped on by whoever drives the giant pigs."

Candace's first impression was: *I've been here before.* Winking lights on medical monitors. Oxygen tubes poked up her nose. A familiar face hovering above hers; the same nurse who had cared for her after she was crippled by the taser strike six months before.

It's all been a dream, she thought. *I never escaped, I never made it home; Paul and I are not going to be married. I'm still trapped and Kevin will torture me again.*

The nurse smiled. "How do you feel?"

"Lucy. Where am I?"

"In your hotel room. In Las Vegas."

Candace reached up and gripped the other woman's hand, deeply glad of her presence. "Are you the medical expert who's supposed to examine me?" She tried to sit up and met a gently restraining palm. The nurse removed the oxygen tubes and began to disconnect her from a medical monitor beside the bed.

"No; a doctor was here earlier. I was called in from Colorado last night. They felt my previous experience would be useful. You've been unconscious for twelve hours."

"Twelve!"

"We've been very concerned. The President has called more than once to see how you're doing. How do you feel?"

"Like my head's been used as a soccer ball. Other than that, all right."

This time, the nurse slid a supporting hand under her back and helped her sit up. She handed Candace a glass of orange juice that the elf drank gratefully, and placed a change of clothes on the bed.

"Do you remember what happened?"

Candace nodded as she pulled on the garments.

"Mr. Maxwell wants to speak with you. I'll tell him you're conscious." The nurse left the room and a minute later Max entered, immaculate in his black suit, a stitched wound on his forehead the only sign of the battle.

"I'm glad to see you awake." He pulled an armchair beside the bed and sat down. "You had us worried."

"Is Bill...?"

"Dead. Yes. Joe will recover."

"The attackers?"

"We killed four and captured one. All hotel employees. There was an incident on the street outside at the same time; a car accident. We don't know if it was a diversion, but the people involved all fled and haven't been located. One of the cars was a pink limo. They'd all been stolen."

Candace tried to smile. "That's the most words I've heard from you at once. I am very sad about Bill. He was a brave man."

"Yes, ma'am, he was. Were those hotel people under your mental control?"

"No!"

"Can you prove that?"

She sighed. "No. Are you going to bring out the thumbscrews now?"

"We don't do that, ma'am."

"You don't: I know someone who'd love to. If I was controlling those men, I wouldn't have warned you of the danger."

"We have come to the same conclusion."

"So, no thumbscrews."

"Perhaps something worse. I'd like you to try your telepathy on the survivor." Max noted her shiver. "Have you encountered people like that before?"

"Yes. In the college dorm. I'm sure you know about that."

"Which man was it?"

"Morris. In a way. Also, someone I didn't see."

"What do you mean by 'in a way'?"

Candace paused to think. "It's not easy to put into words. Morris thought like a normal human, but there was someone, something, looking through from the back of his mind. When Doug started beating him, the watcher disappeared and took most of Morris's mind with it." She shuddered again. "The one I didn't see had nothing human in it. Imagine staring into a black hole in space. I may not be human, but I'm the girl next door compared to that."

"You seem very human."

Candace laughed. "My people are the product of human wishing and dreams. Plus, I've lived among you for the better part of two hundred years. I've had more practice at being human than any human ever gets."

"That tells me a lot. Do you know what made you collapse?"

"Yes. Imagine putting a wet finger in a light socket and turning on the power. To be so near a normal human's death while fully receptive, is like that. Those mindless minds have a draining effect, too. They're not the same as the thing in Morris. Whatever that creature was, it had intelligence. The, the emptiness—" She wrapped herself in her arms, shaking. To her very great surprise, Max reached across and pressed a hand briefly over one of hers.

"I don't want to insist on your examining the survivor."

"But you will." She managed a smile. "I was with the CIA for years; I understand about hard imperatives. Where is he?"

"She. A chambermaid. Can you stand?"

"Yes." Candace rose and though her legs felt like overcooked spaghetti, walked out of the bedroom without assistance.

Not much had changed. Debris still covered the plush carpeting and large bloodstains marked where the attackers and Bill had fallen. Four of the men in black suits waited, weapons in hand.

"We'll go down one floor," Max said, touching Candace's arm; she wasn't sure if he was guiding her or afraid she'd collapse again. "We will have to take the stairs. The elevators are on lockdown."

"That must be making some people very upset."

Again the thin smile. "Hotel management is cooperating, despite their heartfelt sorrow over the inconvenience to their guests."

"Who must be leaving in droves."

"Not really. They can't get past the media swarm in the street."

"Oh! Do they know about...?"

"No, ma'am. You don't exist. The story is that an employee went on a shooting rampage."

Candace could feel the cold emptiness as she went down the stairs with her alert escort. By the time they reached the room where the chambermaid was being held, she was shivering again.

Max paused at the door, which was guarded by two more black-suited men. "Last chance to change your mind, Ms. Batonne."

"You didn't say 'ma'am'."

"If you can make a joke, you're okay. Ma'am." He nodded and a guard opened the door.

This apartment, though luxurious, was smaller than the suites upstairs. Candace followed Max into a living room. A slim young woman dressed in a white smock with the hotel's crest on the breast sat on a couch, manacled hands folded in her lap. Two more armed men watched her silently. Candace noted the well-applied makeup and short, carefully manicured nails that suggested she was ambitious for better things than a chambermaid's life.

"She had an assault rifle hidden in her laundry bag," Max said. "Pulled it out as soon as the elevator door opened.

Luckily, it hooked on a sheet. Gave us a couple of seconds to bring her down."

"Who did that?" Candace sat on a chair facing the young woman, well beyond arm's reach. *Time to be an analyst again,* she told herself, and pushed aside the fear.

"I did."

"Was she able to fight back?"

Max slipped a finger into his collar and pulled it down. A quartet of ugly deep scratches showed through a coating of disinfectant. "She only stopped when we had her cuffed."

"Describe her behaviour since then."

"Docile. Stands, sits, and walks on command. Doesn't talk."

"Do you know her name?"

"Sunny Daley. The head housekeeper showed us her employment records. Her other records—school, medical, tax—are being checked, but so far appear to be legitimate."

Which could mean nothing, Candace knew. She'd passed for years as a born American on the strength of superb, elf-forged documentation.

"Anything else you can tell me about her?"

"A hard worker; cheerful and well liked by the other staff. She tried to live up to her name and was flagged for a possible promotion to the concierge desk."

"Possible, not probable?"

"Ms. Daley liked to party late and was once caught taking a nap in the linen storeroom. Kept on because she's usually reliable. No other blots on her employment record. No known or suspected associations with criminals, terrorists, or questionable personages."

Just a pretty girl who enjoyed life, had a good head on her shoulders and a bright future. Candace leaned a little closer and inhaled. She could pick up hints of cleaning fluid and fresh linen, but behind the scent of warm human girl lingered an unpleasant, metallic odour. "Ms. Daley," she said, "can you hear me?"

Nothing. Only a void where a living mind should've been.

I'm crazy to do this, she told herself. *I could get up, say I can't help, and go back to my comfortable prison. No one will hold it against me. But if I do, I'll never know who took away Sunny Daley's mind and left this shell. I'll never even get close to knowing who did the same to the people who died.*

"Try not to get a twitchy finger and tase me, Max," she said. "Don't interrupt, either." She slowly extruded her antennae. The watching men showed no outward reactions, though she picked up surprise, interest, and in one a brief queasiness. *You and me both,* she thought.

Tuning out the men was like drawing a curtain over each mind. Candace stretched her awareness gradually toward the silent figure, ready to snap her antennae into their sheaths at the first hint of an attack. Softly, she glided into the young woman's mind.

If asked to describe how it felt, she would've drawn a comparison to floating in space in a starless emptiness. She could feel the girl's heart beating, lungs automatically drawing breath, blood transporting oxygen, organs following their prescribed routines. Of consciousness, the compendium of energy to which every cell contributed its fraction, organized and elevated to self awareness in the brain, she found nothing.

She was about to withdraw and describe her findings when one of her antennae tingled and stiffened. In the emptiness, a dark star lurked.

Feeling like a piece of bait in a lobster trap, Candace allowed her own consciousness to drift toward the presence, calling all the while for Sunny Daley, for some surviving fragment of the girl's mind.

Elf.

The recognition of her nature was like a laugh in a locked room, or the brush of a viper's tongue under the sheets.

Candace tried to ignore it and slipped more deeply into the nothingness.

Sunny? Sunny Daley? Are you there? I want to help you. Let me help.

Candace projected as harmless an image of herself as she could, deeply aware that it was close to the truth. She disciplined her thoughts and quelled her fears, putting herself into the clear, calm, detached frame of mind that had helped to make her a successful analyst.

Sunny? Hello?

Help me.

Plea or trap? She floated toward the apparent source of the cry, calling encouragement. A wisp of something human in the empty night touched her mind; raw fear. Plea, or trap? One way to find out.

In the hotel room, the watching men saw her take a deep breath. The lightly quivering antennae stiffened and drew together like psychic dowsing rods.

Trap! The entity struck. It wasn't hiding in the void; it was the void itself and now it collapsed onto her. Candace didn't try to dodge; instinct or hunch or both made her throw her mind forward, like a skier cutting across the path of an avalanche, toward the source of the weak cry for help.

She was no longer on Earth. The hotel room had vanished. In its place an expanse of rolling plain reached out to the horizon of an unknown world. Overhead loomed a startling trio of blue suns. Under her feet, a carpet of soft, azure moss spread in every direction. In the distance an irregular tower of white crystal soared up to the sky.

"Sunny!" Candace spotted the girl huddled on the moss and ran to her. The impact of her feet on the ground, the feel of the wind tugging at her hair, were perfectly real.

The young chambermaid's head jerked up. "Please, help me," she whispered. Candace sensed her mind hanging onto the very edge of sanity.

"I came to bring you home," she said.

"What is this place?" the girl asked as the elf helped her to her feet. "It was all dark before. How'd we get here?"

Damned if I know, Candace admitted privately, and told herself: *If there's a way in, there's a way out. There must be.*

She put an arm around the shaking shoulders. "What happened to you? Do you remember?"

"I—I sat down for a nap, just for a minute, and I couldn't wake up. I was dreaming but it wasn't real dreaming. It was like standing in front of a mirror and watching yourself do things but you're not making yourself do them."

Sounds like a good description of possession, Candace thought. In a level, calming tone she asked, "What did you do in this mirror-dream?"

The words tumbled out. "I took my laundry cart down to the delivery bay. There was this tacky pink limousine waiting. A man got out and hid a gun in the cart. I went up the service elevator. When the door opened, some men were there. I pulled out the gun but it caught on a sheet. One of them knocked me down. I fought—I mean, my body fought. He put handcuffs on me and searched me. Then he sat on me and held me down until more men came."

Candace had to smile. Efficient Max. "How did you get here?"

"I don't know! I felt like when, you know, your boyfriend goes off with another girl and you think the world has come to an end and nothing matters any more."

"You felt discarded."

"Yes." Sunny's terror began to recede and she even offered a tremulous smile. "Are you a Martian?"

"A what?"

"You know. A Martian." The girl waggled two fingers above her head. "Like on the old TV show."

Candace had forgotten about her antennae. "You mean *My Favorite Martian.*" She'd seen a few episodes in the 1960s and had been much amused.

"Daddy collects old TV series. I think they're kind of, you know, out of date, and some aren't even in colour, but I bought him the Martian set last Christmas. We watched it all Boxing Day."

Candace smiled. *Here we are, trapped in an eerie dimension with possibly no way home, talking about Christmas. How strange is that?* "I'm an elf, not a Martian," she said. "But, unfortunately, not the kind of elf that has magic rings."

"This is all a dream, isn't it?"

"More of a hallucination, I think."

"Oh. I had one of those once. My boyfriend at the time put something into my drink. When I got out of the hospital, I told him to go to hell. In front of all his friends. It felt good."

"Was his name Scott, by any chance?"

"Yes." Sunny looked up, startled. "How'd you know that?"

"Just a lucky guess." *Something is working itself out*, Candace thought, a quiver running down her spine. *Something enormous, and we're caught right in the middle.*

"Can you read minds?" Sunny's expression was pensive. "The Martian could."

"Well, yes, I can, but please don't ask me to prove it by telling you what you're thinking. We have strict rules about respecting privacy." *Which I routinely ignore,* she added to herself, but the girl's mental state was fragile enough as it was. They began to walk toward the distant crystal tower.

"Where are we going, miss?"

"Home, given a positively indecent amount of luck."

Sunny's laugh was brief but strong. "I like it that you're not pretending everything's going to be all right. I don't think this is a hallucination. It's just as real as real."

I may have underestimated Ms. Daley, Candace decided.

"And, and thank you for coming to help," the girl added shyly. "I think you scared that monster away."

"I did?"

"I saw you coming. You shone. All bright and beautiful. I thought you were an angel."

Candace could find no words in reply.

"That tower," Sunny said after a few more minutes. "It doesn't look made. It kind of looks like it grew."

"Like a cluster of icicles turned upside down," the elf agreed. "Beautiful, in an altogether weird way."

Sunny laughed again. "I feel that I ought to be screaming. I mean, more than I was screaming before."

"Good thing you were. I might not have found you otherwise." Candace stooped to examine the ground. "Take a look at this." She went down on one knee. "There are tiny icicles here, lots of them."

Sunny bent over to look. "Maybe the big one had babies."

"Who knows? I suggest that we walk carefully. The rule for visiting strange and mysterious worlds is simple: don't step on anything that might resent it and kill you."

"Is that really a rule?"

"I just made it up, but it ought to be a rule, don't you agree? Let's get closer to the building, or growth, or whatever it is."

The two picked their way with care through clusters of milky white spires of varying sizes until they reached the wall of the largest. It soared up three hundred or more feet.

"Odd," Candace said, sniffing. "I smell tobacco smoke."

Sunny copied her. "I can't smell a thing."

"I have a highly evolved nose. It's this way." She followed the faint molecular trail through a narrow slot to a small enclosure.

"Someone's been here!" Sunny pointed. "Look; cigarette butts." She picked one up. "Hand rolled. My Daddy used to do that before he got emphysema and his doctor made him quit."

Candace had picked up another. "Fairly fresh, too. This is only a few hours old."

"How'd you know that?"

"I once read a forensic evidence manual."

"You were a detective?"

"CIA analyst. It's a long story." Candace dropped the butt and inhaled deeply, stretching her senses to the maximum. She caught a wisp of pheromones. "There was a man here; a woman, too, I think."

"I wish I could do that. I could quit my job and go home and become a wine taster like my uncle. What are you doing now?"

Candace had raised her antennae. "It's sort of like listening. If they're still here, I'll—"

"You OK?"

She couldn't answer. Impressions swelled in her mind, flooding it to overflowing. She felt her own identity submerging under the massive tide of information streaming into her brain.

A sharp pain in her arm broke the trance. To her astonishment, she was lying on her back, staring up at Sunny's alarmed face.

"What—?"

"I pinched you," the girl said, her voice thin with fear. "You went all blank-looking and fell over and your feeler things whipped around."

Candace sat up. "The crystal towers," she said in wonderment. "They're alive. They live on sunlight and have minds and there's lots of them but something is killing them and they're afraid and want us to help and I'm babbling." She clapped a hand over her mouth to hold back the surging words, none of which, in any language she knew, could even begin to describe how the contact had felt.

Sunny showed a practical streak by asking, "Can they tell us how to get home? I'd be glad to help them but about all I can do is put a chocolate on their pillow."

Candace lay back on the moss and laughed until her ribs ached.

Sunny sat beside her and leaned against the smooth wall of the tower. "I've an idea," she said when the elf had quieted. "In fantasy stories, people sometimes get what they want by wishing. What if we try to wish ourselves home?"

"Well, why not? There's no harm in wishful thinking."

"Can you tell me where I was? I think it might be important to know that." Sunny listened attentively while Candace described the scene she'd left behind.

"I know that room," Sunny said. "I've cleaned it lots of times. I even remember the couch. A guest barfed on it once and it took ages to clean and the housekeeper was annoyed because I ran late on my schedule." She closed her eyes. "OK, so I'm wearing handcuffs and sitting in the middle of that couch and—"

Like that, she was gone.

Ms. Batonne. Max's voice cut through the wind keening around the tower. *Can you hear me?*

"Yes! Dammit, yes! Keep calling!"

Ms. Batonne. Candace.

She threw herself toward the voice. The strange world disappeared and was replaced by warmth and an overwhelming fatigue. Scents told her where she was: Sunny; human girl with a hint of cleaning products and nothing worse; churning male pheromones; angry and frightened odours from Lucy.

Dimly she felt arms lifting and carrying her.

"Paul?" she whispered.

"Sorry, no," Max's voice said in her ear.

"Is it all right if I faint now?" she asked and without waiting for a reply, did so.

Candace woke to a strong sense of deja vu all over again. She reached up, pulled an oxygen feed out of her nostrils and, with an effort, sat up and looked around. She was in a room that was both familiar and unfamiliar. After a moment, she realized it was the suite allocated to the guards.

She pulled off a number of monitor attachments, swung her legs out of bed and stood up, feeling like she'd been run over a few times. Having a headache was becoming a normal condition.

The door to the living room was shut but she could hear raised voices on the other side. Lucy's was the loudest. Candace made her way closer, using furniture and the wall as supports. The nurse was trying to keep her voice under control, but outrage drove it up.

"...endangering her life, making her face God knows what risks; I don't care if you say she was willing, you both should've known better; you were in charge, you should've stopped it..."

A rumbling reply from a man. Max, Candace guessed, and grinned. He'd met his match in the feisty little nurse.

"The President didn't authorize it!" Lucy's voice grew louder as she approached the door and Candace backed away until she sat once more on the side of the bed. "I can just imagine what he'll say," the nurse snapped as she opened the door and looked in. A relieved smile lit her face. "You're awake!" She flipped on the light and came across to check Candace's pulse. No other nurse in the world had ever had to read the pulse beat made by two hearts, but Lucy did it with the confidence of practice. "How do you feel?"

"All things considered, not too bad. Definitely alive. Is Sunny all right?"

"Her vocal cords certainly are." Lucy pressed sensitive fingers lightly on Candace's forehead. "Your antennae feel swollen. They were curled up like springs when Mr. Maxwell brought you here."

"They've had a busy day."

"You shouldn't have been out of bed, let alone dragged into heroics!"

"But Sunny's OK, is she?"

"You've a friend for life there. She's wearing out the

world's supply of superlatives in describing you and what you did."

"I can use some friends right now." Candace took the nurse's hand. "I never had the chance to thank you for what you did for me. Before, when I was paralyzed."

Lucy blushed. "I was only doing my job."

"You went out of the way to be kind. That wasn't part of your job. I was so scared and alone. It was a comfort that you were there."

The glow of the nurse's pleasure accompanied her to the next room.

Max was waiting with two of his black-suited brethren. For once, he wasn't wearing his dark glasses and the expression on his normally stony face hinted at relief and, perhaps, guilt.

"Ms. Batonne. Thank you for what you did earlier."

"All in a day's work for us elves," Candace said. "Where's Sunny?"

"Sent home to rest."

"Alone?"

"Under discreet surveillance. Also, a doctor will visit her regularly until we're sure she's not in danger."

"Good. And?"

"She isn't facing any charges."

"Almost good enough."

"She won't lose her job."

"But she could have a better one. That girl has a level head and plenty of courage. I'd hire her if I was still working for the Agency."

"We will bear that in mind."

"Very good. Well, gentlemen: I'm alive, in reasonable health, and the target of a ruthless hunt by mysterious creatures that can possess human minds. How do you propose to proceed from this point?"

"Away from here." Max almost smiled. "You said 'elves' just now. Is that what your people call yourselves?"

Melchior's moustache; I'm letting my mouth run away, Candace thought. *This is what comes of breaking cover.* "It's what humans call us."

"Ah." Max nodded. "That would perhaps explain the fat man in the Santa suit who carried you out of the Cheyenne Mountain complex six months ago."

His single-minded pursuit of information reminded her of Paul. "Was that recorded by the surveillance cameras?"

"Yes, just before the power went out. Also by eyewitnesses."

Candace had her own guilty moment. One of her sons had been the culprit behind the global power outage, a fact she'd left out of her conversation with the President.

"Also," Max went on, "an officer reported that you, Santa, and another man disappeared in plain sight."

"Isn't that an oxymoron, disappearing in plain sight?"

"Also, a quantity of what turned out to be reindeer droppings was found on the spot shortly after."

"Meaning what?"

"I hope you will share that information. Ms. Batonne, I understand that you didn't tell the President everything. I understand that there's much more going on than meets the eye."

"Or disappears in front of it?"

Another thin smile. "Trust, Ms. Batonne. It's a shared responsibility."

She thought of Bill. "I consider myself deservedly chided. I wasn't withholding information. I just hadn't gotten around to it yet."

"Understood." Max cupped a hand to his earpiece. "We are ready to go. There's a helipad on the building next door. Our ride is there."

Rather to Candace's surprise no one ambushed them on the trip down the elevators, through the hotel's lobby, and along the street to a neighbouring building. She was tense with anticipation on the ride up to the helipad and relieved to be disappointed.

The sleek helicopter waiting on the pad looked built for speed and covert missions. *A Men in Black special*, she thought, wishing for a cell phone and the opportunity to send a photo to Harald, who was enthralled by the mysterious agents. Max helped her into the cabin and to a seat by a window, his body language saying discreetly that if she balked, he'd be in the way.

"I've never flown in one of these," Candace said, pulling her seat belt snug and gripping the arm rests tightly. "What holds it up?"

"I could give you a technical explanation," Max said, taking the seat beside her and also strapping in. "Personally, I think it's just good luck every time."

Candace laughed in surprise. "Is that supposed to calm my nerves?"

"Mine, ma'am."

"Not a frequent flier?"

"Very frequent."

She caught a quick mental image of fire and screaming metal. Max had survived at least one crash.

"How do you travel on your home world, Ms. Batonne?"

"I take the bus or a taxi." She decided not to mention that the vehicles were pulled by reindeer or polar bears. Perhaps because she didn't enjoy flying inside an aluminum can, and perhaps because she was beginning to like him, she added, "Well, really, I only took the bus when I was a girl. As a mother, I'm entitled to my own chauffeur. We fly, too. But not in one of these things."

The rotors were beating the air now and the craft raised its tail in defiance of gravity. She braced herself. "Are we crashing?"

"No, ma'am, that vibration's normal. I'll let you know if we're going to crash."

"Oh, good! How?"

"I'll scream like a little girl."

The city dropped away beneath them and for a few moments Candace forgot her fear in delight at the many-coloured, sparkling cityscape. Quickly they left Las Vegas behind and desert darkness took over. It always amazed her that a country as heavily populated as the United States could have vast, empty regions. One of which was going to be her new home.

Max pulled a cell phone from a pocket and held it up so she could see the screen. "There's something I'd like to show you," he said, tapping buttons. A photo popped up of the room where she'd investigated Sunny. Max must have taken the picture, because Candace could see the other agents who'd been present, looking in apparent surprise toward the couch and her chair.

"You took this before you brought me down?"

Max shook his head. "Afterwards. Look more closely."

She did, and caught her breath. A ghostly outline of her own body sat in the chair. A similar eerie, Sunny-shaped figure sat on the couch.

"What's this about?"

"I hoped you could tell me." Max slipped the cell phone into his pocket. "You both disappeared at the same instant, leaving behind these impressions. Ms. Daley came back after a few minutes. She said to call your name. We did, and you returned."

"I heard you," Candace confirmed.

"Ms. Daley debriefed us on what happened. Or appeared to happen. Do you have any thoughts on the matter that you'd like to share with me?"

Candace laughed. "If I were a physicist, I'm sure I could impress you with long words and mathematical formulae, but as I'm merely a linguist I'd have to guess that we momentarily shifted phase from this universe to another."

"Well put, ma'am. Was it your universe?"

"No. Our sun is like yours. We don't have blue moss, either."

"What caused it?"

She shrugged. "Contact with an unknown alien entity of unknown powers and unknown origin? In other words, Max, I don't know. Do you?"

"No, ma'am."

They sat in silence for several more minutes as the helicopter droned through the dark, until, more unsettled by the photo than she cared to admit, Candace asked, "Can you tell me where you're taking me?" Prompted by the sprite of mischief, she added, "I hope the shopping's good."

"Can't say, ma'am." Max's foray into conversation and confidentiality appeared to have run its course.

"I'd like to know what happened to the things I left in my apartment back in Langley," she said. "I suppose they were all confiscated. Any chance of getting my clothes back?" Her wardrobe, in her apartment near the CIA's Virginia headquarters, had included many expensive, couturier-designed items, but she wasn't really interested in the clothes. Showing a weakness, her fear of flying in the helicopter, had relaxed her companion's reserve and she was curious to see how far she could lead him down that path. A hint of vanity might do the trick.

"I'll look into it," Max promised but didn't take the bait. His mental guard was strong; perhaps he was having regrets about his momentary lapse.

Wrong approach, Candace decided, and with nothing to look at outside the window, and only winking console lights and her companion's profile to draw the eye on the inside, leaned her head back to have a nap.

Max's profile was, indeed, appealing. *Do I have a thing for handsome secret agents?* she asked herself, trying to relax despite the roar of the rotors, a constant reminder that she was riding in a machine made of thousands of parts sourced from the lowest bidders and not on a simple, reliable, deer or sleigh. *Am I falling in love with my jailer?*

Before Paul, she'd had a carefully chosen succession of lovers. Female elves didn't run the risks that human women had to face in their love affairs: they could spot predators instantly, didn't need to worry about pregnancy, and couldn't catch social diseases. The greatest risk they usually faced was heartbreak when a lover grew old and died.

Am I fickle? she wondered uneasily. Elves' emotional development came much more slowly than that of short-lived humans. In Paris before the First World War, she'd already been decades older than the young men with whom she'd shared the charms of that most life-loving city, but emotionally she'd been an adolescent.

Candace turned her analytical mind on her own life. She noted a steady decline in the number of affairs from the giddy early years in Paris and London. They became fewer, longer in duration, and emotionally deeper. In 1940 they stopped completely after her man, a member of the French Resistance, was shot by the Gestapo.

I was so angry and confused and desperate, she recalled. *I couldn't save Edouard; couldn't stop the juggernaut of evil that swallowed him up. I wanted vengeance; I wanted to make humans pay for my grief. I wanted to mend their flaws so no other woman would ever have to suffer as I did. I wanted to run home and never come back. But the Master had other ideas.*

I'm dreaming, she realized. Her conscious mind obligingly sat back to watch as the memories paraded past:

"Candy Cane." The Master stood up behind his big desk to greet her as she walked into his office, escorted by Glitter. Piled on the surface of the desk was the enormous list of children naughty or nice. He looked to be about half-way through it. Visible beyond the huge window behind him was the City, its crystalline walls glowing in the reflected colours of the aurora rolling in stately waves across the sky.

"Sir. You sent for me."

"I did. Thank you, Glitter. We'll have tea in the salon." Kringle nodded at his assistant, who bowed to him before making obeisance to her with his antennae. She projected a warm fondness at him as he left, receiving in return a surge of love and respect.

The Master led her to an adjoining room where soft couches surrounded a low table. Candace sat straight-backed on one of the couches. She had a good idea, through the mothers' grapevine, of why he wanted to see her but it would not be courteous to let on.

Glitter returned soon with the requested tea and the Master waited until she was served before getting down to business.

"I understand that you speak several languages," he said, helping himself to a large cookie from a plate loaded with sugary cakes.

"Yes, sir. I'm fluent in thirty and in twice as many dialects."

"Just returned from Moscow, I'm told."

"My Russian needed improvement."

"I don't get there as often as I used to, before the Revolution. What's it like now?"

"Grim. No decent shopping anywhere."

She'd worked in a factory, picking up fresh idioms, improving her pronunciation, and trying to avoid the attention of the ever-suspicious secret police. The Cold War was in full spate and to the paranoid state apparatus, spies and fifth columnists lurked everywhere.

"Saved some lives, I'm told."

Candace wondered how he'd found out. "They were just a couple of ordinary girls who were going to be denounced by the factory's commissar. I read his mind. They'd have been sent to Siberia or even shot if someone didn't do something to help them."

"Why was he going to denounce them?"

"They'd declined to recline."

"Ah. I see. The old, ugly story. What happened to them?"

"They got promotions and moved on to other factories."

Kringle smiled knowingly. "Would I be correct in thinking that the commissar had a change of mind?"

"Yes, sir. A drastic change." Candace looked into the russet depths of her cup of tea. "I am, of course, ashamed of having meddled so seriously with a human's mind. It was very wrong of me."

The old man's booming laugh filled the room. "My dear girl," he said, eyes twinkling, "it seems that wherever you go, such constructive meddling happens. Moscow. Berlin. San Francisco. Prague, and many more."

"I take it that I've made the 'naughty' list."

"Impudent, too. The head of the Council had a lot to say on that score."

"We've never quite seen eye to eye."

"Mothers and daughters often don't."

Candace set her cup and saucer on the table with a rattle of fine bone china. "Sir," she said, clasping her hands on her lap, "tell me why I'm here. It's not for chit-chat over tea."

"Good. Very good." Kringle nodded in satisfaction. "You take no nonsense, even from a stubborn old autocrat like me. You know about my operatives?"

"The ones who watch human society? Who keep them from knowing about us and our world?"

"Those operatives, yes. Would you like to become one of them?"

"No."

The old man cocked a heavy white eyebrow. "No? Just like that?"

Candace stood up. "Thank you for the tea, sir."

"He did not die in vain."

The words arrested her steps as she headed to the door. She turned slowly, hands knotted at her sides. "Sir, with all due respect, that's none of your business."

"If he'd lived, would you have stayed with him as he aged?"

"Yes!"

"He'd now be almost sixty years old." Kringle brushed crumbs from his beard. "Have you considered how he might've felt about his own body growing old and weak, while you remained young and beautiful? That he might even have come to hate you for your endless youth?" He took another bite of cookie, watching her with shrewd eyes.

"It doesn't matter now, does it? He's dead. And you can put me at the top of the 'naughty' list because, with all due respect, *sir*, you can go to hell."

Kringle folded his hands comfortably on his ample stomach. "I visit so many children on Christmas Eve: I fill their little stockings with gifts and the next year I come back and do it again, and again. I watch those children grow to have children of their own, and grandchildren. Then there comes a Christmas when their stocking no longer hangs on the mantlepiece. I grieve for them. Do you know, Candy Cane, how I keep my sanity?"

"No."

"I remember them. Every single one. They are all in here." Kringle tapped his head and then his chest over his heart. "And here. Go back to your studies. Go back to learning verbs and nouns in the most perilous places, where an angry young elf can find opportunities to fight the kind of evil doers who killed her sweetheart."

"I—" Rage drained away and shame rushed in to take its place. "I'm sorry, sir. I should not have spoken to you as I did."

"You spoke from the hearts. That's never out of turn. Think about it, Candy Cane. Come and see me again when your hearts say it is time."

It took me years, Candace thought, the dream fading away.

Years to understand that I'll never forget Edouard and never cease to love him, either. Years to understand that I, alone, cannot change the world that caused me such grief. I even learned the hardest lesson of all, that I should not try. Human destiny is humanity's to determine.

She opened her eyes, oddly calmed. The helicopter's rumble was now almost soothing, even if it was bearing her toward captivity. *I'll survive this,* she thought. *I will make it home and Paul will be there.*

Max had left his seat and was talking in a low voice to the pilot and co-pilot. Candace wondered if there was such as thing on board as a washroom. Outside the window, darkness still governed the land, save for a single bright red speck far below that grew rapidly brighter. Was someone camping down there, lighting a lonely fire against the dark?

The crimson dot swelled like a firework. In the pilots' compartment, alarms buzzed urgently. Candace pressed a hand against the window, wide-eyed with sudden terror.

"Max!" The agent turned around at her shout. "Missile!"

I*t is not that I'm afraid of heights,* Paul Gironde said to himself, looking down past his dangling toes. A wandering cloud drifted in an insouciant, *I*-have-nothing-to-worry-about way between himself and the far-off ground. *It is simply that I recognize the potential in gravity.*

The wicker chair in which he sat creaked and swayed in a way that suggested gravity might employ its potential on him in the near future.

Gironde focused his thoughts instead on his porter. The ant, shiny and black as coal, was sized in proportion to the World Tree, which made it about as large as an elephant. Its six legs, each tipped by a strong claw, dug rhythmically into the bark as it raced through the deep grooves and valleys in the Tree's bark. To his left, Gironde saw Kringle dozing comfortably in his chair strapped to the thorax, or mid-body segment, of another ant. A man who spent much of his life in an open sleigh drawn by reindeer through howling winter skies either got used to heights or took a job as a department store Santa.

The ants appeared to be highly intelligent. They communicated using a blend of sign language, a clicking speech, and a model of the Tree with routes to transit stations indicated by coloured threads.

A red dot, glowing in the afternoon light, marked the miniature dragon, soaring lazily on the air currents stroking the giant plant's trunk. Another, larger dot also mounted the currents; a crow the size of a jumbo jet. Kringle had vetoed their booking a seat on one of the birds: apparently they had a habit of occasionally eating their passengers.

"I'm not worried about you," he'd said to Gironde in the ticket office. "You're a lean fellow. Probably stringy." He patted his ample midriff. "But I'd be too tempting. Think what it would do to Christmas if I wound up inside a bird."

"Turkeys would call it simple justice."

"When I was a boy," huffed Kringle, the master of thousand-year-old anecdotes, "we always had fish or a goose for Christmas. North America and its turkeys hadn't even been discovered then."

Chuckling at the memory, Gironde tilted his head back to look at the branch that was their destination. A transit station near the cloud-wreathed tip would, the ticket agent had assured them, lead to the world of the Moon Track and the next leg of their journey. He wondered if the air would be breathable, so high on the mighty plant's stem.

The crow's circling was bringing it closer and something about its motion triggered unease in his mind. Before joining the CIA, he'd flown combat jets.

"It's setting up an attack run," he said aloud and looked for his weapons. They were all out of reach, strapped to the ant's abdomen. "Hey!" He reached over his head and rapped on the insect's back, but if it felt anything through its thick armour, it gave no sign.

The crow banked, beat the air powerfully and came straight toward Kringle's mount. Now Gironde could see its three passengers and his heart leaped in his chest. One was the kelpie, riding in a basket that left only its head exposed. The scarlet eyes were fixed on the sleeping man. The other two were ants. Red ants. Warriors, oversized killers. He could see their enormous pincer jaws snapping in anticipation.

Gironde jerked at the buckles of his waist and shoulder seat belts. Free, he dug his fingers into gaps in the chair's thick wicker and lowered himself until he could reach the wide strap that secured the chair to the ant's back. There was just enough room to slide in a hand and grasp the thick leather.

He let himself swing free and reached down the glistening black carapace toward his bundle of weapons. The long spear jutted point-down: Gironde grabbed the butt and pulled with all the strength of his arm. The spear slid toward him, jammed briefly against a leather satchel, and sliced itself free. Food and the bag of money slipped out and fell toward the now almost invisible ground.

One-handed, Gironde couldn't pull himself back into his chair. Instead, he flailed the spear against the ant's side, creating a loud rattle that he prayed would draw its attention.

It worked: the ant's bulbous eye rolled back, saw the diving bird and its passengers. It shrieked a warning. Kringle's mount squeezed itself flat against the bark as the crow swept past, its reaching claws almost grazing the old man, still peacefully asleep.

Gironde jabbed with the spear as the enormous bird glided past, feeling like a mouse armed with a toothpick. For a moment, as the bird banked for another pass, he thought its efforts would be futile: there was nowhere on the trunk where it could land and it was too wide for the red ants to reach around and use their pincers.

They had other plans.

The two black ants were now sprinting up the trunk of the World Tree, screaming in voices so shrill they rose beyond Gironde's hearing. He hoped they were calling for help but knew it couldn't arrive in time.

The red ants crouched and as the enormous bird again swept past, sprang through the air to land several body lengths above the fleeing black ants. They dug in their claws and opened wide their massive pincers. An anticipatory chittering filled the air.

The black ants stopped, rose onto their back four legs and defiantly opened their small pincers. Gironde readied his spear and felt a brief envy of the still comfortably snoozing Kringle, who wouldn't know a thing as he was torn to pieces.

Flame gushed from the sky, pouring in golden glory over the nearer of the killer ants, charring and splitting its heavy shell. Shrieking, the ant reared up and locked into that position, living tissues cooked. The second red ant tried to escape but another blast of fire caught it. Thrashing in agony, it lost its grip on the World Tree's bark and fell, trailing oily black smoke.

Shaking so hard that he nearly lost his grip on the wicker chair's belt, Gironde looked at his rescuer.

Scarlet wings wide enough for a regiment to march beneath; eyes glowing like the doorways to strange dreams; fire still trickling from jaws agape in a toothy grin.

"You bastard," Gironde called to the dragon. "You glorious, magnificent, size-changing bastard."

The beast's long neck curved in acknowledgement of the compliment. Tilting its vast wings, it slid down the sky in pursuit of the fleeing crow. Gironde watched until the dragon and its prey were mere specks, one of which brightened briefly. The dragon did not return.

Getting back to his seat took the last of his strength. He strapped himself in and closed his eyes until the black ants stopped at the transit station.

Kringle woke up as Gironde came over to help him down from his mount.

"There," the old man said cheerfully. "Now didn't I say this was the safest way to go?"

In the helicopter, consciousness returned to Candace in a wild rush. She was lying on her side, still strapped into her seat. Flickering red and gold light showed wreckage all around. The helicopter's cabin had been ripped almost in two and she lay in the aft section. Her groping hands found the seat belt and sprang the buckle, sending her sprawling onto what had been a wall.

Extending her antennae, she searched for the three men. Two unconscious minds responded. She stumbled forward, finding the pilot by tripping over him. Candace knelt and ran her antennae over his body, sensing the pain signals given off by damaged cells. Both legs were broken but the breaks were clean and his internal organs appeared to be unharmed. She slipped her hands under the man's arms and, drawing on all her strength, pulled him toward the split in the cabin.

She'd forgotten how heavy, how solid a human could be. By the time they were well clear of the burning helicopter, her arms and back ached and she was panting heavily. Nonetheless, she ran back. The fuel tanks hadn't ruptured in the crash, but fire was licking at them avidly.

"Max?" She couldn't make out in the fitful light which contorted shape was the agent. The co-pilot she turned over and quickly released with a cry of horror; half his head was gone.

A slight movement caught her eye. Max lay under the other man's body, pinned by the weight and by wreckage.

"Get out." The agent pushed weakly at the corpse. "Save yourself."

"Screw that." Candace heaved at the body but her hand slipped on the blood-soaked flying suit. When she tried again to get a firm grip, a mass of intestines spilled out. She forced herself not to vomit and this time succeeded in pulling the body off the agent. He was still caught in mangled metal and she tugged at it frantically.

"The tanks will blow any second now," Max said in the same calm voice he'd used when the zombies attacked the hotel suite. "Get out. That's an order."

"There's only one man from whom I'll take orders. I'll not leave you to burn." Heat gusted through the wreckage and she coughed, choking on acrid smoke.

Max grunted, wrenching at the twisted mass of metal that held him down. "Reach into my inside breast pocket," he said. "The key to the anklet is in there. Take it."

"No; I have to get you out."

"Listen to me: this 'copter was stealth enabled. That missile homed in on the anklet. You have to get it off."

Candace could almost feel the searching electronic eye of another flying weapon. Panic rose in her throat.

"Get the anklet off," Max repeated. "Head east; there's a dirt road a few miles from here. Follow it south to the highway. From there you can commandeer a truck or car. I know you've done that before." His eyes closed in pain. "Candace, don't be a fool. Go. Now."

She felt his mind slip into unconsciousness. He was right: she wasn't strong enough to help him and at any instant the wreck would become a pyre. Atavistic terror plucked at her mind. Wildfire, to a cold-adapted race, was mortal enemy.

Candace gripped and pulled, taking advantage of the fear-inspired surge of adrenaline in her system. At first

Max's body didn't move; then, lubricated by the dead man's blood, he slid out from under the contorted metal.

She didn't remember the next minute, of dragging him outside to safety; but at some point realized they were well clear of the wreck. Cold desert air soothed her face and the sky overhead was rich in stars. She threw herself across Max as the fuel tanks exploded, sending flames shooting up a hundred feet, but a brisk wind blew the fireball away from the little group.

With plenty of light from the fiercely burning helicopter to guide her, she turned to the two men. For the pilot she could do little, except to pull off his belt and carefully strap his legs together, to reduce the possibility of further injury if he woke up and tried to move. Max's injuries seemed mainly to be a concussion, plus what promised to be spectacular bruising down one side.

His pocket yielded the promised key, a slip of metal that fit into a slot on the underside of the anklet. The blue light winked off and the device opened. Candace flung it as far as she could into the darkness. If it didn't draw another rocket, it would at least serve as a beacon for rescuers when the fire burned out. She sat beside the men, exhausted by her efforts and afraid for them. Hypothermia was a real danger; the frosty desert air could soon chill and kill two injured people. Cuddling up to them might've helped if she was a human woman, but her body temperature, described by Paul as 'pleasantly cool', wouldn't keep them warm. Dragging them closer to the conflagration wasn't a good option, in case something else exploded.

"Make a bonfire," she told herself and got up to search for tinder. All she could find was scrub and brush and, painfully, cactus thorns. She was pulling one out of her hand when headlights glimmered in the distance.

Rescuers or enemies? If the former, well and good for her two companions, even if it meant her journey would end at the ranch house prison. If the latter, they might finish what the missile had begun.

Paul wouldn't approve of this, she told herself, waving her arms as she trotted toward the bobbing headlights, making sure to silhouette herself against the flames. The cars, three of them, slowed and she lowered her arms, certain they were turning in her direction. The two unconscious men were well hidden in the dark outside the ring of light.

The machines weren't military or government. Two were oversized pickup trucks and the third was a squat, rugged-looking off-road utility vehicle. Hunters, perhaps, who saw the blaze?

The men who climbed out were all armed, but not with hunting weapons. One carried a military assault rifle and in the back of a pickup reared a home-made framework supporting a lean and lethal shape. A missile launcher, Candace realized, and whirled to flee.

Footsteps pounded behind her. She tripped over a bush and sprawled on the dry ground. An instant later, a heavy body landed on her back.

"Don't fry my brain!" hissed a familiar voice.

"Doug?"

"Look, just go along," the youth whispered. "I'll get you out of this." He pulled Candace to her feet, keeping a grip on her arms. "Got her!" he yelled. The other men had returned to their vehicles and now closed in, making the pair the centre of a glaring triangle of headlights.

A door opened in the humvee and a tall, white-haired man stepped down. He was distinguished looking in the carefully manicured style of a professional politician, and a quick look at his mind told Candace that that was exactly what he was. It also told her that he wasn't alone inside his head. Inhuman intelligence watched from the depths.

He smiled, showing teeth as well cared for as his hair. "Good work, my boy."

The man with the assault rifle came up, holding his weapon at the ready. His mind was normal, insofar as a mind obsessed with religion can be said to enjoy that state. "Senator," he said, "the 'copter wasn't supposed to crash. You said the missile would force it to land. I didn't aim to kill no people, government spooks or not."

"The Good Lord decided otherwise," the politician said. "Men who consort with evil must face the consequences. See what He has delivered unto us."

All the hunters came closer to stare. "She don't have horns," said the one with the rifle. "The boy said she had things comin' out of her head."

"You just killed three men," Candace screamed. Even injured, Max and the pilot were safer in the desert than in the hands of these fanatics.

"Three of Satan's acolytes," the Senator said dismissively. His eyes were chill blue and intense.

"Maybe we should get outta here," said another man. "That was a government 'copter. Someone will come lookin' when it don't arrive."

"What about her?" A fourth man, lean and nervous, came closer to peer at Candace. His fingers toyed with the handle of a pistol strapped to his hip.

"She is an abomination!" The words boomed from the Senator's chest. "Brothers, do not be deceived." His hand shot out, pointing. "This *thing* in a woman's form slaughtered my grandson's friends and put his immortal soul in gravest peril."

Doug's hands tightened involuntarily on Candace's arms. She could both sense and smell his fear. "Grandad, maybe I was wrong," he said, stumbling over the words. "I mean, I did think she was a demon or a witch but it wasn't horns I saw. More like feelers. Maybe she's, like, an alien. Out of a space ship. From Roswell." He began to urge her toward the humvee. "I'll take care of her. Besides, I caught her, I get to decide."

"The Bible don't say there's such things as aliens," put in the fourth man. "It does say there's demons and witches."

Mutters of agreement went around the group. Candace could sense the implacable swing of their thoughts.

"The real question," said the rifleman, "is what do we do with her? She can identify us."

There were more mutters of agreement from the men.

"Whatever we do, we gotta do it now," the pistol owner insisted.

"Fear not." The Senator raised both hands in a reassuring gesture. "God will grant the time His servants need to do His work."

"I'll take her to town," Doug said. "Turn her over to the authorities."

"Authorities?" Senator Whallen came closer and regarded the elf with eyes that saw not a person but an object. "The 'authorities' are sons of Satan, nephew, as well you know. Have they not forbidden the teaching of religion in schools? Do they not permit our institutions and culture to be infiltrated and undermined by foreigners, whose false beliefs have no place in a righteous, God-fearing, Christian society?"

The four men blocked Doug's way. "Nephew," the Senator continued, "this creature has corrupted you. Since you came to me, you have talked of nothing else. She has possessed your mind. Because of her, your friend Scott died and poor young Morris is mad. I love you, boy. I won't let you suffer the same fate as those innocents." He beckoned imperiously and one of the men stepped forward and pulled Candace away. Once again, Doug's self doubt held him motionless.

"We do God's work this night," the Senator said gravely. He nodded at the remaining men. "Get a pole."

"Couldn't we just throw her in the fire?" asked the rifleman. He fingered his weapon lovingly. "Or shoot her?"

"Absolutely not." The Senator shook his well-groomed

head. "Beelzebub's power bestrides the world. We must send a message that there are good men who know how to fight evil and who do not hesitate to do so. She must die in such a way that there is no mistaking the message."

"You know best." The man returned to a pickup truck and hauled from the back a long, stout pole and a spade. The bed of the truck was full of wood and wire for repairing or building fences.

"Doug!" Candace twisted in her captor's hands. "Don't let this happen." She watched in growing fear as two of the men dug a hole with practiced speed, tipped up the pole, rammed it down and braced it with earth and stones. *I can't stun them all*, she thought. *I can only do one at a time and the others will kill me when the first drops. They might even kill Doug.*

The young man stood with his arms hanging by his sides, as irresolute as he had been in the dorm room when the possessed Morris murdered his friend. His grandfather moved to stand beside him. If the older man had shouted, or cursed, or threatened, it might have sparked some rebellion. But the Senator put a gentle hand on the youth's shoulder. "My boy," he said, "this is how it has to be. You know what the Bible says: Exodus 22:18. 'Thou shalt not suffer a witch to live'."

"I'm not a witch! I saved your life, Doug, and you damn well know it!" Candace's protest was cut off as she was thrown against the stake. Her head cracked against the tough wood and for a crucial few seconds she was too dazed to act as rough hands grabbed her arms, pulled them behind the post and bound them tightly with a twist of wire.

Doug didn't look at her. "Yes, sir. I know the Bible."

Senator Whallen patted him on the shoulder. "You don't have to watch. Take the humvee back to the ranch. I'll let you know when it's over."

"I should stay, sir." Doug's face worked. "I started this. I should see it through."

"I am proud of you." The Senator lifted his chin. "You made a mistake when you allowed this corrupted creature to tempt you, but with the Lord's help you will rise from the ashes a stronger man."

"He's talking about *my* ashes!" Candace shouted. "This is murder, Doug."

Some of the men brought more fence poles to stack around her feet. Candace kicked at the logs, which only resulted in wire around her legs. When the wood was stacked as high as her knees, a man brought a can of gas and poured pungent liquid around the pile. He sprinkled the last drops on her head like a nightmarish benediction.

In the back of the Senator's mind the lurking entity watched with icy curiosity. *It's studying me,* Candace thought. *It's watching to see how an elf dies. Very well: I have nothing to lose now.* She extended her antennae, bitterly enjoying the startled gasps from the men, and asked:

What are you?

Hungry.

What for?

Minds. Life energy.

Where are you from?

A quick impression of emptiness and strangeness; of the utter cold of outer space and the giant, brilliant whorl of the Galaxy. Candace's knowledge of astrophysics was basic, but she'd heard her four young friends talk about the energy matrix that imbued space itself. The matrix was the creature's home.

Why are you here?

To feed.

On us?

On all that thinks.

You can possess humans.

And others. A strong impression of cold glee. *This cycle of universes will feed us well.*

With that thought came an impression that her brain translated into an image of a loose necklace of glittering beads, spinning and twisting about a central jewel made of many layers. One of those beads was her own universe.

The being was speaking to her again. *We see in human minds what they most fear and with their fears we kill them in their dreams. What do you fear most of all, elf?*

Losing my fashion sense, Candace jeered and took a brief, fierce pleasure in the creature's confusion. *Who are the beings with no minds?*

Our allies. Those who made the beginning, came the puzzling reply and with it, perhaps involuntarily, an image of a building. She recognized it: a cathedral that had recently made the news after the apparent murder-suicide of two of its senior staff. During her stay in the penthouse suite, she'd watched the coverage on TV.

The whole bizarre exchange had taken only seconds. Candace's attention jerked back to the real world as the Senator pulled a long barbecue lighter from a pocket and flicked it. Orange flame leaped at the tip and flickered impatiently in the night breeze.

"My brethren, let us pray," he said. All the men knelt. "With this purification by fire we consign to Satan his daughter, that all Hell may know there are righteous men in this nation who will not be corrupted, nor yield to the corruption of those whom the machinations of Hell have placed in power over us. Yea, though evil be fair of face and sweet of form, we will spare it not, for we are guided by the Lord God—consarn it; this thing has gone out." The Senator clicked the lighter's thumb switch in vain. "I must've used too much fuel at last week's Sunday school barbecue. Does anybody have another one?"

No one did.

"I gave up smoking last year," one of the other men said apologetically. "We could just stone her to death."

"No, no; that's for adultery. We must do this correctly. For sorcery, it has to be fire. Doug, my boy; do you think you could run over there and fetch a torch?" The Senator nodded toward the helicopter's blazing carcass.

"Don't hurry on my account," Candace said in a thin voice as the young man threw a last glance at her and loped toward the fire. Her thoughts took on an odd, fragile calm: *I'm going to die; I'm going to be burned to death. My children won't have the chance to be born. I'll never see Paul again and he'll never know what happened to me.*

Doug took so long to return that she wondered if he'd run away. When he did come back, he walked slowly.

The Senator frowned at him. "My boy, what kept you?"

"Sorry, sir," the youth muttered, holding out a stick of smouldering wood. "I had to find a branch. Everything else was too hot to touch."

"The Lord provides to all who wait in faith," the Senator said serenely, taking the branch. He walked to the edge of the wood pile and looked into the elf's desperate eyes. His expression was sorrowful. "This fire shall not be as hot as the flames of Hell, but perhaps this brief suffering will release your tormented soul from bondage to evil. Endure it, witch, and be freed." He bent down and poked the tip of the torch into the wood pile.

"I'm an elf! Not a witch!" *As last words go,* Candace thought, struggling uselessly against the bindings, *they leave a lot to be desired. I don't want to die. Oh, Paul; we were going to have centuries together—*

Bright flames shot up among the logs as the sparks found drops of gas. A rivulet of fire raced toward Candace's trapped feet.

"Lord have mercy on your soul," murmured the Senator, stepping away from the flames.

"I can't look!" Doug's wail drew the attention of all the men. "Oh, God, give me strength!" He threw himself on the ground, howling.

As a distraction, it was perfect. Max came out of the dark like a night fury. He crashed into the pyre, kicking burning logs away from the stake. Doug jumped to his feet, smashed a fist into the face of the man with the pistol and grappled with him for the weapon.

The rifleman yelled and took aim at the agent. He was close enough for a mind blast and Candace gave him everything she had. The man dropped the gun and fell to the desert floor, blood bursting from his nose. He began to crawl toward the vehicles, mewling.

"Run!" Senator Whallen took his own advice and dashed for the humvee. Doug and his opponent blocked his path and he swerved toward the pickups, making no attempt to help either of his comrades.

With Candace out of immediate danger, Max halted the escape of the rifleman with a quick, brutal kick before turning from the now unconscious man to help Doug. The big youth had a grip on his opponent's wrist and was crushing it. Seeing that reinforcements were coming, the man let go his weapon, broke free with a desperate twist, dashed for the Senator's pickup and vaulted into the back. The fourth man was already on the driver's seat.

"Look out!" Candace's cry came just in time as the machine roared toward the two victors. A side mirror narrowly missed Doug's head.

"You are damned, boy! Damned!" the Senator bellowed. The vehicle disappeared behind a screen of stinging sand and gravel and was soon out of sight.

"Help her," Max said to the young man. He dropped to one knee, breathing heavily. Candace sensed the pain of his battered body and marvelled that he'd been able to move at all.

She went to his side as soon as she was free. "Are you bleeding?" she asked, unsure how Doug would react if she used her antennae to check for wounds.

"Just beat up," he grunted. "You?"

"Not even singed." Impulsively, she kissed him on the cheek. *It's true,* she thought; *I do have a thing for good-looking secret agents.* "Thank you, Max."

"All in a day's work."

"That's my line." Candace stood up and went to the youth, who was looking across the desert in the direction taken by his fleeing grandfather.

"Doug? That was very brave, what you did. Thank you."

The youth shook his head. "I'm not brave. I was running away. Mr. Maxwell stopped me. He said, do you want to live the rest of your life with someone you can't stand? He meant me. I said no, I didn't, and he told me what to do. Are you really an elf?"

"I am." Candace hadn't retracted her antennae and instead laid them flat against her hair, gleaming silver strands on midnight black. "I work for Santa Claus. He does exist."

Doug might not have heard. "My grandfather wasn't always like that. He could be so kind. Tough about what he believed, but he never hurt anyone." Tears gleamed in the young man's eyes. "It's like something pushed him over the edge."

Something did, Candace thought. *Something saw where he truly wanted to go and gave him the push he secretly craved.*

"Will you stay with Mr. Maxwell and look after him?" she asked. "There's another man who needs to be kept warm, too, until help comes."

"What? You're leaving?"

A deadly entity from deepest space, an invasion that she alone of all the people on Earth could track; a cathedral. "I have to. Doug—" She searched for the right words. "You have my admiration as well as my thanks." Candace put her arms around the youth's blocky body and hugged him tightly. "Trust yourself. There's more to you than you know."

She could sense the seed of confidence sprouting in the young man's mind as she walked back to Max.

"You're going, aren't you?" the agent said as she knelt beside him.

"'Fraid so."

"It's my duty to deliver you into custody," he said, wincing, "but my muscles aren't cooperating. Can't even stand up. You know there'll be a manhunt."

"I think you mean 'elfhunt'."

"Don't. It hurts when I laugh. Running implies bad motives. When we catch you again, we'll have to be less nice."

"No swimming pool?"

"No shopping either. Ma'am."

"I'm just trying to save your world, Max. Is that your real name, by the way?"

"It's Maxwell Maxwell. My parents lacked imagination. What's yours?"

"Candy Cane. Seriously, it is. Tell the President there's an invasion happening of creatures that can possess human bodies. They aren't my people. Senator Whallen may be possessed. Likewise those poor souls in the hotel. I'm the only one who can detect them and I can't be of much use behind an electric fence. By the time your people decide to believe me or trust me, it may well be too late to stop them."

Max actually smiled. "I promise, the next time we meet, I'll put my taser on the lowest setting. Good luck, Candy Cane."

"If I find out what's going on, I'll try to send information." She kissed him again. "The Magi be with you."

"Take the humvee," he called as she walked away. "You won't get far in a pickup with a missile launcher in the back."

She was miles distant when she saw in the vehicle's rear-view mirror the bright lights of a rescue 'copter. It reminded her that she was going to need help herself.

"I know just where to find him," she said aloud, gunning the engine.

Far away, the Lady Yseult sat on a carved marble bench in her garden at the Palace of the Rings and waited patiently. A stir in the air drew her eyes upwards. She stood, holding out an arm, and the dragon, once again the size of a hawk, dropped heavily onto her wrist.

"You are exhausted," she said, running a caressing finger along the ruby back. "You did well; very well. Our friends are safe for the moment and the possessed kelpie is released from the grip of the Devourers; may it know peace. Rest now, soon your strength will return." Some communication that went beyond words passed between them. "I know," Yseult said with a sigh. "We can no longer help Kringle and his friend. But perhaps the Powers will yet assist."

She began to walk toward her palace, slowly, mind full of troubled thoughts. "My time is nearly over," she said aloud, causing the dragon to ruffle its scales. "But I will not leave my successor to cope with a catastrophe born of my grievous error. I must, I *must*, find a way." She stopped, gripped by a profound fear. "If I fail, all the worlds are lost."

You've a fucking nerve." Kevin Finnegan stood in the doorway of his apartment and stared at Candace. He was unshaven, had gained quite a few pounds around his belly in the six months since their last encounter, and spilled food had made a long stain down the front of his undershirt.

"Hello, Kevin. It's nice to see you, too."

"Bitch. I lost my job because of you. Lost everything."

"I recall that the last time we met, you tried to cut my throat. Before that, you tortured me. I'd say we both have grievances."

Finnegan's hand tightened on the doorframe. "It was just a rigorous interrogation. Perfectly legal." He scowled. "What the hell did you hit me with, that night? The doctors said the marks looked like hoof prints!"

"Kevin," Candace said crisply, "I'm an elf. I work for

Santa Claus. You were run over by his reindeer and sleigh, which humans can't see unless he lets them. Can I come in?"

Rather to her surprise, he stood aside and let her enter. The apartment was in keeping with its occupant: messy and pungent.

"You here to finish the job?" he asked as he shut the door. "Planning to kill me?"

"No." Candace walked a few feet into the living room. It was piled with papers, charts, photographs and other ephemera, as well as empty pizza boxes, beer cans, and unwashed clothing. A computer station had pride of place in the centre, within a cocoon of tidiness and order. She recalled that he'd always kept his office work station meticulously neat. "Are you still running your website? The one about aliens on Earth?"

"Yes." Finnegan hadn't left the door. He looked like he was on the verge of bolting. "Know about it, do you?"

"I've heard of it. You were wrong about only one thing: we're not interested in taking over your world."

"Oh." Gratification surged in his mind. "Care to say that in front of a camera?"

"That would not be my preference."

"Why are you here, then?"

"I need a place to stay for a few days. To avoid some people looking for me."

Finnegan barked a laugh. "You've got to be fucking kidding! You're on the Agency's 'most wanted' list. I only have to pick up the phone to get my job back." He came closer. She could smell his anger and see it in the red face and clenched fists. "Give me one reason, just one reason, not to turn you in."

Candace faced him coldly. "Knowledge. I'll answer your questions. You'll know, really know, what happened. I won't talk on camera or to any recording equipment. But I'll tell you the truth."

"That won't get me my job back."

"You don't want it. What you really want is revenge on me. What better revenge than placing me in your debt?"

He stepped so close that she could feel the heat from his body. "Maybe that wouldn't be enough."

"Look, Kevin, I detest you and you hate me. But I understand what hurts you the most: that no one believes you."

"You read minds, huh."

"Yes."

"Can you tell what I'm thinking now?"

"I don't look like that naked."

"What if the price of my cooperation is that I get to find out?"

"Would ten thousand dollars in pure gold distract you from your lechery and buy me a safe place to stay?"

"You've got it?"

"I can get it."

"Make it fifty."

"Twenty."

"Forty."

"Thirty."

"Done." He turned and walked into the apartment's small kitchen. "You can keep your clothes on. I like men more than women, anyhow. I just hated it that Gironde only had eyes for you." Candace stood rooted in obvious surprise and he snickered. "Mind reading doesn't tell you everything, does it?"

"I guess not. You hid that very well. Aren't you worried about the people hunting me?"

He grinned. "You've got scruples. You wouldn't be here if it would put me in danger."

"Touché." She followed him into the kitchen.

"Tea?"

"Please."

He filled a kettle, put it on the stove and took a pair of chipped mugs from a cupboard. "Lots of sugar?"

"You remembered. How touching."

"An elf, eh. And the old geezer's real after all." Finnegan snorted. "When I was a kid, I once had a dream that I saw Santa putting presents under the tree. Was that really a dream?"

"Probably not." Candace watched as Finnegan spooned sugar generously into a mug. "He puts people to sleep when he enters a house. Sometimes, kids do waken."

"That was the first time someone called me a liar. On Christmas morning."

"Sorry to hear that. Who was it?"

"My step dad." He handed her the mug. "Want the whole sordid story of my life with a perv?"

She shook her head. "I read it in your personnel file."

"Huh. Boss lady knew all along. Was it you who had me classified as a psychopath?"

"No. But you are one. Low level. You weren't considered to be a threat to the Agency."

"Low level, huh." Finnegan dropped teabags into a pot. "Not up there in the serial killer ranks. Not even good enough to train as an assassin. Just a fucking pest."

"Now there you did excel."

"Huh." He surprised her again by holding out a hand. "Truce?"

She took it gratefully. "Truce."

"Good. The water's boiling. Tea will be ready in a minute. Let's clear off a couple of chairs. You start talking. I'm going to listen until my head explodes."

At the top of a cliff in Ring Six a cruel wind curled around Gironde's face and bit at his exposed skin. The wind felt alive; stroking curious fingers through his beard and into his clothing. He leaned on the shaft of his spear, clenched his teeth and fought to control his shivering. His body screamed for warmth.

Beside him Kringle bent double, trying to catch his breath. "Not my kind of winter world," he panted. The frozen crystals of his breath hung in the frigid air, glittering in the light of a moon larger than Earth's Luna.

Gironde silently agreed. As far as he could see all the world was ice. At the foot of the cliff stretched a plain of wind-scoured crystal dotted here and there by odd shapes that might have been glazed trees or, possibly, glazed once-living creatures. He could feel the moonlight tingling on his skin and wondered about radioactivity. The light lay strongest in a wide band that led far into the distance. Moon track, indeed.

"We should move on," he said. "Can't stay here." *Can't go back*, he reminded himself. Death on huge paws waited for them at the transit station.

"Not my kind of polar bears either," Kringle wheezed, straightening up. "Back home they're quite friendly. Helpful, even. Thousand years of selective breeding by the elves."

"And not crossbred with rabid elephants," Gironde added, looking over his shoulder.

"We've left them behind, at least."

"They were distracted." Gironde tried to loosen his grip on the spear. The shaft was sticky. Blood that looked tarry in the harsh light was freezing his fingers to the sturdy wood. "Too busy eating the staff of the transit station."

"Shouldn't have happened." Kringle shook his head, also looking back. "Magic, you know. Powerful in this Ring."

"That fellow who was waving a stick at them. He seemed to believe they'd stop. He didn't run."

"A wizard. Poor, poor man. At least he died quickly. Probably never felt a thing."

Gironde wondered how long a head bitten off its body would stay conscious and didn't want to find out.

"Good work, by the way," Kringle said. "I never heard the second dire bear creeping up on us. It'll think twice about attacking a man with a spear."

"I only annoyed it."

Kringle pointed back the way they had come. "And now it wants revenge."

Just visible at a distance in the eerie light, two enormous white figures sped toward the pair. One limped.

"Suggestions?"

"The portal to the Way of No Return is several hours from here," Kringle said. He grinned with lips that were starting to crack in the cold. "Best we ride."

"*Ride*?" Gironde wondered if the eerie light was affecting his friend's mind. He peeled his fingers from the spear, turned toward the onrushing beasts and levelled the weapon. "Kris, find a way down the cliff. I'll hold them off as long as I can." *Candy*, he thought, *I tried. I'm so sorry.*

To his surprise, Kringle didn't demur. As Gironde braced his feet on the ice, the old man shuffled away, muttering under his breath.

The dire bears were only seconds off when he said, "Done! Get in lad."

"Get in...?" Gironde turned around.

A sleigh, translucent and shining in the moonlight of which it was made, sat on the edge of the cliff. Ahead of it, prancing on the air, a team of eight reindeer tossed their antlers.

Kringle was already on the driver's seat. Losing no more time, the man from Earth scrambled aboard. The dire bears were close enough that he could hear their snorting.

"Couldn't bring my own team," Kringle said, flicking the reins against the glassy rumps. He looked about to burst with pride. "Doesn't mean I can't improvise. I've even installed a heater."

Gironde gripped the front rail as the sleigh rose light as a thought into the air and accelerated. Behind them a double roar of frustration shattered the chill peace of the eldritch world. "Magic," he said in delighted wonder. "The Swiss Army knife of Hy Brasail!"

Finnegan looked down at the sleeping elf, curled up on his sofa with the cleanest of his pillows tucked under her head. *Two hundred years old,* he thought, *and she looks like a girl.* Candace frowned a little and he wondered if she could sense him standing there.

He backed away, went into his kitchen and put the kettle on for tea. His brain fizzed with so much new knowledge that he couldn't sleep. Other worlds, other universes; fantastic realms unknown to the human race, all clamoured in his skull for contemplation.

He went through the tea ritual with only a fraction of his attention on the task. How much more could he learn before she left? What, if anything, could he do with the information, other than possess it?

Finnegan wandered back into the living room with his drink. She'd offered him thirty thousand dollars in gold to shelter her, and he knew she'd keep her word if he kept his. How much would the government give him? How much could he get from the people hunting her, if he could contact them?

"They'd kill you, Kevin."

He started, almost spilling his tea. Candace's eyes were open and very dark in the half-light of early morning.

"Do you do the mind-reading thing all the time?"

"No." She sat up on the sofa and rubbed her face. "It's instinctive, though, to be alert while I sleep."

"Why?"

Candace ran fingers through her hair in a gesture that was unintentionally sensual. "A thousand years ago, my species lived mainly underground. It was the only reasonably safe place in an environment over-endowed with predators. We had to be on our guard all the time."

"Then you became sentient, thanks to us humans, and started building a civilization."

She smiled a little. "After Peter cleared out the predators."

"Sounds like a tough guy."

"He is. Very. Is there any more tea?"

"I'll make some. While I'm doing that, tell me about the people looking for you."

Candace followed him into the kitchen. "I don't know much about them except that they're horrifying. Neither human nor elf." She leaned against the kitchen counter, arms folded. "Not our usual enemies, either."

"Those demons you described."

"They're connected in some way, but I don't know how. I've never sensed anything like them. I do know they can take control of human bodies."

"Ah. So if I try to sell you to them, I might end up like that?"

Her lips tilted up at the corners. "How much were you going to charge?"

"More than you offered. Sugar's in the tin to your right."

"It's always nice to feel valued."

"Mindless, huh." Finnegan opened his fridge in search of milk. "How do I know you're not lying?"

"You don't."

"Best answer. If you were lying, you'd try to convince me you weren't."

She grinned at him. "Or I'd know that you'd think that."

Finnegan laughed as he poured the tea. He held up his mug. "Here's to old times. May they never return." They tapped mugs together. "By the way, sorry about having you chained. That was perhaps going overboard, what with you being half paralyzed at the time."

"Sorry about your broken nose. I'm glad to see it healed straight. It was Peter who knocked out your tooth, though."

"I got an implant."

Candace sipped her drink thoughtfully. "How much do you think the government would give you for me? Less income tax and deductions, of course."

"I'd probably get a medal and a handshake. They wouldn't want me back at the Agency."

"So it would make sense that if you were going to sell me, you'd make an offer to the others."

Finnegan's hand froze with his tea mug touching his lips. "You've got to be kidding. You just said they'd kill me."

"Kevin; we both worked for the Agency. We know how valuable information is. Right now, I know almost nothing about them."

"You're not an analyst any more! And I quit the Firm."

"But I'm still one of Santa's little helpers and it's my duty to protect my world, any way I can. Whether you like it or not, it's your duty to protect yours. If this is an invasion no one will be safe; not anywhere. We must have more information."

Finnegan swore. "This is the kind of craziness you get into with a fucking conscience! One of the perks of being a psychopath is that I haven't got one. No; boss lady, you're not dragging me into this any deeper. No way. I did my bit and got my ass kicked for it. All pain, no gain."

Candace was silent, her gaze looking into the distance. Finnegan felt his stomach sinking. After a moment she asked, "Do you have a gun?"

"Yes. You can have it. Just leave me out of whatever you're planning."

"I won't need it. You might." She caught his eye and his insides squirmed. "You were raised Catholic. Were you ever an altar boy?"

"Yes, but what the hell does that have to do with anything?"

"You'd know your way around a church. Or a cathedral."

"I told you, I'm not getting involved!"

"We'll also need a car and a stamped envelope."

"Are you sure about this?" Finnegan looked over at Candace, in the passenger seat of his elderly Mustang. She'd been very quiet since they'd left the apartment and during the long, inter-city drive. "If it goes wrong, you're dead or worse."

"I'm sure." Her fingers were tightly interlaced in her lap and although they were still, he could see how pale they were.

"Well, if your investigation tanks and you die horribly, don't come complaining to me."

Candace looked up and smiled. "Kevin. You've a sense of humour."

"Being a psychopath doesn't mean I can't laugh. Someone else's imminent death is hilarious."

"You know what to do with the envelope?"

"Yes. We've been over this."

"Sorry." She looked out the window, at the drab industrial buildings they were now passing on the freeway. "Nerves, I suppose."

"Why are you doing this? Really, I mean. It's happening in my world, not yours. You could go home, shut that wormhole thing and forget about us."

"I don't know that it's only happening here."

"It's still not your problem. Let's hear it: you promised to tell me the truth and hold nothing back."

Candace looked down at her hands. "If you must know, it was my duty to keep humans from ever learning about my world and people. I failed badly. Not only was I captured, I was put through every medical test imaginable: MRIs, X-rays, DNA analysis; you name it. Your government has that record. Proof that my people and my world exist."

"Science fiction writers have been speculating for over a hundred years about first contacts with alien civilizations. So it finally happened. Big deal."

"Oh, come on, Kevin! That general in Colorado thought

I was spearheading an invasion! He put me into the hands of a torturer!"

"Rigorous interrogation specialist."

"I have a feeling we're never going to agree about that."

"Look, it's not like you could've escaped, after that tasering. Who knew it would fry your nervous system? I wouldn't blame myself, if I were you."

"Who would you blame?"

"Gironde. He's the one who tasered you."

"It was in the line of duty. He didn't know how it would affect me."

"Yeah; that must've made it feel a lot better. Where is he now, do you know? Seems to have dropped off the face of the planet since he quit the Agency."

"He did. He's in my universe. We're getting married."

"Well, fuck." Finnegan drove a little longer in silence. "Yet, you want to go play secret agent. Doesn't sound like your honey comes first."

"Low blow, Kevin."

"Telling blows often are. We're getting close. There's the cathedral. Shit; I can't believe I'm doing this. I'm not even getting paid!"

"You asked for the truth. You're doing this for the same reason that you joined the Agency. You want to know what's going on; to be at the centre. You have a very strong and, as I recall, usually unsatisfied desire to know things you shouldn't."

Finnegan spotted a parking space and nosed his car into it. "Nothing like riding around with someone who knows me better than I know myself. Seems like an unfair advantage."

Candace studied the street ahead. A hundred feet away, the cathedral rose up on a landscaped lot set back from the curb. Its dignified tower and façade belied the recent events inside. Yellow police tape criss-crossed the front doors.

"We'll have to find a way in," she said.

"Yeah, yeah." Finnegan popped his seat belt. "Maybe I didn't make it to field officer, but I know a thing or two. Wait a sec." He got out, walked around the car, opened Candace's door and extended a hand. "Come on, darling."

"What?" She stared at him.

"Don't be shy. You're the one who insists on being married in this cathedral."

"Oh. Right." She smiled, accepting the proffered hand. "It's been my dream ever since you proposed, that wonderful night under the stars in Barbados."

"Have you been there?" Finnegan offered his arm as they crossed the street and she hugged it for the benefit of onlookers or security cameras.

"Not a chance. I'd roast in that climate. What if someone notices I have no engagement ring?"

Finnegan reached into a pocket and passed a small object to her. "I thought ahead."

Candace surreptitiously slipped the gold band onto her ring finger. "That's a big diamond."

"It was my mother's."

"I'll try not to lose it."

"Won't bother me if you do. Not sentimental. I kept it to pawn. Although if you do lose it, I'll charge you ten grand. No; twenty."

"At another time, I'd be delighted to haggle. Look: there's an open door."

The door, on the side of the building, stood ajar, shreds of yellow tape hanging from its frame. The pair paused to listen; in Candace's case with more than ears.

"I don't detect anything awful," she said. "There's just one person. I think he's cleaning up."

"According to the news, it was a very bloody killing," Finnegan said with relish, pushing the door wide. "The killer tore out the other guy's throat with his teeth then ripped open his own wrist and bled to death. I'm surprised the cops would let someone mess with a crime scene."

"Maybe they don't know." Candace led the way cautiously down a short corridor that opened into the nave. Stained glass backlit by an afternoon sun shed coloured light that reminded her, with a homesick pang, of the aurora. The murder-suicide had taken place on the steps to the main altar and there, behind a cordon of police tape, a lone figure on hands and knees scrubbed at the carpet. Candace sensed the bewilderment and grief in the man's uncomplicated mind.

"It's the custodian. He's the one who found the bodies," she whispered to Finnegan. "I think he's slightly challenged, mentally. Let's be gentle."

"Sure. Hey, you! What the hell are you doing?"

"Kevin!"

He leaned toward her and muttered, "Good cop, bad cop. Worth a try."

The man scrambled to his feet. He was thin, elderly, and wore an expression of mingled alarm and determination.

"Are you with the police?" He raised his chin defiantly. "This is a house of God. It must be cleansed!"

"We don't have anything to do with the police," Candace said, inflicting a reproachful pinch on Finnegan's arm. "We're hoping to get married here and want some information." With a flash of inspiration, she added, "The cathedral website's down and no one picks up the phone, so we thought we'd drop by."

"I understand." The man's shoulders sagged, with relief and a kind of hope. He gestured at the damp carpet. "This, too, shall pass. What can I tell you?"

"We'd like to have a look around. If that's all right with you," Finnegan said, reluctantly abandoning the bad cop role. "You have a reception hall, don't you? Kitchen facilities for caterers? That sort of thing."

"Yes, we have a fine hall." The old man looked at his handiwork. A pail half full of bloody water, brushes, rags and soap sat on the altar step. He picked it up and headed toward a side door. "Follow me."

The custodian led them downstairs, detouring briefly on the way to dump the bucket down a toilet and throw the rags into a garbage pail.

"When is the wedding?" he asked, escorting the pair into a large room where folded tables and chairs were stacked against a wall.

"June," Candace said.

"May," said Finnegan.

The reluctant partners glared at each other. "We haven't settled on a date," Finnegan said. "It's *her* family's fault. They're an interfering lot."

"Ah, that does happen," the old man said with an understanding smile. "Can't tell you the number of weddings we've had here where the families disagreed. It all comes out right in the end. You just have to have faith and trust in the Lord."

"You remind me of my boss," Candace said. "He always takes the optimistic view."

"Is he a member of the congregation? Perhaps we've met."

"You'd remember him if you had," Finnegan said. "Fat guy, needs a shave, goes into people's houses at night, likes little children."

"Darling," Candace said in a icy voice, "I have to use the ladies' room. Do ask the nice man to show you around some more."

Finnegan's satisfied chuckle followed her as she marched, stiff-backed, out of the room.

I will not let him get under my skin, she told herself, walking so briskly that she overshot her goal; the stairs to the cathedral's crypts. In Europe's old cathedrals, crypts were used for burials. In North America they held heating plants and provided storage. She found a light switch, flicked it on and headed downwards.

Later, she was amazed at her folly in exploring alone. At the moment, though, foremost in her mind was the need to make as thorough a search as possible before the custodian ran out of points of interest to show to Finnegan and began to wonder where she was.

Stone walls covered in layers of paint; conduits on the corridor ceilings to transport air, water, sewage, and electricity; stacks of chairs and worn-out furniture in wayward corners: she wasn't overly familiar with cathedral basements, but didn't see anything alarming. She opened one door and found a storeroom filled with Christmas decorations; opened another and encountered the cathedral's furnace brooding by itself in a nest of hot-air ducts.

A few fruitless minutes later, she paused in a vaulted chamber empty of everything except dust and a mouse that scuttled away. *Poor little hungry critter,* Candace thought, wishing she had some crumbs to leave for it.

There were marks in the dust that she took at first to be rodent-made until a pattern caught her eye. She crouched and swept a hand through the fine powder, trying not to sneeze. Someone had laid a model train track on the concrete floor. The miniature rails curved to form a complete circle about eight feet in diameter.

Her hearts began to pound. In John's garage a steel circle, pegged to the wall instead of the floor, anchored the wormhole connecting Earth with her world. The best elf artisans had made it and it was a thing of both beauty and practical function, but the principle was the same: create a closed, metal circle. A wormhole with such a secured terminal could be used repeatedly, unlike the portal that had caught her at the lake. That meant, in turn, constant traffic from—where?

A trickle of moving air; a wisp of ozone; a hint of sulphur. She raised her antennae and felt the tingle of building energies. The dust eddied and curled, responding to static. Candace's hair lifted as well.

Time to go! She jumped up and backed away from the circle toward the door, but curiosity and a dash of recklessness made her linger, peering around the frame.

The incoming wormhole agitated the dust still more until it erupted with frenzied blue-violet sparks. As the energy field stabilized, the charged particles fell outwards, leaving behind an eye-twisting void in the floor. A shining bronze cylinder rose smoothly almost to the ceiling, completely filling the circle. With it came a terrifyingly familiar impression; four of the non-minds.

A hatch in the side of the cylinder began to open and Candace abandoned her vigil. She ran, praying that she could remember the way to the upper floor.

Luck was on her side: she found the stairs and went up them three at a time, not slowing until she was almost at the kitchen, where the elderly custodian was proudly showing a bored Finnegan the features of a large kitchen range. The ex-officer looked up as she entered and with a quick, casual motion brushed a finger against his forehead. Candace retracted her antennae before the custodian could see them.

"Darling," she said, trying hard not to pant, "we have to go. Now. Right now!"

"I think I've seen enough," Finnegan said, slapping a hand on the custodian's back and incidentally turning him toward the door. "This is just what we're looking for."

"Oh, but I want to show you our pipe organ before you go," the old man protested. "It's the largest in the state. The reverberation is splendid. I could play it for you during your ceremony."

"We'd love that," Candace said, linking her arm in his and with Finnegan's help almost dragging him to the flight of steps leading to the main floor. "We have to go, however. I, um, have a wedding dress fitting. Can't linger. You know how bridal salons fuss if people aren't on time."

Finnegan cast a quick look back the way she had come.

His free hand dropped into the jacket pocket where he kept his pistol. "Of course," he said, "it wouldn't be *fitting* for you to be late."

He was enjoying himself. *Psychopaths!* Candace thought. *He's loving it that I'm scared.*

"I should take your names and phone number first," the old man said, practically flying up the steps with the two gripping his arms. Alarm began to stir in his mind and Candace slipped in a subtle thought. "Oh, dear," he gasped. "I'm afraid the police are back from dinner. Here, let me show you out. I'm not worried about myself, but I doubt they'd be pleased to see strangers. I wouldn't want you to get into any trouble." He led them quickly to the side door.

"As it's dinner time," Candace said, stepping with relief into the sun and fresh air, "why don't you let us give you a ride home?" She didn't want to leave the old man alone in the cathedral with whatever had just arrived.

Finnegan's brows drew together, but he took the hint. "Sure; won't be any trouble."

"I live across the street," the custodian said, nodding at a small house. "Perhaps you'd like some tea? We can talk about the date for the wedding." Another subtle mental nudge from the elf and he said, "My goodness; I'm hungry. Would you like to stay and eat with me?"

"Not today," Candace said with a smile that she hoped didn't look forced. "We'll see you home and be on our way. My friend—my fiancé, I mean, and I have a lot to discuss."

As soon as the old man was safely behind his front door, she hooked her arm in Finnegan's as they headed to his car. "If I say 'run', don't hang around."

"What did you find?"

"Tell you in a moment."

Once they were inside the car, she described what she'd seen and sensed in the crypt.

Finnegan put his key in the ignition but didn't turn it.

"Want to stay and see if they come out?"

"No, but I suppose we must." Candace stiffened in her seat. "What is it about these people and limousines?" A large grey specimen had just rounded the corner and was pulling to a stop in front of the cathedral. Four figures, all apparently male, emerged from the side entrance and climbed in.

"They're coming this way. Get down as low as you can," Finnegan said. "I've an idea. I'll let them see me." He rolled down his window. As the limo pulled even with the Mustang, he stared very deliberately at the tinted windows. The long grey vehicle didn't slow, but the driver's head did turn in his direction.

"What was that about?" Candace remained crouched out of sight.

"That was so they'll recognize me when we meet again."

She cautiously sat up and looked at the retreating tail lights. "What do you have in mind?"

"Getting rich."

Her eyes widened in shock as she stared into the round black muzzle of his gun, pointed at her head.

"You should've seen the look on your face." Finnegan threw back his head, guffawing. "Priceless." He pushed the old Mustang over the speed limit, grinning.

Candace made an effort not to sulk, without much success. "Try looking into the business end of a gun held by someone who hates you and see how funny it is. I could've melted your brain, Kevin!"

"I figured you'd read my mind first, to be sure. Anyhow, it was worth it. You went so pale you were green."

"I don't think much of psychopath humour."

"Live and learn, grasshopper."

"Oh!" Candace fumed in silence for the next several miles, until Finnegan pulled off the road at a fast-food restaurant.

"Want something to eat, or would you rather sit there scowling?"

"I'll have you know, I am very seriously piqued," she replied, her sense of humour reviving. "A large soft drink, please, and, why not; a slice of humble pie."

"Kinda sorry we never went on a date," the man said, placing her drink order and his own for a hamburger and fries. "You can be fun. Back at the Agency, you were all career woman and boss lady. Very businesslike and serious."

Candace accepted the frosty cup he handed her and took a long pull before saying, "Spend a few years on an alien world as a double agent and see how it tickles your funny bone."

Finnegan spoke around a large mouthful of hamburger. "While we're being chummy, let me say that I don't hate you. Never really did. You were what I wanted to be and wasn't. Brilliant, respected, moving fast up the Agency ladder, trusted with important secrets, canoodling with Gironde, all that."

"Canoodling?"

"You know what it means."

"Kevin, you are positively confiding in me. I'm flattered."

"Yeah, well." He swallowed and wiped a hand across his mouth. "This is a backassed way of saying that I'm not going to sell you out. I've got a feeling that if I hang around and help you in your socially responsible, idiotically noble quest for information, it'll be to my advantage."

"More grist for your website?"

"Fuck the website!" Finnegan slammed a palm on the steering wheel. "You were right in what you said earlier, that I want to know secrets. That's the real price of my cooperation. Keep me in the loop; make me part of what you're doing." He reached into the breast pocket of his suit jacket and pulled out the stamped envelope she had asked him to provide. It now contained a letter from her, authorizing the release of thirty thousand dollars in gold to him from her account in the City. The address on the front read simply, "Santa Claus, North Pole." She'd assured him that the letters-to-Santa interception unit in the post office would pick it out and forward it.

"This is how serious I am. Keep the money."

Candace took the envelope, turned it over in her fingers and handed it back. "You gave me shelter and that was what the gold is for. Helping me is dangerous. You could be killed. Or worse. Confronting those creatures head-on won't be the same as giving me a ride. I never meant to put you in serious danger."

Finnegan was silent for a moment. "Look," he said in a sober tone, "I know what I am. I've read books about it; I know my brain doesn't work like yours—like a normal human's brain, I mean. God alone knows what goes on in that elf head. I wouldn't want to change. All that guilt normals feel? All that remorse, shame, and fear? They can keep it."

"They feel empathy, kindness, and compassion, too," Candace said. "They know what it's like to love and be loved."

"I don't know what that's like, so I don't miss it. Here's why you need me: I'm not afraid of anything."

"Which is why psychopaths often get hurt."

Finnegan waved a dismissive hand. "I'm not stupid. I can assess risk. It just doesn't bother me. Do you want someone at your side who's shitting himself, he's so scared, or someone whose heart rate won't speed up a tick?"

Candace sipped her drink, not noticing its flavour. The driving force of a psychopath's existence, she knew, was the craving for control, for power; but despite their terrifying public image as serial killers, most didn't depend on physical violence. They were manipulative, lied as easily as they breathed; were callous, skilled mimics of the emotions they couldn't feel and, as Finnegan had said, were unaffected by danger to themselves or others. They often sought high-risk, high-stakes jobs such as test pilots, stock brokers, or charismatic politicians. Talented ones could be top surgeons, able to carry out difficult, technically complex surgeries and never once be distracted by the unnerving responsibility of holding a human life in their hands. Their failures could be spectacular, as their self assurance frequently marched miles ahead of their ability, but Finnegan's past failures owed more to his jealousy than to incompetence.

I can never trust him, Candace thought. *If he sees it to his advantage to betray me, he will.* "Tell me," she said, "what was the greatest moment in your life?"

Finnegan chewed his hamburger a moment before answering. "All right. I should've seen that coming. It was when you were my prisoner. Roles reversed. You, powerless. Me, the big man at last. I felt like a god."

"Glad you were happy. I wasn't having as much fun inside that freezer."

"You'd have preferred water boarding? I knew the cold wouldn't hurt you. So it got stuffy. Didn't kill you."

"I almost suffocated! More than once, as you damn well know. I was nearly dead by the time I was rescued. I have nightmares about it."

"Man, this sucks. Take a girl for a nice drive, give her an engagement ring, show her an interesting time, buy her dinner, and what happens? She whines. This is why I don't date more often."

I want to laugh, Candace thought. *I should hate him, and I want to laugh. Talk about manipulative.* Yet, she could see in his mind that he was as sincere as he had it in him to be. That could change, of course; there was nothing in his nature to hold him to his word if he saw an advantage to himself to break it. But she did need help and he was what she had.

"All right," she said, "let's work together. I'll do my best to keep you in the loop. Now it's your turn. I could rummage around in your brain and find out what you're planning, but as we're working together I'll extend to you the professional courtesy of staying out of your head."

Finnegan cracked his knuckles. "Good. I'll extend the courtesy of no more practical jokes involving guns."

"No more practical jokes! Period."

"Still the boss lady." He grinned. "Here's my idea: we make you look really roughed up. Blood and bruises all over. I take you back to the cathedral, in the trunk of the car. When those people return, I approach them and offer a deal: you, for wads of money. They'll want proof. I open the trunk, show you to them, say I tortured you until you told me everything, including how to find them. We trade. I pretend to drive off. They take you inside. I follow, with my gun. You do the mind reading thing. I rescue you before they take you away in that bronze cylinder to wherever."

Candace winced mentally. "Your plan has interesting points," she said, with a determined effort to be polite. The 'really roughed up' portion definitely lacked appeal. "They'll want to know who you are, though. Why you were hunting me."

"Rogue ex-CIA officer. Fell from grace when you escaped. Became obsessed with you. Probably a bit crazy. Finally tracked you down. Made you pay."

She nodded. The advantage of a cover story that was close to the truth was that there was less likelihood of a stumble. "There's a problem, however: I can't read their minds."

"Huh! Why don't I shoot them all and then we use the wormhole ourselves? Find out where it goes."

"And with luck, how to come back. But killing them would be murder. There are still humans inside those bodies, even if their personalities and minds have been suppressed."

"Well, what the fuck, let's just go back and use the thing ourselves."

Candace brightened. "I like that plan. Simple. Easy to understand. So insanely dangerous that it might just work. But we need a contingency plan in case they come back. Perhaps a modified version of yours." She thought for a moment, drumming fingers on a knee. "Where can we get some food colouring and an egg?"

Sunset was muting the cathedral's brown stone walls to a warm sienna when the two returned.

"How's your makeup?" Finnegan said as he guided the Mustang down the street. There was no sign of the limousine and the church's parking lot was empty. A police car now sat in front of the building. A quick glance showed that the side door was closed and resealed.

Candace pulled down a sun visor and examined her face in the small mirror on the reverse. "Flaking a bit, but not too bad." Twin rivulets made by mixing green food colouring with egg white imitated the kind of bloody wounds that ripping out an elf's antennae would make. She'd drawn the line at 'really roughed up'.

"Can you feel the old guy?"

She extruded the delicate organs. "Napping. Thank the Magi."

"What about the Magi?"

"It's an elf thing."

"Religion sucks."

"I thought you were an altar boy!"

"I signed on to butter up my mother. Then I skipped Mass a lot, to piss off my step dad."

"Well, it isn't religion," Candace said, miffed. "It's more like, like, not religion." Changing the subject, she said, "That officer's awake, but he's drowsy." She concentrated again. "OK, he'll see two forensic unit specialists going in. People he's expecting."

The man eyed her antennae. "Gotta get me a pair of those things."

"Put it on your Christmas wish list."

Finnegan parked the car in the same spot as before and followed her past the police car, resisting, she was relieved to see, any whim to test the illusion she'd planted in the officer's mind.

The side door was unlocked. They pulled it open, ducked under the yellow tape and entered the cathedral.

In the nave, footprints in the deep pile of the altar carpet suggested that real forensic experts had been at work, probably greatly frustrated by the devoted custodian's cleanup efforts. Candace hoped he wouldn't face any charges.

Finnegan looked around. "Can you tell if anybody's home?"

"Just us."

He sniffed. "You sure? I smell french fries."

Candace pulled a hand from a jacket pocket and opened it to reveal a wrinkled ocher chip. "Sorry. I took one of yours. There was this mouse..."

"Don't explain. It might hurt my head."

The bronze cylinder was still there when they reached the crypts. Candace tossed her gift into a corner and was pleased to see bright, tiny eyes watching from the shadows. Animal minds were difficult to read but the hungry little rodent's interest was keen.

"What now?" Finnegan examined the hatch. A recessed button in the centre sank deeper when he pressed it and the hatch slid open. Weapon in hand, he poked his head inside the cylinder. "It's standing room only. No seats. I don't see any controls, either." He eased himself warily inside.

Candace joined him. "It might be on autopilot." She shut the hatch. "Feel anything?"

"Should I? You're the one who commutes between dimensions."

"Perhaps it's activated from the other end." She opened the hatch and stepped out. The french fry and mouse were gone, but otherwise there was no change.

"Is anticlimax a good or a bad thing?" asked Finnegan. "I say we go back to the car and wait."

"Agreed." Candace kept her senses on full alert as they retraced their steps to the nave, but no one else was in the cathedral and she said so.

"Are you sure?" Finnegan paused, frowning, near the foot of the altar steps. "Then who took away the tape? Who dried out and smoothed the carpet?"

"I'd have sensed—" A glimmer of the truth caused her antennae to curl backwards. "We need to get out."

The side door was shut and the rusty hinges groaned when they pushed it open and stepped into the sunlight.

"Cop's gone," Finnegan observed. "Hell, so is my car!"

"We weren't in that cylinder above a minute," Candace said. "Toto, I don't think we're in Kansas any more."

"What? This state isn't Kansas. Oh, I get it; a reference to *The Wizard of Oz*. Were you comparing me to the dog?"

"I saw the movie when it came out, in 1938. Or maybe it was 1939. I liked Toto. This doesn't look like the Emerald City. My home town looks like it when the aurora is green, but we're not there. We're here. Not there."

"Your mouth's going on a ramble. You're scared." Finnegan held his gun at the ready. "We need to look around." He led the way to the street. Change had struck here, too. Some houses were clearly vacant, their lawns and gardens overgrown. Cracks in the pavement sheltered miniature forests of weeds and grass. A sense of neglect hung over the street.

Candace ran to the custodian's home. "He's not in," she said after a quick scan for the old man's thoughts.

Finnegan rubbed grime from a window and peered in. "Yes, he is. Take a look."

She did, and recoiled. Dim though the interior was, she could see a couch in the living room and on it, in a position of peaceful repose, a skeleton, wrapped in decaying shreds of clothing.

"That cylinder," Finnegan said. "Did it move us forward in time?"

"I don't know. We need to find a newspaper." Candace led the way at a jog toward the nearest intersection. "In time travel stories there's always a handy newspaper lying around that gives the date."

"Or I could check my cell phone." Finnegan fished one out of a pocket and thumbed its buttons. "No signal. Hey, there's a car!"

A vehicle moved through the intersection ahead of them. The pair chased it around the corner and saw other cars, all heading for the parking lot of a nearby school. Men, women, and children were entering the building. Most carried sleeping bags, blankets, rolled-up mattresses and pillows.

Finnegan slipped his gun into a pocket. "Look at this," he said, pointing at a large, weather-worn sign.

"'Slumber Party Headquarters'," Candace read aloud. "What does that mean?"

"There's an easy way to find out. When in doubt, ask the guy with the clipboard."

Sure enough, at the entrance a man stood checking off names on that universal badge of authority. He looked up and smiled as the two strangers approached.

"New in town?" he asked in a friendly voice. "We're pretty full here, but I'm sure we can squeeze in a couple more." He stared quizzically at Candace's forehead.

"Thanks," she said, rubbing at the green tracks with her hand. "I, uh..."

"Got hit by a bird. Twice," Finnegan said with a wide grin and the clipboard man clucked his tongue sympathetically.

"The water's still on if you'd like to wash up, ma'am,

though it's not hot. I'm sure one of the other ladies can lend you a towel. There are some extra sleeping bags inside if you haven't got any of your own." He ran a finger down his checklist. "I don't suppose you'd be willing to take monitor positions? I've a slot open from four to five a.m."

"We'd love to." Candace nudged Finnegan as he opened his mouth to refuse. "Put us down for that time. Would you happen to have a newspaper? We're a bit out of touch."

"Sure. Got one that's almost fresh." The man reached into a duffle bag by his feet and pulled out a thin tabloid. The front page headline declared in massive type, *ATTACKS DROP!* "Heroes like Helm and her team mates create hope for us all," the man said with a pleasant smile as he handed the sheets to Candace. He turned away to check off the next arrivals.

"It's yesterday's date," she said, reading the paper as the two walked into the building. "We haven't moved in time."

"Then where the hell are we?"

"I think it's an alternate universe. One very similar to yours."

"But different."

"Yes." They'd reached the school's gymnasium, where scores of people were laying out bedding. Scattered throughout the room were hard, straight-backed chairs, some already occupied by people with serious, focused expressions. "No one here looks like they've had a good night's sleep in ages."

"I've never seen such deep under-eye bags," Finnegan agreed. "Looks like a prize-fighter's convention."

"Their thoughts are normal on the surface but underneath is fear, deep fear. Of sleeping."

"Of what?"

"Yaaaaaah!" A small child appeared suddenly in front of the two. "You're bogeymen in disguise!" He brandished a plastic toy sword. "I'm Helm and I'm gonna kill you!"

A girl child rushed up. "No, you aren't!" She wore an Ancient Greek-style helmet made of tin foil topped by a bristly crest that in another life had been a push broom. "You can't be Helm, 'cause she's a girl. I'm Helm. You can be Sword."

"Sorry, sorry!" A harried-looking woman intervened. "They're always hyper before bedtime." She caught sight of the newspaper in Candace's hands. "Isn't it wonderful? They say that attacks have dropped off sharply worldwide. We haven't had one in this group for a whole week!"

"Real glad to hear it," Finnegan said. "We're new to town. Didn't bring any sleeping bags."

"We've taken monitor duty from four to five," Candace added.

"Oh, that's so nice of you. I'll find something for you to sleep on," the woman promised, herding her offspring away.

"I know you'll want to stay," Finnegan said. "What if we can't get back?"

"I'm willing to bet that the cylinder is a shuttle. There's something else I'd bet on: whatever happened here is going to happen on your Earth, too."

"Yeah." Finnegan looked around at the tense, weary people. "Scouts. That's what those four men were. Scoping out the new territory."

Candace was holding up the tabloid again, as if reading. "They're called Mindeaters. They attack sleepers and cause lethal nightmares." She looked around at the people preparing for bed. "Everyone now sleeps together. If an attack comes, the monitors, those people on the chairs, try to wake them up. If that doesn't work, they're rushed to a hospital."

"You got all that from the paper?"

She tapped her now green-free forehead and nodded slightly at a nearby group. Folding up the paper, she handed it to him. "I've met those horrors before. They feed on fear and death energy. They're from outer space or, or some kind of space. It's difficult to describe."

"Yet you want to hang around."

"Kevin, they've killed millions of people here! Millions. This civilization is hanging on by its fingertips. Ours—yours, I mean, will suffer the same fate. Mine too, I think. I've a hunch that they've made some kind of alliance with the demons I told you about."

"Which aren't really demons, just a strange life form."

"But there's something else...something in the background." Her head throbbed. "Do you ever have that feeling of walking through the fog and almost, but not quite, seeing what's there?"

"Yeah; had it all the time when I was working for you at the Agency."

"Sweet. I have heard it said that psychopaths can be very, very charming. It's not something I've experienced personally, but now might be a good time to go charm up these people and learn everything you can."

"At last, a job I can do."

"In the meantime, I will snoop without shame into these defenceless heads. We can compare results later."

"Yaaaah! Got you!" The boy had returned, now equipped with both sword and helmet. His mother and sister were across the room, laying out sleeping bags. "Bet you can't get away!"

Candace went down on one knee. "I surrender to you, Sir Knight."

"I like knights," the boy said. "My uncle lives up in Canada. He was saved by Camelot Team when a bogey got into his head. They chopped it up with swords and killed it and my uncle woke up. But I still like Weapon Team best of all." The tin foil helmet slid over his eyes and Candace tipped it back with a gentle finger. "I saw Helm on TV last week," the child went on, eyes shining, "and Sword, and Spear, and Shield, and Axe, and Arrow, and Castle. They all got big medals but Helm got the biggest."

I think I need to meet these people, Candace told herself. *I wonder if Kevin can hot-wire a car.*

"Are you someone special?" the child asked. "People don't travel any more unless it's real important."

"We're on business. World saving, monster slaying; that sort of thing."

"Oh." A pause for deep thought. "You're in a combat team, I bet. Who are you in the Dream World?"

"I'm an elf. One of Santa Claus's little helpers."

The young forehead furrowed. "How can elves fight bogeys? They're tiny and green and give out candy canes."

She laughed. "That's my name; Candy Cane. You'd be surprised how tough little green people can be. We use exploding sugarplums and rapid-fire gum drops and tie up the bogeys with ribbon candy."

A few minutes later, she reunited with Finnegan at the sleeping bags laid out for them.

"What've you got?" the man said, stretching out beside her on his bag. With their heads close together, no one could overhear their discussion.

"They've been at war for about two years. The initial attack was the worst: an estimated billion people died in just one night. A billion people! Maybe half that number more were killed before they worked out a response. They learned that lucid dreamers, people who can wake up in their dreams and take control, survived most often. Some kind of hyped-up biofeedback device called a 'psi box' boosts teams of these dreamers into the minds of people under attack. The fighters all choose symbolic personas to represent themselves in the dreamers' minds. Weapons, warriors, animals, super heroes; whatever works for them. Very recently, the activities of a combat team up in Canada seem to have turned the tide."

"I got something, too," Finnegan said. "Dinner." He

passed a chocolate bar to her. "I traded my tie for these. Real Italian silk, I'll have you know. The barter economy is alive and well here."

"I appreciate your sacrifice." Candace ate her chocolate slowly, only now aware of how hungry she was. The soda had long since worn off. By the time she'd licked the last morsel from her fingers, most of the people in the room had settled on their bedding. The lights didn't dim; nearly everyone had an eye mask or, like Finnegan, slept with an arm across the face. The monitors were in position, alert to any sudden restlessness that might indicate an attack. Even the children had quieted.

Candace listened to the babble of internal chatter and imagery that gradually eased into dreams. *These beleaguered humans are surviving,* she thought. *Perhaps by the skin of their teeth, but it won't be the first time that the human race has made it through desperate peril.* She'd read books on archaeology and anthropology and had never failed to be impressed by humanity's ability to dodge cosmic bullets and even bullets of their own devising. The thousand-year span of elven history seemed meagre in comparison.

Kringle liked to say that the elves' high-speed evolution from their inauspicious beginnings hinted at the heights they could one day reach, and Candace believed him. *But without humans,* she reminded herself, *we would be nothing but terrified primates hiding in our burrows. My duty is to my race, but how can I ignore the race that gave us a future?*

I love them, she admitted in the privacy of her own mind; *I love these wonderful, fearsome, fascinating people. I cannot go home without at least trying to help them.*

She turned on her side. Finnegan had fallen asleep and was snoring lightly. With his face in repose, he was almost handsome. *Damn it,* Candace thought; *I'm doing it again; falling for a secret agent. There must be a scientific name for this complex. Homo intrigus elven susceptibilitis?* She was still pondering it as she fell asleep.

"Wakey, wakey." Candace opened her eyes, momentarily confused by her surroundings. Memory returned quickly. Finnegan was squatting beside her, finger poised to poke again. "It's four a.m. and all's well," he whispered, "except that we have to get up. Our turn as monitors. Remember; the job you volunteered us for? Without asking me if I agreed?"

"Right." She sat up, rubbing her eyes. Sleep had been fitful. She could tune out human thoughts but now and then a powerful image, such as a burst of fear or grief for the dead, broke through her barriers. In the gym's harsh light Finnegan didn't look handsome any more. She had a flashback to the way he'd loomed over her as she lay half-paralyzed and helpless on the hard floor of a walk-in freezer.

Candace took a chair vacated by a monitor and settled down to watch. The secret agent part of her rather hoped for a Mindeater attack and an opportunity to study how they behaved; the rest of her wished for a peaceful night.

Dawn came quietly, her better wish granted. The last shift took over and Candace stood up to stretch. She caught Finnegan's eye and motioned toward the door. They'd learned quickly that slumber party etiquette forbade even low-voiced chat.

"What now?" he asked when they were outside in the fresh air. "Go back?"

"There's a lot we still don't know," she replied. "Where in this world are those creatures headquartered? Wormholes with fancy bronze travel capsules don't make themselves. When the scouts return from spying, who takes the reports? I'm sure there's an organization behind all this and that it has a counterpart on your Earth."

"Yeah." Finnegan's jaw muscles worked. "Going by what the newspaper article said, that combat team up in Canada did something big. Did you notice, though, how little the article said about what, exactly, that was?"

Candace's hearts lifted. "Are you thinking the same thing I'm thinking?"

"It curdles my soul to admit it, but if you're thinking about getting in touch with them, then, yes."

She grinned. "I thought I was going to have to persuade you."

"Yeah, well..." Finnegan thrust his hands into his pockets. "I talked to a lot of people. Charmed them, as per orders. If you can't find friends to sleep with in this world, you die. It's become strictly survival of the nicest. Me, I like living in a world where I don't have to be nice all the fucking time. I also like it where things work and there's plenty to eat. Nobody here is starving, but the system's barely functioning. I don't want home to become like this."

"Canada, then?"

"We'll need to steal a car." Finnegan cracked his knuckles. "Takes me back to my boyhood. I don't think it'll be a problem. There's lots of houses around here where people have died. Lots of orphaned cars, probably."

He was right. The most serious problem the two had was finding a battery that still held a charge. They raided four abandoned cars before finding one that worked. Next, they had to find a way to siphon gas.

"I've always wanted a Mercedes," Finnegan said a couple of hours later, guiding their newly acquired ride down the highway. "I wonder if there's any way to get this through the wormhole?"

"In pieces, I suppose. How far is it to the border?"

Finnegan switched on the car's GPS system. "Surprise, surprise; this still operates." He tapped buttons for a moment. "About eight hours if I push it and you don't drive."

"I'm prepared to do my share!"

"Nah. You'll drive like a lady. I propose a division of labour: I drive, you do the elf thing to the state troopers and border guards."

Candace later added the journey to her life-list of terrifying experiences. Guessing, correctly, that the troopers were reduced in numbers and patrols less frequent, Finnegan pushed the car's powerful engine hard. Towns, cities, and states flew by. He drove with a psychopath's complete confidence in his own abilities, abetted, his passenger was sure, by a squadron of guardian angels who afterwards went on stress leave. The border crossing came into sight even sooner than he'd promised.

"Your turn," he said, slowing the Mercedes to a respectable speed and guiding it to the inspection booth she selected after a quick peek at the nearby minds. "I'm not stopping at duty free, though."

To Finnegan, the inspection had an aura of unreality. The guard politely requested identification and Candace as politely handed him two chocolate bar wrappers. The guard read them carefully, scanned them, ignored the querulous beep from the scanner, returned the wrappers, wished them a pleasant visit to his country, and waved them through.

Finnegan shook his head as he drove the car away from the booth. "That was fucking weird. What did he see?"

"Our passports, all up-to-date and correct."

"Are you sure you're not trying to take over the world? Because if you are, we don't stand a chance."

"I couldn't have pulled that off if he wasn't tired. Did you notice the very large sign we just passed? The sign that says this country's speed limits are in kilometres per hour, not miles per hour? The sign we passed very, very quickly?"

"No," Finnegan said and went back to working his angels hard.

He did slow down hours later on the approach to the hospital and turned sedately into its public parking lot.

"Popular place," he observed as they walked toward the main entrance. "Something must be happening. Look at the camera crews."

Television vans, people with shoulder-mounted cameras, and reporters earnestly talking to their microphones made a cordon near the doors. Security guards kept the media from interfering with arriving visitors, but now and then an outward-bound person was pounced on and interviewed.

"They're hoping for information about that woman code-named Helm," Candace said, picking up the paparazzi's thoughts. "She's the focus of intense world-wide interest. If we want to talk to her, it's not going to be easy."

"Ah, no problem," Finnegan said. "You'll walk us right in."

They walked right in as far as the front lobby, where a lineup stretched twenty feet.

"They have a screening station," Candace said. "Did you leave your gun in the car? I can't trick a metal detector or make all these people see what I want."

Finnegan's hand moved a little toward his pocket. "I may have kept it."

"How about you go put it in the car while I wait in line." The urge to tap her foot, glower at him, or merely scream was strong. She resisted, taking her place at the end of the row while he hustled away.

The lineup moved more quickly than she'd expected. Candace was through before Finnegan returned. *Good,* she said to herself, following the stream of traffic to the elevators and trying to look like she wasn't loitering as she picked the minds of passing hospital staff. She quickly gleaned that the location of the Combat Group's headquarters was one floor above the Emergency department. Patients presenting with Mindeaters in their heads could be rushed upstairs, where a team of lucid dreamers was always on duty, ready to do battle in the Dream World.

She chose her target carefully, an overworked and weary doctor with a pass to the upper level; coaxed him to the elevators with a vague memory of having left behind something that he needed, and rode up with him, as unnoticed as his shadow. The man's pass opened door after door and she followed him into the Combat Group's section, letting him go with a thank-you gift of a comforting sense of well-being.

The doctor had left her beside a door marked 'Observation Gallery'. Curious, Candace opened it. A room with seats for about fifteen people faced a large glass window. On the other side was a chamber straight out of a science fiction movie. In the centre of the room, a contraption aglow with myriad tiny lights hung suspended from the ceiling. The mysterious psi box, perhaps? Spaced around it in a daisy-petal pattern were several gurneys, each crowned by a smaller version of the central device.

As Candace watched, doors to the room opened and medical staff pushed in a stretcher on which a human body twisted against restraints. She caught an almost overwhelming mental stench that physically drove her away from the window and doubled her up, retching. The man on the stretcher was under attack by a Mindeater.

When she was able to straighten up, the scene had changed. A half dozen people had hurried into the chamber and were taking positions on the gurneys. The newcomers were an odd-looking crew, most dressed in medieval-style green tights and jerkins. While nurses fitted connectors from the central unit to the patient's head, with practiced speed the new arrivals did the same to their own. Candace watched, spellbound. The central unit's lights flashed, synchronized with the individual headpieces, and stabilized.

"Caspar's balls!" the elf whispered. All six minds were now inside the patient's head. Candace extended her antennae and watched as the fight unfolded in the realm of dreams. The alien invader had taken the form of a multi-legged, acid-spewing giant insect, tearing at the tender stuff of the patient's mind. The combat team members hurled themselves on it. Bows shot deadly missiles of pure thought. Psychic quarterstaves battered the carapace. Broadswords of focused hate and rage stabbed and hacked. Bit by bit the creature retreated but the team was relentless. The monster's form wavered, changed and changed again, to shapes of deepest nightmare, drawing on the patient's own memories and fears to guide its transformations. Nothing worked. The onslaught gradually tore it to shreds and it died with a soundless shriek that drove the elf to her knees, clutching her head.

In the chamber the patient was now awake, smiling and answering questions posed by the nurses. Team members roused, released themselves from their connectors, and left.

Candace did likewise, so overwhelmed by what she'd witnessed that she forgot she had no lawful reason to be there.

Around a corner was a lounge and several of the team members had gathered with other waiting colleagues to chat and compare notes. A big, blond young man was closest and she walked up to him.

"Excuse me," she said. "I wonder if you can tell me where I'd find Helm—"

The man transformed. His cheerful grey eyes flashed leonine yellow and the hair on his head sprang up like a mane. Fangs sprouted, pushing aside his lips. A basso growl rumbled from his throat. He raised a hand, each digit suddenly tipped by a claw.

The Sherwood Forest team members didn't transform as dramatically but somehow became larger. Bows and arrows appeared in their hands. A chubby fellow in a monk's robe raised a broadsword that glittered wickedly.

"She's possessed!" roared the monk. "Get her!"

Why do things like this happen to me? Candace wondered as the blond youth wrestled her to the floor and held her down. The monk raised the sword over his head with both hands. A ceiling fixture was visible behind the not-quite-there blade. She jabbed at his brain, intending to stun him.

Nothing happened. The sword swept down and passed through her neck.

"That's odd." The monk bent over with a puzzled frown. "The bogey should've died." He poked the blade into her chest where a human heart would be located. "Still zip. Anyone else want to try?"

The sword hadn't hurt her in the least. "If it's not too much of a bother," Candace said to the leonine young man, "might I get up?"

He scowled at her. "Are you with the media?"

"No. I'm here to see Helm. It's very important."

"They always say that." He stood, pulling her to her feet, but didn't release his grip. "Someone call Security. They'll want to know how she got in."

"Down the chimney," Candace said, exasperated. Saving worlds was turning out to be a poor career choice. "Look, I'm really not with the media."

The youth's hand tightened, making her wince. "Are you an assassin?"

"Christmas, no! I'm from an alternate universe. I came here with a companion to ask for help."

"That's a new one," the monk said.

The look on the leonine youth's face was skeptical but not cynical. "She triggered our Silchar devices when she came in," he pointed out, lisping heavily around his fangs. "I think the Commander will want to see her."

Several confusing minutes passed, filled with big men in uniforms, curious Combat Group members in a variety of costumes, and the ever-present blond youth, who hovered behind Candace like a shadow. She was at length escorted to a small room with a table and a few chairs and left there.

After a while she dozed off and into a dream where Kevin Finnegan learned to divide himself like an amoeba and took over the world. A gust of air as the door opened and the noise of someone briskly entering and taking a chair woke her.

"So, who are you?" The large woman now sitting across the table regarded Candace with shrewd eyes. The elf brushed at her mind. It was like Max's; almost impossible to read. The ample flesh hid a strong personality. Behind her stood two guards; a rangy man wearing a phantom white cowboy hat on which a silver star blazed and a woman who gave off an Arctic chill. Candace couldn't read either mind.

"My name's Candace Batonne," she said. "I'm an elf."

"Glad to meet you, Candace. My name's Commander Alpha. I'm the sugar-plum fairy. No games, miss."

"I'm not lying! My companion and I are from another universe. We're here looking for information and, possibly, help against the same enemies. You call them Mindeaters. We don't have a name for them; they've just begun their invasion."

"You asked to meet Helm. Why her?"

"I read her name in the paper. Look; I can prove I'm an elf."

"Go for it."

No one so much as twitched when she extended her antennae.

"Hm," Alpha said, "I haven't seen that kind of Silchar device before. What combat team are or were you with?"

"Team Santa," Candace said and immediately cursed her flippancy. *Mother was right,* she thought. *I* am *impudent. At the worst moments, too.* "Look, I can prove it. Just contact—" The Men in Black. The President. A host of doctors and scientists. Santa Claus. All of them in other universes. "There's a stable wormhole in the States. We used it to come to this universe. I'll give you the coordinates. Put me through an MRI machine. My internal anatomy isn't human. Or stick a pin in my finger. My blood's green."

Alpha leaned back in her chair and relaxed. Her smile was kind. "I'm going to refer you to our psychiatric service. Considering the nightmares that combat teams face every day, it's not uncommon for people to act out their Dream World personas while awake. It's a way of coping. We have some very good counsellors on staff."

"But—"

"The Texas Ranger and Ghost will escort you to a room. Believe me, we understand what you've been going through."

"No, I really am—"

"I've never heard of Santa Team, though. Are you sure you don't want to tell us where you're stationed?"

"I'm not stationed anywhere!"

"Well, not a problem; we'll check with the other hospitals. You said you had a companion. Do you know where he or she is now?"

Probably on his way home, Candace thought. "Please, just let me show you a drop of blood."

"The desire to commit self mutilation can be a side effect of overwhelming stress." Alpha nodded at the guards, who lifted the protesting elf from her chair with sympathetic but firm grips on her arms. "Don't worry about anything. You'll be fine."

The worst of it, Candace told herself an hour later, sitting frustrated, hungry, and bored on a hospital bed in a private room, *is how nice these people are. How kind and understanding. They truly do want to help me. Damn them.*

As prison cells went, the room was pleasant. She even had a telephone, though it wasn't connected. Private bathroom, comfortable bed, view of a park, and her very own security guard on the other side of the door. No sharp objects anywhere, though, and the dinner brought up earlier, a thoroughly cooked hamburger with mashed potatoes, was guaranteed to cause severe elven indigestion.

She passed the time by reading the minds in the hallway outside. All were human but some were shielded, like the Texas Ranger and Ghost. The security guard was one of them, which ruled out waiting until he was sleepy and persuading him to let her out.

A soft tap on the door distracted her from her gloom.

"Come in," she called.

A young woman poked her head inside and asked, "Is this a good time?"

"I am not at the moment engaged in saving the world."

The visitor slipped inside and shut the door. She wore a T-shirt and jeans and had a head of irregularly cut brunette hair that complemented a gamine smile. The sparkling hazel eyes disappeared suddenly as an antique Grecian bronze helmet manifested around her head. Blue lightning played in the black horsehair crest.

"You must be Helm," Candace said.

"Guilty as charged."

"Can you make that go away? I'm just curious. I'm not going to attack you."

"Sure." The helmet vanished. "Alpha said you're on a team that uses a Christmas theme. I was wondering how you fight."

Candace pulled up a guest chair for her visitor. "I'm not on a combat team. Nor am I possessed. I take it those—Silchar devices?—like your helmet appear in the presence of a Mindeater."

"That's correct." Helm sat cross-legged on the chair and studied the other woman with open curiosity. "You seem to be an anomaly."

"How can you tell that I'm not possessed?"

"Your bogey would've died the moment Friar Tuck ran you through with his device."

"Ah. Convenient. I have to rely on old-fashioned mind reading to tell me who's who or who's what."

"Can you really read minds? That would be something new for a device. I imagine people could get all hot and bothered around someone who knows what they're thinking."

"I can only read unshielded minds. Anyhow, human sex fantasies don't interest me."

"Alpha said you're convinced that you come from another

universe. She thinks you're suffering from a serious case of reality displacement."

"Sorry?"

"That you're nuts."

Candace smiled at her visitor. "Were you sent here to talk to me one on one, as a friendly, sympathetic confidante who understands the life and can perhaps lead me out of my sad, deluded state?"

"Ooh, you do go for the jugular. In a very polite way. I admire your style. No, this is business. Could I see those things in your head?"

"My pleasure." Candace extruded her antennae and the young woman hopped off her chair and came closer.

"They're pretty," she said. "Shimmery. May I touch?"

"We don't usually—oh, why not." The elf steeled herself but the other's finger pressure was very light.

"Well, that proves one thing," Helm said, returning to her chair. "Those aren't Silchar energy devices. They didn't manifest; they're solidly part of your head. Alpha said that you think you're an elf."

"Born and bred. Would you happen to have a pin on you?"

Helm folded over the waistband of her jeans and removed a safety pin substituting for a missing button. "Like this?"

"Yes." Candace took the pin and a deep breath and jabbed the point into the pad of her thumb.

"Wow." Helm tipped her head to the side and studied the emerging viridian droplet. "Do you ever tell people to live long and prosper?"

"I'm not sure I understand."

"There's a Trekker team in another hospital but the feelers don't fit that mythos," Helm said, thinking aloud and confusing Candace further. "It's uncommon for a device to alter the user's body, though it does happen. You saw my friend Leo when he went cat." Despite the light words, Helm's expression was sober and Candace had a sudden impression that, gamine grin or no, there was steel in the young woman. "Tell me: does the name 'Gamma' mean anything to you?"

"It's from the Greek alphabet and comes after alpha and beta. Another code name?"

"It's cheating to answer a question with a question."

Candace was starting to enjoy the fencing match. "I propose a fair exchange of information: you tell me who Gamma is and why you're interested, and I'll tell you which state the wormhole is in."

Helm laughed. "I'm supposed to hold the high ground and take charge of the interrogation. What am I thinking now?"

"Nothing complimentary about me, I'm sure. I've a question: where do those 'devices' come from?"

"That's sort of classified. Besides, if you have one, you already know."

Gotcha, Candace thought. "You said a minute ago that my, ah, feelers, aren't Silchar devices."

"The real question is this: Am I chatting with a lady who is engagingly loopy? Or am I verbally sparring with someone from another universe?" Helm drew up her knees and wrapped her arms around them. "If you were in my place, how would you go about resolving this dilemma?"

"I'd contact the American authorities and ask them to investigate the wormhole coordinates. However, that's not going to happen because why would anyone listen to a crazy woman who thinks she's one of Santa's little helpers?"

"Mmm. That's what Alpha said. Just before the CIA called and said they were missing an extraterrestrial."

Mr. Finnegan. Is this the woman?" The officer from the Canadian Security Intelligence Service who was escorting the visiting American official stood aside to allow the newcomer to enter the hospital room.

Candace kept her face calm. The man now regarding her wore a familiar three-piece suit, had short-cut hair and a trim, lean body. She knew him well from several years as his supervisor in the CIA, with one difference: this wasn't *her* Kevin Finnegan.

The counterpart agent pulled a black notebook from a pocket and studied an entry with a finicky self importance that was Finnegan through and through. "Have you run the medical tests we requested to establish that she's an alien?"

"Yes." Revulsion flickered on the CSIS officer's face. After two years of nightly murders, the word 'alien' was synonymous with 'monster'. "She sure as hell isn't human. We know they can possess bodies. Can they also remake them? Is this the next stage in the invasion?"

"No," Finnegan Mark Two said. "This is top secret, of course. She's not a Mindeater. She's from Roswell. A descendant of one of the survivors of the spaceship crash years ago. We've a small colony." He met the elf's eyes. "Nice to see you again, Ms. Batonne. You know you're not supposed to go walkabout without permission. This planet can be very dangerous." Loud and clear came the projected thought: *Play along*.

"I'm sorry," Candace said. "I did so want to see polar bears."

"Well, it was very naughty of you."

The CSIS officer pointed a finger at Finnegan. "Are you telling me that your government has had real extraterrestrial aliens for years and never shared that information with your closest ally?"

Mark Two looked huffy. "Of course we shared it. Haven't you picked up a tabloid newspaper lately? We plant stories all the time. The 'I Had an Alien Baby' spread a month ago was one of mine. That way, when something does happen, like our restless girl here going off on her own and getting into trouble, no one really believes it."

Candace hoped she would be long gone before the governments of the two countries bumped heads on the issue. She noted the Canadian official's skeptical expression and decided it was time to jump in.

"I didn't mean any harm. I was bored, sitting around all day thinking up new inventions."

"They've shared a lot with us," Finnegan said, picking up the cue. "The microchip, for instance." He took the CSIS officer's arm and drew him a little aside. "Normally, the CIA wouldn't be involved with them but our internal security is so shorthanded that I've been seconded to this case. I'm here to take her home."

"I can't release her without authorization from my superiors," the officer said stubbornly.

"Would you please check? I'd like to have a few minutes with her while you do that." Finnegan waited until the official grudgingly left, closing the door behind himself, before taking a deep breath and letting it out in a gust.

Candace said with a smile, "Met my Kevin, have you?"

"This is absolutely the weirdest thing that's ever happened to me," Finnegan Mark Two said as he took the guest chair. "When he called, I thought it was a prank until he started telling me things, stuff only I could know. I flew here right away."

"Where is he now?"

"Waiting outside. He said to trust you. You're really an alien?"

"Yes, but not from Roswell. Was that your idea or his?"

"We came up with it at the same time." The man grinned. "Great minds thinking alike, huh."

Overwhelming curiosity drove her next question. "Does your boss know about this?"

"No boss. One thing about the war: promotion is fast. Go to sleep a junior; wake up the leader of your unit and, hell, its only survivor."

Candace's hearts sank. "Do I have a counterpart here?"

"Not that I know of."

"Who was your unit leader?"

"Is that important?"

"Please."

"A guy named Paul Gironde. Took leave of absence to join a combat team. Bought it a couple of months ago. Are you all right?" Kevin Mark Two's eyes narrowed as he watched her. "He ended well. Took on three Mindeaters in someone's head. Killed two, but the third one got him. Ripped out most of his mind."

"What, what persona did he adopt?"

"You're sure curious about this guy. Some kind of warrior, I think. Ninja or Viking. Why?"

Candace couldn't answer. *He wasn't* my *Paul*, she said to herself. *Not mine*. A huge ache was nonetheless growing inside and she correctly identified it as fear of what might yet be.

"You going to be all right?"

"I—" She found her centre again and managed to smile. "Yes. What next?"

"Well, that's an interesting question." Mark Two crossed his legs and steepled his fingers. "I know my double wants to go home; that's what I'd want in his shoes, which are my shoes, after all. But you could be of great value here. He says you want to protect your world. Why wait for the Mindeaters to go there? Why not fight them here?"

"I came for information. If I don't share that with my people, they'll be defenceless. I must return home." Candace thought of the image of a necklace of jewels. "Going by what I've learned so far, these creatures may be able to move without hindrance between dimensions, as long as they don't take corporeal form. Possess people," she clarified, sensing Mark Two's bafflement. "They've run into opposition in this universe. Now they're spying on your double's world." She paused, thunderstruck. "Oh, of course! They're searching out lucid dreamers. The people who, in this world, form your combat teams. They're going to kill the counterparts; to stop resistance before it can even begin."

"You sure?" Finnegan Mark Two frowned.

Candace jumped to her feet. "We have to warn them!"

"How?"

The simple question rocked her back onto the bed once more. How, indeed. How could she warn a world that wouldn't believe her story?

"Oh, Melchior," she groaned, dropping her head into her hands.

"Wasn't he one of the Magi? What about them?"

"It's an elf thing."

"Religion sucks."

"I thought you—" Candace bit back her reply. Once was enough. "I have to return. Can you get me out of this place?"

"Yes. My double and I have a plan. He's going to act. Any moment now."

A premonition chilled her. "What's he planning to do?" Her question was answered by a clangour in the hallway outside the room. "Oh! He's pulled the fire alarm." It was exactly the sort of damn-the-consequences distraction a psychopath would use in a building full of sick, vulnerable people. Unless, of course, for that authentic touch, he'd really started a fire. Feeling both ashamed and angry, Candace followed Finnegan Mark Two to the door. The guard outside was on his feet.

"Sorry," he began, holding up a hand, "hospital rules require that you remain in—" Mark Two's fist cracked against his jaw. Candace caught him in time to ease his fall as he slumped to the floor.

Up and down the corridor, the doors to the patients' rooms had closed automatically. Staff were hurrying to their emergency stations.

"Fire exit," Finnegan Mark Two said, pointing to the nearest.

Candace ran, with a strong sense of deja vu all over again once more. *Let there be no limousines,* she prayed as they pelted down the stairs.

Mark One's Mercedes met them at the exit. He'd driven across a lawn to reach the door.

"Shotgun!" Mark Two yelled and jumped into the passenger seat beside his counterpart, leaving the back seat to Candace. She didn't have time to buckle herself in before the car leaped ahead, throwing her to the floor.

"Stay down there," Finnegan One said. "Don't let anyone see you."

Rejoining the main road and slowing to a sedate speed, the Mercedes passed a fleet of incoming fire engines and police cars. Mark One turned off almost immediately onto a side street.

"We switch here," he said, pulling in behind an inconspicuous sedan parked with other cars on the shoulder. "We'll change again in a few minutes. That'll throw them off our scent."

They switched three times to waiting cars, which told Candace what he'd been up to during the long day. The last vehicle was a taxi. Finnegan One drove, following directions given him by his counterpart.

Unable to see from her position lying on the rear seat, Candace asked, "Where are we going?"

"There's a small private airport on the city's outskirts," Finnegan Two said. "My plane's there."

Mark One smiled. "You got the civilian pilot's license, I see. I quit the Agency before I finished the training. Where'd you get the money for the plane?"

"Just went to an airport and picked one out."

"Lucky bastard."

"Yeah, well, the former owner didn't complain and

neither did his heirs. All dead."

"There's something to be said for this war."

Candace hoped no one in the hospital had been hurt as a result of the false alarm. She tried to keep anger out of her voice. "You boys are getting along well."

Finnegan Two looked over his shoulder at her and grinned. "Kevin told me you were his boss at the Agency. He said you're a real stunner."

"As in what I do to brains?"

The two Kevins exchanged grins. "That, too."

I ought to fry my own brain, Candace thought, *before I'm shut up in a small aircraft with two of the one man I detest.*

"Cop car," Finnegan One said abruptly, pulling the taxi over in response to flashing red and blue lights. "Probably a routine check. The license must've expired. Better warm up those feelers, boss lady. Watch this," he said with a grin to his duplicate. "We'll be on our way in a minute."

An hour later, Candace sat eyeing the surveillance camera in the interrogation room to which a squad of grim-faced, heavily armed officers had escorted her, and reflected that her career was taking a whole new direction: repeat offender. Arm and leg restraints and the presence outside the room of alert guards made it plain that she wasn't going on any more unauthorized strolls.

One of the officers had brought a can of pop and placed it on a table in front of her, even adding a straw so that she could bend forward and drink. The small kindness was all that kept her mood from sliding completely into despair.

Where the guards had taken the similarly restrained and loudly cursing Finnegans she didn't know and didn't care, although she hoped they were very uncomfortable. The time they'd wasted with the elaborate car-switching scheme had given the security forces an opportunity to coordinate and close in. *No wonder*, she thought, *that my Kevin never made it to field officer.*

The door opened. Candace looked around to see a familiar face.

"We meet again," said Commander Alpha. She took one of the seats on the other side of the table. Helm joined her. The young woman's Grecian helmet was fully visible. Unlike the Texas Ranger's cowboy hat, it looked solid. Candace couldn't see the wearer's eyes, only darkness.

"The pleasure is mine," she replied with weary courtesy.

"I'll cut to the chase," Alpha said. "There's a hell of a lot going on and you seem to be at the centre. Here's what we know: you aren't a human, you aren't a Mindeater, you aren't from Roswell, and you aren't leaving here unless I say so."

"You've that much authority?"

"Yes."

"I propose a bargain: let me go and in exchange you can keep both Finnegans. With my blessing."

"The essence of bargaining is to swap items of equal value. I think you're trying to short-change me. Was the fire alarm stunt your idea?"

Candace sighed. "No."

"Both of your friends say it was. In fact, they said it almost word for word, although they were interviewed separately."

Candace sighed again. "I'm not surprised. Was anyone hurt?"

"A patient had a panic attack and chest pains but the cardiologist says he'll be all right."

"I'm glad of that."

A smile flitted across Alpha's face. "You can stop sighing, miss. I know how to spot a couple of liars."

Helm shifted on her chair. "Those guys, they're not twins, are they?"

"Counterparts. One belongs to this universe. The other came with me."

"Through that wormhole down in the States."

"Yes."

Alpha dug into a pocket, produced a key and handed it to Helm. "This was your idea, so you do the honours."

Candace looked on in surprise while the young woman unlocked the restraints. "Are you letting me go?"

"Not exactly." Helm returned to the other side of the table. "We have our own sources of information and they say you're to be trusted."

The elf rubbed her chaffed wrists. "Your security service said that?"

"No. Have you ever heard of a place called Hy Brasail?"

"Is it a mountainous part of South America?"

Alpha rapped her knuckles on the table. "You dodge well, Ms. Batonne, and I've the impression that you've had long experience in the secret-keeping game. Know this: if I didn't think there's a chance, albeit small, that you can help us win this war, I'd hand you over to anyone who would take you off my hands. I don't believe you were behind the false alarm, but you keep very poor company."

"What, then, do you want of me?"

"We're sending you back," Helm said. "And I'm coming with you."

In the Palace of the Rings, the Lady Yseult walked briskly down a marble-lined corridor. At her side a tall old man kept pace. He carried a long wooden staff that clicked sharply against the polished stone floor in rhythm with his steps. Behind the pair, staying out of earshot but keyed to high alertness, followed the Lady's personal guard.

"You're sure you're all right," the old man said. His voice rang with both authority and concern. "It wouldn't be the first time you've hidden an attack from me."

"Hubert." The Lady's smile lit the air. "You know that I can't die and that any injuries I receive heal instantly. But I thank you for your concern."

The staff rapped on the pavement. "Of course I know that. But all the same, someone just tried to kill you."

The woman made a dismissive gesture with a gloved hand. She was dressed for riding, in a long, divided skirt and snug velvet bodice. A bloodstain and a hole just above her heart marred the green fabric. "I am fine, my love. Don't fuss."

"It is the duty of those who cherish you to fuss," the man replied. "You aren't invulnerable to pain. How many times have evil doers tried to capture you and force you to use your magic for their own ends?" He looked back at the guards. "Yes, everyone in the Rings knows that you cannot be killed. But apparently the Devourers of Minds are not convinced. This attack was only a test. Yseult—" he put a hand lightly on the Lady's arm. "Today, an arrow. Tomorrow, who knows? There are weapons, strange weapons, that might be brought from outside the Rings. The Devourers infiltrate everywhere. Who knows what they may find?"

"Such weapons cannot work outside their proper universes."

"Kris Kringle's people long ago mastered the art of creating universe bubbles that enable him to travel on Earth and perform magic there. If the Devourers conquer his world, the secret of the bubbles may fall into their hands."

"Are you saying that my friend was behind the attack? That he is possessed?"

"Of course not!" Impatiently, the old man struck the floor again with his staff. Small cracks appeared in the polished pavement. "You are the Guardian and I cannot tell you what to do, at least where it concerns the balance of the Rings. But as head of the Council of Wizards, I beg you to be careful. Stay in the Palace with your guards. And me. We can protect you."

The Lady's sherry-coloured eyes sparkled. "You know perfectly well that I can pass through the Rings from Nine to One without leaving the Palace."

"Take me with you, then."

"Hubert." The Lady rested fingertips on the wizard's hand. "I cannot do what I must do without going where I am needed. That includes the inner Rings."

"And no mortal can go there," the old man said.

Yseult leaned closer and kissed his cheek. "I promise to be careful. I just wasn't expecting an attack. Now that I *am* aware, it will not happen again." She touched his hand again and with a reassuring smile turned into her private apartment. The door shut softly behind her.

A flutter in the air above his head made the wizard look up. The little red dragon swooped from the rafters and lit on the door's wide, carved lintel. Some understanding passed between man and beast.

"If they devour *her* mind," the wizard said, "every being in every world is doomed."

"You really don't like flying, do you?"

Candace opened her eyes and looked across the aisle at her traveling companion. Helm had banished the Grecian helmet and in its place wore a cap that hid her mop of brown hair. Although the device was no longer visible, its influence was still apparent and the elf couldn't read her mind.

"I love flying," she said, reluctantly easing her death grip on the arms of her chair. The view out the window of the government jet was a close-up of high-altitude clouds. "Just not in mechanical things." To distract herself, she asked, "Are you a celebrity? I saw a lot of paparazzi outside the hospital." To reach the airport, they'd had to slip out concealed in the back of a delivery van.

"Yeah. I guess I am." Helm's expressive face saddened. "I was shot dead by a possessed person. A friend saved me by using his Silchar device. It all happened in front of a lot of people and cameras."

"Interesting. You don't look happy about it."

"My friend gave me his life. Literally, gave me his life." Perhaps seeking a distraction of her own, the young human said, "What do you fly on, or in, at home?"

"Reindeer and sleighs. Before you think I'm lying, I mean it. That's what we use."

A smile flicked across Helm's mouth. "The natural laws in your universe must be very unusual."

"As far as I'm concerned, they're perfectly ordinary."

"Is your universe the source of our Santa Claus myth?"

"Possibly. My world's had a thousand-year connection with the other Earth, the one that the fatter Kevin comes from. I don't know if there's a counterpart to my universe." Candace described the image shown to her by the Mind-eater of a necklace of jewels orbiting each other. "I think our universes are in a sort of cluster," she went on. "There's a central universe that seems somehow to connect them all."

"Hy Brasail," Helm said, surprising her companion. "I've been there."

"You do get around."

"Speak for yourself!" A pause. "What's Santa like? In this world he's a fantasy, though there was a real man, Saint Nicholas, on whom the legend's based. I've always loved the story."

"He's kind, and wise, and real." Candace fought a swell of homesickness. "We call him the Master, in the old sense of 'teacher'." She turned away for a moment, trying to compose herself. The jet hit a patch of turbulence, which effectively distracted her. A buzzer sounded and the seat belt light flicked on.

"Feels like we're descending," Helm said. "Are you going to be sick? You look green. Don't worry, it'll be over soon."

"Did I mention that I was recently in a helicopter crash? That was over soon, too."

"I could hold your hand, if it'll help."

"It might, at that." Candace gripped the proffered hand in shaking fingers as the jet shuddered its way through clouds. Curiously, the warm touch partly neutralized the dampening effect of the helmet. Images danced in her mind and one in particular jumped out. "The blue place," she said between clenched teeth. "The world with three blue suns. I've been there, too."

Helm didn't withdraw her hand, though the elf felt her tense. "Would it be impolite to ask you to stay the hell out of my mind?"

"I wasn't trying to—what was that?"

"Just the landing gear coming down. You've been to the Silchar world?"

"Briefly. If that's what you call the blue world."

"Did you meet the inhabitants?"

"Yes, and I'm sorry, I'm not trying to read your mind and please don't let go."

"You must've flown in jets before."

"Big ones, but never after surviving a crash."

The human's fingers squeezed sympathetically. "Post Traumatic Stress Disorder. Just about everyone in my combat group has it. Occupational hazard of working among nightmares."

Candace had closed her eyes. The landing was silken smooth, the roar of the braking engines a relief. *Should I add cowardice to my other lack of virtues?* she asked herself as the jet taxied to a halt. *Possibly fickle, definitely insolent, and a miserable failure as a secret agent.* Her mood dipped lower when she saw the long vehicle rolling across the tarmac to meet them. The jet, once a trap, now seemed like a haven and she was slow to leave her seat.

"Let me guess: you don't like limousines," Helm called from the foot of the steps, as the elf hesitated in the jet's doorway. "I don't, either. I was once chased by a limo full of Mindeaters. In the real world, not the Dream World."

"Was it pink?" Candace conquered her momentary panic. "I was chased by one, too."

"At last, something in common! No; mine was black. The Mindeaters seem to have a thing about limos." Helm tapped her head. "If any of the possessed are around, we'll know right away. My Silchar device will light up."

A minute later, "It must be the buttons they love," Candace said, settling herself on a well-padded leather seat. She poked curiously at one of the many available on a polished wooden console, causing her seat to tilt backwards. Both women burst out laughing.

"That's better," Helm said. "I was afraid we weren't going to get along. You're so graceful and poised. I felt like a gawk when we met."

"You did? I felt scruffy and disreputable. As your Commander Alpha said, I kept very poor company." Candace relaxed in the seat, enjoying the luxury of being able to stretch her long legs in a vehicle. "What's happening to the Finnegans, anyway?"

"Extensive debriefings, I believe. Ours will have some strident music to face when he goes home. Yours—I suppose it all depends."

"You know I won't return with you," Candace said. "I have to warn my people."

"Yeah, I kind of figured that." Helm's expression was speculative. "You asked who Gamma is. The Mindeaters are hive creatures, with thousands of individual beings under the rule of one dominant personality. When they arrived at my Earth, they discovered how to enter human bodies and take possession." A cloud passed across the young woman's face. "What they didn't realize is that brains cling to energy. They couldn't easily get out again. The dominant personalities became trapped in the bodies they'd stolen."

"Gamma is one of them?"

"He is. We caught his human body and it's now in prison,

but he can still communicate with the other members of his hive. We've learned that his goal is to take control of our civilization and then farm the human race to provide a sustainable source of food. I imagine he's planning the same for the other Earth, and maybe your world as well."

"Are they always trapped if they possess human bodies?"

Helm shook her head. "They've learned from experience. Drug abusers are now the vehicles of choice. Brain damage smooths the neural pathways and they can get in and out at will. Some prescription meds have the same effect. It's playing hob with our world's pharmaceutical industry."

Candace thought of Sunny and wondered if the aliens had been able to enter her mind while she napped because of the date rape drug Scott had slipped her. She'd found nothing in the young woman's mind to suggest habitual drug abuse. Possibly, the other possessed hotel people had not been so wise and had suffered the consequences.

"What do you know about the others?" she asked.

"Others?"

Candace described her encounter with the terrifying mindless minds.

Helm went pale. "I don't know of them. Mindeaters have at least rudimentary intelligence and personality. The dominant personalities have both, in spades. Shit; this is new."

"They seem to be working together."

"Just when it seemed things were getting better. Any idea where they're from?"

"The Mindeater I had communication with called them 'the ones who made the beginning'. Beyond that, I'm in the dark. What about the other dominant personalities?"

As Helm began to reply, the limousine pulled to a stop in front of an office building and Candace never heard the answer to her question. The pair were escorted indoors to a conference room. Communications must have flown rapidly between the security services of the two countries, because the briefing was quickly over and they were again on their way, this time in an ordinary taxi. The driver was middle-aged, overweight, and altogether nondescript, aside from the communicator discreetly clipped behind one ear and the gun on his lap.

"We sent a team inside less than an hour ago," the driver said as they neared the cathedral. "The capsule is still there."

Candace let out her pent breath in relief.

A few minutes later, she and Helm stood looking at the bronze cylinder. Armed escorts and a videographer kept them company.

"What next?" Helm whispered.

"Well, we pushed this button," Candace replied, demonstrating. The round door opened silently. Both women stepped hastily to the side and the armed guards tensed. "Then we got in," she said, when nothing murderous leaped out.

Helm followed her through the hatch. "Dibs on pushing the next button."

"Sorry, but there's only this handle for shutting the door. I think it automatically activates whatever powers this thing. Shall we?" At Helm's curt nod, Candace drew the door closed and both women waited tensely for a few seconds. "Now we open it again and see if anything's happened."

Helm poked her head out. "We seem to have lost our friends. Nobody here but us and, oh look, a mouse."

"It worked." Candace reached into a pocket and pulled out a cookie she'd saved when snacks were served on the jet. She broke it into pieces and tossed them to the tiny animal.

"What's that about?"

"Call it a reward for a faithful mascot."

"You're strange, but in a nice way."

"The feeling is mutual." Candace stretched out her senses. "I don't detect anyone nearby." She led the way upstairs to the now familiar side door. It opened easily on well-oiled hinges and the pair stepped out into the sunlight.

They walked to the nearby road and paused. Helm caught her breath. Her eyes widened. "It's all fresh and clean." She looked around, blinking away tears. "It's so—normal. Like it used to be. Are you sure that bronze thing isn't a time machine? Did we go to the past?"

"Quite sure. You've traveled before to other universes."

"Yes." Helm wiped tears away with the back of her hand. "But they were obviously alien. This is home, as it was. Before so many people died. So very many."

"They won't die here." Candace wondered if her companion would appreciate a hug and, with a little trepidation, put an arm around the young woman's shoulders. The hug was well received. "We won't let that happen. Look, I should head for home but I'll stay, at least for a while, and help you convince people about the danger." *I escaped before*, she reminded herself. *I'll do it again*. She noticed that the police officer had emerged from his car and was approaching them. "He probably wants to know what we're doing at a crime scene. We can show him the capsule. Get things rolling."

Helm had her emotions quickly under control. "Fine. I'll show him my Silchar device, too. That should get some attention."

Candace was wondering what to say to the police officer when it hit her that she wasn't picking up his thoughts.

At the same moment, the officer removed his dark glasses. "Ms. Batonne," he said. "Welcome back."

Candace smiled ruefully. "Mr. Maxwell. Has anyone ever told you that you are very, very good at your job?"

"Yes, ma'am. It's in my performance appraisals." The agent's face was as stoic as usual but his eye held a gleam. "We used the GPS system in that humvee to track you until you abandoned it and started hitchhiking. After that, we tracked the bug I hid in the lining of your jacket."

"That's why you told me where to find a road! You knew all along that you could trace me."

"Quite so, though when you disappeared here, along with Mr. Finnegan, we were very concerned. Ladies, you are under arrest. In case you're thinking about making a run for it, several marksmen have you in their sights and I have a taser. Ms. Batonne, please hold out your right arm."

Helm frowned. "Is he a good guy or a bad guy?"

"Oh, a good guy," Candace said, trying not to flinch as the agent clipped a handcuff around her wrist. "Technically, I'm a possible enemy alien and you're with me, so that makes you a suspicious character."

"Person of interest," Max corrected her, making sure that the bracelet was snug but not too tight. His fingers brushed against her skin and lingered a second longer than strictly necessary. "Have you ever been tased, miss?"

"I don't recommend it," Candace said. "Max, this isn't necessary. I was going to surrender myself."

"Sorry, ma'am. Protocol. You did run." He clipped the remaining bracelet to his left wrist.

"I don't mind your company," said the simmering elf, "but I hope togetherness stops at the bathroom door."

"Discretion is my watchword. I promise I will close my eyes."

"I should go back," Helm said uneasily. "People will be wondering what's happened to us."

"Sorry, miss," Max said. "First, we debrief you."

He guided the two women toward a black car that quietly drew up, installed Helm beside the driver and sat with Candace in the back seat.

"I've never been arrested before," Helm said as the car pulled away. "My mother will be scandalized. But on the plus side, she'll probably never know."

"I'm getting used to it," Candace said. "My life lately has been fraught with interest."

Helm frowned again. "Where are we going?"

"I don't know, but I'm pretty sure there won't be a swimming pool and that the shopping will be abysmal."

"Now you're being cryptic."

"I may have inadvertently forgotten to mention it during our briefings, but currently I'm not on the very best terms with the government of this country."

"Now you tell me!"

Max offered his thin smile. "Ms. Batonne has a well-deserved reputation for evasiveness. And for disappearing mysteriously. Now we see her, now we don't. Our code name for her is 'Poof'."

"It isn't!" Candace felt colour rising in her cheeks.

"Yes, ma'am. I came up with it myself."

"I'm so flattered I could spit. How's your injured side doing?"

"Tolerably well. Please introduce me to your companion."

"My name's Eli Baden," Helm said, turning around in her seat. "I'm from another universe and I'm here to warn you about an impending invasion."

"Really."

"Yes, really," Candace snapped. To surrender herself was one thing; to be arrested put a darker twist on the situation. She hoped it wouldn't harm Helm's mission. "You must've examined that vault in the cathedral."

"We found footprints that appeared to be yours and Mr. Finnegan's. They went to the edge of a toy train track and did not return. Where is he now?"

"Where he deserves to be." Too late, Candace realized how the words might be interpreted.

"Is he dead?"

"Not as far as I know."

"Is he a hostage?"

"To fortune. Like me."

"He's OK," Helm put in. "I'm sure our security people

will be very glad to give him back once they've debriefed him, but first things first."

Candace let her anger fade. "You'll have people down in the crypt by now, I'm sure."

"Yes, ma'am." Max cupped his free hand over his earpiece and listened for a moment. "As you said, your life is fraught with interest. What is that bronze cylinder?"

"It's an inter-dimensional travel capsule. Not mine. We borrowed it to go sightseeing. Why are you taking us to a fire station?" The car had rolled into a fire hall and parked between twin red engines.

"It's both a fire station and a training centre," Max said, opening his door. Tugged by the handcuff, Candace followed him. "There's something here you need to see."

Helm joined them, escorted by the driver, and Max led the way through the building and out the back, to a large yard filled with rescue equipment of various kinds. In the middle was a small, ordinary-looking concrete house. Two of the black-suited secret agents stood on guard in front. Max brought the women to the door and stopped.

"This building is completely fireproof," he said. "It's used to train firefighters how to move through smoke and flame."

Candace tried to make her tone light but couldn't keep a quaver out of her voice. "You're not planning to finish what the Senator started, are you?"

"No, ma'am. My job is to protect you. With my life, if need be."

"I'm sorry." She touched his hand with her fingertips. "Chalk it up to post traumatic stress."

The driver handed a pair of sunglasses to each woman and put on his own. "You'll need these," he said. When everyone's eyes were covered, he stepped forward and opened the door.

A scorching glare like the noonday sun almost

overwhelmed the eye protection. In the heart of the heat and brilliance, Candace made out what seemed to be a seated figure.

"Oh, Ms. Batonne!" wailed the voice of Sunny Daley. "I can't make it stop!"

The Silchar are very literal-minded." Helm looked around the station's homey and comfortable staff lounge where she, Candace, Max, and a stunned-looking but no longer incandescent Sunny had gathered. "They pick out of our minds how we identify ourselves and create a matching energy construct."

"Do you mean," Candace said, "that they took Sunny's name as a statement of fact and turned her into a small star?" She had curled up in one of the room's big, cozy chairs, with a large glass of orange juice in her free hand. The other remained attached to Max.

"I'd bet on it." Helm grinned. "I've a colleague who belongs to a team with a cowboy theme. She took the name Calamity, after the historic personage Calamity Jane. She now can't walk past a lamp without the bulb blowing. Doorknobs fall off, shelves collapse, and computer hard drives fry in her presence. She's a real powerhouse in the Dream World, though. Causes massive calamities to the Mindeaters."

Max hadn't touched the cup of coffee steaming on a small table at his side. "Is this effect permanent?"

"As far as we know, yes."

"It'll happen automatically any time she's near a possessed person?"

"Correct." Helm smiled at Sunny. "It might switch on anyhow until you have the hang of suppressing it. Just keep practicing the mental exercises I gave you."

"What about Ms. Batonne?"

Candace looked up, startled by the agent's question. "Will I develop something like that? I don't feel any different."

Helm gave her a thoughtful look. "You're not a lucid dreamer, are you? You know, wake up in your dreams and take control?"

"I do that," Sunny said shyly. "Almost every night. I like flying dreams the most."

"No, my dreams are down-to-earth." *But Paul is a lucid dreamer*, Candace added silently, *and after he falls asleep I link my mind to his and soar with him through the aurora.*

"Are you all right?" Max was watching her closely.

"Yes. Just a touch homesick. There's a meeting room at home that has furniture like this." She caught herself speculating about sleeping arrangements in the near future.

The agent asked, "Can this phenomenon be used as a weapon?"

Helm nodded. "You've probably seen and felt the maximum force Sunny can achieve on this plane, but in the Dream World she'd be awesome."

"You refer to that as a real place," Max said. "Do dreamers somehow connect to a larger reality?"

Candace listened, impressed, and wondered, not for the first time, who Max really was inside the anonymous suit.

"Without a Mindeater present, dreams are just dreams," Helm said. "During an attack a connection is made to the energy matrix where the aliens live. It's possible to follow that to other dimensions. The physics and math involved are crazy complex and we've only begun to study them."

Max turned to Candace. "Do your people know anything about this?"

"We were aware of the existence of other universes, but these creatures are new to us."

"Do you have any wise men or shamans, people who might have helpful observations our scientists can use?"

"We are but simple folk," Candace said, annoyed. "Our

primitive tribal ways do not lend themselves to such deep learning. However, our *shamans* have an understanding of the quantum universe that makes human physicists look like babies sucking their toes."

Max turned red. "I'm sorry. My bad. I shouldn't have made assumptions."

An awkward silence filled the room.

"I could be on my way home now," Candace said. "I chose to stay and help." She rattled the handcuff. "Get this off me, Max. I have had enough."

"I am under orders," the agent replied, his face turning a darker red. "Until and unless I receive instructions to the contrary, you and I are going to have to put up with each other's company."

Sunny's nervous laugh broke into the roiling emotions in the lounge. "I think it's kind of kinky," she blurted. "I mean, I wouldn't mind spending the night with—what I mean is, it's a good idea, isn't it, to sleep with someone in case one of those Mindeaters attacks?" Her face was almost as crimson as the agent's.

I do believe Ms. Daley has a crush on Mr. Maxwell, Candace thought. Her sense of humour roused. If she was Max's prisoner, it followed that he was also hers, with all the potential for amusement that implied. "I accept your apology," she said with a straight face. "I know we're both going to remember this experience for a long time."

Sleeping arrangements, as it later turned out, were simple: Candace had the left side of the bed and Max had the right. The training centre provided overnight quarters for visiting students, all of them now relocated.

"Do you snore?" she asked, stretched out fully dressed at his side.

"Can't say, ma'am."

"Your suit's going to be wrinkled."

"It'll survive."

"Do you want to make mad, passionate love to me?"

"No, ma'am."

"Why not?"

"You don't really want me to."

"Are you sure?"

"Yes, ma'am. You're trying to push my buttons."

"You must've memorized my psychological profile."

"Yes, ma'am. I wrote it."

"Are you gay?"

"Won't say, ma'am."

"What if I wait until you're asleep, pick your pocket for the key, unlock the handcuff and go poof?"

"I took care to leave the key with someone else."

"Can I air my antennae? They get itchy if I leave them sheathed too long."

"No, ma'am."

"This is the least romantic bedroom banter I've ever had."

"Sorry, ma'am."

"You're really determined not to lose me again."

"Yes, ma'am."

"Did you get a slap on the wrist because I got away?"

"Can't say, ma'am."

"Hardly fair if you did. Who'd have expected someone to shoot a missile at us?"

"I should've."

Candace turned her head to study the handsome profile on the pillow next to hers. "That's asking a bit much, in my opinion." When Max didn't answer, she said, "Did you find out how the Senator and his gang knew where we were going and how to lock onto the anklet's signal?"

The agent took a long time before replying: "Yes."

"I bet it was a mole. A possessed mole. One of your brother agents. Communicating through that hive-mind

Helm described."

"Can't say."

"You forgot to add 'ma'am'."

"Ma'am."

"You really are a very irritating man."

"That is a compliment, coming from a leading expert in the art of being irritating."

Score one for the elf, Candace thought, rolling onto her right side and leaning on her hand, which forced Max to raise his; another tiny victory. "Where are Helm and Sunny?"

"In the room next door."

"Did you catch the mole?"

"Not yet."

"But you will. If those energy devices light up in the presence of a possessed person, you'll find him soon enough."

"Go to sleep, Ms. Batonne."

"I wonder what sort of device the Silchar might give me. As my real name's Candy Cane, perhaps I could destroy the Mindeaters with sugar poisoning."

"Go to sleep."

Candace surprised herself by saying, "The last time I mated, officially, that is, I had eight males. It was very solemn: there was a ceremony, and speeches, and I wore white and knelt in the centre of the Life Room, and the males I'd chosen came in and each made a speech, and then they knelt in a circle around me, and my mother made another speech as head of the Mothers' Council, and after that I addressed the males, each by name, and thanked them, and then we, the males and I, extended our antennae and—" She broke off. Max did, indeed, snore. "How about that: I bored a human male to sleep by talking about sex. There's a first time for everything." She extruded her antennae and gently touched his head, sensing the waves of exhaustion and fear breaking through his conditioning.

Candace put her free arm around him and cuddled close. "I do understand, poor man," she whispered. "You know the invasion is under way. You know that anyone, even your trusted friends, could be possessed; that your world could suffer as terribly as Helm's has and there are only a few of you to stand against all that horror." Waves of drowsiness flooded her own mind. "You're a good man and I like you," she murmured, "and I promise I'll stop teasing you." She was almost asleep before honesty made her add, "As much."

Morning light turned the fire station's kitchen into a friendly harbour.

"Did you sleep well?" Helm smiled at Candace over the rim of a steaming cup of coffee.

"Yes; and you?"

"Not bad. No hot flashes. I see you've been set at liberty."

"I guess Max received new orders." Candace flexed her right hand. She'd awakened alone in the bed, handcuff free. "Where is he now?"

Helm nodded toward the training yard. "In the concrete house with Sunny. I showed them how to test for Mindeaters and since dawn there's been a stream of people getting checked out. That girl will be a godsend to this world. They just need a few hundred thousand more like her."

Candace raided the refrigerator and emerged triumphant with a bottle of apple juice. "From chambermaid to one of the most important people in the country in just a few days. Her future does look exceptionally bright."

Helm winced. "It's too early in the morning for groaners."

"Tit for tat. That was for the 'hot flashes'. You'll be busy today, I expect."

"We've certainly started the ball rolling. I'm supposed to talk later on to some scientists and engineers about psi boxes. Wish I'd brought some designs, but at least I know the general idea of how they work. I am very slightly optimistic about this world's chances."

"Only very slightly?"

A touch of grimness flicked across Helm's mobile features. "Depends on how many assassins have made it here. Mr. Maxwell says they have people searching the media for reports of unusual murders."

"There are ordinary murders?"

"Mindeaters don't follow the conventions. Ghoulish and gruesome would be their style."

"I wonder if that's what happened at the cathedral." Candace filled in her companion about the murder-suicide that had so entertained Finnegan.

"Sounds about right," Helm said. "At a guess, I'd say that the poor soul whose throat was torn out was a lucid dreamer, or else had stumbled onto the transit station. If the possessed body was no longer useful, the Mindeater inside might have deliberately killed it."

"Any more activity with the travel capsule?"

Helm shook her head. "Which could mean either that the enemy knows we're using it, or they've more than one."

"Odd."

"What, in particular?"

"There's nothing for me to do." Candace laughed. "For days now, I've been running. Just when I want to stay and help, I've become a fifth wheel."

Helm grinned. "Enjoy it while you can."

That I will, Candace decided. She finished her juice and wandered into the station's recreation room. A billiard table and a dart board told her how the fire fighters spent some of their off-duty time. She picked up a dart and tossed it at the target. Her aim was accurate; the needle-sharp point lodged close to the centre.

"Nice shot," said Helm, who had followed her.

"I used to enjoy this game." Candace retrieved the dart and collected a couple more from a rack. "When I lived in Paris, my man and I would go to an English-style pub after work. He was good at darts, but I was better."

Helm reached for a few darts. "Play until we're called?"

"Sure."

"How long were you in Paris?"

"Oh, about a hundred years, on and off."

Helm paused in the act of taking aim. "Elves live a long time?"

"Several centuries. I'm sorry; does that bother you?"

"Nah. I'm used to strangeness. In my line of work, we don't think far ahead. Alive today, a corpse or among the walking dead tomorrow."

"I hardly dare ask."

Helm threw her dart. It lodged near Candace's. "They're people who've survived a Mindeater attack, but have lost most of their mental functions."

"I think I've met one. Name of Morris. Can they be helped?"

"I wish I knew."

"By the way, do you smoke?" Candace took aim and hit the bull's eye.

"Strict abstainer. Why?"

"My species goes by the nose. I hope you won't find this offensive, but I'm sure I picked up your scent before we met. On the blue world, inside one of those crystal towers. I found a cigarette butt, which is why I wondered if you smoke."

"You smelled only me?"

"There might've been a man there, too. The traces were faint."

Helm was silent for a long moment. The elf saw the rush of emotions across her face and identified them: grief, shame, curiosity. "Hours. You must've missed us by hours." She shook her head. "It's a small universe."

"Small multiverse."

"Po-tay-to, po-tah-to. Do you ever have the sensation of something going on that's just outside your vision?"

"Lately, all the time."

Helm laughed. "Something else we have in common." She threw and her dart lodged against Candace's. "Tell me more about Paris and your friend."

"I was a model at a fashion house. Edouard was a photographer. He loved British beer and after work we'd often go to a pub on the Left Bank. Of course, the beer supplies dried up after France was invaded, but by then we were both well known at the pub and that's how we were recruited into the Resistance."

"Excuse me: you're talking about the Second World War?"

"It always amazes me that humans number their wars."

"Keeps 'em tidy for the history books." Helm threw again and hit the innermost circle. "What happened?"

What happened. She'd been on her way to the pub one evening for a clandestine meeting when an explosion sent up a fountain of smoke and debris. When she arrived, the pub was burning. Two Resistance men lay dead in the street and Gestapo agents were dragging a third man toward a waiting car. It was Edouard. He broke loose, drew a gun and aimed at an officer in a long, black leather coat, but saw her and hesitated. In that fatal instant, the officer shot him.

He was dead when the Gestapo men dragged her off his body and threw her into a car. The officer jumped in beside her. In his thoughts, sharp as razors, she read his intent: rape and torture until she broke and told everything she knew.

She did nothing until they were well away from the pub, then reached into his head and the driver's to vent her rage and grief.

The car ran into a wall and stopped. She left the convulsing men and fled to a safe house, where she'd long since hidden one of her own special communications devices. Hours later, two reindeer drifted down from the inky night sky. Crystal rode one. Her sister said nothing, not then and not during the return ride to the North Pole and the rift that linked two universes. But all the way, as only elves could do, she'd held Candace's agonized mind wrapped tenderly in her own.

"Penny," Helm said. "Penny for your thoughts. You look so far away."

"I insist on at least a dime per thought. No; it was a long time ago. I went home. Santa doesn't approve of our becoming involved in human wars."

"He's a pacifist, then."

"Yes; when there's peace." Candace went to the board to retrieve her darts. "Is something going on outside?" Both women listened for a second. The sharp popping of gunfire came clearly.

"We'd better stay here," Helm said, but they were already moving.

A blast of heat and a solar glare met them as they entered the training yard. The heat and light faded quickly. A dozen or so shocked-looking people stared at Max, who lay motionless on the ground. Sunny knelt beside him, tears steaming on her face. Two of the agents held a third man who slumped in their grips as loosely as a puppet.

Candace froze, caught by the double impact of emotions old and new. *He isn't Edouard*, she told herself and fought off the paralysis.

Max stirred and sat up. He pulled open his shirt.

"Bulletproof vest," Helm said, her voice shaking with relief inside the phantom Grecian helmet that had flashed into being. It faded slowly into nothingness.

Candace ran over and sank to the ground beside the agent. "Are you all right?"

For the first time since she'd met him, he grinned. "Right as rain, ma'am." Three flattened bullets over his heart testified to the assassin's aim. His face darkened as he turned toward his attacker.

"It's Joe." Candace looked, appalled, at the downed man.

"He was on meds for pain," Max said. "An after-effect of being so near the explosion in the hotel. He shot me and was about to shoot Ms. Daley when she lit up and he collapsed."

"Her device killed the Mindeater inside him," Helm said. "Are you on painkillers, too?"

The agent's jaw muscles tightened briefly. "No. I went off them. They made my head feel fuzzy."

"Good thing you did." Helm regarded Joe's limp form with a sad, experienced eye.

"Is he going to die?" Sunny was still crying. Candace read her shock that what had begun as a thrilling adventure, a chance to play real-life super-hero, had turned deadly. "Can't we do something for him? Ms. Batonne? You can read minds. Please!"

"I, I'll try," the elf said, moving to kneel beside Joe's body. His face was slack, empty. *Now we know who the mole was,* she said to herself. She nodded toward the small crowd of onlookers. "Max, I'll have to use my antennae. Do you want to clear the area?"

"Let them watch," the agent said, going to one knee on the stricken man's other side. "They're important people; they need to know. Do what you have to."

"Right." Candace bent forward to glide her antennae over Joe's head, wary of what might still lurk inside.

There was no alien present. She found instead a welter of scraps; ragged bits of memory and personality drifting like flotsam in an ocean calming after a hurricane. Joe had fought his attacker bravely and the memory still seethed among the bruised neurons of his brain.

It's the conscious mind that's ripped away, Candace realized, closing her eyes to aid her concentration. *There's some brain damage, too. But most of his intelligence is still here, like information stored on the hard drive of a computer.*

She sank deeper into Joe's shattered mind, losing awareness of the crowd of humans watching intently. Slowly, tentatively, she reached into the neural pathways, calming some, stimulating others, seeking the man that Joe had been before the Mindeater ravaged him.

Candace caught a memory of herself, abrim with vitality as Joe had perceived her in the Las Vegas hotel. *Here is my starting point, when he was still himself,* she decided, and like a surgeon delicately repairing torn tissues began to sew new connections between brain and consciousness.

When at last she pulled herself away and sagged into Max's waiting arms, Joe had a mind once more.

"Is he—?" Max's breath tickled her cheek.

"Back. Mostly." Candace wanted only to fall asleep in the strong embrace. "He's lost a lot of recent memory and I'm sure he'll need therapy, but he's here."

"Could you do that again?" Helm was almost quivering with emotions held tightly in check. "We've so many like him."

"I suppose." Candace felt exhausted but, at the same time, lightheaded with elation. "We'll have to talk." Max's warm body pressed against hers and his scent washed over her. *That answers one of my questions,* she thought. *He does love me and is trying not to show it. I hope this doesn't interfere with Sunny's chances.*

The young woman's face brimmed with an emotion close to worship. "That was wonderful! I love the way you're glowing, too. Maybe we'll be, like, double stars."

"I'm glowing?" Candace raised a hand. A soft, forget-me-not blue shine did emanate from her skin and reflected from the tips of the darts that she'd somehow held onto through everything.

"Ms. Baden," Max barked, "is this normal? Is she radioactive?"

Helm came closer. "That blue is definitely Silchar. I've no idea what's happening. They don't communicate with us. They do things as and when it suits them."

"Max," Candace said, "are you fading away or is it me?"

"Hold onto my hand!" The agent's shout sounded faint. The comforting pressure of his body against her back lightened until it was gone completely.

The whole world seemed to wrench itself sideways. Candace fell a couple of feet and landed with a bone-jarring thud on something hard and sharp. "Ow." Her voice sounded flat, swallowed up by the barren, copper-coloured wasteland that now filled her view. She scrambled to her feet, fists clenched. "You damned crystal blockheads! You made me go poof! Right in front of Max! I am not a game piece; you've no right—" She choked on her anger and for want of a better target, kicked the pebble that she'd landed on. She turned, expecting to see an enigmatic crystal tower that could be kicked more thoroughly.

A strangled cry broke from her throat. The coppery tone of the landscape came not from the colour of the rocks but from the light bathing them. Overhead, filling more than half the sky, hung a gigantic red sun. Despite its enormity, the light it cast was so subdued that without being blinded she could see huge sunspots pocking the mottled surface, like the marks of a fatal disease on a bloated face. This star was nearing the end of its long life.

A desiccating wind blew stinging pellets of sand against Candace's skin but she didn't notice.

"There's no place like home," she whispered to the desolation. When nothing happened, she tried again, and again, focusing on Max's face, trying fiercely to project herself back. "It worked before," she groaned, throat aching as the dry air leached away moisture. "Why are there never any ruby slippers around when they're needed?"

There must be a reason why I'm here, she told herself. *Helm said the Silchar don't explain. Maybe they can't.* Candace recalled her brief, overwhelming mental contact with the crystal beings. The struggle to communicate had been two-sided, each entity trying to express thoughts in terms completely alien to their normal thinking. The Silchar lived rooted in their planet, endlessly drinking energy from the triad of suns that ruled their sky, communicating with each other and, briefly, one dazzled elf, in language more like the chiming of a million bells than crude, harsh words. Their first contact with motile creatures, beings that could change location at will, had come with the invasion of the Mindeaters.

Candace's rage cooled. There wasn't much point in staying angry at a species that probably couldn't even understand the emotion. "I hope you know what I'm doing here," she said, in case they were somehow listening. "I hope you know, because I surely do not."

She turned slowly to study the bleak landscape. Barren plains filled most of her field of view. A range of low hills that looked ground down by the ages crossed the horizon opposite the sun and she chose that direction to begin walking, partly in the hope of a better view from higher ground, but mainly to keep her back to the monstrous star.

Very far away, in a place that was neither here nor there, the Lady Yseult paced impatiently back and forth on the parapet of a castle formed of seamless milky stone. On her shoulder sat the little red dragon, tail wrapped for balance around her neck. Above her head a black sky stretched to infinity, unmarred by moon or stars. But stars there were in plenty, breaking in waves against the castle's walls where it sat like an island in the centre of a glittering Galactic whirlpool. This was a dimension that took the form imposed on it by a powerful mind.

The centre of the castle was completely covered by a dome of the translucent material. Within, a Shape writhed slowly, burning eyes fixed with utter hatred on the Lady.

They come, whispered a dire thought. *You can do nothing to stop them. My fragments aid them. All the worlds will fall. I shall be free.*

"I will not allow that to happen." Yseult turned and fearlessly met the creature's gaze. The dragon hissed and stuck out its forked tongue.

Already they infiltrate your realm, the prisoner replied. *You could not prevent it. Proud lady, you are weaker than you know.*

"If I am so weak, Khuluxyxuluhk, leave your prison," the Lady taunted.

The Being inside the castle condensed into a diamond-hard point and hurled Itself at the wall of Its prison. The castle rang like a gong but resisted.

"Leave me," she ordered and the creature sank out of sight.

Yseult turned her attention to the sky. In the dark one star now shone, growing brighter as it neared, taking at length the form of a magnificent winged human, brilliant in forget-me-not blue.

"Rigel," the Lady said with a courteous nod as the newcomer set foot on the castle's stone. "It is good of you to come."

"We are pleased that you wish to ally with us," the angelic being said in a voice that rang like a chime. "Alone, we cannot survive. Together, we may prevail."

The Lady moved a hand and the air silvered, forming into a mirror. Images flickered rapidly across the magical surface. "I have news to share with you," she said. "Of the three Earths in our cycle of universes, two are now under attack but one has defences and the second has been alerted to the danger."

"What of the third?"

"It is as yet unharmed but remains in peril. Of the three, it lies farthest from Hy Brasail and is difficult to reach, but I have succeeded in sending dream images to one in that universe who is a teller of tales; a writer of books. Let us hope that she can convince her people of the danger that hangs over them, before it is too late. Rigel, I have a question for you." The dancing images in the mirror slowed and fixed on a single, small figure moving at a dispirited pace across a carmine landscape. "Why did you send the elf lassie to the demons' world?"

"She desires to be with her mate," the shining being replied. "Did we do wrong?"

Yseult's lips tightened. "That world is deadly to her kind. There is also a concept that perhaps you do not understand, called 'freedom of will'."

"We do understand it," Rigel answered, his glorious face touched by a frown. "We gave her a gift she can use when she wishes."

The Lady sighed. "If she learns what it is! Ah, well; you meant to be kind. At least, I think you meant that." She regarded her companion for a moment with grave eyes. "How much of you is man and how much is Silchar, I cannot guess. How you think is a mystery to me; you are neither one nor the other."

The shining figure began gradually to lose its glow, like flame dying to an ember. The royal wings disappeared and from the blue radiance a duller shape emerged, of a human man in his early thirties. Unkempt hair hung over piercing, dark eyes. "I remember that I was a man," he said. "I remember that I belonged to a Dream World combat team. I think I died during a battle. Or perhaps not. It is unclear."

"You lost much of your mind, I am sure," Yseult said. "What was left, the Silchar appear to have rescued and restored as best they could." She reached up with one hand to stroke the dragon's crimson scales. "They knew that an interpreter would be needed if we are to be allies. The fact that the interpreter needs an interpreter is a moot point."

The man's eyes gleamed. "Are you displeased? I remember that when I was a man, women were often displeased with me."

"I wonder why—no, don't tell me," Yseult said quickly. The man began to shine once more. She turned again to the magic mirror. "As there is nothing we can do to help her, let us watch and hope for the best."

By the time she'd trudged to the top of the nearest hill, Candace's liquid breakfast had worn off and her throat ached with dryness. At least the journey was worthwhile: from her new vantage point she could see, a few miles in the distance, what appeared to be a large fortification, a menacing hulk dyed the colour of dried blood by the ghoulish sun.

She also saw movement. Two figures raced across the desert, chased by a flood of smaller creatures that almost encircled them. Candace dropped flat on the ground.

The two fugitives sprinted in the only direction available to them and made for the hill. The pursuers spread out, clearly intending to surround the elevation and trap them.

Her, also. Candace started to back down the slope but it was too late; the swarm was flowing around the hill, cutting off her retreat. Shrill shouts rang in the air, the first sounds she'd heard other than her own breathing and the crunch of her feet on the plain's hard-packed surface.

The three darts in her hand were all the weapons she had, aside from her mind. No shelter offered itself on the barren hilltop.

If these two attack me I'll try to stun them, she decided, hearts pounding as the noise of rattling pebbles and harsh breathing told her the two runners were nearing the summit. *After that, I'll have to hope that the enemy of my enemy is my friend.*

She tensed, sprang to her feet and almost collided with the two fugitives.

"Paul!"

"Candy!"

"Sir!"

"Candy Cane! My goodness!"

Three voices as one: "What are *you* doing here?"

"We're looking for you," Gironde said, slipping an arm around Candace's waist and delivering a hasty kiss.

"Where the blazes is 'here'?"

"The demons' world," Kringle said. He scooped up a stone and threw it, knocking the nearest pursuer head over heels.

Candace pointed at the horde. "What are those things?" Every one of the thousands of creatures was armed to the teeth; the very sharp and pointed teeth.

"Goblins!" Kringle drew his sword and held it ready.

Goblins. Servants and henchbeasts of the demons. Elf lore told of their viciousness and of the havoc they'd wrought during the great invasion half a millennium earlier. Long after the last demon had been slain or had fled through the rift, the elves had had to hunt down and destroy their abandoned servitors. The last one had been killed by Peter, who tracked it to the lair where it dragged its imp victims. After seeing what the goblin had done to the imps, he'd twisted its head off with his bare hands.

"Take my sword," Gironde said, eying Candace's three tiny weapons. He passed over the narrow blade and readied his spear to receive the charge that was massing at the bottom of the hill.

She waved the sword experimentally. "I've never used one of these."

"Slash," Gironde told her. "With a slash you're bound to hit one or more of them every time."

"I take it you're past the negotiating stage."

"Miles past," Kringle said. "Here they come." A line of goblins began to lumber up the hill. "My dear, do you think you could throw one of those darts? I would direct your attention to that brute with the splash of red on its armour. It appears to be an officer."

Candace overcame a flash of queasiness and flung one of her darts. It lodged in the centre of the goblin's tiny eye. The creature shrieked, wrenched out the dart and rolled screaming on the ground until the relentless feet of its companions trampled it into silence. Something atavistic in her raised its head and howled silently in triumph.

"There's something we should do right now," Gironde said, bracing himself.

Kringle eyed the advancing host, picking targets. "Charge them? Hope to break through?"

"Not quite what I had in mind. Would you please marry us?"

"What, *now*?" Kringle dodged a flying axe. "Lad, we are rather busy at the moment."

"Sir, I agree with Paul," Candace said. "There's no time like the present." She hurled one of her remaining darts into a goblin's face. The creature screamed and fell back, knocking down several more that were forcing their way up the steep slope toward the summit. The third, and last, dart stuck in a goblin's forehead, between projections like stunted antennae. There seemed to be no end to the advancing swarm.

"I'd prefer to die a married man." Gironde slashed the throat of an attacker with the blade of his spear and jabbed backwards to drive the bronze pick on the butt into the belly of a goblin about to stab Kringle. "We don't lack for witnesses."

"People were so looking forward to the wedding," Candace said, swinging her sword and opening a goblin's chest. A gout of blood splashed across her cheek. "I'd hate to think we disappointed them."

"But there's no ring!" Kringle parried a sword blow and

riposted with a deadly thrust.

"I have one." Candace waved her left hand, where Finnegan's diamond sparkled like a ruby under the crimson sun. She almost lost the finger to an axe but caught the missile and returned it to sender, with fatal consequences. "It's the vows, don't you see?"

"What we mean to each other," Gironde agreed, kicking a goblin so hard that bones crunched. He slid a foot under the writhing body and flipped it into the mob. "So if you'd do the honours, we'd really appreciate it."

"Even if not for very long," Candace added.

"I'd best make it quick, then." Kringle ducked the vicious swipe of an axe. "DoyouPaultakethiswoman—hah! got you, you spawn of the devil!—tobeyourlawfullyweddedwifeinsicknessandinhealthforbetterorforworseforaslongasyoubothshalllive, however briefly that may be?"

Gironde impaled an onrushing goblin with his spear. "I do!"

"AnddoyouCandyCanetakethismantobeyour—look behind you! Oh, good stroke!— lawfullyweddedhusbandinsicknessandinhealthforbetterorforworselikenowforaslongasyoubothshalllive?"

Candace whisked her sword through a goblin's neck and kicked the still snarling, snapping head down the slope. "I do!"

"Thenbythepowervestedinme by, well, me, I now pronounce you husband and wife. You may rescue the bride."

Gironde slashed at a goblin that had seized Candace around her knees and was trying to pull her down. As the corpse rolled away, he snatched a kiss from his new wife's lips.

"Not the honeymoon I'd hoped for," he said, whirling to spit another attacker. The creature, tumbling backwards, wrenched the spear from his grip. Gironde drew both of his daggers and braced his back against Kringle's.

"That's all right." Candace took advantage of a momentary lull in the attack to wipe thick goblin blood from her brow before it could drip into her eyes. "Think of the money we're saving."

Below them the horde surged, reforming into a dense wall of weapons.

"Candy Cane," Kringle said gruffly, "get between us. We can shield you for a little while, Paul and I."

"No. I fight beside you and my man."

"My dear. I insist."

"Sir, I'd tell you to go to bloody hell but we're there already."

"Then shoulder to shoulder to shoulder it is," Kringle said, hefting his weapons.

Candace stole an instant to rest her head against Gironde's. "Love you," she said, and a heartbeat later the goblins were on them.

Gironde opened his eyes onto a gray gloom. He lay still, cataloguing the environment around himself: dank odours, hard, cold floor underneath, stone or concrete ceiling, wan light coming from some far-off source.

He turned his head to the left. Kringle sat slumped against a wall. The old man's head was sunk onto his chest and he appeared to be asleep. To the right: thick vertical bars.

Gironde sat up, looking around the cell for Candace. There was no sign of her.

"She's alive, lad," came a whisper. Kringle's head lifted slowly. "You know I'd feel her death. She was unconscious, as were you, when they brought us here. I believe she wasn't badly hurt."

Relief so intense that for a moment he couldn't breathe. "Where's here?" Gironde gingerly felt his head. A proud lump stood out from his scalp but a cautious examination told him that his skull wasn't broken. And that the wound hurt like hell.

"Their citadel. The dungeon. Do you remember what happened?"

"Vividly." The screaming horde charging up the hill; Candace fighting furiously as savage hands dragged her to the ground; throwing himself into the seething mass; a brief glimpse of a swinging club. "Why didn't they kill us? We killed plenty of them."

"Timely intervention." Kringle stretched out his legs. A metallic rattle accompanied the movement. Belatedly, Gironde realized that he, too, wore fetters. "We weren't fighting the lords of this world, only their servants. Apparently, the lords want us alive. For now."

Gironde struggled to his feet. Swaying with dizziness, he stumbled to the cell door and shook it, knowing even as he did so that it wouldn't yield.

"They won't hurt her, lad. Not yet, at any rate."

"What do you know of them?"

"Too much." Kringle stretched again, working stiff muscles. Even in the dim light, Gironde could see that he was covered in dried blood.

"Are you hurt?"

"Bruised everywhere a man can be bruised." A low rumble in his chest proved that his sense of humour was intact. "And you? That was a nasty clip you took to your skull."

"It's still in one piece." Gironde returned and sank down beside his friend. "Tell me about these lords."

"They're demons. Or what we call demons. Back on Earth, sorcerers now and then manage to open doors that allow them to cross over. Wormholes; that's what young Bart and Martin call those portals. In Earth's universe they convert quickly to a pure energy form. Burning devils from a distant hell. When I was Bishop of Myra, I didn't truly believe that demons existed. I thought of them as a politically useful means of frightening the lay folk into attending church. I suppose," Kringle went on with a rueful chuckle, "that I was technically correct. The fact that there really were evil entities trying to invade was beside the point."

"Any idea what they'll do to us?"

"Going by what they've done on those occasions when they've invaded my—our world, I'd say torture, death, and dinner."

"Dinner?"

"With any luck, we'll be dead first."

"I see." Gironde bent over to examine the manacles on his legs. "These have a simple lock."

"Could you pick it?"

"With a piece of wire and a few minutes, yes. Got any wire?"

"Sadly, no."

"Why would they separate us from Candy?"

Kringle turned his face away for a few seconds. "You have the right to know," he said so quietly that Gironde could barely make out the words. "You are her husband, after all, and you know that in six months, she will give birth. Unless she dies by her own hand."

"Why—?"

"Don't mistake me, lad," Kringle said quickly. "I know she'll do her utmost to escape. But once the demons understand her condition, they will do *their* utmost to keep her close. And alive. You saw the goblins. Didn't they look vaguely elf-like to you?"

Gironde stiffened. "Are you saying that those little monsters were elves?"

"A long time ago, hundreds of years it was, an elf woman was taken captive in a raid. Her name was Star. You know that when an elf dies, I feel it. Star lived for over a year in the demons' world. Long enough to be bred to something vile."

Gironde sucked in his breath with a hiss.

"Candy Cane's children will be a treasure trove. You'll recall the circumstances of their conception, when elf and human energies played equal parts. They'll be like nothing we've ever seen in our world. I have no doubt that they'll be raised as soldiers and turned against their own race. If one happens to be female, she'll be used, like her mother, to breed more."

Gironde longed to stand, to pace, to burn off his anger with action. Years as a secret agent had taught him remorseless self control; to hold the anger in until the right moment came for explosive, lethal release.

He hoped it would come soon.

How I envy human women, Candace thought, lying flat on her back on the floor of her cell. *What a blessing and a relief it must be to be able to weep. Yet if I could cry I might never stop, so perhaps it is better that I can't.*

There was no light in the cell. She'd crawled around it earlier, feeling with her hands. The chamber was about eight feet in diameter and made of rough stone. A trickle of water flowed down the wall and into a narrow slit in the floor that, from the odour, also served as a latrine. She was sure that now and then a peephole slid open with an almost inaudible rasp.

Elf folklore was rife with tales of creatures that hunted in the dark. Ancestral burrows had been kept brightly lit by glowing, insect-like domestic animals as a defence against predators. Darkness meant danger and grief.

I will not despair, Candace told herself fiercely. *Until I am utterly sure that they are dead, I will believe they are alive.*

In the meantime, she had to stay sane. She searched for some way to distract herself and found one in recent experience. "I'm going to write a book," she said to the darkness and her own aching soul. "I shall call it 'Prison Cells I Have

Known: One Elf's Recent Memoirs'."

We look forward to reading it.

She sat up with a jerk and immediately groaned from the pain of abused and bruised muscles. "Who are you?"

Whispers of laughter, soft and wicked.

Candace crawled to a wall, pushed herself slowly to her feet and stretched her arms up, biting back more groans. The ceiling was beyond reach. She clapped her hands and listened to the echoes. At the bottom of a well, perhaps? Or an oubliette, a prison for the forgotten.

She seeks to know her surroundings.

"I can hear you," she said. The whispers came to her mind, not her ears. "Show your ugly faces."

She thinks we are ugly.

"Where am I? Who are you?"

She poses questions.

Candace slid down the wall, too weary to feel provoked. "Oh, have it your way."

She is no fun.

They wanted fun, did they? An idea quickened her spirits. During the 1870s, like many of her sister elves she'd lived in Paris, the fashion hub of Europe. When the Franco-Prussian war broke out and the city was threatened, Kringle had ordered them to leave. Most had returned home, but Candace had gone to London and spent several months as governess to a Victorian family's large brood. The experience had left her with a lasting fondness for human children and an arsenal of some of the most irritating poems and songs ever composed.

She smiled in the darkness and began to sing: "Three blind mice, three blind mice, see how they run."

She sings.

"They all ran after the farmer's wife."

What farmer? What wife?

"She cut off their tails with a carving knife."

Is this instruction?

"Did you ever see such a sight in your life?"

We see no tails and no knives.

"As three blind mice." The inimical power of nursery songs lies not in the lyrics or the music but in loudly singing them over and over, preferably off key, until adult nerves crack. She'd almost fled London and returned to war-torn France before it dawned on her that her little charges were merely trying, in their blithe and innocent way, to drive her mad. After that, blessed with a fine voice of her own, she'd entered with joy into the duel. Children love adults they cannot bully. When the war ended, to the family's heartfelt sorrow she'd returned to her job in Paris. For decades, though, she'd secretly followed the progress of the children's lives. As old age closed in on them she'd attended their funerals one by one, a grieving, veiled lady in exquisite black mourning; a mysterious family legend.

She started over: "Three blind mice, three blind mice."

She enjoys herself.

"See how they run."

She mocks us!

"They all ran after the farmer's wife..."

Candace kept count of the number of repetitions. The increasingly agitated mental voices fell silent after ninety-six. She reached two hundred and thirty-five, pausing only now and then to lick drops of water from the wall seep, before stone grated on stone high above and a few beams of reddish light oozed into the cell.

Climb.

A rattling noise preceded a rope ladder unrolling down the shaft. Candace caught it and with difficulty started up, pausing frequently to rest her aching muscles. Eventually, her slow progress annoyed her captors and they hauled the ladder up.

Hard little hands seized her at the top and pulled her

over the rim of the pit. She stood and took note of her surroundings, which consisted mainly of armed goblins and stone walls.

Come, growled one of the creatures in her mind. Elves couldn't read demons' thoughts and it surprised her very much that the goblin was telepathic. It led the way past a barred door, down a corridor and through an archway into a courtyard. Candace tried to linger and get her bearings, but was urged on by pointed objects clutched in many fists. She wondered if she could snatch a weapon, fight her way through the mob and escape. But escape to where? Only one thing interested her at that moment, and that was the fate of Paul and Kringle.

Overhead, the grossly enlarged sun spread across most of the sky. The air was cold, bone dry, and smelled like sour, corroded metal.

The guards prodded her across the courtyard and into the keep, where they followed a maze of passageways through the hulking building. Trophies hung on the walls, some of them so caked with dust that in the dim light she couldn't make out what they might have been. The stone underfoot sloped inwards, worn down by centuries of passing feet.

The oppressive sense of age ended when they reached a massive metal door easily twenty feet high and ten across. A goblin rapped on it with a mailed fist and twin panels swung inward onto decadence.

She noted the tapestries first: long sheets of heavy embroidered silk agleam with threads of gold and silver in the light cast by ornate hanging lanterns. The images nearest the door were bucolic: hunting parties mounted on strange creatures, riding through lush landscapes of towering trees and many-hued flowers. As Candace was pushed further into the chamber, she saw more of the tapestries, these depicting the hunt's progress: odd-looking hounds scenting the quarry; the chase through the forest; the quarry brought to bay; the quarry begging for mercy; the killing and the butchering.

"Do you like my tapestry, elf?"

Candace pulled her horrified gaze away from a hanging showing the hunt feast. The speaker sat on a towering throne of carved black stone at the far end of the room. Flames from the many lanterns glittered in the man's yellow eyes. He would've been very tall when standing, and lean to the point of emaciation, though the strap-like muscles lining the long bones looked diamond-hard. White hair flowed over his shoulders and cinnamon-coloured skin.

"Is that supposed to be you on the thing with—" she paused to count "—sixteen legs?"

"It is. Such steeds run faster than the wind that howls around this castle. They are fleetest when chasing game in the forest."

"In your dreams. This world is barren."

"Not as much as you think." The man rose to his feet, with such an economy of motion that one instant he was prone, the next on his feet. "We still hunt quarry."

"Me, I assume?"

As the demon lord stepped gracefully down from the dais, the goblins released her and crouched obsequiously. Candace's hearts hammered. Looking into the citrine eyes was like trying to read the gaze of a tiger. A starving tiger.

"Perhaps." He stretched out an arm and ran a finger tipped with a black talon very lightly along her cheek. She jerked her head away and the needle-sharp talons in response flicked forward to clamp about her throat, holding her motionless. "You have annoyed my little ones," he purred. "Singing to them when they looked to bathe in your fear."

"I'd be happy to sing for you, too. Have you ever heard 'Twinkle, twinkle, dying star'?"

The talons bit, just enough to draw blood. He collected a drop, touched it to his tongue and bared his teeth in an elated smile. "I have other uses for female elves." He turned and glided back to the throne, arranging himself on it like a copper statue. "The taste of your blood says that you are gravid."

"That's no concern of yours."

"Oh, but I disagree. Do you know who I am?"

"You're a demon."

"Not quite." The golden eyes glinted. "I am *the* demon; the quintessence, the fountainhead, the culmination, the King."

"The thesaurus." Candace folded her arms. "I take it that I am addressing the current racial mouthpiece?"

The demon's teeth clicked together and he hissed. "We are legion. When one falls, another rises. Yet we are also individuals. I, this self, have been King for ten times a hundred years. I have killed all who challenged me." He inclined his head toward the tapestries. "I had those made in honour of an ancestor of mine who ruled in a time so far gone that mountains have worn down and risen and fallen again; a time so far behind us that our sun has grown old."

Candace didn't reply. For all that she, or any other elf knew, the demons might well possess a racial memory going back millions of years. Or else he was living in a fantasy.

"What happened to the two humans who were with me?"

"The humans?" A cruel chuckle. "I dined well on their roasted hearts."

Candace reached the top of the dais in one leap, crashed into the startled demon and pinned him against the throne. Her hands clamped about his throat in a steely grip. A fury like nothing she had ever experienced filled her mind, driving out reason and replacing it with a primitive, consuming zeal. Always, in the ancestral burrows, the last and strongest line of defence against predators had been the females.

The astonished look on the creature's face changed quickly to terror. Cartilage crackled under Candace's fingers. She didn't feel the black claws tearing at her arms, her body. Nothing mattered in that moment except the overwhelming need to destroy the enemy.

A tidal wave of screeching goblins threw themselves on her, fighting for a piece of elf and getting in each other's way. Eventually, numbers prevailed and she was torn from her prey.

"You, you dared! Dared to touch me!" The words rasped in a harsh whisper from the demon lord's half-crushed throat. "You do not need hands or feet to bear your young, elf. Or eyes, or a tongue. I shall pick your meat from my teeth with toothpicks made from your bones and you will watch; I shall sauce my food with the sound of your screams; and when we take your world I shall hang what is left you in a cage that you may watch the extermination of your race!"

Candace laughed wildly, still full of the killing rage. "You can't make me watch if you eat my eyes!" Blood pooled under her legs where she knelt on the floor. She half rose to continue the battle but the goblins dragged her down. The demon lord stumbled hastily backwards.

He's afraid of me, she thought. An icy calm descended and pain began to make itself known. The pool of blood was rapidly enlarging. Her last thought before the world slipped away was: *I'm dying. This is becoming a habit.*

Lucy?" Candace blinked at the blurry face hanging over her own. Her vision cleared and the face resolved into a strange woman's. Cinnamon-coloured, lean, white-haired; xanthous eyes full of hate.

"Be silent, elf." The demoness backed away, lifting her feet high as if stepping over something on the floor.

"Where am I?" Candace looked around. She lay on a cot in a room that, from the cut stone of the walls and stale odour, was part of the ancient keep. Two armed male demons stood watchfully behind the demoness.

"Silence!"

"Don't worry; I'm not in a singing mood." She sat up and held out her arms, searching for wounds. Very faint lines marked where the demon lord's talons had ripped. Candace peeked under the plain white shift she was wearing and saw only her smooth, whole body. "Whom do I have to thank for the healing?"

The demoness' palm smacked her face. "Speak not, elf! Were it my choice, you would be meat in the pot. My husband the King has a whim to keep you alive, that you may pleasure him with longer suffering. You were like to die too swiftly."

Candace repressed an urge to drive a fist into the other's silk-covered abdomen and instead swung her legs over the side of the cot. "Oh!" Scattered across the floor were at least a dozen goblins. Dead goblins. "You need to speak to whoever does your cleaning." She leaned quickly backwards and the demoness' hand flew past her face. "Don't do that again," she said, standing up. Slender though the elf was, she still outweighed the demoness and had a longer reach. Both guards stepped closer, hands on their sword hilts.

"The King has given you to me," the creature hissed, radiating an icy anger. "You will serve me or you will return to the pit and there you shall rot until your spawn are born."

"Ah. You want my children."

"I do not!"

Candace looked at the goblins. "But your lord does." She nudged one of the corpses with a bare foot. Dead, the little monster was shrunken and pathetic. No two of the goblins were alike. Some had long arms and short legs or the opposite configuration; some had twice as many fingers on one hand as on the other; some had two eyes, or one, or several; and all had short, twisted stubs sprouting from their heads. Mutated, inbred, biologically worn out. No wonder the demon lord wanted her children.

"You used these to give me bio-energy," she said, appalled. "You killed them to heal me."

"What of it?" The demoness pointed a peremptory finger at the cold stone floor. "Bow, slave!"

"They were part elf. They couldn't have connected with me if they weren't." Bio-energy, transferred from elf to elf through the sensitive antennae, could heal injuries at miraculous speed. In sufficient intensity, it could trigger conception. It was never given without consent; never used save to restore health or create life. Outrage and anguish warred in Candace's hearts. "They must be Star's descendants," she said. Every elf knew of the kidnapped woman, the one who had never come home. "They were my *kin*!"

The demoness smirked. "My husband dragged her here with his own hands, killing all who tried to defend her. It was he who sparked new seed in her while she fought and screamed in vain. But it was I who tore the stalks from her head. And so I will do to you, if you do not know your place. Kiss my foot. Now." She pointed again at the stone floor.

Candace opened her mouth to deliver her heartfelt opinion and possible last words. Prudence intervened. She did not know the fates of Paul or Kringle, and there was only one way to find out. She dropped her gaze and said, "Yes, mistress." Kneeling, she bowed until her forehead touched the tops of the demoness' gold-embroidered slippers. "I am yours to command."

It is a strange feeling not to be recognized," Kringle said in a low voice, shuffling along beside Gironde. Their ankle fetters, joined now to wrist chains, made walking awkward, even with the incentive of sharp spears at their backs.

"You're certainly not all the man you used to be." Gironde tried to memorize the twisting passageways and wondered if the guards were deliberately taking a roundabout route to confuse them. Or, possibly, the ancient stone pile had been so rebuilt and repaired and added onto during its existence that it no longer had a logical design.

"When we get home," the old man muttered, "I'm going on a diet. Sugar and spice and everything nice and plenty of it. Six meals a day, plus snacks." The long trek through Hy Brasail and the demons' world, plus a week or more of imprisonment on miserably inadequate rations, had whittled him down to a slim shadow of his former jolly self. On top of that, dirt had dulled to a tawdry grey the iconic silver-white hair and beard. Gironde was sure his own appearance was as unappealing. He longed to scratch his beard, if only to dislodge several hungry life forms.

The procession reached a pair of towering doors. Guards swung them open, revealing a large chamber lined with tapestries. Gironde couldn't see much of the images through the crowd of male and female courtiers filling the room. They wore splendid garments of spun metal and silk and moved in an odd, flickering manner, like living candle flames. Their eyes, in a dozen shades of gold, followed the two prisoners avidly.

Kringle leaned closer. "I think we're about to have an audience with the rulers of this land."

"Silence!" A tall demon in armour glared at them. He rapped a spear butt on the floor and in a carrying voice announced, "Talking beasts for Their Majesties."

"Talking beasts, indeed," Kringle growled. "I'll give them a piece of my mind, I will, and may they choke on it."

The men shuffled into the room, the crowd drifting apart to let them through. They were goaded toward a dais at one end. If the courtiers were resplendent, the man and woman on the two high-backed thrones dazzled with their jewels and towering crowns.

Overdone and tacky, Gironde thought and grinned. If Candace were there, she'd have had something astringent and funny to say about the demonic fashion sense.

"It laughs," cried the crowned woman shrilly. Every amber eye in the room turned toward him. "Great lord, will you permit this crawling animal to mock us? Let it be killed at once."

Kringle dropped to his knees with a crash of chains. "Mercy, oh exalted lord of infinite wisdom! T'was but the rictus of terror and awe that such low mortals as we feel in the presence of glory. Kneel," he added in an almost inaudible aside and Gironde dropped to the stone floor.

"Let them approach," said the king. "On their bellies."

"Crawl, lad," Kringle whispered. "I know these folk. You cannot exaggerate their vanity and arrogance." He set an example, squirming forward with a scraping of chains and much loud, pathetic wheezing. Mocking laughter rippled through the court.

Gironde followed, catching onto the method behind Kringle's performance. Making themselves comical, even despised, might be their best chance for survival.

"Let the younger beast stand," the king commanded. Guards hauled Gironde to his feet. "How came you to our world, animal?"

In the dungeon, they'd gone over what to say. "I don't know," he said. "I fell. The world just dropped out from under me. Can I go home now? Please?"

More cruel laughter. Gironde looked up, wondering if it would help the cause to snivel. The female demon was leaning a little forward, a sneer on her face. But what riveted the man's attention was the figure kneeling quietly at the side of her throne, eyes cast downwards, hands folded in the lap of a simple white shift.

Candace's eyes flicked up, met his gaze for a flashing fraction of a second and dropped again.

Gironde didn't hear what the king was saying through the angry hum of blood in his ears. There was no mistaking the meaning of the steel collar around her slender neck.

"Steady, lad," Kringle whispered from the floor.

He pulled his eyes away and whined, "We mean no

harm." The crowd erupted into screams of laughter.

"They mean no harm!" The demon king rose to his feet. "Their feebleness amuses me. Let them live until we find some other way in which they may amuse us." Loud laughter followed them as the guards dragged them out of the room. Gironde caught one last glimpse of Candace, her eyes still downcast but her pallor saying everything.

On a rickety wooden pier stretching across the mud flat that had once been the bottom of Rainbow Lake, Bart studied the air a few feet away. He could see, like a mirage on a hot summer's day, the queer shimmer that marked the interdimensional portal's current location. Like a mirage, it didn't stay long in the same place.

Around the perimeter of the lake the elves had built weapon emplacements and barricades. If the demons came through before the final defence was ready, they'd meet a concentrated blast of fire.

"Is that thing working?" he asked Princess.

She checked the readout on the detector she held in her hands. The device was unique, invented only a day earlier. On its screen, the rip between the worlds registered as a multi-hued, vibrating oval. "Of course it works," she said. "I did the math."

"When you weren't issuing new names." The youth turned to look at the airy metal towers rising around the lake's perimeter. When the ring was completed, generators also under construction would deliver an enormous electrical charge and create an energized field that would, it was hoped, seal the rift permanently. Elves feared and avoided electricity, being even more vulnerable to its burning power than humans, but they'd be far away when the new weapon was unleashed.

"Oh, there's lots of time," the girl replied. "I mean, time's not the same here as there, is it? They could come home any second."

An imp ran past on the mud, kept from sinking by flat pieces of wood strapped to its feet. In its arms it clutched a thrashing fish. Other imps were likewise engaged in rescuing creatures stranded in puddles. They tossed the animals across a new dam into the reservoir behind it and bustled back for more.

"Careful, Pinky," Princess called. "Don't go so near to the portal."

The imp waggled its antennae in acknowledgement and hurried on with its gasping burden.

"Pinky?" Bart whispered, leaning closer.

"I'm into colours now," Princess said. "I used up all the flower, bug, and jewel names I could think of."

"I see. That explains Ragweed, Bluebottle, and Labradorite."

"Well, they don't seem to mind. Are you scared?"

"Yeah. You?"

"Petrified. I mean, it was exciting when it started but it's all real, isn't it?"

"Scary real. Do you want to go home?"

Princess's indignation trumped her fear. "Are you kidding? What have I got to do at home but read stupid texts from Alison and her friends? All they ever want to do is shop."

"I thought you liked shopping."

"I do, but they buy crappy stuff and think it's great. Once you've shopped in the City, you're spoiled for quality."

"Hi, guys." Harald came trotting down the pier, Tiddleums riding as usual on his shoulder. "General Peter asked me to tell you that you shouldn't be so near to the portal and would you please return."

"We're testing the detector," Princess said. "Can't do that without coming out here."

"When I said 'asked me to tell you', and 'please', he didn't put it exactly like that. He used words that were short and crisp and maybe in medieval Latin. But, you know, easy to understand if you factor in the scowl, the gritted teeth, and the threat to have you sent back to the City under guard for your own protection."

"Yet here you are," Bart said.

"Yeah, well..." Harald fidgeted. "I thought maybe I should tell you before the cops get here." Elven police were burly males who ate a special diet that built muscle. Although individually smaller than any of the human youths, they made a formidable pack.

"Peter must sure be hot under the collar," Princess said, pointing. Shugger was running toward them at full speed.

"Guys, better move it," he shouted, going so fast that momentum almost sent him off the end of the pier. Bart's long arm shot out and prevented a head-first sprawl onto the mud. "Thanks, bro. There's something happening. The elves say they can feel it with their antennae."

"That's true," chirped Tiddleums. "It tickles."

"It's not the wormhole," Princess said, holding up the detector. The oval was unchanged.

"No; look, it's closer." Bart pointed at the the screen. A deep violet rimmed the edges. Pulsing ripples drove threads of colour across the pane. "Something's happening. Here, where we're standing."

Princess swung the device in a circle. "He's right," she said, voice cracking.

Harald said, "Maybe we should, like, run for our lives?" Parenthood had given him feelings of responsibility.

"Mother is glowing a beautiful blue," Tiddleums said proudly.

"Grab him!" Princess snatched at her friend's arm. Harald's form was shimmering.

"Got him," Shugger said, holding out a hand to Bart for

extra support. The tall youth gripped his arm and managed to take one step toward the shore before the world whirled and went black.

Gironde was asleep on the floor of the cell when a sound in the corridor woke him. He passed instantly from drowsiness to full alertness and rolled to his feet, straining to see in the weak light from the guards' station.

"Candy!" He could at first make out only a slim white shape beyond the heavy bars, but he'd have known her anywhere, anytime.

At the sound of his voice, Kringle stirred and sat up. "I was dreaming of dinner," he said grouchily and then, realizing who the visitor was, scrambled to his feet.

Candace reached between the bars and gripped Gironde's hands. She was trembling. "I thought you were both dead! Until I saw you in the throne room, I didn't know what had happened to you."

Gironde pulled her closer for a kiss. "We're getting out of here. I don't know how, but we will."

Her smile flashed in the dim light. "That's my man. I knew there was a good reason why I married you."

"Here I thought it was just for my charm and devastating good looks."

Kringle said, "Are you free to move about this castle?"

"No. I'm supposed to be on an errand for the Queen right now. I'll have to run to make up the time."

Metal glinted around her throat and the old man pointed at the steel collar. "What does the writing say on that abomination?"

"I was told it says 'I belong to the Queen. Touch me not.' I have her protection for the next six months. After that, I'm pretty sure what will happen." She glanced down the corridor. "The guard is changing. They take their time about it.

We have another couple of minutes. If I'm caught here—I don't know what they'd do, but it would probably leave a mark."

"Have they hurt you?" Gironde couldn't make himself release her hands.

"A few slaps, nothing worse. The Queen doesn't want to spoil her new possession. Everyone else has to make do with goblin servants, but she has her very own elf slave. She shows me off as much as she can. I've seen a lot of the castle. It's only the tip of a huge iceberg."

"How so?" Gironde felt himself slipping into secret agent mode; a chill, clear calm separate from his emotions.

"There's an entire world hundreds of feet below the castle. Enormous caverns, a city, even whole forests and farms. I've only been there once, but I saw enough to know it's technologically advanced. This castle is draughty and inefficient and falling down in places, but I gather that it has enormous political importance. The King and Queen live here to assert their domination. Every stone in the place comes from some other fortress that they've conquered. Every stone has a story to tell." She gave a low laugh. "I've heard scores of them. It must've been a long time since the Queen had a fresh pair of ears to bore. When she's not recounting the history of glorious past massacres, she likes to go over recipes."

"Recipes?"

"Boiled, broiled, braised or roasted elf. Marinated elf. Fried elf. Today it was elf tartare."

"Any talk of man burgers?"

"Not yet. But if they try to feed you up, I suggest you go on a hunger strike." She glanced down the corridor. "We've perhaps a minute more."

Kringle said, "Can you bring us weapons or a key?"

"I'll try."

Gironde added, "Do they know who we are? Where we're from?"

"I don't think so. Your performances in the throne room seem to have convinced them that you're nothing but an pair of miserable human wretches, scooped up by accident when the trap they sprang at Rainbow Lake failed." Candace again paused briefly to listen. "The trap did work, partly," she went on. "It transported me to Earth."

"Earth!" Kringle's eyebrows shot up. "That shouldn't be possible."

"Agreed, sir. I haven't time to tell you what happened next. But this I know; they weren't trying to catch John. It was Gumdrop they were after. They wanted an elf; any elf. They were hunting on behalf of new allies. I've met them."

"That means there's a wormhole back to our universe," Gironde said.

"In the city below. Somewhere."

"Will you be all right, at least for now?" His hands tightened on hers.

She laughed wryly. "The King and Queen had a politely ferocious argument about me at dinner last night. I was waiting on her and heard it all. I think he's had second thoughts about the wisdom of keeping an elf around. He wants to hand me over soon to the new allies, as a goodwill gesture."

"What caused the change of heart?"

"I tried to kill him."

"Good girl!" Kringle beamed.

"The Queen had a hissy fit and said she wouldn't give me up until after my children are born. He said that would be too late."

"Any idea what he meant by 'too late'?"

"Not yet." She looked down the corridor. "I'd better go."

"Take care, child." Kringle reached past the bars to touch her face lightly.

With deepest reluctance, Gironde released her hands. Candace leaned forward to give him a last, quick kiss and warm smile. "Don't worry about me. I'll be fine." She glided away.

Kringle waited until she was out of both hearing and mind reading range. "Think she's telling the truth about how they're treating her?"

Gironde pressed his forehead against the cold metal bars. "I don't know. She lied expertly for years when she worked at the CIA as one of your secret operatives. If they're abusing her, she'll hide it well."

"I fear you are correct." Kringle sighed. "The last time they invaded, we succeeded in over-running one of their camps. We found their prisoners, what was left of them. Candy Cane's own grandmother, Star, led a flying squad to cut off the demons' retreat before they could escape through a portal with the rest of their captives. She succeeded but was herself taken; dragged through the portal just as it closed. We were not able to reopen it."

"It must've been hard on you. Knowing she was alive."

"Harder than anyone can imagine."

"How did she die?"

"Quickly. That much I know. But, as you now know, not soon enough."

Release her." The demon queen watched as guards cut Candace loose and allowed her to slide limply to the floor. She walked closer and kicked the moaning elf in the side. "I can bring you back from the brink of death any time I wish. This, you know."

Candace tried to raise herself. "Mistress, I was lost, only lost; the castle is so big and I don't know it well. I am sorry my message was delivered late. Please, show mercy. It won't happen again."

"That it will not." The demoness kicked her again, contemptuously. "You beg for mercy. Your predecessor was never so weak. Even maimed, she tried to escape. Twice we brought her back. On the third attempt, when she could not evade us, she leaped from the castle walls." Another kick, harder this time. "Degenerate flesh! My lord is foolish to think he can wrest new blood from the likes of you."

"Yes, mistress," Candace whimpered. "I beg your forgiveness."

The demoness bent over her. "Do you think your lies and pleading deceive me? My lord's throat still pains him. You do but bide your time and await your chance. You pretend to submit and make great show of humility, but I know better. I will make your submission real, elf; I will break you. I will make you kiss the foot of death so often that you would rather betray your own people, even your dearest love, than risk my wrath." She beckoned to the guards. "Continue until I bid you stop. Bring more goblins: they will be needed."

Night of a sort had fallen over the castle. The bloated sun never truly set. As the planet turned away, the horizon all around gradually lit like flames under a cauldron, an omen of the future.

On the stone floor at the foot of the queen's huge bed, Candace lay curled. The cold did not bother her, but searing memory kept her awake while her body cried hopelessly for sleep.

Can fear become so intense that it warps the brain itself? she wondered drearily. *In a month, a week, or less, will I be as she wishes; so afraid of another agonizing near-death, another resurrection, that I'll do anything to avoid it, even betray Paul and the Master?* She sat up, moving slowly to keep the chain linking her collar to the elaborate, wrought iron bedstead from making noise. The queen sometimes woke and took a whim to send a message or to have a snack fetched from the kitchens.

The racket from the centre of the bed echoed off the stone walls. For a being who seemed at times to be as much wavering energy as matter, the demoness had an uncommonly coarse snore. Perhaps because of it, the king slept in his own bedroom. Candace had learned that he rarely slept alone. Asserting his droit de seigneur, his overlordship, on the wives, daughters, husbands and sons of demon nobles took up much of his time and effort. He was a dedicated monarch.

At least he hasn't tried to screw the livestock, she told herself, trying to squirm into a more comfortable position. *Not yet, at any rate.* Listlessly, she ran a finger over the bed's iron filigree. Like the clothes of the castle's inhabitants, it was an over-the-top extravaganza of ornamentation. Somewhere along their timeline, the demons had lost the creative spark that gives energy and purpose to a species. Originality had been replaced by excessive display, and an obsession with the real or imagined glories of the past now took the place of innovation. Their existence, like that of their sun, was nearing its end.

Which explains their lust to conquer my world, she thought, tugging fretfully at a loose fragment of iron. *Fresh start on a fresh, new planet under a young, healthy star.*

She gave the shard of iron an angry jerk and the piece snapped off. Candace almost threw it away before the words 'lock pick' popped into her mind.

A padlock attached the chain to a ring on her collar. After several fruitless minutes spent probing the lock with the iron scrap, she pushed it out of sight under the bed and sent exploring fingers across the filigree. Her search was rewarded by a long, thin piece that broke free after a few minutes' determined tugging.

As a CIA analyst, she'd never needed to become expert in the more esoteric spy skills, but she'd read all the manuals. She used her teeth to bend the tip into a hook and got to work.

Like many other things in the castle, the padlock was deliberately antique. The key, out of reach around the queen's neck, was a simple one and Candace had as a matter of course memorized its shape. The lock clicked open after some delicate manipulation. She gathered the chain and lock and laid them on the floor with only the slightest clink of metal on stone. Free, she rose soundlessly to her feet.

Her first impulse was to kill the creature snorting in the bed; to wrap vengeful fingers around the corded neck and throttle her. Sober second thought changed her mind. Even with rage doubling her strength, she'd only bruised the king's neck. Retribution would have to wait.

The remnants of the queen's supper sat on a side table; a tray with covered golden plates. Concealing the piece of wire under a lid, she took the tray and padded on bare feet to the door. It opened quietly on well-oiled hinges and she stepped into the hallway and closed the door behind herself. The guards outside were watchful; assassination was a constant threat to the planet's overlords, but they were used to seeing her come and go at all hours. Candace ignored them and hurried away as if on yet another errand to fetch a late-night snack.

After a week in the castle she knew the roundabout route to the distant kitchen, an enormous chamber on the main level. Huge fireplaces served for cooking, the wood to fuel them brought up from the subterranean world via an elevator controlled from below. She'd considered the possibility of scrambling into an unused fireplace's chimney and hiding in the castle's maze of flues, though death by smoke inhalation would be a risk.

Now, she walked past the busy night staff and headed for a cabinet where the savoury tidbits that the queen fancied were stored. The cooks looked up only long enough to register that she was there, as familiar to them by now as a pet piglet trained to fetch and carry, and went on with their task of helping the castle's butcher cut up a leg of meat on a large wooden block. She was deeply relieved to see a hoof on the end of the leg.

Candace stepped aside to let a cook pass, on his way to pitch a tray of scraps down the kitchen's garbage chute, a round hole in the stone floor with an open trap door. She'd asked a cook one day where the waste went and the demon had grunted, "Farms on the first level. Compost." He'd added, with a snide grin, "Grinding machine at the bottom, elf. In case you're thinking of going down there."

She selected several items from the larder then moved briskly about the kitchen, adding condiments to the tray. A sudden distraction caused by the chief cook angrily protesting the butcher's appropriation of his staff gave her an opportunity to tuck a knife and a chopper under a napkin. The under cooks, used to such professional disputes, went stolidly about their tasks as she pattered out of the kitchen with her burden.

This was the riskiest part. The route to the dungeons lay in the opposite direction to the royal chambers. She relied on the tried and true technique of spies everywhere: look like you know where you're going. Luck was on her side; she passed only one person, a noble lord much more interested in his own business than in a slave girl carrying a tray.

That left one obstacle to pass: the guardroom at the entrance to the prison level. She took a deep, steadying breath at the top of the long flight of stairs that led to the dungeon and started down, deliberately rattling the dishes as she went.

Sure enough, at the bottom a guard came out to intercept her.

"What's this, elf?" He frowned at the golden dishes. "Does the Queen know you're stealing her dinner?"

Candace bobbed a curtsey. "Please, my lord; my mistress sends her leftovers to the prisoners. She says they are too lean."

"That they are. Scrawny, in fact. Good only for soup." The demon lifted the lid of the largest dish and sniffed appreciatively.

Candace curtsied again. "I'm sure a bite or two won't make a difference to them."

The guard took the bait and picked out a handful of the best morsels. "Get on with you, girl," he said, jerking his head toward the cells. "Don't linger." He carried the food into the guardroom and she heard him talking to a companion.

Candace almost ran down the row of cells. Kringle and Gironde were the only prisoners, kept at the far end of the range where any noises they made wouldn't irritate their jailers.

"Paul! Sir!" In the dim light she could barely see the two men, sleeping back to back on the floor. "Oh, wake up, do!" When neither man roused, she extended her antennae and hurled the mental equivalent of a kick at their brains.

Gironde jumped wild-eyed to his feet, hand going automatically to where his shoulder holster used to ride. "Candy!" He stumbled to the bars. Behind him Kringle sat up, holding his head and cursing softly.

"Paul, can you pick locks?

"Yes." He took the iron wire she handed him and crouched to work on his fetters.

Kringle accepted the chopper and twirled it in one hand. "Is that food edible?"

"It's not made of people. Some kind of hoofed animal. I've seen their flocks." Candace passed a golden dish though a feeding slot to the old man, who wolfed the contents.

"Is there any more?" Gironde took the plate she offered him and emptied it with a few desperately interested gulps. He gave it back and kicked his fetters into a corner of the cell. "Kris, stand still and I'll have you free in a moment."

"Can you open the door?" Candace ran a finger over the thick, grimy lock plate.

"Give me a minute." Having freed his cell mate, Gironde bent and worked at the mechanism. A minute stretched to two, then three. Candace was almost dancing with anxiety by the time he stopped, holding up the now badly bent and twisted wire. "The lock's too damn stiff. Have you anything else?"

"Try this knife." Kringle had appropriated both weapons. "Perhaps the point?"

"Hey! Girl!" The guard's shout echoed in the corridor. "What's taking you so long?"

"Go," Gironde said urgently. "I'll keep trying. We'll get out and take care of the guards."

"Hide in the chimneys," she whispered. "I'll find you."

"Chimneys!" Kringle pulled a long face. "I hate chimneys."

Candace smiled as she hurried up the corridor, remembering just in time that amusement wasn't the best expression for the guard to see on a slave's face.

The demon barred her way with an outstretched arm. "I told you not to linger."

"Yes, my lord." She kept her head bowed. "My mistress ordered me to wait and make sure the prisoners didn't steal the dishes."

"Oh." The guard took it in stride that two men under lock and key in a prison cell might try to steal. Or else he didn't wish to take the chance of questioning the order. "If *she* sends you back with more of those leftovers, you stop at the guard station first, do you hear?"

Candace curtsied. "Yes, my lord." The guard dropped his arm and she ran up the stairs.

Bypassing the kitchens, she hurried toward the royal apartments. Until the two men could escape from the cell, she had to act as if nothing out of the way was happening. All of their lives now hung on fortune's caprice but, with any luck, the queen would still be asleep. She could put back the tray, dishes empty as the queen had left them, reattach her collar to the chain and it would appear as if she'd never left the room. The guards at the door would know, but had no reason to comment. When she needed another lock pick, the ornate iron bed would no doubt supply one.

She rounded the last corner and stopped in dismay. The king and two of his courtiers were walking up the hallway toward her. Candace immediately pressed herself against the wall, head bowed submissively, and waited, hearts pounding, for the trio to pass.

To her alarm, the king paused in front of her. "See how meek this wild elf is now," he said. "Not the same untamed creature that tried to kill me!" The courtiers laughed obligingly, their chromatic eyes sliding over her. "There are those who believe that elves cannot be broken," the King went on, "but my wife has proved that it is indeed possible. When we have conquered the elven world, I shall have her train for me a harem of their most beautiful women."

"Have you bedded this one, sire?" asked one of the courtiers matter-of-factly.

"Not yet. Girl, put down that tray."

Candace smelled a sharp, ominous change in his odour. She set the tray on the floor and straightened up, clasping her hands to control their tremor.

The king stroked the back of a talon sensuously along the curve of her neck. "When not trying to kill me, she's pleasing to look upon. Let us see what we have here." The knife-sharp nail turned, slipped under the top of her shift and with one quick jerk, slit it down to her waist. The king pulled the cloth away from her shoulders and ran his palms over her exposed skin. "Is it not strange," he said, "that the delectable female form is so similar across the worlds?"

"All other females are but poor reflections of the perfection of our own women," a courtier said dutifully.

"True. Yet where is it written that pleasure cannot or should not be taken with a talking beast? Is it not the highest honour for a lesser being to be permitted to couple with a greater? If I take this elf to my bed, I elevate her above her natural level. To raise a mere beast to the stature of concubine is a noble act, do you not agree?"

The courtiers did, with polite enthusiasm.

"My lord," Candace whispered. She was trembling with both fear and the effort of hiding a white-hot fury. "The Queen—"

"Snores and is ugly," the demon king said curtly. He jerked the shift down, baring her to the hips, and pushed her against the wall. "What I give, I can take away."

Endure it, Candace urged herself as his hands and mouth leisurely explored. The sheer strain of concealing her emotions pushed her to the verge of fainting and she swayed.

"See how eagerly she responds." The king let out his breath with a satisfied hiss. "Girl, you will do." He turned to a courtier. "Instruct my chamberlain that she is to be prepared for me."

"And your wife?" said the other demon. "Will your wife not be angry that you take a slave to your bed, when you have not visited hers for many a night?" The courtier either had a death wish or held a high enough position that he dared to speak his mind.

"I do but pleasure myself with animal flesh. It is no more than scratching an itch. When I have congress with my wife, it is a divine sacrament."

"I recall," the courtier said, "that your most exalted wife ripped the stalks out of the head of the last such animal flesh with which you pleasured yourself."

"That is true." The demon king thought for a moment. "I fear that my wife does not understand the high importance of assisting our new friends. With their help, we will be able to complete our conquest. I will not need the spawn this elf bears within her. Instruct my chamberlain that as soon as I have finished with her, she is to be conveyed to the Lowest Level." His talons inflicted a final squeeze that sent drops of blood trickling down Candace's torso. "They seek to know an elf's mind by taking one apart; the condition of the body is immaterial."

"As are they," the senior courtier said with a laugh. The three moved casually off, leaving Candace still leaning against the wall, shaking from head to foot.

It is not to be borne!" The queen stormed about her chambers in an excess of furious energy. "He prefers to couple with an animal, rather than with me! His own wife, his equal! Did I not bring the power of my tribe to his aid when he was no one, a princeling, a mere gatekeeper? Was it not I who raised him to glory and domination?"

"Entirely true, my lady," said the King's chamberlain, who had arrived only a minute earlier to deliver his unwelcome message. "His Majesty respects and loves you, so much so that he does not wish to pollute your royal body with acts of mere carnal lust." Two of the Queen's ladies in waiting, who had arrived for the morning ritual of dressing their ruler, nervously murmured tactful agreement.

The demoness glared at Candace, kneeling on the floor at the foot of the great bed. The elf strove to keep her face expressionless. She'd made it back to the queen's bedroom, changed into a spare shift, and re-attached herself to the royal bedstead in the nick of time. The chamberlain had arrived only minutes later.

"I will not give her up," the Queen spat. "She belongs to me!"

"Majesty, it is only for a night," the chamberlain pleaded.

"Do not think to deceive me. He means to take my servant. I will lose both her and my stature, to be treated in so light a manner by one who owes me so much." The queen bared her teeth at her ladies in waiting, witnesses to her humiliation. Both looked terrified.

"Only for a night," the chamberlain repeated in less suave

tones. "Your Majesty; when the conquest is concluded, the noblest of our enemies will be your slaves. I am sure His Majesty will give you your pick of the finest."

"After he has debased himself, and me, by coupling with them? I will never take his castoffs." The demon queen stopped in the centre of the room and appeared to be trying to compose herself. When she turned, a feral smile twisted her lips. "Very well. I see that I must bow to the inevitable. Tell my lord that his consort will deliver to him what he wishes. Tell him he shall have his elf to enjoy. And," she said, "tell him that I desire no hard feelings between us. I invite him to dine with me this evening and will make a present to him then of this talking beast."

The chamberlain smiled in relief, bowed, and left the room.

When the door had shut behind him, the queen beckoned to one of the ladies in waiting. "He shall indeed enjoy his elf," she said, fixing on Candace an eye like a shard of topaz ice. "Send for the chief cook and the butcher."

The dry, crunching noise made by the rusty cell door lock yielding to the tip of the knife sounded too loud in Gironde's ears. He froze, listening, but no response came from the guard station.

"Good work," Kringle whispered. "After you, Air Marshal."

Gironde eased the cell door open and stepped into the hallway. The knife hung from his right hand and in his left he held a bundled mass of fetters. The heavy steel chain and cuffs could be used as a club.

He was conscious of the older man at his back as he went light-footed toward the guard room. His muscles still ached and complained but obeyed his will, despite weakness caused by starvation and inactivity. *Like old times as a secret agent*, he thought and grinned like a wolf.

He held up a hand and both men froze. At the far end of the corridor, sounds and a burst of rough laughter told them that the guard was changing. They'd timed their escape attempt to coincide with this: it would be hours before the next shift arrived and the prisoners' flight discovered.

Gironde heard the scuff of booted feet on the stairs leading up. He edged forward, matching his steps to the receding noises.

The two demons who had just arrived were settling down to a board game when death on soundless feet entered their room. One died instantly with a knife in the back of the neck. The other jumped to his feet, reaching for a sword rashly placed out of reach on a shelf, and went over backwards with a mass of chain in his face.

"If I may?" Gironde said to Kringle, holding out a hand for the chopper.

"It would be my pleasure," the old man said, with a courteous inclination of his head as he passed over the desired object.

The demon, fumbling for his sword, discovered that it is impossible to shout for help when head and body are going in separate directions.

Gironde stepped aside to avoid the blood fountain. "Where to now?"

"Upstairs. Find a chimney."

"You mean that?"

Kringle's eyes twinkled among the deep creases that weight loss had left in his face. "Your excellent wife knows that I have a certain expertise about chimneys. Big old buildings like this castle have brick flues to carry out smoke and gasses. They're large enough to crawl in and often have small nooks for a sweep to turn around or to pile soot. Good hiding places." He picked up the guards' lantern. "This castle is so big that I'm willing to bet our lives that only a fraction of the flue system is full of smoke."

"How will we find Candy?"

Kringle tapped his forehead. "If she's able to move around, she can find us. I'm part elf, remember?"

"Ho, ho, ho," Gironde said.

Candace stumbled beside the castle's butcher, towed along by the demon's strong grip on her arm. Since leaving the Queen's apartment she'd used every stratagem she could think of to break free: tripping him, digging in her heels, clawing; biting, trying with her free hand to snatch the cleaver clipped to his belt.

The demon's muscular calves knocked hers aside; digging in her heels only got her dragged; his leather coat was impervious to her nails; attempts to bite earned a violent shaking, and when she grabbed for the cleaver, the demon simply lifted her off her feet and held her thrashing and helpless. The kitchen, its wooden chopping block, and the King's dinner date drew ever nearer.

"I don't suppose you'd take a bribe to let me go," she panted. "I know where the Queen keeps her jewels."

The butcher made a noise deep in his chest that could have been laughter. "What need have I of baubles?" he said. "Or of risking *her* hatred?"

"The sun," Candace said. "You know it's going to explode. I could help you escape."

"The beast cannot escape from me, yet it thinks it can flee this world." He squeezed her arm so tightly that she yelped in pain. "You will not see our conquest, but you will be there. In His Majesty's gut." His chest rumbled again.

The invasion must be soon, Candace thought, the analytical part of her mind surfacing through a haze of terror. *Stall for time!* she urged herself. *If Paul and the Master have escaped their cell and hidden in the flue system, they might find me before it's too late...* "I'll be digested and expelled long before the invasion starts," she said, probing, despite her fear, for more details about the impending attack. "I had to clean the Queen's commode every day. I know how fast her digestion works. I'm sure the King's is no different."

The butcher snorted. "It matters not at all. Elf flesh is a delicacy that we do not waste. Fresh or pickled, dried or smoked or salted: the King can eat his fill tonight and there will still be enough of you for the victory feast days from now."

Days from now, echoed the cool, analytical Candace. The other Candace wailed, "The Queen doesn't really want to lose me; she'll soon change her mind. You'll have her gratitude if you hold off."

"Not in a thousand years has she changed her mind," said the butcher. He gave her arm a hard jerk. "Never once has she stayed an execution. Do you think, little beast, that *I* do not know?"

She did: the butcher's other job was executioner.

The kitchen was getting closer; she could smell smoke from the fireplaces. Candace shot her last bolt: "I'm poisonous," she said. "You saw me bite the chief cook. I bet he's dead by now." In the Queen's chambers the cook had tried to seize her before the butcher could. She'd bitten him hard enough to feel his finger bones crack under her teeth.

A gleam of pleasure at his rival's misfortune passed across the butcher's face. "I slaughtered and ate beasts during our last invasion," he said. "They did me no harm."

The arrogant words triggered Candace's fighting reflex. A flurry of punches to the butcher's well-padded ribs with her free hand left him undamaged and herself winded from being hurled against a stone wall. "You only ate males," she wheezed. "I'll make the King sick. He could even die."

"Elf, you are lying."

"It's true!" Candace improvised desperately. "I was sent

here to assassinate the King and Queen. You must've heard how I attacked him. It was our plan from the start. We knew about the portal and the invasion. I volunteered to be a sacrifice. *I* planted the idea of having elf for dinner in the Queen's mind. So I could poison both of them."

"And now you turn coward?" The demon's heavy lips lifted in a sneer.

"The King—so masterful, such a mighty lord, I was overwhelmed by his glorious power." She hoped that the goblins who had saved the King from her attack hadn't gossiped about their cringing lord. "Surely you know that he wants to grant me the honour of becoming his concubine. No elf has ever been raised so high." *Am I laying it on too thickly?* she wondered. But the butcher seemed interested.

She shot a pleading glance from under her lashes. "Perhaps my beloved master will even make me his new queen when he conquers my world. A slave queen, of course," she added hastily, seeing the demon's scowl. "I could be so helpful; I know all our secrets, all our hiding places, everything. You don't wish to anger the Queen, but she needn't know; you could hide me somewhere, serve up something else—those two humans; she won't know the difference." *I am gambling that Paul and the Master have escaped by now,* she told herself. *May the Magi help them, and me, if they have not.*

Thought was creeping behind the butcher's small eyes. She encouraged it some more: "Think of His Majesty's pleasure at finding me alive. Why, he would reward not just you, but your whole tribe."

"There is something in what you say." The demon's sharp teeth flashed in a grin. "Something that stinks worse than the Queen's commode. *Her* tribe is also mine. Think you that I am a fool?"

"I had hopes," Candace retorted. The kitchen entrance loomed ahead of them. *Time to think of some last words,* she thought in despair. *Would a primal scream do?*

Inside the smoky chamber, the kitchen staff were going about their usual duties. They looked up in surprise as the butcher strode in with his prisoner.

They can't yet know that I'm to be dinner, Candace thought, and shouted, "Help me! He's gone crazy; he's trying to kill me. Stop him; the Queen will reward you for saving me."

One or two of the cooks exchanged glances as the butcher heaved her onto the chopping block, but no one budged.

"You, bring me a knife," the big demon ordered, pointing with one hand at a cook and with the other pinning Candace against the scarred wood. "Someone else, fetch a bowl for the blood. The rest of you—"

Whatever he meant to say turned into a grunt as Candace's foot slammed against his jaw. The heavy hand pressing her down loosened a fraction; she wrenched free, slithered off the chopping block and darted for the door.

The butcher's angry roar was followed by his cleaver. It skimmed over her shoulder and almost hit the King's chamberlain, standing in the kitchen entrance.

"What—?" The chamberlain flung out his arms, blocking the elf's dash. She sprinted instead toward one of the unused fireplaces, several cooks and goblins in pursuit. Ducking under the stone mantlepiece, Candace leaped blindly into the darkness, reaching for a grip on the chimney's bricks. Her fingers scraped against masonry made slick by centuries of soot and she fell back into the grip of eager hands.

"Stupid little beast," fumed the butcher as she was dragged back and thrown across the block, a cook anchoring each limb. "I would've given you a quick death, but now I will flay you alive."

"Best to leave the skin on," said the chamberlain, coming closer. He'd picked up the cleaver but did not offer it to the butcher.

"Has *she* changed her mind?" asked the butcher. "Am I to return and gut the beast in front of her, for her amusement?"

"No, no." The chamberlain held out a scrap of paper. "This is the menu Her Majesty wants for tonight."

"Do you mistake me for a cook?" growled the butcher. "I give orders to vat rejects like you and your tribe; I do not take them. To fetch and carry and obey; that is the only worth of your kind."

An angry ripple passed from head to foot through the chamberlain's body. "The chief cook has broken bones that must be set, and *she* told me to give this to you and hurry back because there are preparations, many preparations, to be made before the invasion and *she* can't spare me for very long..." As the butcher began to read the menu, the chamberlain's amber eyes locked onto Candace's. His face lost its courtier smoothness in a rush of emotions she couldn't read.

He is trying to tell me something, she thought. She tipped her head inquiringly toward the butcher. In an odd pantomime, the chamberlain's gaze went from her to the butcher and back. He nodded once, hard.

"Does your neck pain you?" the butcher asked, having caught the movement. He snorted. "Your tribe bob and grovel like goblins." He waved the menu. "Why is the head to be roasted whole and served in a covered dish?"

"It is so that Her Majesty may present it to the King at the end of the meal," the chamberlain said. "As a surprise, you see."

A mordant grin slipped across Candace's face. *How will the King react when he finds he has eaten his intended paramour?* she wondered. *Get angry, or ask for seconds?*

The big demon snorted again and tossed the paper onto the floor for a goblin to pick up. "Enough," he said. "Go run your little errands. I have work to do." He selected a knife from a nearby rack, tested its sharpness with a thumb, and returned to the block.

Candace looked into the copper-coloured eyes as the demon placed the razor-sharp edge across her neck and thought: *This is the last sight I will ever see.*

"The collar's in the way," the chamberlain said, coming up behind the butcher.

"So it is," the demon grunted. He slid a fat thumb under the metal ring and forced it up, tilting the elf's head back and exposing her throat.

She closed her eyes, trying to visualize Paul's face, but in a last burst of defiance opened them again, just in time to see the chamberlain split the butcher's skull with the cleaver.

The corpse toppled, spewing a foam of brains and blood. The chamberlain dropped his weapon and stepped backwards, eyes huge. His body shivered violently. "Release her," he said hoarsely.

The cooks obeyed immediately. Candace slid off the block, wondering if he wanted to kill her himself.

"Please..." the creature croaked. He stepped forward and held out his hands in appeal. "Please," he said again, "You must help us. You are our only hope!"

We were made to serve," the Chamberlain said, squatting in a bright puddle of robes beside Candace, who sat slumped against the wooden block. Her body felt like one massive bruise and shock had set in. She could not have risen to her feet even to save her life.

Now I know how Max felt after the helicopter crash, she said to herself, catching back a laugh. She recognized the onset of hysteria and willed herself to be calm as the Chamberlain continued with his story.

"Our purpose was to help our glorious Makers escape the death of the sun." He turned away to check the progress of the cleanup. Several cooks were dragging the heavy corpse of the butcher to the garbage chute. A crew of goblins followed, mopping up spatters and dribbles.

"You weren't among the rebels?" Candace asked.

Air hissed between her companion's teeth. "My tribe was swept along. When the killings started, many of us resisted. Those who did were among the first to die. Even now, if any show the slightest sign of regret or rebellion—well, you saw; the Queen brought you to the last execution."

"I recall it vividly," Candace said, her thoughts skittering away from the gruesome memory. "What happened?"

"There was a dispute among the Makers. Most were committed to the Great Journey, but a few wanted instead to try opening a portal to another universe."

Candace absently rubbed an itchy ear tip. "Great Journey?"

The Chamberlain ignored her question and continued with his story. "The method was new, untried, and dangerous. A quick way to escape if it worked, but catastrophic if it didn't." He broke off again as the cleanup crew heaved the butcher's body over the side of the chute. It hung there for a second, stout legs jutting at the ceiling, before dropping out of sight.

"Some servitors were still growing in the vats," the Chamberlain went on. "They were the most powerful, the most complex; they would hold the greatest responsibility during the Journey. The dissenting Makers interfered with their programming so that they could instead open portals."

"Humans have a saying," Candace put in, "that the road to Hell is paved with good intentions. Did the King and Queen belong to that batch?"

"A spoiled batch, a corrupted strain," the Chamberlain snarled. "My tribe's role was to care for the sleepers. We would never be absorbed; we would always keep our identities. When a suitable world was found, we would help our Makers build a new civilization."

"And were you content with that?" Candace immediately regretted the words. *For a thousand years, we elves served the human race's dreams and fantasies of Christmas,* she reminded herself. Until one of her own sons had upset the apple cart, her people had been happy with their role. "Sorry. No offence meant."

"Who knows what we might have become? The Makers always rewarded loyalty. Perhaps they would have helped us find a home of our own."

Despite her soul-deep antipathy to the demons, Candace felt a twinge of pity for the creature. *If he's telling me the truth,* she reminded herself, and asked, "What is it that you think I can do for you?"

"Be our ambassador to your people." A golden spark lit in the demon's eyes. "We no longer have a choice; we *must* use the portal. What would it avail us to escape a starburst, only to die fighting your kind?"

"You'd scarcely be welcomed," Candace agreed. "By now, I'm sure they'll have prepared defences around the portal."

"That's why you have to go through first."

She laughed. "I see. I tell my people that you've had a change of hearts and are now ever so friendly, guide you past the defences, and then you kill us and take our world."

"Elf, I have saved your life," the Chamberlain reminded her. "If *she* finds out, mine will be forfeit. Her wrath will extend to my tribe as well." He gestured at the cooks standing nearby, listening. "You care about your people. Can you not believe that I care about mine?"

"But you still are what you are," Candace whispered. She closed her eyes, exhausted to the marrow of her bones. *All I wanted was to go home and be with my man,* she told herself. *Now I am being asked to make a decision that could destroy my people.* Resentment flared. *This is all the Master's fault. I should never have let him talk me into giving up modelling.*

"It is not a jest," the Chamberlain said indignantly as she succumbed to her mood and laughed again. "Yes, we are what we are, but it is not *this.*" He seized a handful of his robes and shook the shining cloth. "I was made for a grand

and glorious purpose, but now I must prance about in useless finery and grovel before a mere door opener who calls himself a king!"

"Why?" Curiosity momentarily distracted Candace from her own situation.

"When the last of the Makers died, we no longer knew what to do with ourselves. Then *she* found a purpose for us; in foolish old tales of kings and queens; of wars and battles and conquest."

"You can't deny that your people seem to have thrown themselves into their new roles."

"Many did," the Chamberlain agreed. "Any who objected, died." He deflated a little. "I am sorry about the invasion and the harm to your people. It will be different this time."

"Of course," Candace said, sarcasm saturating her voice. "This time, you'll win."

The demon shivered but held onto his temper. "No. This time, only *my* tribe will pass through the portal." He glanced toward the kitchen door. "I must go back. I will tell *her* that I could not find the butcher. My people will hide you until we can speak again."

"Wait," Candace said as he stood to leave. "The invasion. When will it take place?"

"Only the King and Queen know for certain," the demon replied. "Perhaps when they realize that you have disappeared, they will hold off. They may think that the butcher kept you for himself; his gluttony for elf meat is well known."

Candace gritted her teeth and said nothing.

"*She* will want to punish him," the Chamberlain went on. "Everything will wait while they search."

"The two humans who were captured with me. Can you free them?"

"The portal will only access your world," the Chamberlain said, shaking clinging dust off the skirts of his robes. "The humans are of no use."

Candace folded her arms. "Help all three of us, or I don't

even think about helping you."

The demon's eyes narrowed. "We wondered about it; an elf female in the company of two humans. We thought they'd been caught by accident, but if they matter to you—"

She groaned inside, realizing the advantage just given away. "I feel sorry for them," she protested. "Poor things; harmless, really."

"Perhaps." The Chamberlain stared down at her. "All the same, I think it will be in our best interest to make sure the humans can't escape." His smile had ice in it. "I meant what I said earlier. We only wish to flee the sun's death. I will do what I must, to make it so." He beckoned to a cook. "Take your cohort. Go reinforce the guards in the dungeon. Do not let the humans out of your sight."

"What about dinner?" asked the cook, looking at the pots bubbling over the active fireplaces and then, speculatively, at Candace.

"I'll tell *her* that you're helping to search for the butcher and the elf," the Chamberlain answered. "Go!" When the last of the cooks and goblins had trooped out, he said, "We need to hide you."

"Up the chimney?" Candace glanced at the cold fireplace. Dislodged soot still rained down.

"No. First place searchers will look. Climb down the garbage chute. There are handgrips on the side. If you're careful, you won't slip. Stay out of sight until I return."

"Can't move," Candace said, pointing at her still disobedient legs. "Paul, dear, don't kill him."

"Who are you talking—" The Chamberlain's scowl stretched into a terrified grimace as a soot-blackened arm clamped across his neck.

"Are you all right?" Gironde said.

"Peachy," Candace replied, voice catching between a laugh and a sob. "Near death experiences are just a hobby with me. Let him go, Paul. Before he dies of fright."

More soot showered into the fireplace and Kringle's

dangling feet appeared. Grunting noises suggested that a millennium of experience with chimneys perhaps wasn't enough. He landed in the firebox in a black snowstorm.

"The humans," said the Chamberlain, stepping quickly to the side as the grip on his neck eased. "They are *here*."

Gironde knelt beside Candace and gathered her into his arms. "You know this guy? Can we trust him?"

"Probably not," she said, swept by a giddy and, under the circumstances, irrational wave of relief. "But we may have to."

The Chamberlain was still staring at the newcomers. "I gave no orders to release them," he said. "That means—" He whirled and ran in the direction taken by the cooks.

"Nervous fellow," said Kringle.

"Paul," Candace said, "the dungeon guards. Did you...?"

"I may have been a trifle harsh. I take it we should get out of here?"

"With all due haste."

"Can you walk, darling?"

She tried, but her quivering legs still refused to obey. "I'm afraid I'm out of commission for a while." Agitated noises echoed up the hallway leading to the dungeon.

Gironde stood up with her in his arms. "We can't go that way without running into a mob. Kris, can you see another way out?"

The distant noises were rapidly growing louder. "Through that door there?" Kringle nodded at the kitchen's main entrance.

Candace shook her head. "It leads to the busiest part of the castle. We're bound to run into guards."

"What about going down that?" Kringle moved toward the garbage chute.

"They'll shut the cover and trap us, and at the bottom is a grinder."

Gironde started toward the cold fireplace. "Up the chimney again."

"I can't climb," she reminded him. "They'll send armed goblins after us or light fires."

Kringle pulled a knife from his belt and planted his feet. "We fight, then."

"There must be a way out!" Gironde turned in place, searching the stone walls desperately for an opening.

Candace tucked her head against his and drew his scent deeply into her lungs. *At least I shall die with him*, she told herself. "I wish there was a way out, my love," she murmured.

"There!" Gironde half ran toward a wall. A wooden door, so grey with age that it blended with the stonework, beckoned.

"What?" Candace stared in disbelief. "That wasn't there before! I'm sure I would've noticed."

Kringle reached the door first and jerked it open. "There's a stairway here, going down." He sidestepped to grab a lantern and returned to lead the way onto a landing. "May I suggest you hurry?"

He shut the door only a second before a flood of angry demons and goblins poured into the kitchen. Holding the lantern under his rags to stop stray beams from leaking through cracks in the ancient wood and betraying them, Kringle started down the stone stairs. Gironde followed, carefully feeling for each step.

They'd descended a hundred or so steps when a flare of light and a burst of noise told them that the door had been discovered. The two men continued to pick their way into the darkness as fast as they dared.

After another hundred steps, Gironde whispered, "Where the hell are the exits? We haven't passed a single one."

"This stairwell must go somewhere," Kringle said. "The dust is ankle-deep. No one's been here for ages."

Gironde's arms, legs, and back were on fire. Candace wasn't heavy, but days of inactivity and hunger had drained his muscles.

"Set me down," she said. "I'm better now. I think I can

walk. Also, I hear them coming." The sound of voices carried distinctly. Gironde slipped his arm around her waist: despite her claim to feel better, she stumbled often. Soon, he crouched and, against her half-hearted objections, lifted her onto his back.

Kringle, now following, had lost count of the steps. His legs wobbled and the lantern in his hand shook, sending weird shadows rolling across the walls. Behind them a loud crash said that at least one pursuer had lost his balance and taken a tumble, but the sound was alarmingly close. Both men forced strength into their limbs and hurried their pace.

Neither saw in time the end of the steps.

To Kringle, one instant his friends were ahead of him; in the next, they were gone. His involuntary forward lurch tipped him over the edge. As he fell, his life passed before his eyes, and passed, and passed: a thousand years of history. He was into reruns when something gripped his body like an enveloping bath of water, slowing his fall.

He landed on his rump and sat open-mouthed for a long moment, coming to terms with the startling fact of being alive. His lantern had blown out during the fall and the darkness was absolute.

"Sir?" Candace sounded very close by. Her voice quavered. "We're alive. Paul and I."

"Oh, good." Kringle breathed deeply several times. "Does anyone have a flint and steel?"

"I left mine at home." Gironde's voice was the only one that sounded calm.

"That, that was familiar," Candace said. "I've felt it recently. Sort of soft and hard at the same time."

"*What* was soft and hard?"

"Darling, it was a pentacle's force field. I was inside it."

"Alone?"

Kringle started to laugh and the laugh rolled out of his chest and boomed up the long shaft. It was contagious. When they had all quieted, he said, "Any idea how far we've fallen?"

"At least two miles," Gironde said. "I did a lot of skydiving, back when I was in the military. I started counting as soon as we began to fall. Unless terminal velocity is different in this universe, I'm pretty sure about the distance."

"Handsome, brave, strong, and can count," Candace said. "Did I choose well or not?"

Kringle managed to rise to his feet. "It might be a good idea to move."

"True. Company could be coming." Gironde's feet scraped as he, too, dragged himself painfully upright. "This surface we're on. I think it's metal."

"Don't trip over me," Candace said from near the floor. "I'm crawling. Ow!"

"Sweetheart, are you all right?"

"I hit a wall."

Both men froze in place.

"And I smell fresh air."

Gironde inhaled deeply. "I can't smell anything but dust. Can you follow it?"

"Bloodhounds have nothing on me." Shuffling sounds marked her progress. "This way," she called after a moment. "I can't feel any obstacles. It's smooth metal."

By degrees, following the faint air current, she led them into what hand claps and echoes suggested was a larger chamber.

"There are objects in here," Candace warned them. "I can sort of sense where they are. It's like seeing a shadow on a shadow."

Kringle grunted, having walked into one. "How are you doing that?"

"I think I'm rediscovering my roots. I suppose antennae

evolved in the very distant past to help us find our way through burrows and keep track of each other in the dark. This is so strange. For a human, it would be like finding out you have a tail after all."

"Damn," Gironde said. "I was hoping no one would notice mine. Aside from that, I think I can feel controls on top of this hard thing I've just cracked my knee against. Feels like a tombstone. About half my height. Rectangular. Smooth."

Candace said, "Do you suppose we were caught by some kind of anti-gravity device? An ancient drop-shaft of some sort?"

"Here there be mysteries," Kringle replied. "Back in the day, I'd have attributed it to the merciful hand of God."

"Right now, I'd welcome the hand of God with a flash-light in it," Gironde grumbled. "Is that fresh air trace getting any stronger?"

"Yes." More scuffling from Candace. "Much stronger. I'm running into debris, though. Broken rock and torn metal. Some of these chunks are big. I think the ceiling may have partly collapsed."

A guttural voice growled not far behind them.

"Company!" Kringle half turned. "Paul, are you still armed?"

"I've got a knife. You?"

"Knife and cleaver. Candy Cane, let me give you one of these."

"I'm OK," Candace said. "There's lots of nice, jagged pieces of stone I can throw and I also have teeth and a very, very bad attitude toward demons." Loose stone clattered as she picked her way across the floor. "Is anyone else feeling a terrible urge to sing nursery songs?"

"At moments like this, I always go with grand opera," Gironde said. "I can feel the air flow now. Kris, how about you?"

"Yes; on the side of my face. I'm moving toward it."

Rattling noises marked Candace's progress. "I'm going up a rock pile," she told them. "You might find it easier to lie down and sort of slide. There's a door here, partly blocked, but I think you can make it through." A moment later, her excited voice called, "I see light!"

That, plus the pursuers now stumbling and cursing behind them, was all the incentive the two men needed. The doorway was almost completely blocked by fallen masonry or stone, but guided by Candace they squirmed through and into a tunnel. As she had said, a faint glow showed in the distance. The way was hazardous, littered with debris that caught at their feet and slowed them down, but the lure of the light helped them ignore bruised shins and stubbed toes.

Candace reached the opening first and stood framed in the carved arch of a doorway. "Balthazar's bones! This is incredible."

When the men caught up, for several moments they almost forgot about the hunters behind them. They stood on a ledge overlooking a valley that Gironde estimated to be at least five miles across and perhaps twice that long. Light poured from above, illuminating an idyllic landscape of rivers and ponds, trees, green fields and what appeared to be small settlements.

Kringle stared in awe. "Did we fall into another universe?"

"I don't think so." Candace shielded her eyes with a hand and looked up. "There's no sun. The light's distributed evenly across the sky. Light strips, perhaps? Colossal light fixtures?"

Gironde put an arm around her shoulders. "Is this what you saw before, when the Queen took you below the castle?"

"No. Not at all. The ceiling was much lower. They had huge greenhouses full of stubby trees and even pastureland, but nothing on this scale." She tilted her head, listening. "Do you hear that?" A sound like a gong came from the valley. "I wonder if someone's seen us."

"More to the point, does anyone see a way down?" Kringle peered over the lip of the ledge. "It looks like a landslide happened here. If there was a path, it's gone now. Just a sheer, forty-foot drop."

Gironde looked at the cliff face above his head. "We could go up. There's a decent-sized crack and lots of handholds." He crouched, leaped, and caught a projecting rock. A boost from Kringle helped him scramble onto a smaller ledge. "The path's still there," he called from his vantage point. "We can work our way along this crack and get to it."

"After you, my dear," Kringle said to Candace, holding out his cupped hands to give her a boost. Gironde pulled her the rest of the way and she started along the narrow path. "My turn." He spat on his hands, took a tentative grip on a projecting rock and started slowly to climb.

"They're here!" Candace's shout galvanized the old man. He swarmed up the rock like a spider, heaved the last couple of feet by the younger man's grip on his clothes, just ahead of two demon guards who had emerged from the tunnel. One bared his teeth in a lean smile, drew his sword and fiddled with the hilt. The blade began to emit an electronic hum.

"Those weapons aren't as antique as they look," Candace said urgently.

"The female beast speaks the truth," one of the guards shouted. "Come down. Surrender yourselves and perhaps we will show you mercy."

Gironde's reply flashed past his head, nicking an ear on the way, and tumbled like a meteorite into the valley below.

The guard hissed, clapping a hand to his wounded ear. "I will gut you, animal, and eat your heart raw. But first, we will play with the female and you shall watch." He easily ducked the chopper Kringle flung. The weapon struck the ground and bounced over the edge of the cliff.

Yellow eyes agleam, the demon slashed with his sword at the wall of rock. The humming blade slid effortlessly into the solid stone. Another swipe and a large chunk fell off, undercutting the ledge. The three fugitives moved along it as quickly as they could but it was clear they would not make it out of range before the ledge collapsed.

A piece crumbled under Kringle's foot. Gironde's quick grab kept him from falling but the collapse had begun. With a grinding roar, the ledge gave way and spilled all three fugitives.

Candace rolled almost to the feet of the second demon. He grinned, exposing sharp teeth, and reached for her, dagger in hand. He continued forward, still grinning, and dropped heavily across her body, a feathered shaft protruding from the back of his skull.

"Archers!" she shouted and tried to push the corpse away, before recognizing its value as a shield against the projectiles that now clattered about them. The demon with the sword spun around to face the unseen enemy and sprouted three arrows in his chest. Gironde scrambled to his feet and kicked him, launching the creature over the drop. Prudently, he threw himself flat and covered his head.

"Yield thyselves!" A female voice rang from the valley below.

As Gironde crawled over to tug the corpse off his wife, Kringle eased himself to the edge and in as loud and clear a voice as he could muster, called, "We are not your enemies, and we thank you for slaying ours." He poked his head cautiously over the rim. "We cannot descend."

A long pause was followed by a shout of "'Ware above!" and the arrival of an iron grappling hook that Gironde caught before it could slide back. He pushed a prong into a crack to secure it, noting as he did so that the hook was made of hand-beaten iron.

"I'll go first," he said, standing up, though his skin crawled in anticipation of imminent perforation.

Candace also stood. "No, I should. They might be less likely to shoot at a woman."

"Or more likely, for all we know." Kringle solved the dilemma by grabbing the rope attached to the hook and swinging himself over the edge. "If I don't make it, go back to the shaft and try to find a way up." His shaggy head disappeared as he slid down the rope into the trees crowding the foot of the cliff. A moment later, they heard his shout of "Next!"

"I've never done anything like this," Candace said as, with her husband's help, she eased her way over the lip.

"Just remember that I love you," Gironde told her. "Hold on tight and when you get to the bottom be sure to stand there so I'll have something soft to land on if the rope breaks."

Sputtering with mingled laughter and indignation, she slid down the rope and out of sight.

Gironde checked the grappling hook one final time before going over the edge. The rope was made of natural fibres and that, plus the arrows and hand-beaten metal, told him something about the people he was about to meet.

There were a good thirty of them under the trees when he reached the ground; human-shaped people with light mauve skins and upright crests of white hair, every one armed with bows and arrows as well as swords. But the one who immediately caught his attention was almost a third again as tall as the others, as slim as Candace and definitely female. She wore a helmet that showed only the gleam of her eyes and a suit of chain mail so finely made that it clung like skin. The crossbow in her hands was also finely made, and pointed directly at his heart.

"Whence come ye, strangers?" she demanded. "Are ye friends or foes of the piss-eyed people?

Gironde, hands in the air, looked at his companions. The impression the trio made had to be at best miserable: two filthy, bearded, smelly, lousy men in tattered clothing and one woman, lean to gauntness, in a dirt-covered, torn tunic.

Kringle opened his mouth to speak but it was Candace who stepped forward instead, an intent expression on her face. Her antennae slid out and quivered in the still air.

"You're an elf," she said. "You're a mother, too. But I don't know you, and I know everyone."

"That's because she's dead." Every head turned toward Kringle. Under the grime, his face had become very white. He lowered his hands and bowed deeply. As he straightened, tears ran down his face and left pale tracks. "It is good to see you again, Star."

Out of hell and into an unexpected heaven. Candace sat beside Gironde on a comfortable divan in the garden behind Star's simple, elegant home. Flowers filled the air with their scent and fruit trees cast a gentle shade. A large pond added coolness and now and then a flicker of bright movement from its fish-like inhabitants. The household staff had just removed the remains of dinner and served goblets of a tangy, refreshing wine. Overhead, the subterranean world's ceiling was cycling toward an artificial dusk.

She leaned closer to her husband, trying to draw his scent deep into her lungs without being too obvious about it. Life at the moment was very good.

"Guests, is there aught else I might be honoured to provide you?" The old elf smiled at the three visitors from the surface.

Gironde shook his head and with his free hand patted his stomach. "That was the best dinner I've had in weeks."

"You ate so little!"

"Give us a day or two and we'll eat like gluttons," Kringle promised. He lay half reclining on another divan, barely able to move. "That excellent cook of yours may not be able to keep up with us." Like his friends he'd eaten slowly, aware that taking in too much food too quickly could rupture a shrunken stomach.

"You, grand-daughter? More of anything?"

Candace smiled and shook her head, trying to cope with an emotion she'd never before experienced: shyness. Now bathed, collar-free, and dressed in one of the older elf's robes, the family resemblance was easy to see. Both women had black hair, blue eyes, and the same tilting smile. Beyond that, the elder elf was taller than her descendant and her ears rose to proud points. Candace had had to explain that her own ears had been altered by cosmetic surgery so she could pass for human. There were other differences: Star's high, sharp cheekbones and inhumanly long fingers reflected an older elven body type, less modified by the force of human fancies. *The original model versus the current year's,* Candace thought and wondered, *Would Paul have fallen in love with me if he'd known what elves really look like?* And, with a pang, *The look to which I might revert?*

She found her voice and said, "Grandmother, the Queen said that you leaped from the wall of the castle and were killed. What really happened?"

Star's face clouded. "Just as she said, save for this: I struck upon a slanting rock that helped divert the force of my fall. I must otherwise have perished. Nonetheless, my bones were broken in many places. I recall naught of what happened next, though the under folk later told me: how they came from one of their secret tunnels and found me; how they bore me back to this hidden fastness and nursed me. It was many months e'er I could walk again. Many more before I ceased to grieve for my lost home and set my mind to doing what I could for my new friends."

Kringle bowed his head. "I thought you were dead. I would never have stopped searching for you if I had known you lived."

Star's smile was kind. "It was not my death that you felt." She touched her forehead. "It was this little death, when the Queen tore out my antennae. I do not blame thee, old friend."

Candace felt queasy. "They never grew back?"

"Never. I retain some ability to hear thoughts, but it is muted."

"Perhaps—"

"Yes, grand-daughter?"

"Perhaps I could try a healing. I don't know how much bio-energy it would take, but I might have enough."

Star shook her head. "Thou art still much fatigued and weakened by thy ordeals. Later, when thou art rested fully; yes, I would welcome the attempt." She leaned forward to set her goblet on a low table. "But for now, there are matters more pressing."

Gironde slipped reluctantly into secret agent mode. "Do you think the demons will try to investigate the drop shaft?"

"Of a certainty they will," Star said. "This I know: they believed their underworld to be all that exists. They knew naught of this one. Did they have but the merest suspicion, they'd have sought it e'er now."

"Do you know who built this cavern, and why?

"Aye; it was the lost race that once ruled this world. I have deciphered some of their writings, though most were destroyed in the war in which nearly all perished. Long ago, they saw that their sun was growing old. As it swelled, they built many shallow caverns, such as those below the castle, and moved their civilization underground. But they knew it would not suffice forever. When the sun enters its death throes, its fiery breath will scorch this world.

"Next, they built a mighty fleet of ships to travel the empyrean, carrying all their race to a new world. Why they abandoned this plan I know not: perhaps they could find no way to propel the ships through the aether. While I was a prisoner on the surface, the King, thinking to impress me, took me to the castle's observatory and showed them to me through a great looking-glass. There they hang in the sky, a score of orphaned stars."

"They discovered a way to open a wormhole to our universe," Kringle said. "That must be why they abandoned the starship plan."

"Wormhole?" Star laughed. "T'is a pleasing conceit! I think you have the right of it. Why seek an uncertain fate in a perilous realm when salvation may lie not the length of an arm distant? Yet, it was not to be."

"What caused the war you mentioned?"

"They were great fabricators, not only of caverns and machines but of living things. They bred to aid them a servant race, gifted with the skill of manipulating energies and half pure energy themselves. Yet that was their undoing. Perhaps, in their haste, they erred and created a deadly flaw in the servants' natures, for instead of aiding their creators, the new race fell upon their masters." Star paused to pick up her goblet and take a long sip. "In the terrible war that followed almost all the masters died, leaving the servants heirs to their works, but not to their greatness."

Candace said, "But what about this cavern?

"They did not believe in raising all their buds in one crèche. They built this shelter as a haven in case the ships could not be completed in time. So far below the surface, they thought some might survive the sun's devouring reach."

"A fail-safe refuge," Gironde said. "Are there more besides this place and the caverns under the castle?"

"I know of none other. I have thought much on it and believe that when the creators began to fear their servants, they built this refuge in greatest secrecy."

"What of the people who live here with you?"

"Their ancestors were children, hidden here when the

war reached its most fierce. No doubt their parents meant to return for them. None did, and the children grew up ignorant of their heritage. Some learning they regained, but only a little. They saw enough of the war to pass onto their own children a great fear of the servant race, whom they watch in secret and take much care to avoid. Thus they have existed for centuries. Here, in truth, they have all they need."

"Know ye aught about the allies the King seeks to please?" Kringle fell easily into a speech pattern familiar from his long-ago youth in medieval Europe.

Star shook her head. "I know of no allies." She smiled. "I fear that my tales of old times are putting my grand-daughter to sleep."

Candace tried to blink away the fatigue weighting her eyes. "No, I'm fine." Her treacherous extra eyelids ignored her will and slipped out. From an increasing distance, she heard Paul say, "I'll put her to bed."

Half against her will, Candace slipped into a welcome and warm darkness.

Rising with his wife in his arms, Gironde inclined his head toward Star. "Thank you for dinner and everything else. I look forward to hearing more of your story." He nodded to Kringle and strode away, following one of the household staff.

The old elf sipped her wine thoughtfully as the couple disappeared into the house. "She is very beautiful, my grand-daughter. Also, very like a human."

"As the Christmas story strengthened, so the people changed. Candy Cane lives in both worlds."

"She was one of your spies, was she not?"

"A special operative."

"And now, married to a human." Star's mouth twitched. "How the world I understood has changed. The worlds, I mean. Master Kringle, there is more that I must tell you. Now that the upper folk know of the drop-shaft, they will come seeking the place to which it leads. They will seek it with great fervour."

"Because of the sun?"

"Aye. Its end is very near."

"Which also explains their efforts to reach our world. They flee, or die."

"As must we. Deep though this refuge lies, I would not trust it to the sun's mercy. You said 'our world'. It has been a long time. I wonder if I would even know it. Is there a place there for me and my gentle folk?"

Kringle set down his wine glass. Tears stood in his eyes. "Always and for ever."

"Home." Star's expression was pensive. "How shall we reach it? I have taught the arts of war to my people, that they might defend themselves if ever the surface dwellers came, but of battle they have no true knowledge. This cannot be said of our foes, who war constantly among themselves. Indeed; the castle above us and its subterranean demesne are the last that survive; all others have been conquered and destroyed. I had hoped the demon-folk might kill each other as they killed their own masters, but now time is of the essence and we cannot wait for that happy outcome."

"You have ways to reach the surface, do you not?"

"Aye. We have long had the use of two shafts. As for the one down which you fell, from what you have told me I think it was not completed, for there should have been access ports along the stairs. Of the others, one will lift and one is good only for descending. We use them sparingly. The power that lights this great cavern, that makes the rivers flow and the air to move, comes from the heart of the world. It is yet strong but will not last forever."

Overhead, the ceiling had darkened. "The under folk live short lives compared to you or me," Star went on. "No greater than a human span, and to them there is no change in this land. But I know that the light is dimmer and the rivers less swift than when I was brought here. More, the invisible shield that binds the stone above our heads is weakening. Rockfalls have become commonplace." She sighed. "Even if this refuge can survive the sun's fiery breath, it will become a tomb."

"You love these people very greatly, I think."

Her smile was tender. "As you love the elven folk. You were a good teacher, Master Kringle, and set me a worthy example to follow."

"You used to call me Kris."

"When I was brought to this world, a captive, I knew you would not abandon me. To all of us you were as a god; wise and kind and good. When the Queen mutilated me I despaired, for I knew you would think me dead. Yet here you are." The elf rose and crossed to sit beside the man. She placed a hand on his. "Kris. What ever shall be, I am glad that you have come."

Kringle looked in surprise at the long fingers resting over his. A pink flush raced over his skin and his tired eyes brightened. A glow, almost lost for centuries, rekindled in his heart. Slowly, as if cupping a flower, his fingers closed over hers.

"As am I," he said.

Candace woke in the night, called to wakefulness by the conflict of fear and hope. A dear and familiar scent seemed to surround her and her subconscious mind cried out for verification that she did not lie dreaming on hard stone floors.

Paul curled spoon-wise against her back, his arms holding her in a ring of safety, his breath a soft caress. For a long time she lay quietly in the warm embrace, wanting the moment to last forever. She ran a hand lightly over her husband's muscular arm, remembering how she had yearned for its protection, and was content.

Paul stirred, inhaling the scent of her hair. He began to move his hands lovingly and Candace relaxed until his fingers stroked the fresh scabs dotting her body and breasts.

He woke fully. "What caused these?"

"The King."

"Did he—?"

"No. His idea of foreplay. Nothing worse."

"He's mine." The words were light but the anger behind them was as hot as the surface of the sun.

Candace rolled over, kissed him, and for long minutes they thought only of each other.

"What next?" she asked as they lay together in the afterglow. "How will we get home?"

"There's the wormhole."

"Located we don't know where in the city cavern and no doubt heavily guarded."

"You said the Queen took you to the city. Tell me about it."

"It reminded me of a honeycomb. Most buildings reach to the ceiling. They're in a concentric pattern; residences and factories on the outskirts, important civic buildings at the centre, including an enormous courtroom. That's where the Queen took me; she and the King were presiding over the execution and trial of a rebel lordling."

"Did you mean to say that the execution was *followed* by a trial?"

"As far as I could tell, the mere fact of accusation was proof of guilt, or perhaps the Queen simply didn't like him. The execution was treated as a protracted form of entertainment." Candace's mouth twisted in revulsion. "The whole population was obliged to attend, including the condemned man's tribe mates. They had to stand up and praise the justice of his condemnation."

"Or else?"

"Exactly."

"How did you reach the city?"

"There's an elevator, but it can only be activated from below. Well guarded, too."

"We'll find a way."

Candace snuggled closer and rested her head on his shoulder. "Maybe my grandmother and her people know."

Gironde stroked her hair. "Speaking of whom; I wonder how many there are."

"Grandmother thought about two thousand."

"Thought, or said?"

Candace grinned. "You're getting used to elf communication. It was in her mind while we were talking." More soberly, she added, "She fears for them. They've been her world for five hundred years. Getting them to safety is her one goal, but until we came she had no means other than possibly reaching one of those starships, and even the demons don't know how to do that."

"Or they'd have done it already."

"Yes. The command centre must've been destroyed in the war."

Gironde's hand fell still as an idea stirred in his mind. "Probably. But if you were in charge of something so vital to your race's survival, wouldn't you build a backup?"

"I would."

"Where would you put such an installation?"

"Under Cheyenne Mountain."

"Bad girl! As Harald would say, this is, like, serious stuff."

"I haven't had much to laugh about lately. Remind me of something funny."

Gironde thought for a moment. "How about that Christmas office party at the CIA when everyone brought their kids? You dressed up as an elf and gave out candy canes. I wondered what the joke was."

She did laugh. "Yes; and you drew the short straw and had to wear a Santa suit."

"And when that kid said I sucked as Santa, you laughed so heartlessly that one of your plastic ears fell off." Gironde leaned over and kissed the tip of her nose. "That was when I began to fall in love with you."

"Slowpoke; I was already wild for you." Candace sighed, comforted by the memory of a sane and happy time. "But that gives me an idea about where I'd put the installation." She entwined her fingers with her husband's. "I'd choose the safest possible place."

"Close to whatever you held most dear and guarded most carefully?"

"Yes; the place where I hid my children."

"I wonder if I bruised my knee on part of the answer to our problem."

"I sensed a large room. There was a lot of fallen rock, plus that object you hit. But I don't think it operated the shaft."

"You sure?"

"Oh, ye of little faith! Elf communication, again. Grandmother's two working shafts are under a ruin hundreds of feet outside the castle. The controls are basic: step here to go up; jump there to go down."

"They've tunnels, too, don't they? She said that when she leaped from the parapet, the under folk came from one to rescue her."

"A whole network of tunnels! Some reach into the city cavern itself. The under folk use pinholes in the walls for eavesdropping."

Gironde folded an arm under his head and considered. "Time's the issue. We could try to repair the installation and access a starship, but that could take more time than we have. God, I'd give anything to have Bart and Shugger here!"

"I wish they were here too, though I'm glad they're not."

"Especially as the demons are no doubt trying, right now, to figure out if the drop shaft we came down is active. They must have an idea of what it is."

Candace shivered. "If I were in the Chamberlain's shoes, I'd keep it to myself. I wouldn't put it past him to order some of his people to take the plunge. They do have communication devices. I once saw the cooks use a sort of walkie-talkie to call down for supplies."

Gironde sat up in bed. "They could be there now!" He threw back the sheet and reached for his clothes, intending to grab the nearest weapon, run to the cliff and climb back up the rope.

"Easy, my hero," Candace said. "The guards who met us at the foot of the cliff stayed behind, just in case, and some went up to block off the exit." She also sat up. Dawn light was spreading across the cavern's high ceiling. "I'm sure we'll have a council of war over breakfast, but there's something you and I need to do first."

Gironde smiled, understanding. "Continue our honeymoon."

"While we can."

Breakfast and the anticipated council of war were in progress when one of the under folk arrived at a run with news from the surface.

"The King and Queen are at war!" The scout's eyes shone with excitement. "She has accused him of plotting to set her aside and rule in his own name."

Star almost dropped the the bowl of fruit in her hand. "Those tidings are most gladsome. What else?"

"She has pledged that she will kill him, choose another husband, and lead the invasion of the elves' world. He, in turn, claims that she is a traitress who means to help her own tribe to escape, but no others. The tribes have rallied to him and he now controls the castle and most of the caverns, but she and her forces immediately seized the portal chamber and fortified it against attack."

"She is no fool," Star said grimly. "What matter the rest while she holds that?"

Gironde asked, "Will the Queen use it?"

"I don't believe she can," Candace said. "From what I overheard, the King's tribe is the only one that knows how to operate the wormhole device and that was why she married him in the first place."

Kringle stroked his beard for a moment. "So they're at an impasse. What do you suppose will happen when her followers find out she can't save them?

Gironde said, "They'll desert to the King."

Star shook her head. "I think not. The Queen will destroy the device rather than lose it: such is her nature. She must possess all, or nothing. Her followers' only choice is to cling to her and hope that she can, by force or cunning, seize the victory."

"If I were in her shoes," Kringle said, "I'd give the King's people an ultimatum: hand over his head, or else."

"Oh, don't talk about heads," Candace said with a shudder. "I know how she likes them served." She leaned into Gironde's hug. "The King was going to have me sent to the 'lowest level' of the city cavern. That must be where the wormhole generator is located." To her grandmother, she said, "Are there any tunnels near the portal chamber?"

"None near enough. Years ago, when I became aware that that the sun will soon burst, I instructed our diggers to tunnel in that direction, but we have not made much progress for we must dig very slowly, that no sound betray us, and the stone is hardest granite. Even if we proceed without caution from now on, it will take days to break through."

"Gunpowder might help," Gironde said. "I could make some; I know the formula."

Star's ears twitched appreciatively. "As do I. Charcoal we have, and saltpetre, and brimstone."

"But if their wormhole apparatus is as delicate as ours," Kringle cautioned, "an explosion could very well disable it if we try to blast a way into the chamber. Do you suppose that chamberlain fellow will keep the drop shaft a secret?"

"I believe so," Candace said. "He must be very cunning, to have survived centuries under the Queen's rule. He'll want to to find out where the shaft leads."

"We have two options, then," Kringle said. "Attempt to reach the portal and use it to get home, or see if we can activate—is that the correct word?—a starship and escape in that."

"I favour the first option," Gironde said. "There are too many unknowns in the second. We don't know why the ancients abandoned the starship plan. We don't have any means of reaching them, unless they can land, and while I'm qualified to fly a jet I am regrettably untrained as a starship pilot."

"You obviously don't play the right computer games," Candace said. "How I wish Princess and Harald were here! There's another problem with the starships, though: they can't take us home."

Gironde nodded. "Whatever we do, we'll need to commit to an all-or-nothing escape attempt. We won't get a second chance. If anything can reunite our enemies, it'll be the knowledge that they could lose their own escape route. Once we've captured the wormhole mechanism and opened the rift—and I, for one, don't know how to do that—we'll have to hold the chamber while people pass through." He turned to Star. "Could your folk be ready to evacuate quickly?"

"I have so trained and prepared them, in case the need ever arose."

"Can they swim?" Candace asked. "The portal was under water when I was snatched."

"By now the lake will be drained," Kringle told her. "The mud could slow them down, though."

Gironde turned to Star. "Any idea how long it will take to move your folk from here to the surface?"

"We have practiced with our lifting shaft. Fifty people can rise one after the other; the mechanism will not accept more until the last clears the shaft. To raise two thousand people will take a day, at least."

Gironde rubbed his chin, calculating. "Can we get into the castle or the caverns through your tunnels?"

"Nay. There are none in the castle and those that penetrate the underworld are very narrow; one must squeeze inside. Most are mere listening posts. Our largest tunnel passes from the lifting shaft to a crack in the ground near the place where I fell. We might hide several hundred folk at a time in that tunnel, though, and more in the hills."

"But we'd still have to get them inside." Kringle pulled at his moustache. "Assuming we succeed in that, we'd have to fight our way to the portal chamber."

"Past fanatic opposition," Gironde added. "Our casualties would be horrible." All fell silent, no one wanting to admit that escape might be impossible.

Candace asked, "What if we wait? They might kill each other off." She turned to the older elf. "Grandmother, how sure are you about the sun?"

"Very sure. One of our larger tunnels leads close to the observatory. It was there that I found, and later deciphered, last messages from the lost race. Once I understood how they measured time, I knew. Indeed, since I came to this world I have seen the blemishes grow and spread like a cancer on the sun's face. I cannot be certain as to the day, but it will be soon."

Kringle tugged again at his moustache. "What about the shaft we fell down? Could it be reversed? If so, we can move people up and hide them in the castle. Most of the enemy are likely to be down in the caverns."

Gironde stood and began to pace, unable to remain still. "We'd still have to get control of the elevator."

"I've an idea." Candace fought to hold her voice steady. "The King may not know that I was supposed to be his supper. I could surrender myself to his people and say that when the trouble started, I hid in the castle. He's sure to want me brought to him, down below. Then I could watch for a chance to activate the elevator."

Gironde's quick intake of breath belied the evenness of his voice. "If he does know that you were in the kitchen, he'll want to know who killed the dungeon guards. He'll know it wasn't his own people."

"Two crazed, wild-eyed humans did it. I was ever so afraid of them. They forced me to go with them but I escaped and hid, hoping to reunite with my beloved master."

Kringle raised a skeptical eyebrow. "Would he buy a tale like that?"

"Aye." Star's expression hardened. "Such is his vanity."

Gironde came behind his wife and rested his hands on her shoulders, feeling the tautness of the muscles under her skin. "There are a thousand ways this plan could go wrong."

Candace reached up and gripped his hand. "Do we have an option?"

Gironde looked at his friends. "If we can get enough people into the caverns...we'll need a distraction to draw attention away from the elevator."

"Gunpowder," Kringle said. "Pack it into the listening posts. Should be good for a few spectacular explosions."

Reluctantly, Gironde nodded. "Our first order of business, then, must be to see if the drop shaft can be reversed. Everything depends on that."

"Also, it will take a day or two to make the gunpowder," Star said.

"There's more." Candace swallowed, trying to ease a

throat dry with dread. "I'll go to the Queen. Taunt her. Tell her it was the King who saved me; that I was his spy all along. I'm sure she'll believe me. It's how she'd think."

"To what end?"

"Provoke an attack. Get her out of the portal chamber."

"Over your dead body. No." Gironde's jaw muscles looked sculpted in marble.

"Not if you're there. Call me unrealistic, but I don't think anything terrible can happen to me if you're nearby."

"Nothing like, for example, falling down a two-mile-deep shaft?"

"My love, you are a model of encouragement."

"My signature characteristic," Gironde replied. "Still, it would be quite a help to know what's going on."

Candace sighed. "I wish I could find someone who could tell me. Oh, *Christmas*."

She had time for one agonized look at her husband before the world once again dropped out from under her.

Are we dead?" Princess's voice shook. The darkness that surrounded her was punctuated by the sounds of five terrified people breathing rapidly. "If we are, I'm awfully sorry about that lipstick from the drugstore."

"I think you have to ask forgiveness *before* dying," Bart replied, voice rasping through a taut throat.

"It was just one lipstick. Alison dared me to take it. Am I going to be damned forever?"

"I'm sure there's an appeal process," Bart said, reaching toward the sound of her voice and finding her hand. It felt warm and alive.

"If we're dead," Shugger said, "I wanna haunt my parents."

Harald reached up a shaking hand to give his small friend a reassuring pat, nearly knocking the elf off his shoulder. "Are we haunting each other right now?"

"Mother feels alive," Tiddleums chipped in. "Mother smells alive, too."

Not much reassured, Harald groaned, "General Peter's gonna kill us."

Shugger snorted. "I wouldn't want to be in his shoes right now. He's probably wondering how to break this to our parents. My Gram's gonna rip him into tiny pieces."

"She'll have to wait in line," Bart said. "My mom will be there first. Second, I mean. After Harald's folks. And John." A pause. "Does anyone have a flashlight?"

"Yeah." Shugger dug in his bottomless pockets. A few seconds later, a white LED beam lit his face from below, eliciting a panicky squeak from Princess.

"Guys, we're not dead," Bart said firmly. "The portal must've sucked us in somehow. The question is, where are we?"

"Duh, the demons' world, of course," said Harald. "Why's it dark?"

"Because the lights aren't on?" Satisfied that his friends were unhurt, Shugger turned the flashlight's beam on their surroundings.

"I smell an elf mother," Tiddleums said.

"Where?" Princess looked around eagerly.

"It was days ago." Whiffling sounds and the glimmer of light on his thread-like antennae said that he was investigating. "I think there were two humans." Another sniff. "One was the Master."

"Oh, well, we'll be all right, then," Harald said, shoulders relaxing so much that the elf almost slid from his perch.

"I also smell demons."

"Or not. Shug, where are you going?"

The youth was on his feet. "It's Martin; how often do I have to say it? I'm looking for a light switch."

"I'm coming with you!" Princess jumped up and quickly became part of a compact group hugging the flashlight's glow.

"You're stepping on my heels," Shugger complained as they shuffled through the room.

Bart swallowed through a still tight throat. "I'll go last. I'm the eldest. Also, the biggest."

"Great." Shugger waved his light around. "If we hear a bloodcurdling shriek, we'll know it's you dying nobly, defending us to the last drop of your blood as it's sucked out through your pores."

"Stop it!" Princess said. "You're scaring the elf."

"No, he isn't." Tiddleums' look of indignation was lost in the dark. "There's no one here but us."

The little group halted and sheepishly peeled apart, though not very far apart.

"It's a cave," Shugger said, playing the light over nearby objects.

Princess snapped, "Yeah? Share with us why you think so." In her view, bossiness was a good antidote to fear.

"What else would it be? I mean, just look." Shugger continued to wave his flashlight about.

"It looks a real mess," Bart said. "Half the ceiling's come down. Hey, Shug; sorry, I mean Martin; shine that thing over there." Bart pointed at the object that earlier had so offended Gironde's kneecap. "That looks like a console, doesn't it?" The two youths moved closer to investigate. "These don't look like any kind of controls I've ever seen," Bart said, gingerly touching one of the knoblike projections on top. Nothing happened.

Tiddleums tugged on Harald's ear for attention. "Would Mother like me to turn on the lights?"

"You know how?"

For answer, the imp slid down, scampered across the floor and, almost out of the flashlight's range, jumped into the air. He slapped a tiny hand against a dark patch on the wall. Circuits unused for centuries began to flicker to life.

Harald beamed. "When you want something done right,

ask an elf."

"I was going to do that," Shugger grumbled as the imp strutted back. He blinked as the space slowly brightened. "Maybe this isn't a cave after all." He clicked off his flashlight. The now well-illuminated chamber was circular, about fifty feet across, and cut out of solid rock. A round metal disc about half the diameter of the room occupied the centre of the floor. A matching disc was set into the ceiling directly above.

"Guys," Harald said in excitement, "I know what this is."

"Yeah, I saw that movie too," Shugger said quickly.

Bart shook his head. "Uh uh. It was a TV show."

"Fan site. On the Web," Princess interjected.

"Teleportation device," Tiddleums said. He had climbed again to his friend's shoulder and now sat there kicking his heels.

Bart's eyebrows shot up. "How'd you know that?"

The elf wriggled a little, pleased by the attention. "My other mother teaches at the Hall of Advanced Learning. Her course is called 'Humans: Imagination Today, Reality Tomorrow'. We watch your TV shows and movies all the time, to understand how you think."

"How we think? That rules Bart out," Shugger said with a grin.

"I have a brilliant, cutting reply on the tip of my tongue," the tall youth replied. "I'm just not sure you'd understand it."

A round of genial pushing and insults followed.

"Guys, this is great for breaking up the tension," Harald said after a moment, "but it's not getting us home." He turned to Princess. "Why don't you, me, and Tid look around, and maybe Bart and Shu—Martin could open up that two thousand and one thing and find out what it does."

"Two thousand and one thing?" Princess arched an eyebrow in imitation of her heroine, Candace.

"Yeah, you know, like the big black slab in the movie 'Two Thousand and One, a Space Oddity'. I watched it with my parents one night. It was really old. The effects weren't even digital."

"You got the name wrong," Bart said, with the superior wisdom of almost two whole years' seniority. "It was 'Two Thousand and One, a Space Odalisque'."

Princess tried for another eyebrow arch. "Guys, always thinking about sex. You're both wrong; it was 'Two Thousand and One, a Space Obelisk'." Changing the subject, she said, "Look, we can't start pulling stuff apart. What if the owners object?"

"Not likely." Harald pointed at the rubble on the floor. "Look at all the rocks lying around, and the dust. I bet no one's been here in years."

"I can't sense anyone nearby," Tiddleums put in.

"Right." Princess cracked her knuckles. Repenting of her earlier timidity, she had flipped to the opposite extreme and was now aggressively ready to take on the world. "First, let's establish a defensive perimeter."

"Where?" Bart looked around. "Not many options." He nodded toward the shaft entrance. "Who wants to explore that?"

Tiddleums did a backflip off Harald's shoulder and scurried toward the shaft. Cries of "Don't!" and "Wait!" were followed by a group scramble in his wake.

"It's just a big hole," Shugger said moments later after a hasty examination of the shaft's base. "How far up does it go?" His flashlight beam disappeared into the dark and his voice echoed off the smooth walls.

"There's another metal plate here," Bart said, pointing at the floor. "Maybe we shouldn't make a lot of noise," he added to Harald, who was enthusiastically clapping his hands and listening to the retreat of the echoes.

"No one's going to hear," the youth said, but nonetheless stopped.

Bart again pointed at the ground. "Look, there's footprints in the dust. People were here. Maybe this metal plate is a kind of elevator." A quick prowl revealed nothing recognizable as a control panel and the little group drifted back into the main chamber.

"OK," Princess said when they were once again assembled, "we know that Santa and Mr. Gironde and Candace were here, and some demons. But where did they go?"

"Follow the footprints," Shugger said, doing so. "They end here." He looked at the wall of fallen rocks.

A stunned quiet stretched out, as the little band absorbed the meaning of the jumbled stones.

"They're dead," Princess said. "They must be under this shit." She tugged at a rock, setting off a small avalanche and blocking the gap that Kringle, Candace, and Gironde had earlier squeezed through.

"I can't smell them," Tiddleums said. He slid down and, obeying Harald's admonition to be careful, investigated the heap. "They must've gotten through. Maybe this all came down after."

"Or they blocked it themselves," Bart added.

"To keep something out?" Shugger kicked at the rubble. "Or something in?"

Candace kept her eyes tightly closed. *I should be used to this by now*, she told herself. *Being yanked across dimensions with never a "May we?" or an "If it's quite all right with you," or even an "If it won't be too terribly inconvenient and completely ruin your day, just when you found Paul again."*

Reluctantly, she opened her eyes. She was in what was clearly someone's bedroom. A large, four-poster bed filled much of the space. Small tables dotted with knickknacks and jewelry said that it was a woman's room, as did the discarded clothes tossed over a chair. One of the garments was marked by a bloodstain. A fire cast a warm glow over the room and on the auburn hair that the room's owner was brushing.

She had her back to Candace but paused, the brush halfway through its sweep. Without haste she finished the stroke and set the brush on a dressing table, with a faint clink of silver on marble. She turned around.

"T'is the elf lassie," she said. Her tone was amused. "Are you here to visit?"

"To—what, no, no I'm not. I just wish—I wished—oh, those crystal *imbeciles!*"

Yseult rose, went to a long bell-pull hanging beside the bed and tugged it firmly. A moment later a woman opened the door and stepped into the room.

She spoke briefly, eyes sliding to Candace.

Yseult replied, gesturing at the bloodstained gown. The woman scooped it up and left, shutting the door quietly behind herself.

"I have sent Willow for wine," the Lady said, pushing a chair toward her visitor. "I think you may need it."

Candace sank into the soft upholstery. "What language was that?" Her head was spinning and the offer of a chair had come just in time. "Did she have leaves in her hair? Were her leaves hair? Were they hairy leaves? I'm sorry, I'm babbling. I'm not even sure which language I'm babbling in."

"English," the Lady said, pulling over her dressing table stool until the two women were almost knee to knee. "I learned it from one you know; a lass named Helm."

"Ah, yes; she gets around. Like me. We get around. Whether we like it or not. 'Round and 'round and 'round. How do you know that I know her?"

Yseult took Candace's hand in hers. "They mean well, the Silchar. You wished, I take it?"

"On a star," the elf said, still fighting delirium. "On my grandmother. I can't read your mind. It's like looking into a mirror. Did that woman really have leaves in her hair? Her fingers were thin. Twiggy."

"Willow is a dryad," the Lady said. Some calming influence passed from her to Candace, whose whirling head began to settle.

With clarity came memory. "The kids," Candace said with a horrified moan. "I *wished* for them. They could be anywhere now. In danger."

"I will look for them," Yseult said. "But there is something I must do first." Rising, she returned to the dressing table and picked up a wand of polished wood. "I know that it was not your intention, but your arrival has made a rent that must be mended. I have sent for someone to keep you company until I return. I will not be long." She smiled, and vanished.

"Was it something I said?" Candace asked the air. Extruding her antennae, she listened for nearby minds. There were several outside the room. Some were agitated, others wary. One blazed, and this mind came closer rapidly. As she drew a breath to wish herself back to Paul's side, the door opened.

The dryad entered, with a tray bearing a bottle and a golden goblet. Setting the tray on the table, she poured a generous cup of ruby-coloured wine and offered it with a graceful curtsey. Still rattled, Candace accepted the drink and had gulped down half of it before the dryad left the room.

Her place was taken by the owner of the fiery mind, an elderly man, wiry and thin, with diamond-sharp eyes. He carried a long staff in one hand and with the other was trying to pull a housecoat over his night shirt.

"I seem to have inconvenienced people," Candace said. An armed soldier poked his head into the room; the old man said a few words and he withdrew, closing the door. "Your language sounds familiar. Medieval Welsh roots, perhaps? I think you are here to do something I won't like, if I try to do something you won't like."

Having mastered his coat, the newcomer leaned on his staff and smiled; a friendly smile but with an edge that suggested she was correct.

"I appreciate the hospitality, but I think I will leave now," Candace said, rising.

The old man tapped a finger on his staff and quite against her will and very much to her surprise, she sat down again.

He pointed at himself and said, "Hubert Rothsay."

Candace mimicked the gesture and said, "Angry and confused elf."

"Elf?" A spate of words that almost made sense included one she knew: 'Kringle'.

Her hearts leaped. "Do you know him? I can't read your thoughts. I can't get up, either. What did you do to me?"

This time, his reply did make sense as her mind drew on its vast bank of linguistic knowledge.

"All right, I get it; I should wait here quietly until that lady returns."

Rothsay spoke again.

"And not make any wishes."

A few more words.

"And finish my wine."

Candace was deep into a third cup of wine when the Lady returned, in a soft puff of air that stirred the flames in the fireplace.

"How fares my guest?" she asked Rothsay, who rose from the dressing table seat he'd appropriated.

"I'm fine," Candace said before the wizard could speak. "'S good wine. Ver' good wine. Powr'ful. Head spinning. Good thing I'm stuck to this shair. Chair."

Yseult glanced at the wizard. "Hubert, did you...?"

"My love. I would never meddle with a fine vintage. All that I did was to give her more. She is sloshed."

"I unnerstan' every word," Candace said, waving the goblet and spilling wine over the lip. "C'n learn a new language in no time at all. Know thirty. You're a bad, bad man, taking 'vantage, plying an innocent girl with strong drink. In a bedroom. What if I wish you into a frog?"

"The result could be interesting," Yseult said. "But I think that it would be a poor use of your Silchar gift."

Candace tossed back the last drops in the goblet. "Lemme go," she said. "Want Paul. Wanna tell 'im I'm OK. Wanna rescue kids."

"As to leaving," Yseult said, gently prying the golden cup from Candace's resisting fingers, "that may not happen quite as soon as you would like."

"Why not?" Candace watched with a scowl as the goblet was returned to its tray. "Paul'll be crazy with worry. Not fair. Jus' found him again. I wish—"

"Not this time," Rothsay said, again tapping his staff. Candace's voice froze in her throat. "Very sorry, my dear, but the power unleashed by your last wish cut through the Rings like a sword through flesh. We cannot risk that happening again."

Yseult resumed her seat and once more took Candace's hand in hers. "I have mended the rents," she said, "but you must understand, there are beings in some of the Rings that would wreak havoc if they escaped their proper realms."

The wizard's forehead creased. "Did any elementals...?"

"No. All are secure. Likewise the Fay. But they would've felt the tearing and will now be alert for another opportunity. Do release her voice, Hubert. Drunk though she is, I think she will be wise."

"Screw'd up again, haven't I?" Candace said, her mood lurching toward an inebriated cheerfulness as the wizard lifted his spell. "'S a talent I have. Are you going to kill me? Everyone else has had a go. Open season on me." Her eyes widened. "I think I'm passing out."

"And so you are," Yseult said, catching her as she slumped forward. "Hubert, help me get her into my bed." With the wizard's aid, Candace was soon tucked in beneath a silken coverlet. The Lady regarded her guest with her ageless eyes. "Poor brave lass," she murmured. "I have watched her ordeals. She has lost so much faith in herself, yet now she must face the greatest challenge of all: godhood."

Did you hear that?" Bart looked up from the black slab he was examining.

"Hear what?" Shugger, trying to prise open the back of the artifact with the blade of his pocket knife, kept on with the task.

"It sounded like screaming. Sort of a reverse Doppler effect scream; you know, like something very far away getting closer." Bart cupped a hand to his ear. "There it is again. It's like someone's stopping just long enough to inhale and then scream again."

This time, Shugger did look up. "Yeah." Both youths turned toward the shaft entrance. "It's coming from there."

"Guys!" Harald hurried over, Tiddleums standing on his shoulder, pointed ears cocked forward. "Something's happening. Tid says he can hear a noise."

"Whatever it is, it's coming fast," Princess said, joining the group. "Everybody, gear up!"

"I've got my high-velocity heat-seeking quantum laser vapourizer ready," Bart said sarcastically. "Maybe we should all hide instead?" He nodded toward the tumbled heaps of ceiling debris.

"Not while we have rocks." Princess quickly picked up a fist-sized pair and adopted a bristling, ready-for-anything stance.

Shugger didn't budge. "If someone's falling down that shaft they're going to be a splatter, not a threat."

"Yuk." Harald backed away. "I don't want goo all over me." The noise sounded very near. "Should we switch off the light?"

"Too late," Tiddleums said. "It's here. And it's not dead."

A scramble followed for hiding places among the boulders.

In the silence that now gripped the room, the racket emanating from the shaft could be heard clearly.

"It sounds like someone giggling," Bart whispered to Shugger.

"Or sobbing," the other youth agreed. "Or laughing."

"It's having hysterics," Princess said. "Why isn't it smushed?"

"Parachute?" Harald suggested and received a poke in his ribs.

Shuffling noises announced the newcomer's entry.

Peeking cautiously out from behind her shelter, Princess saw it first. She gasped and clapped a hand over her mouth, but the being didn't hear over its own bubbling laughter.

Turning to Bart, she mouthed, *It's a demon!*

The tall youth replied, *Are you sure?*

Princess rolled her eyes, then remembered that Bart hadn't been there when a demon calling itself the Gingerbread Man had burst into living flame and tried to kill her, along with the other two youths and Candace. She'd sprayed it with fire extinguisher foam, causing it to shrivel to cookie size, and Harald's dog had eaten it. The room was sorely lacking in extinguishers and dogs. Princess nodded firmly.

The creature sank to the floor in the centre of the room. It was still gibbering but now and then the watchers could make out the words, 'I'm alive I'm alive I'm alive', interspersed with more bursts of shrill laughter.

Bart stood up, tugged down his shirt, stepped boldly out from his shelter and walked up behind the creature.

He tapped it on the shoulder and said, "'Scuse me."

The demon's head jerked around. It half staggered to its feet before sinking back to the floor and lying still.

"You scared it to death," Princess complained, coming out from behind her own shelter. "Now we can't ask it questions."

"It's only fainted," Bart said. "I can see it breathing. What are you doing?" The girl had pulled off her belt and was briskly tying the demon's feet together. She was quickly joined by her other friends.

"You didn't see one of these things in action," Harald said grimly. Even Tiddleums was using his own belt to bind the demon's thumbs together.

"If it catches fire like the last one did, these won't hold long," Shugger said, adding an extra knot to the tough leather strap now wrapped around the creature's arms.

"If it catches fire," Princess said, "we'll spit on it until it's soggy."

"Or pee on it," Harald added. "I hope everyone had lots to drink before we got here."

Shugger crouched beside the prisoner. "I don't get why we can understand it. I mean, we're in another universe, aren't we? Shouldn't it speak another language?"

"It's the star-gate effect," Harald said. "When you go to another world through a wormhole, you can understand what they say. It's science."

Princess snorted. "That's just from a TV show. This is *real*."

"TV's real," Harald protested. "The producers must've gotten the idea from somewhere. Maybe the Men in Black told them."

"There are no Men in Black!" Bart copied Princess and rolled his eyes. "Dude, you gotta get out in the real world more often."

"Like right now?"

"OK, real worlds."

Princess bent over the captive. "I think it's waking up. Guys, get ready."

"Um." Harald's hand dropped to his pants zipper. "Maybe you could, like, look away?"

"Why?" said the girl, before blushing pink. "I *meant* pick up rocks or something."

"He's not on fire," Bart said and, like Shugger, crouched

beside the demon. "Hey, buddy, can you hear me?"

"Vile human spawn! Putrid dregs of the offal pit!"

"OK, I guess that means yes," the tall youth said. "Look, we're not going to hurt you."

"Much," Princess said, sensing that the demon would interpret kindness as weakness. "What's your name?"

"We are all one! Our name is legion!"

"Everybody needs a name," Princess said. "I'm going to call you 'Burnie'."

Harald said, "How about 'Sparky'? When that guy caught on fire in your house last Christmas, he went up like a firework."

"Yeah, I *love* being reminded that my home burned down," Princess snapped and for a few seconds the conversation devolved into a stress-fuelled shouting match.

"What *I'd* like," Bart interjected in a loud drawl, "is some help with this guy." The demon was wriggling like a panicked snake toward the shaft, evading the youth's snatches.

"Reverse!" squawked the creature as its head and shoulders crossed the threshold. It began to drift upwards like a helium-filled balloon.

"Got you!" Bart's hand clamped about the demon's foot. "Oh, shit; something's got me." The fingers of his free hand scrabbled for purchase on the edge of the doorway as he began to float. It took the efforts of his three friends to drag both back.

"That was kind of neat," Harald panted a few minutes later, above the demon's ongoing vituperation. "Hey, Burnie, how come you knew how to make the elevator work?"

The demon's citrine eyes narrowed. "It was a lucky guess," he muttered. "I do not like this place. It whispers of time gone by." A cunning expression slid across its face. "Let us go up. My lord will welcome you, spaw— brave human nobles. Such warriors as yourselves are seldom seen. He will want to do you honour."

"Burnie, you must be pretty thick," Princess said. "In fact,

I think we'd better make sure you can't go up there. Let's tie him to a rock or that black thing."

Shugger lifted the squirming demon and pushed it against the rectangular structure.

"Release me!" The creature's eyes widened in fear. "I remember what this is."

"Oh, stop whining," Princess said. "Honestly, you remind me of Alison."

"We're out of belts," Shugger said. "Let's sit him on top. We can sort of hook him onto those projecting things." He heaved the now thrashing prisoner onto the console's flat top and with Bart's help secured it.

"No!" The demon shuddered. "These are absorption points—" It froze and sat like a cringing statue, mouth still open. A soft, golden glow began to emanate from its skin. With the light came heat that rapidly grew intense.

Harald took a hesitant step toward the creature. "Should we get him off there?"

"You do it. I'll watch." Shugger pulled a smartphone from a pocket, switched on its camera and pointed it at the strange tableau. "I bet this goes viral."

"I don't think they have Wi-Fi® here," Bart said absently, attention focused on the demon. "Look, he's actually dissolving; he's going all misty around the edges. That black box is sucking him in!"

"Spawn!" screeched the demon. The paralysis broke and it writhed desperately. "Pull me away. I will reward you; I will spare your lives."

"Spawn yourself," Princess said. "This is like what happened to the demon at my house. He's turning to energy. But more slowly."

"Think he'll explode?" Bart said.

Everyone backed away, instinctively clumping together in the centre of the metal plate on the room's floor.

Minutes passed. The now incandescent demon stopped

struggling. Like a bright liquid it flowed into the projections on the black structure until nothing remained but a blob of shapeless solid matter that wriggled briefly and lay still.

Harald broke the silence. "Well," he said in a small, awed voice, "that was interesting." Cautiously, he moved forward and poked the glob. "Feels like a hot gummy candy."

"Gonna eat it?" Slugger looked in satisfaction at his smartphone. "When they discover our dead, shrivelled bodies, at least this'll show them what happened."

"I love your optimism," Princess said. "You do have a point, though. There's nothing to eat down here. Or drink." She looked toward the shaft. "We may have to go up. Demons or no demons."

"Let's try clearing away those rocks instead and see what's on the other side," Harald said. He patted the black console. "So long, Burnie. Hope you're happy, wherever you are. We really have to go find some food and water."

"Your command is received," said the demon's flat voice from the air. "Systems reactivation is in progress. Life support is now online. Environmental warming is in progress. Kitchen facilities are online."

"Guys," Princess said, "this metal plate we're on; it's doing something."

Bart looked up. "The plate on the ceiling; it's vibrating."

Tiddleums grabbed Harald's ear in both hands and squeaked, "Something's been acti—"

The syllables "—vated" hung like a whisper in the air of the now empty chamber.

Gironde picked up a heavy stone and passed it to Kringle, the next in line of a bucket brigade clearing fallen rocks from the tunnel leading to the drop shaft. He bent and straightened mechanically, body and mind focused on the job at hand.

"Lad, take a rest," Kringle said, noting the perspiration dripping off the younger man's face.

"When I know she's safe," Gironde replied.

"I'd know if she was dead," Kringle reminded him. "Wherever Candy Cane is now, I'm sure she's finding out what she needs to know." He shook his head. "Though I certainly would like to know how she gained the power to make wishes come true."

"Want that power for yourself?" Gironde wiped an arm across his face, leaving streaks of dirt.

"No, lad," Kringle said mildly, understanding the fear behind his friend's untypical snappishness. "I am content with who and what I am." He accepted another stone and turned to pass it to the next person in line. "But I have enough imagination, and experience, to understand what such power means. You and I, Paul, know that we can trust Candy Cane with our lives. It seems that someone else trusts her even more than we do." He paused to take a deep drink of water from a cup handed to him by one of Star's people. "After you've been around for a few centuries you'll feel it too; the certainty that there's so much more going on than we can see."

"Kris the philosopher," Gironde said. He stepped out of the line and bent over, hands on knees, breathing hard. Two days of good food and rest hadn't made up for the ordeal in the dungeon. "Where do you and I fit in all of this?"

Kringle joined him. "We love her, lad. Whatever is coming, and I'd bet my sleigh and reindeer it's something that young Harald would call 'mega *awesome*', she will need us." He slapped his friend on the back. "She is the fire, Paul. You're her fuel. Perhaps I'm the hearth."

Gironde managed a grin. "Not the chimney?" He straightened up. "Let's get back to work. We need to find out what's cooking."

Morning light streaming in a window of the Lady's suite in the Palace of the Rings gleamed on breakfast dishes in a dining nook and stuck needles of pain into the eyes of a hung-over elf.

"What possessed me to drink so much, so fast?" Candace whispered, holding a hand over her eyes. "I guzzled like there was no tomorrow. Oh, wait; maybe there *won't* be one. Lately, I've been kidnapped, trapped in a pentacle, wrapped in duct tape, chased by monsters, arrested, in a helicopter crash, almost burned at the stake, arrested again, abducted again, stranded on a world about to blow up, slashed to shreds, enslaved, more than half killed, nearly raped, beaten up, almost *eaten,* and dragged across dimensions." She groaned. "That doesn't even begin to describe what Paul and the Master and the kids must be going through because of me." She folded her arms on the table and rested her aching head on them. "I feel like the heroine in a book written by a demented author who gets a kick out of torturing characters."

"Your lack of moderation is understandable," Yseult said, placing a small glass full of a white liquid before her guest. "The author's, perhaps not so. Take this; it will help."

Candace obediently swallowed the concoction, gagging on its acrid taste. "Was that a magic potion?"

"Acetylsalicylic acid. Made from Willow bark. You can thank her later."

"Fairyland has aspirin. Who'd have guessed?" Candace reached for a glass of fruit juice to rinse away the taste. "My wish. It was to find someone who could explain to me what's going on. Would you, please?"

"Where shall I start?"

Candace thought for a moment. "We were trapped and I wished for a way out. A door appeared in the wall. Just like that; out of nowhere. It led to a stairway. Were that door and the stairway there all along, but somehow hidden?"

Yseult poured herself a cup of tea and sipped as she ordered her thoughts. "I think not," she said after a moment. "A wish empowered by magic must express itself; it has no option otherwise. But it will seek the simplest way. My guess is that the shaft down which you fell was always there. A door to it was the answer."

"And if there had been no convenient shaft?"

"The wish would have found another way; perhaps the ceiling would've collapsed on your enemies, or an escape portal opened to a new dimension. But more energy would've been required to power the wish, and the potential for unwanted side effects would therefore have been all the greater."

"Is that why, in fairy stories, wishes often backfire?"

"You have the right of it. The making of devices that can grant wishes to the user is forbidden in most realms of the Rings."

"Speaking of which, the wizard said that I cut through the Rings like a sword through flesh."

"Hy Brasail is the gateway to many universes," the Lady said. "I do not allow all who want to enter to do so." She frowned. "To break through from outside, as you did, took immense power."

"I'm very sorry. Believe me, I had no intention of doing harm. I don't even know how I did it."

"Your wish drew its power from the Silchar world, an inexhaustible source of energy."

"And potential cataclysms."

A smile touched the immortal woman's lips. "That is true."

"Something else that's true." Candace glared at her hostess. "I never told you that we fell down a shaft. How did you know that?"

"I was watching."

Candace clenched her fists. "So I'm today's entertainment, am I?"

The look Yseult gave her would have squelched anyone not as hung over. "Lass, whether you like it or not, you are caught in great events. Yes, I watched you, as I watch Helm and many others." She took a moment to refresh her cup of tea. "The fabric of life is vast beyond comprehension. In a thousand years, even I have glimpsed only a small corner of that great tapestry. But this I do know: the gift the Silchar entrusted to you will be of utmost importance in the times to come."

"Ah, good. More impending doom. Did you arrange to inflict that 'gift' on me?"

The Lady shook her head. "Hy Brasail is all my care; my will and my writ do not extend beyond it. But there are Powers other than the powers you know."

"How very mystic."

Yseult's eyes sparkled. "Indeed."

"Can you tell me more about these 'powers'?"

"Will you sleep more peacefully at night if you know?"

"Cryptic, too. I think you just told me to back off."

"I do not doubt your strength, but it has been tested sorely. Will you take my assurance that you will be happier if you come to that knowledge on your own?"

"I believe you." Candace slowly unclenched her still knotted fists. "But I am also sure that you deliberately dropped a hint." Angry sapphire eyes met imperturbable sienna. "Are you playing with me?"

"Never. Choice moves the worlds. Fate is driven by decisions. If you decide not to ask, your life will be none the worse for it. If you do insist, you will place on your shoulders a great burden."

Candace once more wished, silently, that she could cry; could spill out in tears all her frustration and anguish. "I must learn everything I can," she said in a voice that did quaver. "I'm not just gratifying my curiosity. As one of the Master's secret operatives, it was my duty to help keep my world hidden from humans. But I failed, and now I have a debt to pay."

"Was it up to you, alone, to protect your world?"

"No, of course not." Candace looked out the window, to where the sun drew a silver brushstroke along the surface of the River Hant. "I look like a human, don't I? But I'm not human. I'm an elf mother. My people are my purpose. A human would say that it all went wrong on my watch, so I'm responsible. I can't disagree."

"Does it matter? The rift between that Earth and your universe has closed."

"A debt is still a debt. By the way, was that a coincidence? The rift closing at just that time?"

"The closing was a natural event." Yseult set aside her teacup and rested her hands on her lap. "The opening, not so. You already know that a thousand years ago, a race desperate to flee from a dying sun tried to breach the wall between your dimension and theirs."

"And made a mess of it."

"The shock wave from that botched attempt tore open many fissures, including the one that Master Kringle later used to visit Earth at Christmas."

"How ironic: someone's bungling kickstarted my race's rise to sentience."

"Even from an accident, good can come."

"Now, why did the word 'enigmatic' just go through my head?"

The Lady ignored Candace's jibe. Her gaze shifted for a moment to a vista only she could see. "There were other consequences. The shock wave nearly shattered a prison I had made to hold a fiend that is a foe to all that lives. I remade the prison and it has held firm since. But some fragments tainted with the fiend's nature did fly through the weakened walls of the dimensions. The shards grant power to any who touch them, but also eat away human substance until nothing remains but the essence of the beast."

Candace exclaimed, "Scott's weird crystal! That's where it came from." She shuddered. "The mindless minds, too."

"I see there is no keeping secrets from you."

"Mystic, cryptic, enigmatic, *and* annoying."

This time the Lady's smile was almost impish, the look of a girl who had long ago roamed light of heart over the heather-covered hills of Scotland.

Candace ran a hand through her hair. The hangover was fading, but her head throbbed with the impact of new knowledge. "I'm very, very glad I didn't touch that crystal. What about the creatures that Helm calls Mindeaters—how do they fit into all of this?"

The amusement faded from Yseult's face. "The Devourers? They are terrible and indeed to be feared, but, for all that, they are no more evil than any other predatory animals."

"Do those 'powers' you mentioned have anything to do with their turning up now?"

"Heaven forfend, if Hell not forebear."

"I'm running out of adjectives to express acute exasperation."

"I have answered your questions," Yseult said, rising to her feet. "Some understanding is best gained in its own good time. Speaking of which, it is time for you to go home."

Candace followed her toward the suite's door. "Am I going to have to be careful about using the word 'doubleyou-aye-ess-aitch' for the rest of my life?"

"You are, and you will be."

"I've screwed up over and over! If you've been watching me, you know that."

Yseult paused with her hand on the doorknob. "Have your sufferings blinded you so severely? I think of a troubled young man whose life you saved and to whom you gave confidence and courage. I think of a despairing young woman whose mind you guided safely home. I think of

Master Kringle, who trusts you completely, whatever you believe to the contrary. I think of so many others, your friends and even your foes, who were enriched by knowing you. And I think of your own true love, who read your heart and adores you with all of his. If you do not believe in yourself, believe in them."

Candace was silent as the Lady led her through the Palace's marble halls, out into a formal garden and down a path. She was not very surprised when the path ended at a door set in a frame.

"Here is where you leave Hy Brasail," Yseult said. "And here is also your last chance to ask me questions."

"The kids. Were you able to find them?"

"I did: they appeared to be well. My looking glass showed them gathered about a table laden with food and drink." Mild perplexity crossed her face. "One youth was clad in silver cloth from head to toe."

"Harald," Candace said. "It has to be. Where were they?"

"I cannot say; and before you use another adjective on me, I do not know. Have you more questions?"

"Just one," Candace said. "Is there a limit to the power of wishing?"

"None of which I am aware," the Lady said soberly. "But always, there are consequences."

"Every Christmas, humans pray for peace on Earth. What if I granted their wish?"

"It would happen, possibly through the extermination of all life on that world. Remember; a wish will seek the easiest solution. Once outside the Rings you may wish as you choose, but take care. Also, I most strongly advise you to keep to yourself the nature of your Silchar gift."

"Paul, the Master, and my grandmother may have guessed it already."

"On their discretion you may rely, but common knowledge of your power will invite greedy attention of the worst kind."

"Thank you," Candace said. "I really don't know what else to say."

"'Tis enough." Yseult hugged her tightly. "Go in peace, and as my friend." She pushed open the door.

Candace stepped through and almost knocked down a startled elf holding an armload of freshly laundered towels.

I still say it looks silly." Princess folded her arms and stared down her nose at Harald. The scorn bounced off him.

"You don't know anything about style," he said, pirouetting in front of a mirror. "If I wore this to a sci-fi convention, people would line up to take my picture."

"Yeah, to post online as an example of what not to do with tin foil."

"Ah, you're just jealous. You could've made anything and all you came up with was pink yoga pants and a fluffy purple sweater with kittens on it."

Princess flushed. "Well, I let my mind wander a bit."

Harald sniffed. "What really gets me is that they meow. Too freaky."

Privately she agreed, but honour demanded a comeback. "I like pink and purple," she said, with a toss of her curls. "I like kittens, too, and at least they don't need to be fed." She ran a hand over her sweater, causing a chorus of plaintive squeals. "If you go outside in that metal outfit, you'll be hit by lighting."

"No lightning in space," Harald said, tugging at the high collar of his suit to smooth a crinkle.

"I *know* that. I was just testing to see if you knew. You have your head in fashion magazines all the time. *I* read about science."

"I've seen your bookshelf at home. What kind of 'science' books have cover pics of guys with big muscles and tight jeans? Plus," Harald went on with glee, "they're always kissing women who aren't wearing bras."

Recognizing defeat, Princess opened her mouth to utter a scathing remark as she marched out, but her exit was spoiled as the doorway behind her irised open. Shugger, Bart, and Tiddleums stepped through, the latter riding on the tall youth's shoulder.

"We found the bridge," Bart said. "Or what looks like one. Geez, this ship is huge!"

"Burnie said it's meant to carry thousands of people in hibernation," Shugger said. He was dressed in a form-fitting coverall laden with gadgetry, some of it functional, the rest copied from television and movies. He looked ready for any engineering challenge, real or improbable.

Bart had chosen to stick with his favourite black, but like his friend had opted for snug and dramatic. In Princess's opinion, perhaps a little too snug in certain places. She tried not to peek too often.

Tiddleums wore his usual outfit of soft trousers and jacket, but had embellished the garments with miniature tools. He ran along Bart's extended arm and jumped to Harald's shoulder, where a small chair had been incorporated into the clothing.

"We gotta decide what to do next," Shugger said, taking a seat at the table in the room the group had made its headquarters. "I mean, it's great, exploring and finding out stuff, and—"

"And not dying," Bart put in. "I thought we were goners, back in that cave. Good thing we ended up here and not in space."

"And figuring out how to use the matter-maker machine," Shugger went on, determined to complete his thought.

"You mean the replicator," Princess said. Television had infused her with deep wisdom about the equipment needed for treks between the stars.

Harald abandoned his mirror. "We just think about stuff and the machine makes it happen. I'd call it a mental matter molder."

"Reality revising replicator!"

Bart forestalled the impending Battle of the Alliteratives by saying, "*I* call it a real lucky break." As the eldest, he felt keenly the responsibility to be right most of the time. "If we hadn't figured out what it was and how to use it..."

"Tid figured it out," Harald said, with a reproving scowl at his friend and a sideways smile for the elf.

The justice of this claim met with general agreement.

"But what do we do now?" asked Shugger. "We've got a spaceship—"

"A fleet of *twenty* spaceships," Bart corrected him. "That's what Burnie said."

"After Tid asked him," Harald reminded his friends. "What do we do next?"

"Find Santa and Candace and Mr Gironde," Princess said. Her face brightened. "Maybe they're on board!" She raised her voice. "Burnie, who else is on this ship, besides us?"

"No one," said the disembodied voice of the demon.

"Well, that means it's up to us to find them," the girl said. "Rescue them."

"But there's only one teleport platform on the whole planet," Shugger objected. "Burnie said there are supposed to be others, but he can't detect them. What if they can't get to it? How can we let them know they should try?" He pulled a cell phone from one of his many pockets and held it up. "This doesn't work here."

Bart looked around at his friends. "We could go back, clear away those rocks..."

"Nope." Shugger put away his useless phone. "Burnie said the transporter isn't working properly. It's one way only; ground to ship."

"There's something we *can* do," Tiddleums called from his perch. As all eyes turned to the elf, he stood up to make himself better heard. "We can take the ship down to the surface."

Shugger asked, "Are you sure?"

"Oh, yes. The ships were designed to land when they reached a new world. They'd be broken apart and used to build cities. Burnie told me."

"But if they can't get back into space, that's no help," Princess said.

Tiddleums raised a tiny hand for attention. "They can, at least once. Burnie said that the Makers were big on safety. If a world turned out to be no good for settlement, they'd leave and try somewhere else."

"So where are these 'Makers', then?" A silence followed Shugger's question.

"We could ask Burnie," Harald suggested after a while.

"Tried." Shugger thrust his hands into the deepest of his pockets. "He only seems able to answer questions about the ship and its operation."

"Well, something bad must've happened," Princess said. "No one came to fix the transporter. And the demons live here."

Harald cleared his throat. "Maybe this isn't a good time to mention it, but there's a really gross-looking sun outside. Tid and I found a porthole, while you guys were off exploring. And while you were making kittens," he added with an arch look at Princess. "The sun's covered all over with blobs like tar. You can look at it without even squinting and the blobs are coming together so fast you can see it happening. I think the demons maybe aren't the worst of our problems."

Bart stifled a groan. "Burnie," he called, "is this ship able to travel? Can it move?"

The answer came promptly. "Sub-light functionality is at ten percent. Full functionality will require the input of master control units."

"I think that means we need more demons." The young man wiped damp palms on his black shirt. "Burnie, is the sun likely to go nova?"

"Yes," came the prompt answer.

"Well, in astronomical terms, that could still be years from now. Centuries, even. How long before it blows?"

The answer was given in a unit of time that none of the group understood.

"Try again," Princess commanded. "Use the rate of radioactive decay of, um, uranium as a base, it must be a constant in every universe, then convert to temporal functions, as follows." She rattled off instructions while her friends listened, trying not to look as impressed as they felt. "Then reduce the equation to a measure of time, using the twenty-four hour scale I just gave you," she said, "and tell us how long until the sun goes nova."

"Operation concluded," said the demon's bland voice. "Three hours."

Candace sat in the centre of a couch in the Mothers' meeting room, deep under the elves' city. Holly sat to her left, struggling to maintain the frosty dignity proper for the head of the Mothers' Council, while at the same time clinging to her daughter's hand. Crystal sat on the right, an arm flung around her sister's shoulders. The room was packed solid with people, both elves and humans.

I am home, she thought. Her antennae pulsed with the love and relief that surged around her. *I am where I belong. I don't ever want to leave. But I must.*

"You can't go back. You don't need to." Crystal, who had picked up the thought, spoke aloud for the benefit of the human guests. "The Master and Paul will come through the portal. They'll find a way. The Master has never, ever, missed a Christmas. He won't let the children down. You'll see."

Holly said nothing, but her hand tightened until Candace winced.

"They're not alone," she said, and described the situation

of Star, her people, and the four teenagers, in a series of flashing images for the elves and words for the humans.

"My mother is alive," Holly whispered when she was done. The fingers wrapped around Candace's shook.

Peter rose to his feet. "Candy Cane, how long were you in the demons' world?"

"Hard to say for certain, but it felt like about eight days. Maybe nine."

"Here, it's been three days. We can't waste a moment. In that accelerated timeline, the sun could already have—"

"Exploded?" John, Princess's father, jumped to his feet. "Sun be damned. My kid's there. I'm willing to go after her and the others. That door Miss Candy Cane returned through; could we use it?"

"No. It just opens to a linen closet now," Candace said. "Only the Master knew how to work it. But there's another option." Mindful of Yseult's warning, she'd buried awareness of the wishing power firmly behind a mental shield. "I, ah, overheard some code words while I was serving the Queen. Words that could reverse the portal at Rainbow Lake. We could transit through. They, the demons, won't be expecting that."

"We're ready," Peter said. "I can lead an assault team through the moment it opens."

Candace had to shout over the uproar of voices volunteering for the mission. "It's best if I go first, alone."

"But you said the Queen has control of the portal chamber," Peter pointed out.

"I'll negotiate with her. And then with the King. Arrange safe passage for our friends and Star's people, in return for letting the demons come here. Unarmed, of course." *I could simply wish the demons dead,* Candace reminded herself, but the idea jarred her soul. *I live for my people. The Chamberlain lives for his. What consequences might follow my wishing for the death of an entire species? I'll wish them to someplace safe in the multiverse instead*, she decided.

Holly released Candace's hand and stood up. "I remember what they did during the invasion. They cannot come here. I will not have it. Not even to see my mother again."

Thoughts passed so swiftly among the assembled elves that Crystal's efforts to translate lagged behind. She summed up for the humans: "No way. Never."

"Pretty sure they won't be welcome on Earth, either," John said. "The one that attacked last Christmas boasted that they'd turn us into seven billion torches."

"The Queen won't negotiate," Peter said. "She'll take you hostage. I used to be a dictator. I know how people like her think." He drew a deep breath to help force out his next words. "Would any of those code words you heard close the portal?"

"But that would trap—"

Silence, both verbal and mental, fell over the gathering.

On the bridge of the fleet's flagship, Bart asked his friends, "Do I say, 'Make it so'?" By common assent he had been elected Captain on the basis of his age, scientific acumen, and the fact that he looked the best in a starship officer's uniform.

"I think that phrase may be copyrighted," said Harald, who had designed their uniforms. He'd kept his own silver theme but acquiesced to his friends' preferences. Every major television and movie starship drama was represented somewhere in their outfits. To his credit, he'd managed to turn motley into style.

"You can't copyright an expression," Princess said, adjusting her peaked cap to a more flattering angle. "Like, what if I copyrighted every word? No one could speak without paying me royalties. If I were a writer, that's what I'd want to do. I'd soon have all the money in the world."

Shugger growled, "I hope no one has copyrighted 'Shut up' and 'Let's go'." He fidgeted on his chair, fighting a case of basophobia, the fear of falling. The group had discovered that the ship's bridge could be made fully transparent. As far as Shugger was concerned, he sat in the centre of a bubble with a dorsal view of the ship at his back, his feet hanging high above a planet, and scarlet hell over his head.

"All right, all right." Bart wiped damp palms on his trousers. "I'm just nervous. Okay, here goes." He took a deep breath. "Burnie, take us down to the surface. Land us near that castle thing. Make it so. Please."

No one spoke as the view began to change, the sere landscape slowly broadening until it edged out the narrow bands of starry blackness around the dying world.

"We're not descending in a spiral," Harald said after a while. "We seem to be going straight down. Is that safe?"

"I don't care as long as we stop before we make a crater," Shugger replied. He pulled his gaze away from the view swelling below his feet and looked back over his shoulder. "Hey, we have company. The whole fleet is following."

Behind them, shining like diabolical fireflies in the light of the mad sun, nearly twenty enormous vessels followed in stately formation.

"I bet I know why," Princess said. "Burnie's the only control unit. The other ships are slaved to him. What he does, they have to do, too."

"Can we stop it?" called Tiddleums from his perch on Harald's shoulder. "Or do we need to?"

"We are turning," Shugger said, eyes still fixed on the world beneath his soles. "Should we be turning? I think something's going wrong."

His observation was vindicated by a stomach-twisting lurch. The view of the planet skewed to the side.

"Burnie!" Bart jumped to his feet and kept moving upwards as the vessel's artificial gravity field failed. "What's going on? Stabilize the ship!"

"Cannot," said the emotionless voice of the demon. "Control functions are overextended."

"Well, separate this ship from the fleet."

"Cannot..." the demon replied, its flat voice now scratchy. "Require the input of a master control unit..."

The voice stopped but the spinning did not. Streamers of superheated plasma licked the tumbling ship and a deep vibration quickly smothered the faint noises made by five people too terrified to breathe.

You are *not* going alone." Peter had to look up to meet Candace's eyes but that detracted not a whit from his authority.

"I have to," she said, resisting an internal squirm at the lie. She turned to look at the army, waiting on a wide wooden platform that had replaced the rickety pier over the bed of Rainbow Lake. "If the portal room is small and we all try to go through, we'll be crushed. No. I must go first. As a scout."

"You'll be killed or captured immediately."

"I'll be quick. They won't be expecting me. I'll have the advantage of surprise."

"I've fought demons before. I know how fast they can react."

"I'll be *really* quick."

"You could give me the code to open the portal."

"What if *you're* killed?"

"Name a better fighter than me." Peter's heavy brows drew together in a scowl. "I've been around elves for a thousand years, Candy Cane. I know you're hiding something."

Candace silently cursed Peter's insight. Her plan was simple: Go through the portal, wish the demons far away, rescue her friends.

"General," she said, "I know you think the portal should be destroyed. And it will be, once everyone is safely home." She drew a deep breath, uncertain what to say next. An hour of sometimes acrimonious argument had yielded grudging permission to make a foray into the demons' world. "Please. Let me go alone."

"No. I'm coming with you."

"But you're in command, you have to stay with the army."

"My seconds know what to do."

Candace recognized defeat. "Just the two of us, then."

The hard lines on Peter's face softened and he placed a gauntleted hand lightly on her shoulder. "I'm sure you have your reasons for wanting to cross alone. But this is our war as well as yours. We all want to do our part."

She looked again at the army. Humans and elves bristled with weaponry of many kinds. No one could say for certain what armaments would function best in the natural laws of the demons' universe. Peter, a believer in the tried and true, wore a full set of plate armour and carried a sword.

And he'd spoken the truth. It wasn't only her war. Again she felt a spurt of guilt, this time because she'd tried to usurp the retribution that rightfully belonged to all her people. Many of the elves in the raiding force were survivors of the demons' foray half a millennium earlier. "I'm sorry," she said and meant it.

She was treated to one of Peter's rare smiles, an upward twitch at the corners of his lips. He drew his sword. "Proceed."

During the hectic time while the army readied itself, she'd taken a moment from briefing Peter and his officers about the demons' underground city to work out the phrasing of her wish. Candace whispered the words and a curtain of mist immediately formed in the air; not part of her wish but a useful phenomenon that visibly marked the portal's location.

It stabilized and hung shimmering just above the platform. Candace nodded to Peter. "After you, sir."

He sprang through. She followed so hard on his heels

that she ran nose-first into the back plate of his armour.

Swearing under her breath, she stepped to the side and froze, as Peter had done, at the tableau in front of her.

The portal chamber was small as she had feared, perhaps a half-dozen strides in diameter. In the centre stood a waist-high rectangular black block crowned by stubby knobs.

Dangling above it by a rope attached to his ankles was the King. Gripping his writhing body were the Queen and the Chamberlain.

Two demon guards collected their wits and lunged at Peter, swords drawn. His blade flicked twice and then there were two fewer persons in the room.

Stepping away from the nearer corpse, he said, "Candy Cane. Interpret for me what's going on here. If you can."

"Help me!" The weak cry came from the King.

"Shut up!" The Queen's palm struck his contorted face and sent him spinning. The Chamberlain stepped away, eyes flicking from her to the two interlopers.

"I think there have been some exciting developments," Candace said.

Ignoring the dripping sword in Peter's hand, the Queen marched toward her. "Tell me how you opened the portal, slave!"

Peter held his sword protectively in front of Candace. "Watch your language," he said. "I have strong feelings about the word 'slave'."

The Queen's thin lips curled."Do you think I fear one armed fool?" She jerked her head toward a door on the far side of the room. "I have an army at my command!"

"No, she doesn't," bleated the King, still twirling slowly. "They're on the run."

"But I have you, my dearest love," the Queen said with a smirk. "When you have opened the portal to the elves' world for me, your followers will bend to my will and to mine alone. They will have no choice." She beckoned to the

Chamberlain. "Hold him against the absorption points. As for you, slave..." The golden eyes that turned toward Candace gleamed fiery red at their centres. "I shall make you pay such a penance as no living being has ever endured. I shall kill you a thousand times, with tortures you never dared to imagine. I shall crush your soul; I shall—"

Candace dodged around Peter's sword and lunged for the creature, mind filled by a single pure desire to tear her limb from limb.

The Chamberlain got there first. Candace crashed into him and bounced back toward Peter, who swung her behind his armoured body as the two demons clashed.

The Queen's shrill screams for help brought no response. She twisted in her foe's grip, talons gashing his body. With an enormous effort, the Chamberlain lifted her off her feet and slammed her across the top of the rectangular block.

Candace clapped hands over her ears as the Queen's shrieking ratcheted up in volume and pitch. Awestruck, she watched the thrashing body undergo the same transformation that the four youths had witnessed earlier. Above the glowing, melting form, the King whimpered and tried to curl his body away.

Several minutes later, the Chamberlain, swaying with pain, knocked the gelatinous blob that was all that remained of the Queen off the block. He kicked it across the room.

"I told you," he wheezed to Candace, "that I would do whatever it took to save my people."

"Yes, starting by betraying me," the King said. "Let me down and I will pardon you."

The Chamberlain sank to the floor. "Don't kill him," he said in a faint voice. "Only he can open the portal from this side."

His wounds were grisly; Candace could see internal organs through flaps of shredded skin. A flare of compassion eased her anger at losing her own chance for revenge. "I can help you," she said.

The wounded demon seemed not to hear. His mouth stretched in a triumphant grin. "One thousand years of... her. No more!"

Candace bent closer. "Let me help you," she said again. The aureate fire in the Chamberlain's eyes was fading.

"Candy Cane." Peter, sword still drawn, loomed over her shoulder. "If you can help him, do so. We're going to need someone who can talk to his people. Go ahead. Wish him well."

"What? How did you—"

"I'm good at reading lips." Peter's free hand again touched her shoulder. "Later, I hope you'll share with me those very interesting parts of your story that you left out earlier. Right now, we need him."

Feeling both chagrined and relieved, Candace nodded. *Take baby steps,* she reminded herself, and said, "I wish the Chamberlain's bleeding to stop." To her relief the blood flow from the dying body ceased. Gingerly, she picked up a strip of skin and pushed it into place. "I wish this piece of skin to grow back. Quickly." Behind her, Peter caught his breath.

Growing more confident by the minute, Candace nudged internal organs into position, tucked gobbets of flesh where they belonged and aligned hanks of skin.

So caught up was she in this work that she didn't notice new arrivals. When at last she sat back on her heels, her sister Crystal and Princess's father, John, were watching over her shoulder.

"When neither of you returned, we feared the worst," said John, leaning on the baseball bat that was his chosen weapon.

"We volunteered to go through," added Crystal. "Well, really, Mother said no, but we went anyhow. She yelled that if we're not back in thirty minutes, she'll order the portal closed. There's only fifteen minutes left."

"Our time," John added, with an anxious glance toward

the gateway. "Five minutes here. We'd better move. Look; you can see that the army's been pulled back. I don't think your mother will hesitate."

Candace did look: the wooden platform over the lake bed was empty. She took a step toward the portal but stopped, as a familiar and loathsome mental scent filled her mind.

Crystal could feel it too: the younger elf gagged. "What are *those*?"

Moving inside the thin veil of the gateway were sinuous shapes. To Candace they resembled strips of the night sky, gliding in the nowhere space between worlds. Hungry. Famished.

"They're called Mindeaters," she said, backing away from the portal. More and more of the monsters appeared until they swirled like a shark feeding frenzy. "If we try to go through now, I think that whatever comes out the other side won't be us any more."

"Time's up," John said. Beyond his pointing finger electrical fire lit the sky around the lake bed.

Candace flinched as the portal vanished, leaving the group staring at a featureless rock wall.

"Oh, Mother," said Crystal. She pressed a clenched fist to her mouth. "What do we do now?"

"Candy Cane?" Peter had not taken his eyes off the Chamberlain for more than a second. "Can you open it again?"

"She can't," the demon said, eyeing Peter's sword. "Only a member of *his* tribe can."

"Won't somebody let me down?" pleaded the King. "He tells the truth. I will open the portal for you."

Don't let him! The voice that rang in Candace's mind sounded as if it came from very far away.

Crystal had caught it, too. "Who the hell—" she began.

"Listen!" Candace jumped to her feet and extended her antennae to their maximum. "Sister, just listen. I think it's important."

...master control unit, said the voice, coming and going as if shouting against a contrary gale. *Too powerful; one such as he...thousand years ago...ripped...*

"I hear you," Candace said to the air. "You're telling me that if he opens the portal for us, it'll cause a disaster." She caught a flashing sense of distant relief before the contact ended.

"What was that about?" asked Peter.

"Advice from a friend," Candace replied, wondering what it had cost Yseult to force her warning across the dimensions. "I can open a portal." She turned, the words forming on her lips.

The room shook and a low, rolling *boom* echoed back and forth in the chamber. Fragments of stone fell from the ceiling.

"Is it happening?" Crystal turned in panic to Candace. "The nova, I mean."

Peter cupped a hand to an ear. "That was a bomb. I know the sound. And there goes another."

"The attack's started," Candace told him. "We were going to make gunpowder and set off explosions. Cause distractions. The Master and Paul can't be far away!"

Peter cocked an eyebrow. "Can you get us to them?"

"Sure. I wish—" Candace managed to say, before a piece of the crumbling ceiling hit her head.

Well, that was *very* interesting."

In the starship control room, Harald peeled a hand off the arm of his chair and wiped it across his forehead. He looked around at his friends, most of them still caught in the paralysis of shock. Only Tiddleums, clinging to his companion's ear, had enough composure to stand up. Harald tried to emulate him, but noticed that he was sitting in a warm puddle and decided to keep his seat for the moment.

"Burnie!" The elf shouted through a miniature megaphone made for him by the ship's replication unit. "Give us a status report."

"The entity known as 'Burnie' has been subsumed," replied a distinctly female voice. "Ship life support functions are maximal. Fleet inter-communication functions are maximal. Sub-light propulsion functions are maximal. Hyperspace propulsion system is non-functional. This is the report of the Quest for Exo-solar Environments New Initiative Implementation System. At your service."

Princess recovered enough aplomb to say, "The Quest for Exo-solar...that's a mouthful. If Burnie's gone, I think we should call you something simpler. If you put the initials together you get, um, 'Queenie'. Does everyone agree?"

Everyone did.

"What now?" asked Shugger. Like Harald, he had chosen to remain seated. The view in the transparent control room now showed cracked ground underfoot, a decaying castle-like structure in the distance, and the same ferocious crimson sky.

Bart stood up, surreptitiously brushing a hand as he did so across the seat of his pants. Looking relieved, he pointed at the castle and said, "What do we do now?"

"Wait for our friends," Harald replied. "I mean, if we go out exploring we could get lost or maybe there's no air or there's microbes or the sand people will shoot us."

Shugger forgot the damp state of his own trousers for a moment as he focussed on the distant castle. "I see movement," he said. "I don't think they're sand people. They're not in single file."

Princess rolled her eyes. "You guys. This is *real*. It's not a movie." Squinting, she also studied the crumbling ruin. "It's obvious: We've gone through a wormhole to another world. One with a red sun. Like Krypton." Her eyes lit up. "Maybe we'll have super powers!"

"Krypton's a gas," said Bart the scientifically minded. "Anyhow, Harald's right; if we try to find our friends, we could get lost. We have to wait for them to come to us. Even if Burnie said there's not much time."

Harald got to his feet. "In that case," he said, backing toward the control room's entrance, "There's something I have to do right now."

"Me, too," Shugger muttered, copying his friend's crab-wise shuffle.

Princess waited until the two youths had exited before rising, performing an elaborately casual stretch, and sauntering backwards to the door. "Just going to visit the matter maker," she said. "I'm tired of this outfit. Think it's time for a change."

"What's gotten into them?" Bart asked as the door shut on the sound of her running feet. Alone on the bridge, he clasped his hands behind his back and pondered what no one had wanted to say; that escaping an exploding star might be impossible.

Consciousness returned to Candace, bringing with it a vicious headache and the curious sight of feet moving rapidly to and fro. An instant's confusion resolved into awareness that she was slung over John's shoulder, and he was running.

Looking about, she saw that they were in the underground city.

Chaos reigned. Thunderous explosions, the shattering roar of collapsing stone, and screams of terror filled the air. The King, trotting at the tip of Peter's sword, was shouting but couldn't be heard over the din.

"I wish myself to be fully healthy right now," Candace said, and then added her own voice to the cacophony as assorted bruises, sprains, fractures, and abused brain cells slid, popped, or squeezed into their proper positions.

The brief agony was followed by euphoria; a sensation of radiant vigour. Candace resisted the urge to hang limply and relish the wonderful and long-absent feeling, and instead patted John's side to get his attention.

"She's awake!"

Peter half turned at the other man's shout. "Over there!" He pointed at an archway and they ran for its shelter. "Can you get us out of here?" he asked Candace as the other man set her down.

"I think so," she said. "But what about them?" She waved a hand at the crowds of terrified demons and goblins.

"Your mother made it plain," Peter replied. "They don't come to our world. I'm not about to disagree with her."

"Please," the Chamberlain begged. "Just my tribe. There's only a few of us."

"And me," the King said. "Now that *she's* gone, I'm the last of the specials. I matter more than they do."

The Chamberlain turned snarling toward him but before he could speak, a small cluster of demons in cooks' outfits saw him and broke from the mob. More followed them until a panic-stricken throng surrounded Candace and her companions.

The King shot a nervous glance at Peter. Getting a curt nod, he raised both arms for silence. "Tell me what is going on," he ordered in a loud voice.

A noble clutching a broken arm stepped forward. "Sire," he said, "the city has been invaded. The enemy have seized the elevator; we cannot escape to the surface. And just before contact with the castle was lost, we learned that the sun is swelling—"

His voice was briefly smothered by the clamour that followed.

"What about these?" Peter gestured at the crowd.

"You cannot abandon us." The Chamberlain's despairing

eyes were palest citrine. "I swear to you by the Makers; help us escape and I will serve you as faithfully as I would have served them." A kind of dignity settled on him. "To serve is my nature. For a thousand years I have had to obey those I abhorred. It would be an honour and a pleasure to serve one I admire."

"You abhorred *me*?" The King goggled at his erstwhile servant. "Well, that explains the treason. Consider yourself dismissed from my service."

"I—" Candace struggled with wildly conflicting emotions: pity for the doomed creatures; loathing for them, too; the burn of growing panic; fear of making a mistake. "Oh," she exclaimed without thinking, "I wish I knew what to do!"

And she did.

Later, she attributed the knowledge that filled her mind to Yseult's mysterious Powers. But now, *Get them to the surface* rang in her head and she said in response: "I wish all the dem—all the people here that I call demons, I mean, and the goblins, to be outside, safely on the surface of the planet."

"Sister," Crystal said into a silence now broken only by the occasional crash of falling rock, "what in Balthazar's name did you just do? Where did they go?"

"And," Candace went on, trying to ignore the distracting mental pulse of her sister's intense curiosity, "I wish that my grandmother and all of her people, and General Peter, and Crystal, and John, and the Master, and Paul, also be safely on the surface of the planet."

Alone in the empty city she asked herself, *Can I stop the nova?*

This time there was no voice in her head; only an understanding that she should not try.

"All right, then," she said to the air. "In that case, I wish to be with my husband."

"What the hell!"

Candace took an involuntary step back from the angry face suddenly confronting her.

"Why the blazes can't you leave me alone?" bellowed Kevin Finnegan.

Looking around, she saw that she was in the familiar messy environment of his apartment.

Words utterly failed her.

"I went through fucking hell, thanks to you," the man blurted, face reddening. "I was squeezed for hours—days—by every security officer in two fucking countries and two fucking universes! I was locked up, charged with falsifying a passport—that should've been you, not me—and with trespass and carrying a concealed weapon and car theft and illegal use of a goddamn fire alarm and when I was so wrung out I couldn't even piss, they took me back through the wormhole and dumped me here and told me to keep quiet or else and God damn it, you still have my mother's ring." Finnegan pointed at the gold and diamond band. "Are you here to give it back? If you aren't, I swear I'll bite your damn finger off and I'll do it so fast you won't even have a chance to wiggle those fucking antennae!"

Still wordless, Candace tugged off the ring and handed it to him.

Finnegan clenched the jewel in his fist. "And I haven't been paid," he went on. "Thirty thousand in gold. You were lying about that, weren't you?"

Indignation fought through Candace's shock. "I wasn't," she said. "My order was received. I checked."

"Well, I haven't received anything."

"I'm sure...soon," she stammered, backing away from Finnegan and, more importantly, from the ring that had now assumed a staggering new relevance. *But I married Paul!* cried her outraged spirit, countered by a coldly analytical: *With Kevin's ring. Oh, bloody* Christmas. *I am a bigamist.*

"I have to go," she said, trying not to shriek. "I was just checking in...glad you're home safe...good place to be; sorry about the ring. Really, really sorry. You've *no* idea how sorry."

She ran into the washroom, shut the door, locked it, and said, "I wish to be with Paul. Paul Gironde. Not just any Paul Gironde; I mean the one I married. The man that the Master, Kris Kringle, Santa Claus, pronounced me married to on that hilltop where the goblins attacked us and I'm about to start raving and anyhow, that's what I wish!"

The sun was indeed swelling. Candace involuntarily backed a step away from the insanity filling almost all the sky.

"Darling," said a beloved voice, "that's my toe you're standing on."

Several seconds passed before Candace reluctantly freed herself from her husband's embrace. "Where are we?" she asked. "And what have I missed?"

"We're on the roof of the castle," Paul replied. "You've missed a busy couple of days. Your grandmother started evacuating people to the surface shortly after you disappeared. She had no choice; the cavern's collapsing. Luckily for us, the drop-shaft we fell down now very conveniently goes up. And then there's this." He tugged her hand and led her to a parapet. "Take a look."

Candace followed the direction of his pointing finger. "Mushrooms?" she asked. "Gigantic mushrooms?"

"Space ships," Paul said. "I counted twenty. Your doing?"

Candace shook her head, dazed. "Don't space ships pop up all the time? Like mushrooms?"

"Call me crazy, but I bet the kids are involved. Some of Star's people said the ships came tumbling down like meteors, all over the sky, then suddenly formed themselves into a squadron and landed as neat as you please." Gironde pointed beyond the fleet of grounded vessels. "What I really came up here to see is *that*."

Candace followed the line of his finger. "It's just a moon," she said. "Rising over the horizon."

"Whatever it is, it's not good news. I think the planet's breaking up." A violent twist of the stone under their feet was accompanied by thunder as one of the castle's curtain walls collapsed.

Candace's antennae tingled powerfully. She turned her head and nudged her husband's arm. "Darling," she said, "You'll never guess what just arrived."

It was Gironde's turn to follow the line of her finger. His jaw dropped. Gleaming like towers of blood in the scarlet light, two mighty pillars rose from the rubble.

"What. The. Hell." Gironde stared at the pillars. Remembering the World Tree, he tilted his head back and back, following their line into the sky.

"They're greaves," Candace said. "Ancient armour. On legs. Very long legs."

"Female legs," her husband added. "Nice legs."

"Dear." Candace reached for his hand. She also tilted her head back. Above the legs, a kilt; above that, a bronze cuirass bound by a leather belt from which hung a sword. Still higher, a shield and spear and over it all, its top brushing the stratosphere, a helmet with a towering black crest laced by cobalt lightning.

"I know her." Candace clung to the quaking stone of the parapet with her free hand and stared in awe at the giantess. "It's Helm."

"Who?"

"Someone whose life is even stranger than mine."

The castle shook again as the giant legs moved. A gale whipped about the roof and blew the couple off their feet.

They picked themselves up with difficulty, the castle

under their feet shaking like a dog scratching off fleas.

"The horizon's *rising,*" Candace shouted over the thunder of falling masonry.

"No it isn't," Gironde said. "The castle's sinking into the cavern. We have to get out of here, fast."

A few hasty words and the castle transitioned to a crumbling mass in the distance. As Candace watched, gigantic cracks opened in the earth around it and spread like spiderwebs in all directions, snaking around the grounded starships and the tight-packed cluster of Star's adopted people, among whom the pair now stood. On a distant pillar the demons and a flock of goblins clumped together.

The noise was intolerable. Having lived much of her life with her ears trimmed to human shape, Candace had almost forgotten how well an elf's pointed ears captured sound. She saw her grandmother double over in pain, hands pressed to her skull; saw Kringle step forward and cover her hands with his own. An instant later Gironde's palms closed over Candace's ears, reducing the thunder to merely awful.

The castle disappeared, flinging up an enormous veil of dust in its last moments that blocked off view of the giant Helm, still striding away. More ground slid out of sight, but there was something peculiar about the subsidence. Rock and earth plunged into the collapsing caverns, but left the ships and the clusters of terrified living beings standing on narrow pillars.

Of course, Candace realized with a thrill. *I wished for everyone to be* safely *on the surface.*

But they could not remain safe for long. Candace made her way to her grandmother's side. "I can move us," she shouted. "Are all your people here?"

"Aye, all my folk," the older elf replied. She pointed toward the demons. "I know not what to do about them."

Candace's hearts sank. Automatically, she reached for the reassurance of Paul's hand. "I can't—I won't—take them home with us. I just can't."

But the Chamberlain saved my life, she reminded herself. *Even if he's no sweetheart, he cares about his people as much as I care about mine and Star cares about hers.*

Kringle joined her, adding the warmth of his arm around her shoulders. "I have always found it pays to err on the side of compassion," he said. "And generally, to do it quickly."

A sickening twist of the rock under their feet gave spice to his words. Candace clutched Gironde's arm. "I wish," she said, "to have the Chamberlain here, in front of me. And the King."

"What—" The Chamberlain reeled from his sudden dislocation.

"Listen to me," Candace said, but the demon's eyes swivelled away from her.

"Makers," he said in the awe-struck tone of a pilgrim beholding the Holy Grail. "They are Makers!" He flung himself flat on the ground before the nearest of the mauve-skinned under folk in an adoring puddle of bright silk.

"Interesting reaction," Kringle said.

Star nodded. "Aye. We have long known from our spying that some of the demon folk mourned in secret for their creators, but were held silent by the chains of terror."

The King looked worried. "I didn't start the rebellion," he mumbled. "It was all *her* idea. She made me help. I killed no one."

"Liar!" hissed the Chamberlain, scrambling to his feet.

"Well, perhaps I did, but only in self defence because they were trying to stop me from killing them."

"Excuse me." Gironde stepped forward and confronted the King. "You and I have a certain matter to resolve regarding my wife." The sound of his fist cracking the demon's proud, arched nose came clearly over the thunder of the still-collapsing castle.

Candace put a restraining hand on his shoulder as he stood with fists clenched over the now prone and bubbling

King. "I consider myself avenged. I called him here because I think we're going to need him."

"You will," the Chamberlain agreed. "*She* was created to coordinate all ship operations, at least that was the plan before the erring Makers tried to reprogram her and brought disaster down upon us all." He glanced at the starships in their orderly rows. "The absorption point computer read her program, corrected it, and put her where she belongs."

"Just in time, too," Kringle said. He pointed at the King. "What about him?"

"He was made to control the hyper engines. Without him, the ships cannot reach light speed and escape this world before the sun bursts. Even with him integrated into the system, it will be very close."

"Oh, all right." The King, still prostrate, waved a hand. "I consent. It's too dangerous to stay in this form. You, slave girl—I mean, Grand Admiral," he added hastily as Gironde's fists knotted again, "Put me into my engines. Please."

Candace obliged.

"Thy magic may yet save us all," Star said. "By my daughter's command, the demon-folk may not enter your world. Yet there is a choice." She touched her forehead to the younger woman's. This near, her thoughts were a love-warmed susurration. "It is my joy to have met thee, but my home is no longer among Master Kringle's folk. I will stay with the people of my hearts. Do you cast the demon-folk, and me and mine, into those great ships. They were meant to journey together. I shall end my days with them, wheresoever they go."

"And I will come with you," Kringle said.

Candace felt as if her soul would tear in two. "But Christmas—!"

Kringle cupped her face in his broad hands and kissed her brow. "Dearest child, my courageous and sweet Candy Cane. Don't forget, you now have the ability to help me commute."

"And us to get home," put in Gironde. The scarlet light of the dying sun had become blinding.

Candace looked at the starships. "But the kids—"

"Can be collected later. Sweetheart, we have to go. *Now.*"

He was right. She shut her eyes against the glare and shaped her wishes. An instant later, only she, Paul, John, and Crystal stood on the pillar. Yet she lingered before phrasing the wish that would take them home, as the squadron of starships lifted lightly from the ground and hovered for a second, before accelerating heavenward so fast that the concussion created by their speed toppled all the pillars, save the one on which the little group remained, protected by the lingering aura of safety.

Candace threw her arms about her husband and spoke her last wish in that world.

There was an instant of dislocation and the horrible red glare was replaced by the sane and kindly light of her own world's sun.

"Home," said Crystal, and sank onto the rough wood planks of the platform covering Rainbow Lake.

Candace joined her as their mother led a cavalcade of elves and humans onto the platform. The elf matriarch threw dignity to the winds, flung her arms around her daughters and hugged them. Nearby elves rocked on their heels, swamped by the strength of her love and relief.

After a few moments, Candace said, "I have to go rescue the kids." She reluctantly extricated herself from her mother's embrace and stood up. "I'll only be a minute."

Gironde stepped forward. "I'll come with you. I've got a feeling that 'just a minute' is a way of saying 'something is sure to go wrong'.

Candace kissed him. "Darling, I've got the hang of it. Trust me." She took a step backwards and said, "I wish to be with the kids."

I'm really getting used to this, she told herself with some pride as the world around her changed instantly. The lake bed and defensive towers had vanished. In their place, a sun shed a pleasant warmth over an ordinary suburban landscape of houses, trees, and gardens. She looked around for the four teenagers.

None was in sight. But regarding her with wide eyes were two children, a boy of about nine or ten, and a girl of perhaps six. The boy was pulling a wagon loaded with boxes of cookies and canned drinks.

"Er," Candace said, with a sinking feeling that something had indeed Gone Wrong. "Hello, children. I'm looking for some friends. Four teenagers. Have you seen them?"

The little girl pulled a finger out of her mouth. "Are you a bug?" she asked, staring in fascination at Candace's antennae.

"No, dear." *The next time I wish, I'll have to remember to name the kids I mean,* she scolded herself. "I'm an elf. You must be lost. Do you want help getting home?"

"You came out of nowhere," the boy said. "You can't be an elf. They're little and have pointy ears. Well, your ears *are* pointy, but I think you're really a bogeyman."

Bogeyman...

"Okaaay," Candace said. "Now I know which universe I'm in." She sank down on one knee to talk to the children face to face. "Do your mommy and daddy know you're not at home?"

"They're out," the boy said. "Our babysitter's watching TV."

And obviously not watching you, she thought. *Time to get these poor mites back to where they belong, and then get to where I belong.*

"Did you come from the Dream World?" the boy continued. "My Auntie Eli fights the bogeymen there."

"Auntie Eli...oh, Helm! Why am I not surprised." Candace smiled at the children, with an amused conviction that it was indeed a small multiverse. "Is she here?"

The boy shook his head. "She's at the hospital." He

pointed toward a distant building on which a hospital sign could just be made out. "We're going there now."

"We have to save the world," piped up the girl. "It's very important. The lady with the baby dragon said so."

"The lady with..." Candace caught a confusing melange of impressions in the children's minds, but one image stood out clearly: "Yseult. I should've guessed. Kids, I'm here to take you home. I'm sure that's what the lady with the baby dragon would like me to do. What are your names?"

"I'm Sarah," said the girl. "He's Nick. But we're not supposed to talk to strangers. Mommy and Daddy said so."

"Good advice. It's OK to talk to me, though. I work for Santa Claus. My name's Candy Cane, but you can call me Candace."

"The lady said not to trust anybody we don't know," the boy insisted.

Candace laughed, grateful for a light moment in an otherwise stress-riddled day. "I know her too, so that makes us friends. Come on, kids." She stood up, holding out a hand, and the little girl slipped a small paw into hers.

"But we haven't saved the world yet!" The boy pointed at his wagonload of snacks. "I know it's a long walk to the hospital. That's why I brought survival rations. We have to go there."

"I think it best that I take you home," Candace said. "When we get there, we'll phone your aunt at the hospital and you can tell her about saving the world. Or we'll call your mommy and daddy." *Then I'll give that babysitter hell,* she decided. *And maybe Yseult, too.*

"I want to go home," the little girl said suddenly. "That car has bad people in it."

"Car?" Candace turned to look.

A black limousine sped up the street toward the three. She caught a foul whiff from the minds inside and said, "Oh, *Christmas.*"

Kevin Finnegan smiled at the code displayed on his computer screen and poised a finger over the 'Enter' button. Planting this virus marked a small but significant step in his campaign to oust that arrogant bastard, Paul Gironde, and open his job to someone more deserving, namely himself. It wasn't even illegal, at least from his point of view. Showing his mastery of covert computer infiltration would impress the bosses upstairs at the CIA.

A gust of air a few feet away sent him leaping to his feet. A woman, holding the hands of two scared-looking children, now stood in the middle of his living room.

"No time for questions, Kevin!" the woman said. "Just look after these kids for me; I need a place where they'll be safe and that's here. I won't be long. You can name your price. I'll explain when I get back." She nudged the children toward him, muttered something under her breath, and disappeared.

Finnegan stared blankly at the children, who returned the look. After a while he said, "What's going on? And who the hell was that?"

Kevin Finnegan whistled under his breath as he played with his gold. The wafers, each stamped with a hallmark guaranteeing 99.999 percent purity, were smooth and cool under his touch as he stacked and re-stacked them. They'd arrived minutes earlier by ordinary parcel post; he'd half expected a courier mounted on a reindeer.

He was twiddling one to catch a sunbeam when a swish of displaced air told him that he had a visitor.

"Hullo, Kevin," Candace said. "How are the kids?"

Finnegan swept the wafers into a pocket as he jumped to his feet. "I'm not giving these back! A deal's a deal."

"I don't want your gold. Are the kids asleep?"

"What kids?"

"Not funny, Kevin." Candace's antennae, until then laid flat against her head, stiffened and pointed at him. He was uncomfortably sure that his mind was being read. "You haven't seen them," she gasped. "I brought them to the wrong universe—"

She reached his sofa in two quick strides, snatched up the pillow she'd slept on only a few days earlier, buried her face in its muffling thickness, and screamed.

"Bad day, huh?" Finnegan tapped a finger against the gold in his pocket and reflected that if he played his cards right, there might soon be more. "I'll go make some tea."

Far away in the Palace of the Rings, Yseult stepped back from her mirror and with a gesture dissolved the image of Finnegan's apartment.

She walked to a window and looked out at the city beyond. Night had come and thousands of flickering lights shone against the darkness.

"So the Powers have acted," she mused to the ever-attentive dragon. "She wished to bring the children to a safe place and did so. But it is also a warning most dire: the two realms already infected by the Devourers are in even greater peril than I thought, for there to be no safe place within them to hide the children. Only the third Earth, the one farthest from Hy Brasail, is safe. For how long, though?"

Overhead the sky, responding to her mood, grew grey with clouds and a cold rain began to fall.

"And my time is near and there is no new Guardian to follow me," she said to the city growing remote behind a silver curtain of celestial tears.

Fear Me.

Yseult whirled, astonished, toward her mirror. Fiendish eyes glared at her in triumph before fading slowly.

Fear Me.

THE STORY CONTINUES WITH HELM IN

Psychological Warrior

A PREVIEW FOLLOWS:

CHAPTER ONE

Helm dropped warily into the Dream World and paused to get her bearings, disoriented as always by the transition from the world she knew to someone else's reality.

An instant later the Mindeater lurking in the dreamer's brain sensed her presence and struck. The ground under her feet transformed into a pit of boiling quicksand. A flash of burning pain; she thought with urgent speed and the viscous liquid transformed into cool, lime-green jelly.

The image was too weak; the Mindeater restored the quicksand and she floundered desperately, knowing that death here would be as real, as final as death in the waking world. She slapped her arms against the still hot mass, trying to think of a countermove before it engulfed her.

Green equals trees; trees equal jungle; jungle equals vines. She reached up, snatched a dangling vine from the forest that had appeared with her thought and dragged herself out of the quicksand, kicking frantically as the bubbling fluid changed, gelled and became a sheet of ice gripping her foot. The vine writhed in her palm and transformed into a fanged serpent that twisted about and lunged for her fingers.

She cursed under her breath and concentrated, forcing the gleaming gold- and brown-striped body into limpness, into green, and at last into a vine again.

"Shield! I need you—quick!" Her voice cracked through the howling sandstorm that sprang without warning from the sleeper's dim memory of a desert vacation and almost in the same instant her second in command appeared beside her.

Not in human form, though; Shield manifested as a dome of heavy, transparent Plexiglas that extended down through the pool. Dark forms wriggled under the ice and pain shot briefly through Helm's trapped foot.

The world inside the bubble steadied. She concentrated again, calling up a favourite image; pink bathtub frothing over with rose-scented bubbles and the soap bobbing just beyond her questing toes. Belatedly, she realized she had left her clothes on and was sitting fully dressed in warm, scented water.

"You look so comfortable," purred Shield's contralto voice from the wall. "Next time, wait for the rest of us. You're not fighting this war by yourself, you know."

Helm grinned to hide the sting of the criticism, concentrated again and shaped about herself a remembered sunny meadow from her uncle and aunt's farm, drawing on the ability of her photographic memory to perfectly recall any image she had ever seen. Relentlessly she forced the image to remain fixed, forming in her mind the field as her memory offered it; hay blowing knee high against her sun-browned leg; frothy white Queen Anne's Lace dancing on the soft breeze and a bluebottle fly darting between stalks of purple loosestrife. The image steadied, strengthened by the thousand tiny details she conjured against anarchy. The Mindeater's attack persisted though; a tugging at her mind, a subtle perversion of the pure golden sunlight into something vile and mad.

Shield manifested as a slender woman in her mid thirties with calm brown eyes and an engaging quirk on her lips. "Ready for the others?"

Helm nodded, squelching a brief, menacing ripple in the ground. The rest of Weapon Team began to appear; Castle almost at once as a comfortable-looking, motherly woman in her late fifties; thin, tense young Spear and rugged Axe. Axe had fixed his broken nose, Helm noted, and was considerably taller and more handsome than in reality. Arrow flicked into being almost at the corner of her eye and edged toward the group. Her dream self was the furtive and silent child of the streets that she had been and not the sleek young woman she now was. Helm tried not to notice as she slipped close to Spear and hoped the young man would keep his mouth shut.

Sword popped into being so suddenly that Axe jumped and briefly reformed into a ball of fire. Helm ruthlessly reshaped the fireball back to human. She let him keep his handsomeness, though; there was no point in antagonizing him. Sword smiled and waved; he had few vanities and looked almost himself, a bit less grey in his hair, perhaps, but his small pot belly was unashamedly apparent.

That left Caduceus, the group's healer. He arrived late, as usual, wearing the black suit and white collar of his discarded priesthood. Almost as an afterthought the clothing wavered and changed to a nondescript grey sweatsuit.

"Where's the bogeyman?" Spear growled, sullen as always. His hands and eyes were never still; watching him was like watching a jumping spark.

"The attack has just begun." Helm put firmness and confidence into her voice, knowing that her apparent body faithfully mimicked the one lying torpid on a couch in Psychic Combat Group 1111's headquarters. A mirror began to waver in the sunlight but she dismissed it before it formed fully. She needed no mirror to know her own slim, small body with its shoulder-length fall of dark brown hair and clear hazel eyes. Some team leaders used their ideal bodies in combat but Helm never did; the face and figure of a glorious woman warrior wouldn't make her one in truth, if she lacked the necessary inborn skills. *I am reality,* she thought, *and the team knows it. Even though reality is also what you make of it, here in the mind of a dying man.*

"The dreamer survived the first attack last night because his wife managed to wake him up," she continued. "He couldn't tell us everything that he saw; he chewed his tongue badly during the attack and he was too shaken to write clearly. We did learn there was just one of them."

The ground heaved again. Shield and Castle flicked out of sight without needing to be told though they were still with the team; Helm could feel them like tingles along her nerves. "Arrow, find the dreamer," she continued. "Spear, Sword—you know your roles. Caduceus—" She turned, spinning effortlessly, her toes not quite touching the warm earth. "Go with Arrow. Keep alert for the bogeyman. Axe—" she hesitated. "Axe, stay with me."

"I'm no babysitter," the big man growled, adding a provocative leer.

Helm met his cold eyes with coldness of her own. "I'm going to let the bogeyman manifest," she said. "I don't want you wandering off. You'll be first strike."

To her relief, but not to her surprise, he nodded and his belligerence faded. *Borderline paranoid,* she thought even as she turned her attention to the coming battle. *Afraid I'll leave him behind if he provokes me too much. As he's convinced I left Mace and Rampart.* She put those memories firmly away, knowing them for weaknesses that the Mindeater could exploit; took a deep breath and let the sunny field go.

She stood on top of a cliff, a cliff so high that God might have perched there to plan the creation of the world. Clouds drifted miles below, twinkling with lightning storms like dirty cotton balls crisscrossed by static electricity. The light was dull red from a low and swollen sun. Helm blinked, astonished as ever by how *real* it all looked. The presence of a Mindeater dispelled the tunnel vision quality of a true dream, without destroying its dangerous potential. There was nothing to tell a helpless dreamer that the landscape about her was false. Millions of sleepers had believed their nightmares and died of terror before anyone realized that humanity was under attack. As far as Helm was concerned, she stood on the rocky peak of a monster mountain, sun-fried stone baking the soles of her running shoes and a wind with a nasty edge sniping at the skin of her exposed hands and face.

She turned around slowly, concentrating on the scrape of small, rough pebbles under her feet, and studied the bleak landscape behind her. The mountaintop stretched back into forever. The sun had moved and now squatted on the distant horizon. The sky was suffused with the rust-red light that leaked from the morbid globe. Thick, clotted drops trickled down the sky, coiling and curling toward her ankles. The ends of the trickles writhed up into clawing hands, needle-pointed nails lacquered a vile magenta.

"The patient's father committed suicide," said Shield from nowhere. "He cut his throat in the family's kitchen. The patient was a boy then. He came into the room just as it happened. In his dream last night, he was wielding the knife."

Helm shook her head, irritated at letting the ghoulish sight distract her. "I know. I read the file. But thanks for reminding me."

"Going to do something, boss lady?" Axe's sneer was sloppy, far too wide for a human mouth. He'd seen his share of blood, she knew. He'd put his wife in the hospital twice before she'd gotten the courage to leave him and lay charges. He'd had a choice of the Combat Group or prison.

"Yes. I'm going to let you deal with that." She pointed at the tendrils writhing toward them. "Have fun." She turned again, managing not to flinch as a gigantic axe materialized in the gory heavens and whistled down in an arc that missed her head by a fraction of an inch. The blade chopped noisily into the grasping tendrils and the severed portions writhed briefly and erupted into steam. The steam turned into silver dust that drifted harmlessly to the stony earth, sparkling in the ruby light. Axe's brutality made him good at this sort of work. Helm forgot about him and returned her attention to the valley.

It had changed, which was nothing unexpected in the Dream World. The nature of the change was a surprise, though. Gone was the stunning depth. Practically at her feet a gentle paradise stretched out invitingly. Grass swayed over a vista of soft green hills that rolled into a misty distance. The breeze was perfumed by wild roses and by a hint of sea that wafted over the hills. Gulls danced in the china-blue sky and Queen Anne's Lace shaded golden coins of buttercups and primroses.

"Sword?" Helm stayed where she was, though the grass nearly touched her feet, still on gravelly, hot earth. She felt her comrade's presence an instant before he materialized beside her. "Your opinion, please."

"Fighting you with your own weapons, I believe," he said, hooking a finger under his brown, worn belt and hitching up his pants. The gesture was so natural that Helm smiled. He squinted into the distance. "Didn't I see some of this before?"

"Some of it's mine." She scowled at the Queen Anne's Lace. "The rest of it must be coming from the patient's memories."

"I think he's asking for help," whispered Arrow, appearing without warning to Helm's right. She crouched down, bobbing a little with the wary nervousness of a wild creature and peered at the emerald grass. "It's nice."

"Nice enough to turn into teeth and eat you," Helm warned. "Don't forget, if you're hurt here, you'll carry the hurt home." Arrow said nothing, but shrank away from the edge of the grassland. "Did you find the dreamer?" Helm asked.

The younger woman's form wavered like a reflection in water stirred by a breeze. "I tried, Helm, I really did. I can't get through. He's everywhere and nowhere."

Which could mean, Helm thought bleakly, *that the bogeyman has infiltrated so thoroughly that we've already lost the patient.* "Never mind. We'll do what we can. Castle?"

"Yes, dear?" The voice in the air was calm and pleasant. Castle never saw the Dream World as the others did; to her it was a vague, foggy realm in which figures moved like shadows. That very blindness was her strength. In some way she was as psychically invisible to the Mindeaters as they were to her.

"I'm going to try a probe. Please be ready in case we have to retreat." Helm focused on the tall stalks of Queen Anne's Lace with their nodding, flat heads of intricate white flowers and 'fixed' them in her mind. Next, the gulls dancing in the sky and then the fresh green grass...

Gulls don't have six inch talons. She opened her mouth to yell and the hills did it for her. They reared up roaring, the gentle green swells cracking open. Molten lava spewed out, rolling in bubbling crimson streams through the shrivelling grass. The buttercups and primroses puffed into steam. Through the avalanche of lava the Queen Anne's Lace continued to sway, a product of Helm's mind that the enemy could not alter.

Weapon Team reacted instantly. Shield became a wall of steel, curving up and over to block the lava. Spear, Sword, and Arrow flung themselves into the sky, looking like their namesakes now, and wrought havoc among the bat-winged creatures that the gulls had become.

Axe waited with Helm behind the wall. His job was to protect her while she tried to impose order on insanity, but for the moment neither did anything. The others would have to blunt the manic fury of the attack first.

"I've a lead!" Caduceus popped into view, dressed half in clerical clothes and half in a devil's costume. A macabre, gloating face hovered behind his own. Helm stared into the empty eyes and banished the face, aware that the Mindeater was feeding on her companion's self doubts. "I think he's in a tree house. Early childhood memory, he felt safe there from his father; couldn't be seen."

Helm looked up quickly. The aerial battle had ceased and the lava flows were frozen rivers of crimson incongruously spotted with the bobbing white heads of her flowers. She waved at the team and they regrouped around her, some in human form and some, like Spear, holding their fighting shapes.

"We're going in deeper," she said, sensing the land under her feet beginning to gather itself like an earthquake in the making. "Arrow, Spear, when I make a breach go in fast but don't get cut off. Look for the patient in a tree house. He'll probably be a child. Shield, Sword, follow up. Hold the breach as long as you can. Ready, all?" She waited only a second for Weapon Team's terse agreement, and struck.

Dimly, she felt her real body arch on its well-padded couch, the muscles along her spine responding to the huge effort of her mind. She wiped out the landscape; volcanoes, lava flows, carcasses of horrid birds, flowers and grass and sky; and left nothingness in its wake.

This was far more difficult than creating images. She visualized fog and mist blotting out everything but her companions, all of them except Castle now in their fully human forms. That done, she stabilized the mist, smoothing it out and making it as blank as a sheet of clean, fresh paper.

A venomous pen tried to scribble on the emptiness. Helm shoved it aside, gesturing to Caduceus. He moved forward into the paper whiteness, she behind, Axe at her side. Spear and Arrow danced off to the right and left, taking care not to get too far away. The others fell into position at the rear.

More shapes rolled by on the mist. None was concrete; they were fragments of nightmares, hints of fears, tinges of woes and hatreds. Weapon Team walked in a cocoon of mist through a valley of insanity.

"Caduceus?" Helm fought the urge to whisper but the pressure on her mind was becoming intolerable as the cocoon slid onward through the Mindeater's defences.

"Nearly there." The ex-priest did whisper, his lean face contorted with effort. "I can feel his soul crying." He beckoned and the team obediently followed, Helm maintaining the protective wall although she could sense her distant heart pounding with the strain. "Here!" Caduceus's triumphant shout was scarcely needed. They all saw it at the same time; a shadowy, great old tree forming out of the mist.

Spear and Arrow flung themselves forward even as Helm gratefully let the mist go. She heard Axe's bellow and sensed Shield soaring up to block a potential attack. An instant later all was silence.

Recovering from the momentary weakness, she quickly checked her new surroundings. She stood in the yard behind an old-fashioned house built of wood. A covered porch encircled the house and a rocking chair creaked busily but emptily in the shadows near the door.

In the centre of the yard was a huge tree. It was an elm, one of the fine old trees that Dutch elm disease had long since destroyed in the real world. Here it stood in its prime, green-laden branches sweeping up to the sky. A small, neat tree house could just be seen inside the leafy canopy and a homemade rope ladder dangled from the miniature porch above.

Helm stepped to the foot of the tree and looked up. A freckled and terrified face stared down at her from a window in the side of the tree house. "Hello." She smiled and showed her empty hands. "Don't be afraid. We're here to help you."

The boy, about ten years old, shook his head. "You aren't," he piped. "You're with him. I know you are." He turned his head toward the rocking chair that was now reaching frenzy on the porch. "There's nothing real here. It's all nightmares like the shapes on the wall when it's dark and nobody comes when I call. You're nightmares too."

"No, we aren't." Helm focused on the tree, making it as real as she could. The boy she left alone. Patients had to want to be rescued; she couldn't force the will to live. "Can I come up and talk to you?"

The boy appeared to be considering the matter. Behind her, Axe shifted uneasily. Shield had vanished from view though her presence was apparent. Shapes moved eerily in the fog that surrounded the yard.

"Well, all right. But you have to come up by yourself." The boy leaned out of the tree house and pointed at the ladder. "It's only strong enough for one person at a time, you know."

"I can see that." Helm smiled reassuringly and took hold of the ladder, made of bits of mismatched wood and scrounged rope. She put a foot onto a rung, noting absently that a projecting tree root near her other foot had a bad case of rot. "Don't be worried. I won't fall." If necessary she could even fly up, or ride an escalator, or grow twenty feet tall. But anything like that could upset the dreamer and give the Mindeater an opening to use.

"I don't like this." Shield spoke unexpectedly near Helm's ear. "The bogey's not moving."

She replied with the minimum of breath, "It's gathering its strength. We've got to take this chance and pull him out while we can." She climbed higher, keeping a friendly smile on her face and trying to maintain eye contact with the boy. Even so, she couldn't help noting how the tree's bark was rough and split and scabbed with a greyish moss.

Another metre. The boy's anxious face lightened as she approached. *He's a cute lad,* she thought, liking the way his black hair tumbled over his ears. She gained another rung and held out her hand. The child reached down with his own grubby fingers, smiling in relief—

"Helm! *He's* the bogeyman!" Shield's shout came only an instant before the roar of the revolver that materialized in the child's fist. Helm had a single, terrifying glimpse of the gaping barrel and of a flash of fire that singed her cheek as she flung herself backward. She tumbled wildly, confusion reigning about her.

"I've got you. Baby, baby, I'll look after you." Castle's warmth surrounded her and held her like a glove. For an instant Helm wanted to hide in the enveloping comfort and safety and cry for sheer relief. It didn't matter what form the Mindeater's weapon had taken; there had been real power and real death behind it.

Fear for her comrades intervened. She wriggled out of the older woman's loving embrace with a muttered thanks and shot back to the combat.

In her momentary absence, Misrule had seized control. The tree still stood but a thick, hideous vine, a demented version of the liana that had saved her from the quicksand earlier, enwrapped it, strangling the tree and sucking out its life. Spear and Arrow darted persistently at lashing tendrils. Sword had been caught in one but was sawing at it with good effect. A gigantic Axe caught the light of a nonexistent sun as he swung back for a devastating stroke at the entangled roots of tree and vine.

Helm launched herself at him, understanding lending a burst of strength. "Axe, don't! The *tree* is the dreamer. You'll kill him! Damn you, *listen*."

It was far too late. The wicked, huge blade swung toward the mass of roots, driven by the ungoverned rage that made

Axe so dangerous in real life. Helm faltered, still shaken by her clash with the Mindeater. She flung up her hands in a dazed attempt to ward the giant blade away from the helpless tree.

Shield did it for her. The deadly blade slammed into a wall of glittering blue steel that sprang up to intercept it at the last instant.

There was a soundless roar, a lightless glare, a mental shriek of pain.

Helm lowered her arms stiffly. The world had become very still, almost like a painted, two-dimensional backdrop. Even the Mindeater seemed stunned. Shield lay motionless in human form on the ground at the foot of the tree. Her eyes were closed and Helm could not see her breathe. Axe lay shivering on the dry earth nearby, moaning softly. Both figures were terrifyingly transparent.

Helm turned in place, spinning above the ground. She felt curiously detached from the combat, like a spectator watching a movie. There were no emotions to deal with, nothing but a vast cold.

She looked at the tree, clutched so cruelly by the thick, strangling vine. Rot and mould clung to the weathered bark. Gashes scored the rough surface and sap dribbled steadily from the wounds to puddle on the bare soil. Tendrils from the vine probed into the wounds, drinking the stuff of the living mind.

Emotion returned with a rush; memories flooding in of all the dead, of all those she had seen over the last two years screaming their way out of life without ever waking. From somewhere deep in her soul Helm drew the strength to push aside that grief and rage. She shoved her emotions into what she privately called her cold room and drew over herself the iron mask of necessity.

"Sword, you others—" she tried not to look at her two stricken team mates lying on the worn earth "— *get* that thing." The words came out hard and flat and crisp and Weapon Team leaped to obey. Sword chopped furiously at the root of the vine. Spear lunged and stabbed and Arrow became a dart moving and striking so fast that even slow motion would have shown a blur.

"Helm?" Caduceus was pressed against the tree, silver hair stuck flat against his head and clerical collar stained with unreal sweat. "I can reach him—he needs our strength. He's fighting as hard as he can."

She stepped closer and placed her hands on his shoulders. Touch wasn't really necessary, but as a symbolic gesture it meant a lot. She focused on the embattled tree, pushing more and more of herself into the cold place until there was just the tree and her hands on the rough black cloth of the healer's jacket, and her own mind.

Green, she thought, accompanying the word with the most powerful images she could summon. *Rich, deep green, the green of maturity, of childhood left behind, of experience and strength and the flower of life.* Dimly, she felt her body again arch on its couch, heart racing, and hoped the life-support team was alert. *Thick, brown bark,* she continued, feeling as though the image was flowing from her mind to her arms and down into the tense body in front of her. *Strong, healthy bark, the tree's natural armour. Under it, a sound core of life's experiences; a caring and decent wife, three children, the respect of peers; the nourishment of love.* The sounds of battle faded. All she knew was black cloth, the towering presence of the tree and the steady drain.

Help is at hand. You're no longer alone. We understand. We know. Your father hated himself, not you.

Was that my thought? Helm fought the mist beginning to pluck at the edges of her overtaxed mind. *Or Caduceus's?*

I hated him. The voice speaking in her brain was childlike.

I know. Caduceus's mental tones sounded as cigarette-roughened as in life, and as kind. *You don't need to any more.*

Your father is gone. You are alive. We are here to help you. Let us help.

It's a nightmare, isn't it? This time the voice was more mature, speculative. *A Mindeater attack?* A pause. *Is my wife all right?*

She's fine. She got you to the hospital. Can you help yourself?

Now the voice was strong, resonant. *Let me at the bastard.*

Caduceus abruptly pulled away from the tree. Helm let go and dropped to the quivering earth beside Shield's body. Before her and above her, the tree struck back at its tormentor. Branches lashed downward with untreelike flexibility, seized the writhing vine in twigs that grew into massive hands. They wrenched.

The vine, already tattered from Weapon Team's attentions, stretched. The tree grew taller and roots boiled through the soil. The vine abruptly came out of the ground with a scream like nothing ever emitted by a human throat. The elm continued to grow, its wounds closing as tendrils were ripped out. Rot and mould faded away. There was no longer a tree in front of Weapon Team. A man stood as tall as the sky, the vine stretched between his vengeful fists.

The Mindeater tried to change form, to slip into something that could elude the giant. Helm concentrated on it, aware of her team mates doing the same, forcing it to keep the vine shape.

The battle ended an instant later as the body of the Mindeater tore in two. With a howl that left them all mentally stunned, it died.

Helm wasted no time in congratulating her team or the patient, but began the mental code sequence that would return them all to waking state and their own bodies.

ABOUT THE AUTHOR

Kass Williams's love of fantasy came about in part as a byproduct of working as a writer and editor, mainly for the Government of Canada. A daily diet of expressions like 'horizontal proliferation' and 'constitutionalization' naturally led to writing fantasy in her off hours as a way of staying grounded. Other experiences in her 38 years in the workforce were more fraught and resulted in her non-fiction book, *Workplace Bullying: A survival guide.* In her alter ego as Katherine Williams, she and her book have been featured on television and radio and in newspapers across Canada. She has been a guest speaker on this subject at seminars for employment equity organizations, unions, conflict resolution professionals, and others.

www.ingramcontent.com/pod-product-compliance
Lightning Source LLC
LaVergne TN
LVHW041107080826
845145LV00007B/1722